NIGHT OF THE DRAGON

WORLD OF WARCRAFT®

NIGHT OF THE DRAGON

RICHARD A. KNAAK

POCKET BOOKS

New York London Toronto Sydney

Pocket Books
A Division of Simon & Schuster, Inc.
1230 Avenue of the Americas
New York, NY 10020

First Pocket Books paperback edition November 2008

POCKET and colophon are registered trademarks of
Simon & Schuster, Inc.

Cover art by Glenn Rane

For information about special discounts for bulk purchases,
please contact Simon & Schuster Special Sales at 1-800-456-6798 or
business@simonandschuster.com.

Library of Congress Cataloging-in-Publication Data is available.

Manufactured in the United States of America

10   9   8   7   6   5   4   3   2   1

ISBN-13: 978–0–7434–7137–4
ISBN-10:   0–7434–7137–7

This one is for Evelyn, Mick—and definitely Chris—invaluable partners in the crafting of Azeroth's many tales

NIGHT OF THE DRAGON

PROLOGUE

He was trapped . . . trapped . . . trapped . . .

The darkness of his prison closed in around him. He could not breathe, could not move. How had this happened? What were the foul little creatures who had somehow managed to ensnare him? Vermin capturing a leviathan! It was impossible!

But it had happened . . .

He wanted to roar, but could not. There was no sound here, anyway. The silence drove him mad. He needed to be free! There had to be some escape—

A blinding emerald light enveloped him. He shrieked as it painfully ripped him from his prison and thrust him into the beyond.

But that shriek turned into a mighty roar of relief mixed with fury. He spread wide his magnificent, shimmering wings, his gargantuan, teal form filling much of this new place in which he found himself. Jagged, almost crystalline protrusions erupted along his spine and head, the latter creating an impressive crest akin to those worn on a warlord's helm. Huge, glittering white orbs—more like pearls than eyes—swept over a massive cavern filled with toothy projections thrusting from both the rounded ceiling and the rough floor.

And then his baleful gaze fell upon the vermin that had dared—somehow!—to trap his greatness. A subtle magenta aura suddenly radiated from him as he bellowed his righteous fury.

"Foul little worms! Foul little gremlins! You would dare make of Zzeraku a caged pet?" As Zzeraku cried out, his already ethereal body grew more translucent. He fixed on a small party of his captors. They were ugly

little things that moved like squashed draenei but were scaled in some places and furred in others. They had vicious little mouths filled with sharp teeth and wore hooded and armored garments. Their eyes were red like molten earth and despite his obvious threat to them, they did not appear properly frightened.

It was clear to Zzeraku that they knew very little about nether dragons.

"Foul little worms! Foul little gremlins!" he repeated. His body suddenly crackled with lightning the color of his wondrous self. He reached out a taloned paw as if to wipe away the creatures, the lightning suddenly shooting forth from it.

The first bolts went oddly astray, turning from the little creatures at the last moment. At the same time, the foreheads of each briefly revealed a strange, glowing rune.

Without hesitation, the captive nether dragon cast again. However, this time the lightning struck the ground *around* his tormentors. Rock and dirt exploded everywhere, the snarling little beasts thrown with the rest. Their hissing bodies scattered through the air with pleasing effect. *"Foul little worms! Zzeraku will squash you all!"*

He summoned more of his power. Veins of dark azure suddenly crisscrossed his chest. The lightning crackled more violently.

From somewhere to the side, a long, sinewy strand of silver energy looped around his left forelimb, tightening painfully.

Startled, Zzeraku forgot his own intended attack. The nether dragon was a creature of energy; the strand should have slipped through him. He snapped at it, only to receive a vicious jolt to his jaws. His limb dropped, suddenly bereft of all strength.

As that happened, his other forelimb was likewise snared. Zzeraku tugged in vain, the slender magical strand so very powerful.

The nether dragon's body swelled, the blue veins that distinctly marked Zzeraku now nearly black. He took on an even more transparent appearance, as if fading away to mist.

The silver strands flared.

Zzeraku let out a pained roar and fell forward, crashing on the cavern floor as if made of flesh and bone. Cracks ran across the stone. A crevasse opened up, into which two of the tiny creatures tumbled to their doom.

The others ignored the fates of their comrades as they set into motion two more silver strands. Five of the vermin at a time wielded the sinister threads of energy as if gigantic whips. The strands soared unerringly over Zzeraku to the opposing side, where the ends were seized and guided into the ground with small emerald stones.

"Release Zzeraku!" the nether dragon roared as the strands flashed and his body suffered renewed agony. *"Release me!"*

The new strands forced him to flatten against the floor. Zzeraku struggled, but his magical bonds kept his powers entirely in check.

All around him, the scaly figures rushed about, adding dread line after dread line until they had all but enshrouded him in them. Each cut into the nether dragon's body, simultaneously burning and freezing him. Zzeraku shrieked his fury and pain, but nothing that he did could alter his situation.

The creatures continued to feverishly work, evidently uncertain as to the strength of the strands. With the emeralds, they constantly readjusted the bonds, often to the nether dragon's further torture. One chortled at his pain.

Zzeraku managed a last burst of energy at that tormentor. Black energy surrounded the creature, who now shrieked with satisfying fear. The nether dragon's magic crushed the one captor into a pulpy mess that then solidified into ebony crystal.

Immediately, another strand fell across his muzzle, clamping it down. The glistening leviathan fought, but his jaws were held as tight as the rest of him.

His captors continued to scuttle about the huge cavern as if in great anxiousness, although Zzeraku could no longer imagine it had anything to do with him. He let out a frustrated hiss—a sound muffled by his sealed muzzle—and tried yet again to free himself.

And yet again, it was to no avail.

Then, without warning, the squat, scaly creatures paused in what they were doing. As one, they stared at a point to the nether dragon's side but well beyond his sight. However, Zzeraku could still sense that someone approached, someone of tremendous power.

His true captor . . .

Those around him dropped to the ground in homage. Zzeraku heard a slight movement that might have been the wind if not for the fact that no wind could reach this accursed place.

"You have done well, my skardyn," came a voice that, despite its feminine allure, touched what passed for the soul of the nether dragon like the coldest ice. "I am pleased. . . ."

"They obeyed their orders well," replied a second, more masculine speaker. His voice held a clear contempt for the creatures. "Though they opened the chrysalun chamber too soon, my lady. The beast nearly escaped."

"There was never a need for concern. Once here, escape for this one was impossible."

The feminine voice drew nearer . . . and suddenly a small form stepped into sight before Zzeraku. A pale figure clad in a form-fitting gown the color of night paused to study him and be studied in turn. She reminded Zzeraku of another, one who had tried to befriend him and taught him something beyond the absolute chaos he had known in the realm some called Outland. Yet, the nether dragon could smell that this being, while similar in some ways to the one he recalled, was also very different in others.

Long, ebony hair flowed down past her shoulders. She kept her countenance to the side, as if not paying particular attention to the captive beast even though Zzeraku knew full well that she did. What the nether dragon could see of her features were flawless in the way his friend's had been, even more so.

Yet the coldness Zzeraku felt from that half-lidded gaze made the giant struggle anew.

The edge of her red lips curled up. "You need not trouble yourself so, my little one. Rather, you should make yourself comfortable. After all . . . I've only brought you home."

Her words made no sense. Zzeraku strained at his bonds, seeking escape . . . escape from this tiny figure that somehow so frightened him.

She turned to face him directly, in doing so revealing that the left side of her visage was draped by a silken veil . . . a veil that fluttered aside just enough when she turned to let the nether dragon see the horrific, scorched flesh beneath and the gap where once an eye had been.

And although she was a mere speck in comparison to the girth of the nether dragon, the image of her ruined countenance still magnified Zzeraku's anxiety a thousandfold. He wanted to be away from it, wanted never to see it. Even when the veil settled over the marred area, the nether dragon could still sense the horrific evil beneath.

Evil that far outshone any that he had known in Outland.

Her cold smile stretched farther yet, farther than her face should have allowed.

"You shall rest now," she said in a tone that demanded he obey. As Zzeraku instantly began to lose consciousness, she added, "Rest and have no fear . . . after all, you're among family here, my child. . . ."

ONE

*S*o quickly passes time when one manages to live to be so old, thought the robed figure as he sat in his mountain sanctum surveying the world through an endless series of glimmering globes hovering around him. At a gesture from their creator, they shifted about the gargantuan oval chamber. Those he most desired came to rest before him just above one of a series of pedestals forged by his magic from the stalagmites that had once filled this place. At the base, each pedestal appeared as if carved by an artisan, so perfect were the lines, the angles. However, as they rose, they transformed into what was more the dreams of the sleeping rather than the result of physical labor. In those dreams, there were hints of dragons, hints of spirits, in the shaping, and at the very top something resembling a petrified hand with long, sinewy fingers stretched up, almost but not quite grasping the sphere above.

And in each of the spheres appeared a scene of much relevance to the wizard, Krasus.

The faint rumble of thunder managing to reach his hidden sanctum gave great indication to the turbulent weather without. Shrouded this foul eve in violet robes that had once bespoken of the Kirin Tor, the lanky, pale spellcaster leaned close to better view the latest scene. The sphere's blue illumination revealed in turn features akin to those of the high elves—a people now all but extinct—including the angular bone structure, the patrician nose, and the long head. Yet, despite also bearing the handsomeness of that fallen race, Krasus was clearly not of any true elven lineage. It was not merely that his hawklike face had lines and scars—most notably three long, jagged ones running down the right cheek—that no elf of any sort could gain unless he had lived well past a thousand years, nor the exotic black and crimson streaks in his silver hair. Rather, it was his glittering, black eyes—eyes like no elf nor even any human—that told of an age beyond any mortal creature.

An age possible only for one of the eldest of dragons.

Krasus was the name by which he went in this form, a name that many knew only as once a senior member of the inner circle of Dalaran's ruling council of wizards. But Dalaran had failed to stem the growing tide of evil despite the best of efforts, as had failed so many other kingdoms during the wars against the orcs and the subsequent one against the demons of the Burning Legion and the undead Scourge. The world of Azeroth had been turned upside down, with thousands of lives lost, and yet was still only barely in balance . . . a balance that looked more and more fragile with every passing day.

It is as if we are trapped in a never-ending game, our lives hinging on the roll of a dice or the turn of a card, he thought, recalling catastrophic events even further in the past. Krasus had witnessed the collapse of civilizations far older than any existing now, and although he had had a hand in helping salvage something from many, it never seemed enough. He was only one being, one dragon . . . even if he *was,* in truth, Korialstrasz, consort to the great queen of the red flight, Alexstrasza.

But not even the great Aspect of Life herself, his beloved mistress, could have foreseen all that happened or been able to stop those events from taking place. Krasus knew that he placed a far greater burden upon himself than he should have, but the dragon mage could not relent in his efforts to help the peoples of Azeroth, even if some of those efforts were doomed to failure from the start.

Indeed, there were even now many situations that drew his attention, situations with the potential to wreak utter havoc upon his world . . . and at the core of those problems were his own kind, the dragons. There was the vast rift leading into the astounding realm called Outland, a great portal that in particular both fascinated and disturbed the blue dragonflight, keepers of magic itself. From it had already come a mysterious cure for the madness that had long engulfed the blue lord. Yet although the Aspect of Magic, Malygos, was now completely lucid, Krasus did not at all like the path the leviathan's mind had now chosen. Outraged at what he felt was the younger races' destructive misuse of magic, Malygos had begun to suggest to the other Aspects that a *purge* of all those wielding such power might prove necessary to preserve Azeroth. In fact, he had grown quite adamant about it the last time he, Alexstrasza, Nozdormu the Timeless One, and Ysera—She of the Dreaming—had gathered in the far-off Northeast for their convocation at the ancient, towering Wyrmrest temple in the ice-bound Dragonblight—a significant, annual ritual originally begun to mark their combined might managing to overcome the dread Deathwing more than a decade ago.

With mounting frustration, Krasus dismissed the image that he had been viewing and summoned the next. His thoughts, however, were still focused inward, this time upon the last of the four great dragons, Ysera. There were rumors of nightmarish things happening in the ethereal realm of which she was mistress, the almost mythic Emerald Dream. Exactly *what* was a question no one could answer, but Krasus was beginning to fear that the Emerald Dream was a problem potentially more disastrous than any other.

He started to dismiss the next sphere without even really glancing at its contents . . . then belatedly recognized the location revealed.

Grim Batol.

All thought of Malygos and the Emerald Dream vanished from his attention as Krasus surveyed the sinister mountain. He knew it too well, for he had been there in times past and had sent agents serving his purpose into the very heart of the accursed place. In Grim Batol, his beloved mistress had been enslaved by orcs—the same barbaric race, oddly enough, that would prove such beneficial allies thirteen years later when the demons of the Burning Legion returned—utilizing a sinister artifact called the Demon Soul. The Demon Soul, unfortunately, had been able to bend her will to the Horde because it had been forged by the Aspects themselves, only to be perverted by one of their own. Alexstrasza had produced young for the orcs for their war efforts, young who became the brutish warriors' mounts in battle. Young who had perished by the scores in combat against wizards and dragons of other flights.

Through his guidance of the impetuous wizard, Rhonin, the high elf warrior maiden, Vereesa, and others, Krasus had been instrumental in releasing his queen from captivity. Dwarven fighters had assisted in wiping out the remaining pockets of orc resistance. Grim Batol had been emptied out, its evil legacy forever eradicated.

Or so all had thought. The dwarves were the first to feel the darkness that permeated it, and so they left almost immediately following the orcs' defeat. Alexstrasza and he had decided then that it was the duty of the red flight to seal off Grim Batol again. This despite the irony of the fact that, having already guarded it since the ancient Battle of Mount Hyjal, the red dragons' presence had made it so simple for the orcs arriving there to enslave them with the Demon Soul.

And so, despite some misgivings on Krasus's part, crimson behemoths had once again stood sentry around the vicinity, making certain that no one wandered in, either by accident or thinking to make some use of that evil.

But then, only recently, the sentries had sickened for no reason at all, and some had even died. A few had gone so very mad that there had been no choice but to put them down for fear of the devastation they might cause. The red flight had finally done as all others had, abandoning Grim Batol to itself.

And so, it had become nothing but an empty tomb marking the end of an old war and what had turned out to be a very, very short period of peace.

Yet . . .

Krasus eyed the darkened scene. Even from so far away, he could sense something radiating from within. Grim Batol had become so bathed in evil over the centuries that there was no redeeming it.

And from it had come rumors of late, rumors that hinted of the baleful past rising from the dead. Krasus knew them all. Fragmented tales of a huge, winged form barely seen in the night sky, a ghostly form that had, in one case, wiped out an entire village miles from Grim Batol. In the light of the moon, the teller of one tale had claimed to see what might have been a dragon . . . but one neither red, black, or any known color. Amethyst it had been, something impossible and so surely of the frightened farmer's imagination. Still, those with distant sight, mostly agents of his, had reported strange emanations in the sky above the mountain and when one—a trusted young male of his own flight—had dared try to track those emanations back, he had utterly vanished.

Too much was going on in the rest of the world for the Aspects to focus upon Grim Batol, but Krasus could not let it rest. However, he could no longer rely on agents, for sacrificing others was not generally his way. This now demanded his own effort, no matter what the outcome.

Even his death.

Indeed, at this point there were only two others he would have entrusted even with the knowledge, but Rhonin and Vereesa had troubles of their own.

It was up to him alone, then. With a curt wave of his hand, Krasus sent the spheres flying into the shadows above. Death was no fear to him, who had seen it and nearly experienced it far too often. He wanted only that—should it happen—it at least would mean something. He was more than willing to die for the sake of his world and those he loved, if that was what was required.

If such is required, the dragon mage pointed out to himself. He had not yet even begun the journey. Now was not the time to think of his demise.

The search must be done with stealth, Krasus considered as he abandoned his seat. *This is no mere happenstance. There is something going on that threatens us all; I feel it. . . .*

If it had been another time, if it had been the Second War, Krasus would have known who to blame. The mad Aspect once called the Earth-Warder or, more specifically . . . Neltharion. But no one had called the immense black dragon by his original name for millennia,

a much more apt one having arisen after the first of the insane behemoth's monstrous plots.

Deathwing, he was called now. Deathwing the Destroyer.

Krasus paused in the midst of the huge cavern, taking a deep breath
in preparation for what was to come next. No, Deathwing could not
be blamed for this, for it was nearly positive that he was this time dead.
Nearly positive. That was far better than in past incidences when the
black dragon had only been presumed *likely* dead.

And Deathwing was not the only great evil in the world.

Krasus spread his arms to each side. It did not matter whether what
lurked in Grim Batol was simply the culmination of ages of past evil or
some sinister new foulness; he would find out the truth.

His body swelled out of proportion. With a grunt, the mage fell to
the floor, dropping on all fours. His face stretched forward, his nose and
mouth melding together as they formed a long, powerful snout. The
robes Krasus wore shredded, the pieces flying up into the air, then immediately settling all over his body, where they became hard crimson-
colored scales.

From Krasus's back burst two small, webbed wings that grew as his
body did. A pointed tail sprouted. Hands and feet twisted into powerful
paws ending in a sharp set of claws.

The transformation took but the blink of an eye, but by the time it
was done, the mage Krasus was no more. In his place stood a magnificent red dragon who nearly filled the cavern and who was dwarfed in
size by few of his kind other than the great Aspects.

Korialstrasz stretched his vast wings once, then leapt up toward the
stone ceiling.

The ceiling shimmered just before he reached it, tons of rock becoming as if water. The crimson dragon dove into the liquefied stone
unimpeded. Powerful muscles lifted him ever upward as he drove full
pace through the magicked barrier.

Seconds later, he burst into the night sky. The rock solidified behind
him, leaving no trace of his passage.

This latest of his sanctums perched among the mountains near what remained of Dalaran. Ruins appeared below, yes—far too many ruins of once-proud towers and powerful keeps—but there was something much, much more astounding enveloping most of the fabled realm. It originated from where the Kirin Tor had ruled and spread equally in all directions. It was the desperate attempt of those that remained of the inner council to resurrect their glory, to rebuild their might while aiding the Alliance against the Scourge.

It was what appeared to be a vast, magical dome, a dome of shifting energies, but especially those that gave it a shimmering violet or gleaming white appearance. It was utterly opaque, giving no clue to the efforts within. Korialstrasz knew what the wizards planned and thought them mad for it, but let them do as they must. There was still the hope that they would succeed. . . .

Despite their own not-insignificant abilities, the council of wizards was utterly ignorant of the dragon almost in their midst. When he had been a part of their order—one of its secret founders, in fact—they had known him only as Krasus, never as his true self. Korialstrasz preferred it that way; most of the younger races would have found it impossible to deal directly with such a mythic beast.

Shielded by his magic, the dragon flew over the fantastic dome, then headed southeast. He was tempted to veer toward the lands of the red flight, but such a delay might prove costly. His queen might also question his journey, even forbid it. Even for her, Korialstrasz would not turn back.

Indeed, it was for her in great part that he sought to return to Grim Batol.

The dwarves were a motley group, even compared with how dwarves often were seen in the eyes of humans or other races. They themselves would have preferred a better state of affairs, but their duty demanded that they ignore their discomforts for the sake of their people.

Squat but powerfully built, the dwarven warriors numbered both males and females, although those not of the race might have had some difficulty discerning the physical difference from a distance. The females lacked the thick beards, were of slightly lesser builds than their counterparts and if one listened close, the voices were a little less gruff. However, they were known for fighting with as much determination, if not more sometimes, than their mates.

But male or female, they were all grimy and exhausted, and this day had seen two of their comrades lost.

"I could've saved Albrech," Grenda said, her lips twisted into a frown of self-recrimination. "I could've, Rom!"

The older dwarf to whom she spoke bore more scars than any of the rest. Rom was commander and the one with the most knowledge of Grim Batol's legacy. After all, had he not also been leader years ago when the wizard Rhonin, the high elf archer, Vereesa, and a gryphon rider from the Aerie had aided his forces in ridding the foul place of the orcs and freeing the great Dragonqueen? He leaned against the wall of the tunnel through which he and his band had just run, catching his breath. He had been young not that long ago. The past four weeks here had aged him in a manner unnatural, and he was certain that it was the sinister land's doing. He recalled the reports concerning the red dragons and how they had suffered even greater before finally having the sense to depart barely a month back. Only dwarves were hard-headed enough to march where the very realm itself sought to kill them.

And if not the realm, then whatever black evil that had now burrowed deep into the dread caverns.

"There was nothing that could be done, Grenda," he grunted back. "Albrech and Kathis knew this might be."

"But to leave them to fend for themselves against the skardyn—"

Rom dug under his breastplate to retrieve his long pipe. Dwarves went nowhere without their pipes, although sometimes they had to smoke something other than what they generally favored. For the past two weeks, the band had been making due with a combination of ground brown mushrooms—the tunnels were full of those—and a red weed found near a stream that was their best source of water. It made for a tolerable smoke, if not much else.

"They chose to stand and help the rest of us get our task done," he replied, stuffing the pipe. As he lit the contents, Rom added, "and that was to bring this stinkin' creature back with us. . . ."

Grenda and the rest of the party followed his gaze to their prisoner. The skardyn hissed like a lizard, then snapped sharp teeth at Rom. It— Rom was fairly certain the thing was male, but did not wish to grant the skardyn even that much identity—stood slightly shorter than the average dwarf, but was a little wider. All of that extra width was muscle, for the scaly creatures dug through earth with their clawed hands as not even the most powerful of Rom's people could.

The face that stared out from under the skardyn's ragged brown hood was a macabre mix of dwarven and reptilian features, the former not at all a surprise to its captors—for skardyn were descended from the same race as Rom and his comrades. Their ancestors had been Dark Iron dwarves, accursed survivors of the War of Three Hammers hundreds of years earlier. Most of the traitorous Dark Irons had perished in that epic confrontation between dwarf and dwarf, but there had always been rumors that some had escaped into Grim Batol after their leader—the sorceress, Modgud—had cursed Grim Batol just before being slain. As no one had desired at that time to hunt any possible remaining foes in a place blackened by magic, the rumors had remained just that . . . until Rom had had the misfortune to discover the truth in them shortly after arriving.

But whatever links there had been between Rom's people and the skardyn's had long ago become so intangible as to be nonexistent. The skardyn retained the general shape and some traces of facial similarity, but even where they had once sported beards, coarse scales now covered everything. Their teeth were, indeed, more like those of a lizard or even a dragon and their misshapen hands—*paws,* to be precise—also resembled those of the two beasts. The thing that the dwarves had captured was also just as likely to run on all fours as it was on two legs.

That did not mean that the skardyn were merely animals. They were cunning and well-versed in weaponry, be it the daggers they carried on their belts, the axes—unchanged since the War of Three Hammers—

or the metal, palm-sized balls wickedly spiked that they either tossed by hand or threw using slings. Still, if disarmed, they were also more than willing to utilize their teeth and claws, as had been disastrously proven the first time the dwarves had encountered them.

That time, the verification that these were the descendants of the Dark Irons had been proven by the garments, which still retained the markings of the treacherous clan. Unfortunately, it had proven highly difficult for Rom's force to capture any of the creatures alive, so fierce did the skardyn fight. Three times before this had he organized missions to take a prisoner, and three times had the dwarves utterly failed.

And three times had others under Rom's command perished.

That last damned streak still held with the loss of two fine warriors this night. However, at last the mission had something to show for its efforts . . . or so he hoped. Now, at last, Rom believed that he had a source by which he could at last discover what could be so malevolent and powerful that even dragons fled in fear of it. What darkness commanded the skardyn with such absolute mastery that the abominations would die for it?

And what now howled its anguish as unsettling lights and energies radiated from the desolate peak?

The skardyn spat as Rom leaned close. Its breath was awful, which said much considering the stenches to which dwarves were used. Rom discovered another change that further pushed skardyn and dwarves apart; the prisoner had a double-forked tongue.

None of these alterations were natural, but rather the result of living in a place so saturated with evil magic. The dwarven leader peered grimly, matching the bloody red gaze with his own stern one.

"You filth can still speak the language," Rom rumbled. "Heard you use it before."

The prisoner hissed . . . then tried to lunge. The two hefty guards holding its arms had been chosen by Rom for their strength, but they were still hard-pressed to keep the skardyn in place.

Rom took a deep puff of his pipe, then exhaled deeply in the creature's face. The skardyn sniffed longingly; one trait that apparently had not changed was the love of the pipe. When first the dwarves had checked the bodies of dead ones, they had found curled pipes carved not from wood, but crafted from clay. What exactly the skardyn used to fill those pipes was another question, for the only substance anyone had discovered on the skardyn had smelled like old grass and mulched earth worms. Not even the hardiest of Rom's followers had been willing to try it.

"You'd like a smoke, would you?" Rom took another puff, then again blew it in the creature's face. "Well, just talk with me a little, and we'll see what we can do . . ."

"Uzuraugh!" snapped the prisoner. "Hizakh!"

Rom tsked. "Now that kind o' talk will only get you turned over to Grenda and her two brothers. Albrech, he was *Gwyarbrawden* to them? You know that old word? Gwyarbrawden?"

The skardyn stilled. Dwarves counted their blood connections in many ways. There was the clan, of course, the most prominent of ties. Yet, within and without the clan there were other bindings, and the ritual of Gwyarbrawden was foremost among the common warriors. Those who swore Gwyarbrawden to one another marked themselves as willing to cross all of Azeroth to find their comrade's slayer, should that happen. They were also not averse to making the death of that slayer long and harsh, for Gwyarbrawden was a justice all unto itself. Clan leaders did not publicly acclaim its existence, but neither did they condemn it.

It was a part of dwarven society that very few outsiders knew about.

But skardyn were not outsiders, evidently, for the wild, crimson orbs flashed toward a grinning Grenda, then back to Rom once more. Legends concerning Gwyarbrawden quests often finished with extravagant descriptions of the prey's lengthy death. It did not surprise Rom to know that such grisly stories would still circulate among this creature's kind.

"Last chance," he said, taking another puff. "Going to talk so we can understand you?"

The skardyn nodded.

Rom hid his anticipation. He had not been entirely bluffing about Grenda and her brothers, but giving up the prisoner to them might have meant finding out nothing. True, Grenda would have done her best to wring some word out of the ugly thing, but he could not discount one of the three perhaps too eagerly pursuing Gwyarbrawden and killing the skardyn before that happened.

With a final glance at Grenda to remind the captive of what awaited it if it did not answer, Rom said, "The veiled one! Your comrades brought her something, and now Grim Batol echoes with a roar like that of a dragon . . . only no dragon's been seen here in months! What's she up to in there?"

"*Chrysalun* . . ." The single word escaped the skardyn with a hoarseness that made it sound as if speaking was a rare and terrible effort for it. "Chrysalun . . ."

"What by the beard of my father is a chrys—chrysalun?"

"Bigger . . ." the prisoner rasped, its tongue darting in and out. "Bigger inside . . . not out . . ."

"What pile of tailings is that beast spouting? He mocks us all!" one of Grenda's brothers snarled. Although not twins, her siblings looked even more like one another than most dwarves did, and Rom always had trouble telling which was Gragdin and which was Griggarth.

Whichever he was, he followed his declaration by charging forward, ax raised as best the tunnel allowed. The skardyn hissed and struggled anew.

It was Grenda who blocked her impetuous brother. "No, Griggarth! Not yet! Put the ax down now!"

Griggarth shrank under his sister's admonition. She was the mistress and they were her two hounds. Gragdin, who had no reason to, imitated his brother's reaction.

Grenda turned back to the skardyn. "But if this filth doesn't make more sense with the next word he utters . . ."

Rom seized control again. Finishing the last bits in his pipe, he tapped the ashes out, then muttered, "Aye. One last time. Maybe a different question'll stir you right." He considered, then said, "Maybe something about the tall one and what his ilk would be doin' here of all places."

His suggestion had a disquieting reaction on the skardyn. At first, Rom thought that it was choking on something, but then he realized that the damned beast was *laughing*.

Drawing his dagger, Rom thrust the point under the skardyn's brown, scaly chin. Despite that, the prisoner did not let up.

"Be still, you blasted son of a toad or I'll save them the trouble of flaying you and—"

The ceiling caved in. Dwarves scattered as tons of rock and stone tumbled down.

And with it came three massive figures not only armored in brass breastplates and guards, but scaled even more than the skardyn. Worse, these imposing giants—nearly nine feet tall by Rom's expert reckoning—were far more deadly and far more unexpected than the descendants of the Dark Irons had been.

"What are—" cried one dwarf before a huge, arced blade cut through his midsection, breastplate and all.

Rom knew what they were, if only by description, but it was Grenda who cried out their foul name. "Drakonid!"

She lunged toward the first, her ax already out. Looking as if someone had melded a dragon and a human into one vicious warrior, the black-scaled drakonid she moved against swung at the dwarf with the already-bloodied weapon. As it struck her ax, the blade flared, cutting through good dwarven workmanship as if through water.

Only Rom's swift action saved her. Having launched himself toward the monstrous figure at the same time that Grenda had, he was there in time to shove her aside. Unfortunately, the confines of the ruined tunnel did not give him enough room to avoid being struck by the blade meant for her.

The dwarf screamed as it *burned* through his wrist. He watched with amazement as his hand fell to the ground, where it was trampled under the drakonid's massive, three-toed foot.

If there was anything fortunate to come from the terrible wound,

it was that the magic of the blade also cauterized the cut. That, combined with dwarven endurance, enabled Rom to throw his strength
into a one-handed swing.

The ax cut into the armored hide near the shoulder. The drakonid
let out a growl of pain and backed up.

Laughter rung in Rom's ears, laughter that less and less sounded like
the skardyn's and more like something far more sinister. He glanced
over his shoulder to where the prisoner should have still been held.

But the guards lay dead, their eyes staring blindly and their throats
cut. Their axes remained harnessed on their backs, and their daggers
were still sheathed in their belts. They looked as if they had simply
stood and waited to die.

Or had been bespelled . . . for what stood where the skardyn had
been was no magic-degenerated dwarf. Instead, the figure stood as
tall as a human, but was slimmer of build. His long, pointed ears were
clue enough to his identity, but his crimson robes and fiercely-glowing
green eyes—the sign of demon taint—verified to Rom's dismay just
how big a fool the commander had been.

It was the very blood elf about whom he had been asking.

Rom's hunt for a prisoner who could give him information had been
turned into a trap for the dwarves. His pulse raced as he imagined his
followers slaughtered or, likely worse, captured and dragged back into
Grim Batol.

With a war cry that resounded in the ruined tunnel, he charged the
blood elf. The tall figure eyed the powerful dwarf with disdain, then
held out one hand.

In it, a twisted wooden staff materialized, the head ending in a fork
in which a huge, skull-shaped emerald matching the blood elf's evil
orbs flared.

Rom went flying back, the dwarf colliding with the wall behind
him.

As he dropped to the ground, Rom uttered an epithet that would
have burned the ears of any human, much less one of the elven races.
Through his blurred vision, he saw dwarves desperately trying to make

a stand against the powerful drakonid. It was not that the dragon men were unstoppable, but his people seemed to be moving sluggishly. Gorum, a fighter whose swiftness was second only to Rom's, hefted his ax as if it weighed as much as he.

The blood elf . . . it . . . it has to be the . . . blood elf . . . Rom struggled to rise, but his body would not obey.

Worse to him than even his own certain demise was his failure to his king. He had sworn an oath to Magni that he would discover the secret of what was now going on in Grim Batol, but all Rom had accomplished was this horrific debacle.

That shame managed to get him to his knees, but from there he could rise no farther. The blood elf turned his attention from Rom, yet another insult to the dwarf's honor.

Rom managed to seize his ax. He struggled against both the spell and his own pain—

A horrific roar that shook the walls rose above the tunnels, causing *everyone* to look up.

The effect on the blood elf was greatest. He cursed in some tongue Rom did not understand, then shouted to the drakonid, "Up! Quickly! Before it gets too far!"

The dragon warriors crouched, then leaped up and out of the tunnels with astounding agility for their immense size. Their leader tapped the bottom of the staff twice on the ground—and vanished in a brief burst of golden flames.

Rom abruptly found it possible to move, if somewhat wearily. Slowly, the conditions of his comrades registered. There were at least three dead and several others wounded. He doubted that the drakonid had suffered much more than one or two cuts each, none of them threatening. If not for the mysterious roar, the dwarves would have been lost.

Grenda and one of her brothers came to his aid. Sweat drenched the female warrior. "Can you walk?"

"Hmmph! I can run . . . if I've got to, girl!"

It was because of no sense of cowardice that he suggested running. There was no telling if the blood elf and the drakonid would return as quickly as they had left. The dwarves were in disarray and needed to retreat to a location where they could recover.

"To . . . to the slope tunnels," Rom commanded. Those tunnels were much farther from Grim Batol, but he felt them the best choice. The ground of the region there was full of rich veins of white crystal—highly sensitive to magical energies—which would make it difficult for even a mage like the blood elf to scry for them. In a sense, the scouts would become invisible.

But not invincible. Nowhere was it completely safe.

With Grenda's assistance, Rom led the dwarves off. Glancing over his battered followers, he saw again how much the very brief struggle had cost them. If not for the roar—

The roar. As grateful as he was for that interruption, Rom wondered at its origins, wondered about that . . . and whether or not what had been the dwarves' salvation was the harbinger of something far, far worse.

TWO

Korialstrasz soared over Lordaeron, forcing himself as best he could to pay no mind to the turmoil below. He was determined to reach the opposing side of the Baradin Bay without even the slightest delay. It was of the utmost importance he do that. The dragon dared not allow himself to become embroiled in any part of the continuous struggle against the Scourge. That had to be left in the hands of other defenders. He could *not* become involved . . .

And yet . . . more than once the immense red dragon failed in his resolve. Korialstrasz could not let the innocent suffer nor allow flagrant strikes by the undead go unpunished.

Nor, when he sighted it toward the end of that shrouded day, could he let the massing of hundreds of the twisted and decayed servants of the Lich King remain untouched.

It was just as he first smelled the distant bay that he saw the macabre army preparing to march . . . an army built from the scavenged body parts and corpses of more than a thousand good souls. The rusted and dented armor of paladins hung upon fleshless frames and empty eye sockets stared out from under helmets. By the builds of some of the undead, the dragon saw that the Scourge was not prejudiced against one sex over the other, nor of young over old; all who fell were potential soldiers for its evil master.

And neither did the fact that some of these had once been women and children have any more meaning for the enraged dragon, who dove down among the ghouls, unleashing his full and terrible fury. A river of flame coursed across the center of the unholy ranks, decimating scores in a single moment. Dry bones made marvelous kindling for a red dragon's fire, and the inferno quickly spread as some undead tumbled into others.

Korialstrasz attacked well aware of what destination this army of the Scourge had in mind, none other than the shield covering Dalaran over which he had not that long ago flown. The wizards were a foe that Arthas, the Lich King, could not let recoup. The dragon had expected such an assault before long, though the Scourge had moved swifter than even he had calculated.

And so, they thus enabled the red dragon to do his former comrades in the Kirin Tor one daring favor before flying from Lordaeron.

Skull-faced warriors fired upon him with bows of many makes, but their shafts fell far short. They were not used to aerial attacks of such monumental nature. Korialstrasz banked to the north, then struck the lines there, first diving down and raking the ground of warriors, then sending another burst into those still standing.

He finally sensed magic stirring from the back lines and responded accordingly. Lesser dragons might have fallen prey to the Lich King's spellcasters, but Korialstrasz was far more experienced. He immediately noted the location of his new foes and focused his own considerable magic on the spot.

The ground there erupted, a huge forest of grass tendrils a thousand times their normal size and thickness bursting all around the casters, lesser liches who had once probably been honored wizards until seduced by the dark power of the Scourge's lord. The huge tendrils encircled their prey, crushing and ripping apart the undead before the latter could finish their own treacherous spells.

Thus does life vanquish unlife, Korialstrasz grimly thought. As the consort of the Aspect of Life and, thus, a servant of that cause, it disgusted him to use his abilities so. The Scourge, though, gave him no choice. They were the antithesis of what his mistress represented and a threat to all that existed in Azeroth.

A savage pain in his chest suddenly sent the behemoth spiraling. Korialstrasz let out a furious roar and cursed himself for becoming distracted just like a young dragon, after all. He nearly crashed among the Scourge, managing to pull up only at the last moment. Forcing himself high into the gray clouds, the behemoth eyed his chest.

A black bolt as long as one of his claws lay embedded between the scales. The head was not made of steel, but rather some dark crystal that pulsated. It had struck Korialstrasz just perfectly, digging deep into the so very slim gap. Such a strike was certainly not happenstance.

New pain wracked him. Even though better prepared against it this time, the red dragon barely kept himself from descending.

Pushing himself to his limits, Korialstrasz flew higher yet. What remained of the Scourge below now seemed like a rush of ants. Satisfied that he was for the moment safe from further magical assault, the leviathan focused his own powers on the sinister shaft.

A crimson aura surrounded Korialstrasz. The dragon fed his might into it, fixing on the area where the sorcerous arrow's head lay.

The black bolt exploded.

Yet, Korialstrasz's sense of triumph was short-lived, for a sharp twinge immediately thereafter took him. It was not nearly so bad as the agony he had felt earlier, but harsh enough. He explored the area of the wound, seeking the cause.

Three small fragments of crystal remained. The sorcery used to create the arrow for use against such as him—there could be no other explanation for the weapon's existence—was so potent that even these few pieces caused him great pain.

The Lich King's minions were growing more and more cunning.

With another spell, Korialstrasz expelled the fragments from his body. The effort took the wind from him for a moment, but fury at what had happened to him quickly renewed his strength.

Roaring, the red dragon once again dropped like a missile toward the rear lines. Whoever had cast the black crystal was among those down there.

This time, Korialstrasz set the entire area awash in dragon fire. There was no possible chance of anything there escaping his wrath. The Scourge would learn that dragons were not to be trifled with.

Undead wrapped in flames stumbled in all directions before collapsing. In the center of his strike, the fire consumed the fiends entirely,
leaving only ash.

Korialstrasz looked upon the scene with satisfaction. He had dealt
the Scourge a bad blow with this assault. That would benefit Dalaran
and the rest of the defenders immensely.

Taking a deep breath, Korialstrasz soared on without hesitation toward the bay . . . and distant, beckoning Grim Batol.

On the eastern coast of central Kalimdor, a tall, cloaked figure silently strode into the unsavory town of Ratchet, a settlement begun
long ago by smugglers and now populated mainly by not only their
foul ilk, but also all those others whom various societies had cast out.
The hood and voluminous cloak completely hid both the new arrival's
features and garments. Indeed, it dragged so low on the ground that
even the legs and feet were invisible. While in many places this would
have immediately drawn the attention of all around, in Ratchet such
images were more common.

That, of course, did not mean that other eyes—goblin, human, and
otherwise—were not watching, merely that they did so very surreptitiously. There were those in the ramshackle collection of crumbling
stone buildings and decaying slat huts who gauged each newcomer for
their possible value and others who marked them for possible threat.
More than a few of the unshaven, unwashed figures were here because
others desired *their* demise, and so they were willing to kill any supposed assassin first. That they might slay an innocent was a notion long
willingly accepted by them.

The covered form shuffled through Ratchet, the hood peering this
way and that in the deepening gloom and at last focusing on a weathered sign hanging over the front of what had once been, in another
time, a fairly reputable inn. The faded letters still managed to spell out
the establishment's unpromising name . . . *The Broken Keel.*

With fluid movements, the stranger veered toward the inn. A lanky, scarred man in leather boots and billowing sea garb leaned against the wall by the cracked door. He peered up at the oncoming figure, then silently moved off. The hood shifted slightly, watching his departure, then turned again to the inn.

Although the flowing sleeve stretched to the handle, those close by might have noticed that they never quite touched. Yet, the door swung wide open.

Inside, the goblin proprietor and three patrons stared at the intruder, who, at nearly seven feet tall, stood a hand higher than the biggest of them. The men's garb and the cutlasses at their sides marked them from the stories the newcomer had heard. Bloodsail Buccaneers. Yet, the figure paid no mind to their interest; only one thing mattered.

"This one seeks transportation across the sea," the hooded form declared. For the first time, the four registered some astonishment; the voice sounded neither male nor female.

The proprietor recovered first. The short, green, and somewhat pot-bellied goblin grinned wide, revealing his yellow teeth. He strode back behind the bar, where, despite his girth, he easily leapt up on an unseen bench or stool so as to be able to see over. His reaction was one of mockery.

"Ya wanta boat? Not too many in here! Food and ale, maybe, but we're fresh outa boats, heh!" As he spoke, his stomach swelled, straining farther out of the stained green and gold jerkin and almost completely over the wide, metal-clasped belt holding his weathered green pants up. "Ain't that right, boys?"

There were a couple of "ayes" and a slow nod, the last from one particularly keen-eyed drinker among the trio. Not one of the band had yet taken his gaze off the shrouded newcomer, who evinced no concern, no other emotion.

"This one is a stranger here, true," the figure replied, again in a voice unidentifiable as anything. "But a place where food and shelter are offered is often a place where knowledge of transport can also be found . . ."

"Ya got gold ta pay for this 'transport,' my muffled friend?"

The hood nodded. The sleeve that had opened the door now stretched forward again. It was not a hand that popped out of it now, but rather a small, gray pouch that jingled. The pouch swung from two leather strings that vanished into the sleeve.

"This one can pay."

The interest in the pouch was obvious, but the newcomer did not seem moved by that interest. The proprietor rubbed his pointy chin then rumbled, "Hmmph! Old Dizzywig, the wharfmaster, might be crazy enough to sail you there. Leastwise, he's got boats."

"Where might this one find him?"

"At the blasted wharf, of course! Old Dizzywig lives there. Go left out the door, then around the building. Walk a little bit. You can't miss the wharf and the docks. There's a lot of water beyond 'em, heh."

The hood dipped forward. "This one thanks you."

"Tell 'im Wiley sent ya." The proprietor grunted. "Happy sailin' . . ."

With a graceful turn, the stranger stepped out. As the door closed behind, the figure surveyed the vicinity, then turned as the innkeeper had dictated. The sky was now dark, and while it was doubtful that the wharfmaster himself would wish to set sail at night, that did not matter.

Figures scurried to and from various buildings as the hooded form passed by. The stranger paid them no heed. So long as they did not interfere, they meant nothing.

The dark sea suddenly beckoned. For the first time, the hooded figure hesitated.

But there is no other choice, the stranger concluded. *No choice but to dare one new thing after another . . .*

While there were some larger ships anchored nearby, none were what the stranger sought. A small boat that could be handled by a lone sailor would serve all the stranger's needs. Three ragged but potentially-useful craft sat at the edge of the water, the fine finish of each a thing of the past. They likely floated, but that was it. To their right, the first of the docks stretched out into the black waters. Several wooden crates waited to be loaded on some vessel apparently not yet in port. An old but tough-looking figure that could have just as well have been Wiley's brother, father, or cousin sat upon one box, his gnarled hands working with fishing line. He looked up as the newcomer approached.

"Hmm?" was all he said at first. Then . . . "Closed for night. Come tomorrow . . ."

"If you are Dizzywig, the wharfmaster, this one seeks transport across the sea. Now, not tomorrow." From the voluminous sleeve emerged the coin sack.

"Ya does, does ya?" He rubbed his lengthy chin. Up close, the older goblin was thinner and in better shape than Wiley. He also wore clothes of a better quality, including a purple shirt and red pants that both contrasted greatly to his green hide. His boots, wide like all goblin boots due to the splayed feet of their wearers, were also of better condition.

"Are you he?" asked the stranger.

" 'Course I am, fool!" The goblin grinned, showing that, despite his age, he had kept most of his sharp if yellow teeth. "But as to hirin' a boat, there're some ships that would do ya better. Where's your destination?"

"This one must cross to Menethil Harbor."

"Goin' to visit the dwarves, eh?" Not bothered in the least by the stranger's odd voice, Dizzywig grunted. "None of the ships are goin' there, that's for sure! Hmmph . . ." Suddenly, the goblin straightened. "And maybe you won't be goin', either. . . ."

His slanted, almost reptilian black and coral eyes looked behind his would-be client, who followed the gaze.

Their approach had been expected. The ploy was an old one, even where the stranger came from. Brigands were brigands, and they always sought the tried-and-true paths used before them.

From behind his seat, Dizzywig pulled out a long piece of wood with a huge nail hammered through the head. The point stuck out for at least half a foot. The wharfmaster wielded the wood with an ease that bespoke of years of practice and use, but he did not jump up to give aid to the hooded figure.

"Touch my wharf, and I'll pound your damned heads to pulp," he warned the buccaneers.

"Got no quarrel with you, Dizzywig," one of the trio muttered. He had been the most interested of those observing the newcomer in the inn. "Just a little business with our friend here . . ."

The stranger slowly turned so as to completely face them, in the process sliding back the hood enough for those in front to see the face beneath. The face, the blue-black hair down past her shoulders, the two proud horns that stretched from each side of her skull . . .

Eyes widening, the three men from the tavern took a step back. Two looked anxious, but the leader, a scarred individual wielding a knife with a curved blade nearly a foot long, grinned.

"Well now . . . ain't you a pretty little female . . . whatever race you is. We'll be taking that pouch girlie!"

"The contents of the pouch will not bring you much comfort," she said, discarding both the spell that had hidden her true, almost musical voice and the speech mannerisms she had used with it. "Money is only a fleeting vice."

"We like a little vice, don't we, lads?" the leader retorted. His companions grunted their agreement, greed having overtaken astonishment over what stood before them.

"Let's finish dis before the bruisers catch wind of it," one of the other pirates added.

"They won't be around this way for awhile yet," the first snarled. "But 'tis true I don't fancy payin' the watch off with what we get, eh?"

They converged on their intended victim.

She would give them one more chance. "You don't wish to do this. Life is valuable, violence is not. Let us have peace between us. . . ."

One of the lesser buccaneers, a balding, skeleton of a man, hesitated. "Maybe she's right, Dargo. Why don't we just leave her be—"

He immediately received a sharp, back-handed strike across the jaw from the leader. Dargo glared at him. "What's gotten into you, you son of a sea cow?"

The other brigand blinked. "Dunno . . ." He stared in shock at the tall female. "She done somethin'!"

Gritting his teeth, Dargo turned on her. "Damned mage! That's the last o' your tricks!"

"That is not my calling," she explained, but neither Dargo nor his friends were listening. The buccaneers ran at her, trying with swiftness to avoid any more spells. Common sense would have dictated that they flee from any caster, but common sense was clearly in short supply among these brigands.

A hand—a light blue hand covered in part by an array of copper-colored metal strands—thrust out of the left sleeve. She muttered a prayer for her foes in her glorious native tongue, too long unheard by her from any other's lips.

The leader was again predictable. He thrust the blade at her chest.

She easily dodged aside his clumsy strike without even moving from her position. As he fell forward, she touched him on the arm and used his momentum to send him flying past her and onto the hard wood of the nearest dock.

As he hit, his thin companion drew his cutlass and made a slash at her outstretched arm. The stranger gracefully pulled her limb from danger, then kicked at his midsection with what was not a foot, but rather a large and very tough cloven *hoof.*

As if struck by a barreling tauren, the second pirate went tumbling back like a missile into the third brigand, a stouter pirate with a bent nose. The pair collided hard, then collapsed in a jumble of arms and legs.

She spun about, the shifting of the two tendrils coming from behind her ears and lining her slim but beautiful features the only outward sign of her emotions. Her hand caught Dargo's wrist as he came at her from the dock and turned his force back against his arm.

The buccaneer let out a howl as his shoulder cracked. With his path already leading to the ground, it was a simple matter for her to let the villain fall face first at her feet.

Atop the crate, Dizzywig chortled. "Hah! Draenei women make for some tough customers, don't they? Tough and pretty, that is!"

Glancing at the goblin, she sensed no malevolent intent in his comments. With his occupation, it was not entirely surprising that Dizzywig had apparently seen or heard of her race at some point in the past. At the moment, he sounded honestly curious about her—curious and amused—but nothing more.

The wharfmaster had maintained a neutral stance during the confrontation, an understandable choice, if not her preferred one. The draenei had wanted to keep her activities secret. She was not where her kind should be.

But her oath and her quest demanded otherwise.

Leaning down to Dargo, she whispered, "The bone is not broken."

The anguished brigand seemed not to appreciate that gesture. In truth, she had done as much as she could to avoid injuring any of them, regardless of their wicked ways. Unfortunately, these three had demanded of her a brief exhibition.

But now the trio was more malleable to her advice . . . and abilities. In a level voice, the draenei declared, "It would be best if you all departed and forgot this incident."

The abilities granted her calling added weight to her words. Dargo and his companions scrambled to their feet and scurried off as if hounds with their tails on fire, leaving their weapons behind.

She turned back to Dizzywig. The goblin simply nodded. "Can't make out much under that robe, but you've got the smell of a priest about you. . . ."

"I am of that calling."

Dizzywig grinned. "Priest, mage, monster, man, don't matter to me none just so I get paid. The red boat there," he indicated with a crooked finger. "That's a good craft, if you've got the money."

"I have." The pouch materialized from the depths of her sleeve. "If I can trust that the boat will sail."

"Yeah, it will . . . but not with me in it. You want a crew, you should've held on to that sorry trio, heh!"

She shrugged. "I only need a serviceable craft. I'll make it on my own, if that is what is destined for me."

The draenei tossed him the pouch, which Dizzywig immediately opened. The goblin poured out the coins, his eyes wide with pleasure.

"That'll do . . . just," he said with a larger grin.

Without another word, the priestess strode toward the boat indicated. Its sides were more green than red due to layers of algae, and the wood was well worn, but she saw no weakness in the thick hull. A strong, single mast with a mainsail-foresail combination gave the fifty-foot-long sloop its only source of movement. Climbing in, she also found two sorry emergency oars resting in the hooks on the inside walls of the hull.

Dizzywig no doubt expected her to ask for supplies, but she was growing uncharacteristically impatient and did not want to spend time bartering for what she did not believe that she needed. Bad enough that she had spent futile weeks following a false trail. Secreted on her person was enough sustenance for the journey across.

The wharfmaster chuckled again, and although she no longer faced him, the draenei knew that he wondered what she would do next. For Dizzywig, the stranger was a good night's entertainment, indeed.

Wondering whether he would be disappointed with what she now intended, the priestess extended her hand . . . and began working the lines and the sail for departure with the practiced skill of one familiar with the sea, albeit no sea as the goblin would have known.

When she was done with that, the draenei leapt out. Judging the mass of the craft, she gripped one part of it and shoved.

Dizzywig let out a hmmph of surprise. It should have taken two or three brawny men to break the boat completely free. Fortunately, the priestess had not relied on brute strength, but a careful measurement of balance.

The boat silently slid the rest of the way into the water. The draenei leapt aboard, thanking those who had trained her.

"The sea's no safer than the land, these days. Just remember that!"

the goblin called jovially. Then, with another chuckle, he added, "Enjoy your trip!"

She did not need the wharfmaster to warn her of the dangers. Over the past weeks, the priestess had confronted more than her share of the darkness seeking to engulf this world. More than once, she had nearly been killed during her pursuit, but, by the grace of the *naaru,* she had survived to continue the chase.

But as Ratchet, as all Kalimdor, rapidly dwindled in the dark and the sea enveloped her craft, the draenei felt that she had only tasted the least of dangers thus far. Now that the priestess knew that she followed the *true* trail, she was also aware that at some point, those she hunted would note her approach.

Note it and do what they could to slay her.

So it must be . . . the draenei thought. After all, she had taken up this quest of her own volition, her own desire.

Taken it up even though all who knew her now thought her utterly mad . . .

THREE

They're gone!" the blood elf snapped vehemently. "They're gone!"

The woman in black stared at him from behind her veil. Although he was taller than her by an inch or two, it was he who seemed to have to look up at her, not the other way around.

It was also he who suddenly stifled his anger under her dread gaze.

"An obvious observation, Zendarin, as is the fact that we need not concern ourselves with them. The dear ones have their fates already destined; you know that very well."

"But there was much to learn, much to explore with their making! Much magic of a sort none has ever witnessed!"

The avarice in his gleaming orbs when Zendarin spoke of magic made his companion smile in disdain. "A trifle, blood elf." She gently stroked the veil covering her scorched side. "A trifle to what I will ultimately achieve."

He bowed to her wisdom and her dark glory, but added, "What *we'll* ultimately achieve, my lady."

"Yes . . . what we will achieve, my ambitious mage." The lady in black turned away without another word. The two stood at the mouth of one of the upper cave passages riddling Grim Batol. Despite its location well above the base of the mountain, this entrance was more accessible to the interior than most below—provided one was welcome within. Those who were not would find the path wrought with hidden pitfalls, including sentinels masked by Zendarin's magic.

And woe betide any of those intruders should they be spellcasters themselves. . . .

The blood elf took one last glance over the landscape surrounding Grim Batol. Beyond the immediate desolation surrounding the mountain's base, the Wetlands had returned in force since the years of the red dragons' captivity to the orcs. The lush lands were misleading, though, for they held many natural and unnatural threats that acted as a good buffer against too many intruders. Six-legged crocolisks hunted in the waters, and tribes of gnolls—all fearful of Zendarin and the lady—also kept watch for fools venturing too close. Among the more horrific guardians were the monstrous oozes, gelatinous fiends that absorbed any animal in reach and, in the drier lands to the northwest, saurian raptors that stalked any and all fresh meat.

So full of life, so full of death, thought Zendarin. It was a far cry from the glorious wooded realm to which he was used, a realm to which he looked forward to returning once he had gained all that he sought.

Smothering a curse at the trials he had to suffer for his arts, Zendarin followed the veiled woman. He and the drakonid had spent the last night pursuing prizes he considered so valuable that he had let the remaining dwarves scurry back into their secret burrows like the frightened rabbits that they were. That, after swearing to his mistress that he would eradicate the pests once and for all. The dwarves had become a grand nuisance of late and while both he and she agreed that they could not possibly threaten the ultimate success of the pair's experiments, they could *slow* it. That was why he had devised this plan, this perfect plan.

But Zendarin could not have possibly known that two of those experiments would choose that very moment to escape Grim Batol.

"How did it happen? How did it happen?" he asked, barely able to keep his tongue civil despite being aware of just what she could do to him if merely riled. She had already slain two able assistants for minor infractions, and while she very much needed his skills, he knew that he had to tread warily. Zendarin's companion was very much insane . . . but that did not preclude her also being *brilliant.*

"The dragonspawn watching them were careless. They were told that the two might be immune to some of the binding spells and that at the slightest hint of that, the guards should alert me. The fools apparently were not satisfied that the danger yet warranted that alert."

The blood elf cursed the guards. Dragonspawn were brutishly-efficient in causing carnage and generally excellent at obeying orders. True, they were not as skilled and cunning as drakonid, but that should have not mattered in this situation. The dragonspawn had handled far more difficult tasks than keeping sentry. He could not believe their great error. "I'll tear out their black hearts for this. . . ."

"You need not bother. There wasn't much left of them after the escape. The children saw to that." She tsked, again stroking the veil as she walked serenely through the caverns like a queen in her castle. "Besides, this will all make for an interesting test."

" 'Test'? My lady, they'll wreak havoc that'll bring someone of power investigating. Someone from Dalaran perhaps or—or worse!" Zendarin could imagine quite well just what "worse" might entail. There were powers existing on Azeroth that were greater than all the wizards left in Dalaran or even among his own people combined.

His declaration only made her smile again, albeit this time in cold anticipation. "Yes . . . someone will very likely investigate . . . someone very likely will . . ."

Before he could question her comment, the pair entered the upper level of the vast cavern in which their gargantuan prisoner and the focus of their work still struggled against his magical bonds. The skardyn feverishly toiled around the shimmering leviathan, ever checking both the strands keeping the nether dragon in place and adjusting the new white crystals that their mistress had just set in place for the next attempt.

"Filthy creatures," murmured Zendarin. A blood elf was still an elf when it came to aesthetics. His long nose wrinkled as one of the hooded creatures rushed up to the mistress and handed her a small cube laced with cerulean stripes along each face.

"Obedient creatures," she corrected, dismissing the skardyn. As the dwarven form scurried back to its comrades, she held the cube toward Zendarin. "You see? Just as I required of them."

His disgust gave way to renewed avarice. Zendarin's eyes glowed a fierce green. "Then, it's only the matter of an egg?"

"Isn't it always? Aaah . . . here they bring it now . . ."

Four skardyn appeared below, the scaly dwarves grunting from effort as they held aloft a huge, oval egg . . . an egg stretching nearly a yard in length. It was thick, gray, and covered in a slick, oily substance that dripped down on its bearers. There was no mistaking just what kind of egg it was.

A dragon's.

"They should make haste!" urged Zendarin, aware of the fragility of the prize regardless of how massive it was. "The egg will not remain fresh long. . . ."

His companion began to descend to the cavern floor, her lack of concern well evident. "The coating of *myatis* will preserve it. Myatis preserves *everything* soaked in it, no matter how long."

Aware of how old this egg actually was and the value of it to their work, Zendarin marveled. Indeed, none of what they hoped to accomplish would have been at all possible if this egg had not been preserved through the dark arts in the first place.

Not for the first time, *her* skills astounded him, he who had lived so many centuries and accomplished so much.

He joined her below, just as the skardyn placed the egg on a stone platform set up in front of the bound nether dragon. The imprisoned behemoth managed a muffled growl, much to the amusement of the lady in black.

"Temper, temper . . ." she cooed, as if to an infant.

Relieved of their burden, the skardyn retreated. The platform was much akin to an altar, the top a rectangular slab of ebony-streaked granite that matched in substance the rounded base. The four legs thrusting up from the base to the slab had been carved to resemble dragons rising on their back legs. Where the mistress had originally gained the platform, Zendarin did not know, but he could sense its incredible age and the many spells that had been cast using it. Latent magical energies saturated its stone form, tantalizing the blood elf. The platform had seen much use over its long existence, especially spells that had called for the lives of the innocent if the pale red stains on the top were any indication to go by.

That his own part in this work had required the sacrifice of others did not in any manner disturb Zendarin. Despite everything, he did not consider his acts heinous in the least. Ambitious, yes. Of necessity, yes . . . but not heinous. Like so many of his kind, he was driven by the hunger, the need, to seek out magic . . . at all costs. He considered all he did necessary to achieving that goal.

And that many others would still have to perish in the process was simply a matter that he could not help . . . not that he cared. After all, they were only dwarves, humans, and other lesser creatures.

The lady in black studied the egg for several seconds, as if able to see within its thick shell. She placed the cerulean cube before the egg. Then, with a smile to the captive leviathan, she ran her long, tapering fingers across the protective layer.

The myatis coating sizzled away.

"Join me, dear Zendarin. . . ."

He eagerly stepped to her side, summoning the magic at his command to blend with hers. It was the very nature of his abilities as a blood elf that made him so precious to her and permitted Zendarin to voice, at least to a point, his frustrations. He brought to the mistress a magic uniquely qualified to aid her, for it was based in the almost vampiric siphoning of power from demons and other denizens of the Twisting Nether. Zendarin was exceptionally proficient in that skill, and thus his might was currently at its height.

It also helped that he had at his command those who brought to him *other* sources of magical energy, invaluable servants whom the lady in black could not rip from his control without losing them and him in the process. That was another reason that she tolerated his impatience.

He stood next to her, his hands splayed over the egg in identical fashion to hers. Silently, they linked their magic together, binding it into one unique form. As they did, both the cube and the white crystals burned bright.

Zendarin's companion stretched forth her left hand toward the captive nether dragon.

The white crystals let out a sinister hum. From each emanated a light that struck the nether dragon.

Blue tendrils of energy shot forth from the struggling beast wherever the light of the crystals burned him. Despite the silver strands binding his maw, his agonized moans shook the cavern.

Guided by the sorceress, the blue tendrils dove down, striking the egg in the center. The egg shook and swelled to twice its original size. The shell took on an azure hue.

"Now . . ." she murmured to Zendarin.

As one, the pair threw their own contributions deeper into the matrix of the spell, mixing them with the stolen forces of the nether dragon. The cavern was suddenly ablaze in a wicked storm of violent energies whose focus was the egg. Although immune from most magic through the skillful work of their mistress, the skardyn scrambled to the farthest corners. Still dwarves at their core, they were rightly wary of a possible collapse of the cavern, but wise enough to know the punishment that they would receive if they fled the cavern at this critical moment.

The air crackled. The sorceress's dark locks rose. The veil also lifted, revealing clearly her savagely-burnt profile. The full lips ended in charred flesh that outlined the permanent smile of a skull. Underneath the upper edge of the veil, the ear proved to be little more than a shriveled bit of skin over a hole.

She raised her hands high, Zendarin matching her actions perfectly. They continued to throw their combined power into the egg as the sorceress tore more and more of the nether dragon's essence from him.

The nether dragon's struggles grew more violent. Futile as his attempt was, it still managed to shake the entire cavern. A huge stalactite cracked free, plummeting to the floor far below. A skardyn too slow to register what was happening was crushed underneath it, a death unworthy of notice or even significance to either spellcaster.

Zzeraku—the blood elf remembered the nether dragon calling himself—shimmered, seeming ready to melt into mist. Yet, the strands holding him prisoner did not permit the Outland beast to even escape to death. They held Zzeraku mercilessly, tightening further at the mistress's silent command.

More and more of the nether dragon's magic—and essence, in fact—poured into the swollen egg, where it continually intertwined with that of the two spellcasters. Zendarin almost expected the egg to explode, so out of proportion had it grown. . . .

And, indeed, one side suddenly developed a crack.

But this did not enrage or frustrate either, for, the next moment, it was clear that the crack was not due to their work, not directly. Rather, the cause could be found within . . . a cause eager now to be free.

The egg was hatching.

In the glow of the ensorcelled egg, the face of Zendarin's companion was more monstrous to behold than even those of the skardyn. An inhuman quality filled her expression . . . not surprising, as the sorceress was no more human—indeed, even less so—than the blood elf.

"Yes . . . my child . . ." she murmured, *almost* sounding motherly. "Yes . . . come to me . . ."

Another crack developed next to the first. A fragment of the shell fell away—

From within, an eye peered out . . . an eye such as neither had ever seen.

An eye, despite this being the birth, that spoke of cunning, of evil . . . far, far more ancient.

The bay that separated the lands of Lordaeron, and Dalaran in particular, from where Grim Batol lay, was wide, but should have taken Korialstrasz no more than five hours to cross. Yet, only midway out, the red dragon was forced to land upon a small rock formation jutting out of the turbulent water and perch upon it like a sea gull while he rested. Korialstrasz could only assume that the sorcerous shaft's crystal head had weakened him more than he had expected.

But he had little opportunity for recuperation, for suddenly a storm assailed him, a tempest of such abrupt violence that the crimson behemoth instantly gave up all notion of rest. Dragging himself into the air, he instead continued on his way.

But the elements were clearly against him, for the storm only worsened. As powerful as he was, Korialstrasz was yet tossed about like a leaf. He immediately headed toward the clouds, thinking to fly above the storm, but though he fought hard to reach them, they stayed well overhead.

And that at last warned the red giant that this storm was not so natural after all.

Rather than struggle to reach the unreachable, Korialstrasz tried a more direct flight toward Grim Batol. The moment he did, the wind exploded from that direction, buffeting him so hard that the dragon felt as if he had struck a mountain.

He did not believe in happenstance. This *was* a spell, yes, though whether directed at him in particular or merely to hunt a dragon was a question he had no time to answer. What mattered foremost was escaping it.

Logic suggested that he fight magic with magic . . . and yet, Korialstrasz was not so certain of the wisdom of that. Yet, he could think of no other immediate course. Thus, steeling himself against the raging storm, the red dragon struck at the dark clouds.

No sooner had he done so than he was attacked by a raging hurricane tenfold stronger than before. A barrage of lightning pounded him, and the gale force winds turned the dragon upside down. He could see little past his snout, for the rain fell in a pounding torrent.

And even as Korialstrasz struggled against vertigo, he was painfully aware that it was his own power that had now multiplied the storm's effect . . . just as the mysterious caster had no doubt intended.

Around and around, the dragon spun. The clouds became the sea beneath and the sea the sky. Korialstrasz saw no choice; he could not reach those clouds. There remained but one alternative, even if it was likely the one his unseen adversary wished him to take.

Arcing, Korialstrasz dove into the swirling waters.

He was certain of his error the moment that he submerged, but could not look back. Even despite his keen eyesight, Korialstrasz could see little. The waters of the vast bay turned to black only scant yards beneath him, again, no natural thing. A monster several times his size might be rising up to swallow him and the dragon would not see it.

Some dragons were born to the water, but red dragons were very much creatures of the sky, however well they could swim. Korialstrasz could hold his breath for more than an hour, assuming nothing tried to force that breath from him. Still, the sooner he was back in the air, the better.

Voices began whispering in his head.

A new wave of vertigo overwhelmed Korialstrasz. He could not tell the depths from the surface. The dragon immediately thrust upward, but instead of the storm, all that greeted him was a blackness that chilled to the soul.

And the voices grew stronger, chanting in a tongue Korialstrasz thought that he should know. He fought against their seductive call, aware that each moment he remained caught in their snare made his hopes of surviving monumentally lesser.

Now, there was only the darkness. The deep waters squeezed at Korialstrasz's lungs, which made the crimson leviathan wonder if he had been submerged longer than he thought. There was no sense of time, no sense of place . . . only the chanting voices.

I will not be undone by this! the dragon swore. He imagined another countenance, that of his beloved queen and mate, Alexstrasza. Yet, her image was faded, and growing more so, a dangerous sign.

But that only served to make him more determined. Summoning his strength, Korialstrasz cast a desperate spell.

Light erupted around him, searing away the darkness of the depths. In it, the dragon beheld the source of his troubles . . . *naga*.

He knew their origins, knew them because he was, to his mind at least, in part to blame for their creation. Once, they had been of the night elf race, the Highborne who had served the mad queen, Azshara. When the source of their great power, the fearsome Well of Eternity, had imploded due to the efforts of a few staunch defenders but especially the young druid, Malfurion Stormrage, it had sucked the great capital of the night elves to the bottom of a newly-created sea. With the city had gone Azshara and her fanatic followers, supposedly to their doom.

It would not be until millennia later that Korialstrasz and the world would discover that a mysterious force had transformed those trapped beneath the waves into something worse.

The incredible explosion of light had caught the naga completely unaware. Several swirled about in utter confusion, stunned by the spell's intensity. As naga, they no longer much resembled elves of any sort. The females upon whom Korialstrasz now set his baleful gaze had some vague similarities remaining, mostly in their slimmer, upper torsos and their faces, which retained the long, narrow design of night elves. They were even beautiful, if in a monstrous way. Yet, no elven race sported four wicked arms that ended in long, taloned fingers, nor did any have the wide, veined fins of gold that blossomed sharply from the head all the way down to the naga's tail.

And tails were all there were below the waist, for long gone were the sleek legs. The lower halves were those of massive serpents, segmented and scaled. They twisted back and forth constantly, giving the naga swiftness and incredible maneuverability in the water.

The males had degenerated even more than the females, their heads low and reptilian, with teeth that jutted out from both the top and bottom of the long maw like a crocodile. Their eyes were deep set and narrow, and their crests and fins, which jutted as sharply as spears in places, were of a darker gold and brown shade. Their torsos were less in contrast to their serpentine lower bodies, being also scaled and segmented. Even their arms, massive compared to most creatures their size, were covered so.

There had developed, over the generations, many tribes of naga, but these aqua and black scaled fiends with their golden fins were of a type of which Korialstrasz knew nothing, save that they were clearly both powerful and of evil mind. That was all he needed to know. Naga in general had no love for those who lived above the surface, but these had gone well out of their way to set a tremendous trap.

For what reason it might be, Korialstrasz had no time to consider. The light began to fade, and the naga regrouped.

But now that he could see them, it was a simple matter for the dragon to strike with both his paws and his tail, bowling over the sinister creatures. Several went sinking into the blackness below, but some desperately sought to rework the spell that had nearly done in the behemoth.

Korialstrasz's body flared a bright red. The water around him suddenly boiled. In his mind, he heard the naga shriek as the heat struck. Two males in the forefront were caught full on, their bodies swelling monstrously as they burned red.

A buzzing filled the dragon's head. He looked below to his right, where a female with all four arms raised toward him glowed with magic of her own.

It was a simple matter for him to increase the heat that his body radiated. The female naga fled just before she, too, would have been boiled. The buzzing ceased.

But Korialstrasz's lungs suddenly ached, and he felt the impulse to breathe. He needed air and he needed it without delay. With desperate strokes, the red dragon pushed himself upward.

The surface seemed so far away that the fear that he was still swimming down instead of up crossed his air-starved mind, but he had no choice but to continue the direction he had chosen.

The strain on his lungs grew horrific. If he could just take a single breath . . .

His head shoved above the water. However, even as Korialstrasz filled his starving lungs, he continued to push himself above the sea. Magic and wings greater in span than some other dragons were in length threw him well into the sky.

A sky that, though still overshadowed, no longer stormed.

Despite the naga threat yet high, Korialstrasz was forced to hover for several seconds as he worked to regain not only his breath but his senses. The clouds remained thick, but the sea itself had grown calm, even deathly silent.

A mass of squirming tentacles broke the surface, snaring the dragon by the tail and hind legs and seeking the wings.

Letting out a roar, Korialstrasz immediately focused on the spot from which the tentacles had sprouted and exhaled sharply. The torrent of flame he unleashed was not as strong as he hoped, but it did make the monster beneath unbind one of his legs.

But the rest of the tentacles still tugging at the red giant threatened to pull him under. Korialstrasz beat his wings. He was no ordinary dragon, even if he was not an Aspect. The naga's pet would soon discover that.

And so, incredibly, rather than the sea creature dragging Korialstrasz down, *he* slowly but inexorably pulled the tentacled monster from the depths. First there came a sharp beak, a savage mouth able to bite into pieces the largest warships. Then came a long, tubular head with two unblinking black saucers for malevolent orbs.

A kraken.

How the small band of naga had gotten such a creature into the bay, he did not know. Still, what mattered most was that the monstrous beast weighed heavy on Korialstrasz. The dragon lost momentum. The sea grew near again.

There was no choice. Near to collapse though he was, Korialstrasz exhaled one last time with all the force left to him.

Unhindered by the sea, his powerful blast broiled the kraken. The sea monster let out a chilling shriek as it released its grip and plunged back into the water. The wave it created rose as high as Korialstrasz's tail before subsiding.

The huge red did not rejoice. Indeed, it was all he could do to keep conscious. Despite his horrific weakness, though, Korialstrasz quickly shoved himself in the direction of his goal. Even as short as the distance remaining was, he did not know if he could reach landfall before his remaining strength failed him. Yet, all he could do was try.

All he could do was hope. . . .

The waters remained still as the gigantic red dragon dwindled in the distance, remained still until a single naga head emerged to watch the vanishing leviathan.

The female naga's slanted eyes stared unblinking until Korialstrasz was no more than a distant dot just above the horizon. At that point, a second head, that of a fearsome male, thrust up. The scales on the right side of the male's head were torn near the jaw, the result of the most peripheral of wounds caused by the dragon's sweeping tail. Ignoring his wound, the male peered intently in the direction the female had.

"The deed is done . . ." she murmured in a grating voice. "We will be spared. . . ."

Nodding, the male grinned. The female followed suit, revealing her teeth to be no less sharp, no less savage, than her companion's.

The two naga submerged.

FOUR

The foreboding landscape rising before her on the horizon was called Khaz Modan. The hooded draenei had no reference as to the name's origins, but the mere sound of it made her steel herself. She knew that orcs inhabited this region, but so, too, did dwarves. Both were races of which she knew. And for her sake, if it came to a confrontation, the mage hoped that it would be with one of the underdwellers, not the green-skinned warriors. The dwarves, at least, were allies.

At first, there was no sign of the island settlement for which she hunted, but gradually some shapes materialized on the distant shore. The most prominent of those was the thick, stone wall on the far end of Menethil Harbor that she had already learned protected most of the town from inland incursions. Then, taller structures and huge, shaggy trees made themselves visible through the dissipating morning fog.

One building in particular caught her gaze. Rising above all else, the four towers of Menethil Keep watched over the settlement like stern guardians, their coned tops reminiscent of warriors' helmets. Within their ranks, the almost cathedral-like structure of the main building stood only a story shorter, but was much broader.

And as Menethil Harbor took form before the lone figure, she knew that the sentries in turn were very likely catching sight of her.

Sure enough, only minutes later a ship turned out to meet her. The crew was mostly human, although there were a few daring dwarves aboard as well. Dwarves in general did not do well with the sea, having a tendency to sink like rocks if they fell in, but current times demanded bravery of a different sort.

As the ship reached her, a human leaned over to study the lone intruder. His bearded face stretched into a look of surprise.

"My lady," he grunted. "Not often we get one of your folk in this particular land . . . and certainly not by such means as I see before me." The man leaned closer, revealing for the first time that he wore a tarnished breast plate marking him as an officer. Despite his beard, he was young for his rank, as young as she possibly. The violence of the past few wars had reduced the number of capable veteran warriors on both sides.

"I seek only landfall, nothing more, from Menethil Harbor," she replied. "Will you permit that?" The priestess did not add that, one way or another, she would achieve that landfall regardless of his answer.

Fortunately, the officer appeared a man of common sense. Draenei were allies; why should one not be allowed entrance to an Alliance stronghold? "You'll be having to answer a few questions once there, but other than that, there's no reason I can see to bar you, my lady."

He had a man toss down a rope ladder near her boat. A hirsute sailor scrambled down to take command of the sailboat while another held the ladder in place as the draenei climbed up.

"Welcome aboard the *Stormchild,* temporarily ensconced in Menethil Harbor." Up close, the lead human looked even younger. His eyes were a bright, almost innocent blue, but something about them yet told her that he had already become a seasoned fighter, rather than some young noble commissioned because of his bloodline. "I am its erstwhile captain, Marcus Windthorne. . . ."

He made a sweeping bow, but ever kept his eyes on her. Those eyes invited—nay, *insisted*—she likewise introduce herself. The draenei immediately saw that Marcus Windthorne was not someone easily made a fool, that despite his innocent-seeming eyes.

"I am called Iridi."

He accepted the short reply. "My lady Iridi. There is someone you seek in Menethil Harbor?"

Her head turned almost imperceptibly side-to-side. "No. My task is beyond this place."

"Beyond this place are the Wetlands, fraught with threat. Little more."

"That is the direction I must go."

He shrugged. "I've no reason to stop you, and if those who command Menethil Harbor have no reason, your doom is your own to decide, my lady."

He bowed to her, then turned to the task of command. The *Stormchild* veered about and headed back to the settlement.

Iridi left the bartered boat in the hands of Captain Windthorne, the vessel having served its purpose but of no more use to her. On shore, several dwarves met her, at their head one with a particularly thick, lengthy beard. He and the rest of his band all wore well-honed battle axes strapped to their backs.

"Name's Garthin Stoneguider," he rumbled after she had introduced herself. Garthin performed a perfunctory bow that greatly contrasted with the sweeping one made by the human captain. "Not many draenei hereabouts. None, in fact, lady."

"She's nothing to be afraid of, you old boar!" Marcus cheerfully called from the *Stormchild* as it began to set off from the docks again.

The dwarf growled at the human, but there was a twinkle in his deep, brown eyes that said he and the captain were friends. To Iridi, Garthin added, "As I was sayin', none at all, lady. What brings you to Menethil Harbor?"

"It is only a momentary pause. I must journey beyond for my task."

"And what might that task be? Someone like yourself shouldn't be going out into the Wetlands. There're things worse than raptors there."

She met his gaze. "Your concern is commendable, Master Garthin Stoneguider, but have no fear for me. I go where it is destined that I go."

"I seen your like. Priestess, you are. You commune with somethin' called the noru—"

"Naaru."

"That's what I said," Garthin returned obstinately. "Some mystical beings or somethin'." He shrugged. "We've got no reason to stop you from goin' beyond our walls, but the final word'll be decided by the governing council. You'll have to wait until nightfall to hear from them."

Although her calling had taught her much concerning the value of patience, Iridi did not take well to the thought of waiting for someone else to make a decision on a subject upon which she had already determined her course. She would leave Menethil Harbor and continue on, of that there was no mistake.

Yet, she bowed her head and humbly replied, "As you say. Where might I seek sustenance?"

He chuckled knowingly. "Oh, I'll show you the market . . . and keep you company until the decision's made."

Iridi's estimate of the dwarf rose. Garthin knew that, left alone, the draenei would buy more than she needed for a meal, enough to continue her journey, in fact. Whether she liked it or not, the priestess would have to wait until nightfall.

But, one way or another, she *would* leave the town before morning.

Garthin proved more pleasant of a companion than Iridi could have imagined, the dwarf willing to explain most of what the draenei came across in the market. He also gave her a hint of the troubles the town was facing now.

" 'Tis not just the Horde these days," the dwarf remarked at one point while Iridi pretended interest in some stoneware. "There're other things stirrin' beyond the Wetlands, they say. There've been shadows that blot out the moon and cries like those a demon might make."

Although her eyes were still on the merchant's wares, the priestess listened very carefully. " 'Demons'?"

"Aye, though no one's seen 'em. Still, more than a few scouts've failed to return, and the council's deciding what to do next to investigate. I hear they're sendin' a message to the king," Garthin said, referring,

Iridi knew, to his own kind's ruler. "But I'm of a mind that if he ain't sent someone out already, he ain't goin' to do so now. . . ."

Through moments such as this and other later ones, Iridi gathered enough information to make her certain that she was on the right track. The "demon cries" of which Garthin had spoken were enough by themselves to make her eager to move on . . . if only the council would give word.

They did, but not until late after sunset, as Garthin had said. More important, the word they gave was not the one the draenei desired.

Garthin received the missive from one of his own men, read it, then growled, "You're goin' nowhere, lady . . . but you've company. They ain't allowin' *anyone* to leave Menethil Harbor for the time bein'."

Iridi molded her expression into one of mild disappointment, although deep inside the draenei was already plotting her departure. "I will need accommodations for the time being, then."

"There's an inn that might suit one o' your callin', lady. I'll guide you to it."

She bowed her head. "You are being most kind, Garthin Stoneguider."

He smiled knowingly. "No . . . I'm doin' my duty. You *will* be stayin', lady, even if you end up in the jail. Orders are orders. No one's leavin'. For your own good."

He obviously meant what he said, both about it being for her own good and especially that he would put her behind bars if necessary. Iridi considered carefully her answer; her intention to leave not in the least lessened despite the dwarf's warning.

"If it is to be so, then it will be so—"

But at that moment, horns blared from the walls overlooking the Wetlands.

With a dexterity and swiftness that the priestess found astounding, Garthin drew his ax. "Stay here! I'm orderin' you to do that!"

He ran off toward the wall. Iridi hesitated for only a second, then followed.

Atop the wall, dwarven guards under the protection of the roofed battlements continued to blare on the horns while others held torches up in order to get some view of the dark lands beyond.

And in those unseen lands, Iridi heard snarls and hisses that set her normally-controlled nerves on end.

Garthin stood at the arched gate, where several other dwarves were preparing to march out into the night. More than twenty fighters hefted their weapons and, as soon as the signal was given by one of their fellows above, charged out.

Unfortunately, something much larger tried to charge inside at the same time.

Iridi only caught a glimpse of claws and teeth before the dwarves beat it back, their axes striking one after another with powerful effect. A pained roar echoed throughout Menethil Harbor. Despite that, Iridi caught a glimpse of one warrior suddenly pulled into the darkness . . . and for the first time she heard a dwarf scream in utter horror.

Yet, despite that awful cry, Garthin and the others continued to push into the night, quickly followed by at least two dozen newcomers. Aware of the determination and might of dwarves, Iridi knew that the threat had to be a potent one.

Heedless of either Garthin's orders or the danger without, the draenei priestess rushed forward. As she did, she extended her hand . . . and a staff formed in it, a staff whose head ended in a long, pointed crystal set in a silver base. The crystal flared a bright blue. At the opposing end, a smaller but identical crystal added to the almost blinding effect.

"Here now! Stop!" shouted a guard futilely as she slipped through the gate. Iridi discovered a wide bridge on the other side of the wall, one leading toward the fog-drenched Wetlands. At the far end of the bridge, she made out the shadowed forms of the fighters . . . and other creatures who loomed tall over the dwarves.

She raised the staff and uttered the words the naaru had taught her predecessors long, long ago.

The greater crystal exploded into even more brilliant light. A monstrous community of hisses and roars assailed her ears, and Iridi finally beheld what the dwarves battled.

They were reptilian in appearance, but stood on hind legs. Their front paws ended in sharp, curved claws easily capable of rending cloth, flesh, and possibly even armor. Most were of some reddish tinge with yellow stripes, and all wore what appeared to be bands of feathers around their wrists and throats.

They pulled back as one, the light clearly more than their narrow, burning orbs could take. The dwarves, their backs to the crystal, were able to quickly take advantage of the situation. They plunged into the band of reptiles, swinging their axes hard. Heavy blades chopped into scaled hides, spilling innards and life fluids. Three of the fearsome reptiles fell to the ground, two of which were quickly dispatched by the defenders. The third managed to crawl back, its twitching form ignored as the dwarves fought those still standing.

But even thanks to her startling intervention, the stalwart warriors were hard pressed. Iridi counted at least twenty of the savage reptiles who, despite the dwarves' deadly axes, were giving as good as they got. They had both the advantage of size and swiftness . . . swiftness, in fact, that astounded the draenei. Worse, they used that speed in combination with a clear, organized assault, almost as if they were intelligent. The priestess saw one dwarf cut off from the rest, then surrounded and ripped to shreds before anyone could aid him.

This must not continue! Iridi leapt forward, using the staff as a weapon now. She thrust it into the midsection of one reptile, then followed through with a kick perfectly aimed at an unprotected area just under the snapping jaws.

The beast dropped to its knees. With a free hand, the draenei toppled the reptile completely, sending it into one of its companions.

But then a set of claws tore at her cloak. If not for its voluminous design, those claws would have also ripped out her shoulder. As it was, though, her cloak became tangled in the monster's paw. The reptile dragged her toward it, causing the staff to fall from her grip.

Gritting her teeth, Iridi reached her stiffened fingers toward her adversary's open maw—and suddenly the reptile's head separated from its torso and tumbled into her arms. The body shivered, its death throes almost tossing her aside, but powerful arms pulled the startled priestess free before that could happen.

"You must be mad!" Garthin growled. "Get back inside! The raptors will rip you to shreds!"

"I only wish to help!"

"By getting yourself turned into dinner?" With another growl, the dwarf started dragging her back to the sealed gate.

A savage hiss was the only warning they had before a slavering, stench-ridden form fell upon them. Garthin grunted as a tail whipped across his chest, bowling him over and nearly sending him into the water flowing under the bridge.

The raptor ignored her, more interested in the armored dwarf. Iridi realized that it was likely due to Garthin seeming more of a threat. The raptor assumed that it could deal with the softer, less imposing draenei once the dwarf was dead.

But the reptile had taken no more than a step toward Garthin before the priestess flung herself into its midst. Senses heightened by years of intense training immediately analyzed the beast for any and all vital spots.

One hand hit just below the eye. Her foot struck right under the rib cage.

The raptor crumpled, its breath shocked from it, its nervous system stunned by the hand. Iridi landed atop the fallen creature, then rolled toward Garthin.

The dwarf groaned as she held his head up. His gaze fixed on her.

"Get—inside—" he demanded.

"Let me help you up," the priestess said, ignoring his frustration with her. She glanced around for her staff, but could not find it. Instead, Iridi saw Garthin's ax. She used it to enable the fighter to get to his feet.

"Let me have that," he said in a dark tone. As she obeyed, the dwarf quickly raised his ax high, then buried it in the stricken raptor's throat.

Iridi felt a momentary sense of repulsion, then reminded herself what was going on around them. Garthin had had no choice but to slay the beast.

The dwarf turned to her once more. "Get back inside, or I'll carry you!"

But that choice was no longer available to them. The battle had fallen back to the bridge, and both were now cut off. Although the raptors appeared unable to swim—for surely they would have otherwise crossed the waters and taken the fighters from behind—neither could the dwarves. Despite what Garthin might desire, Iridi would not abandon him for her sake.

But the dwarf would not be ignored. With a grunt, he seized her wrist. "This way!"

Garthin led her toward the right, away from the fight. The dwarf moved with purpose, clearly certain of his destination.

"Those reptiles," Iridi called as they ran. "Does this often happen?"

"You mean this mayhem? Nay! But somethin's got the lizards all riled up enough to flee their own haunts and try to take ours! Swear they'd even go for the ships if they had the brains to sail 'em!"

The priestess was not so certain that the raptors were not capable of doing just that, but she held her peace. "So they attack you out of fear of some other threat?"

Garthin chuckled, though there was no humor in the action. "Fortunate for us, eh? Aye, they started coming a few days back. First a couple, then more, and now, suddenly, this huge lot!"

"Will you have to abandon Menethil Harbor?"

He let out a defiant grunt. "Only when we're dead . . . Hah! Here 'tis!"

They stood before a rock that only the draenei's excellent night vision enabled her to make out. It was roughly the girth of the dwarf, but she saw nothing else remarkable about it.

"Keep an eye out," Garthin commanded.

As she obeyed, he planted one shoulder against the rock. With tremendous effort, Garthin began shoving it aside.

Iridi kept watch the struggle, which had turned into a stalemate, but also glanced back at both her companion's efforts and the misty Wetlands. Her mind raced as she decided her best choice.

"Here!" the dwarf declared triumphantly. The priestess looked down to discover a hole underneath the rock. It was large and obviously the work of skilled hands . . . *dwarven* hands.

She instantly knew what it was for. "It leads into the town?"

"Aye, into or out of it, depending on circumstances! No raptor'll fit in it, assuming that they could ever find it in the first place. There's a way to cover it back up once we're inside . . . or rather, once *you're* inside! Climb in."

But Iridi had already made up her mind. She put a gentle hand on her protector's shoulder. "I am sorry, Garthin."

"About wha—"

He slumped forward, her fingers having touched the right nerve in his neck to make him temporarily unconscious. The draenei immediately hefted his dense form into the safety hole, then slipped the ax in after. Once assured that Garthin would be all right, the priestess inspected the stone. Unlike the dwarf, Iridi moved it back using not so much strength, but rather a sense of balance and direction.

That done, she returned her attention to the fight. Guilt over abandoning the brave dwarves swept over her, and she started toward the bridge. However, at that moment, more figures came charging from the town, while from above, well-aimed bolts began falling upon the raptors. The tide began to turn.

Iridi thanked the naaru for her sudden luck. There was no sign of her staff, but that was not a significant problem at this point. It would be there for her when she needed it.

She headed into the Wetlands, seeking the trail by which the raptors had journeyed from their old grounds. Trace back the reptiles' flight and she was certain that she would find that for which she had been searching.

Or it would find her.

*　　★　　★　　★*

A massive, winged form flew through the night over land and sea. It flew with a manic determination that only partially had to do with its mission. Its mind was in turmoil, the result of other events stretching across much of the breadth of the world of Azeroth. Indeed, the mission it was upon was, in some ways, a relief . . . though it also added new burdens.

The shrouded sky rumbled, threatening a powerful storm. The huge flyer immediately darted upward, passing through clouds and rising up to where the moon shone down upon the darkening cloud cover.

Fatigue already touched the flyer, but it pushed on. It had a certain location in mind before it could rest and would reach it no matter how much the struggle. The vast, webbed wings beat harder, enabling the flyer to cut the miles as if they were nothing . . . which indeed they were to this particular dragon.

The storm stirred to waking below, but above there was only the dragon and moon. The former ignored the latter utterly, though its light well-illuminated the scaled behemoth's path, not to mention the behemoth itself.

And in that light, the dragon's scales shone almost as bright as the moon . . . if the moon were blue.

FIVE

Korialstrasz awoke to the realization that he had been asleep.
It was not what he should have been doing.
His second discovery was that he no longer wore his true form, but was shaped and clad as Krasus.

And as Krasus, he slowly registered his surroundings, a ragged cave perched on the side of a desolate hill overlooking a swampy region. Krasus knew immediately where he was, though how he had gotten here was still a lost memory.

The Wetlands were near his goal, but not exactly on his original path. The dragon mage stumbled toward the cave's edge, then studied the sky. It gave him no clue as to his coming here.

The last thing that he recalled, he had been using what little strength he had to reach the shore. It had been his intention to find a secluded area, then settle down for a short rest.

From there, Krasus had no idea what had happened . . . and that was a rare instance for him. He did not like being at a loss, especially under the circumstances. In addition, Krasus had no idea exactly how long he had been asleep. A dragon could sleep for minutes, hours, days, weeks. . . . It all depended upon circumstances.

This trek has been a troublesome one from the first breath on. That cannot be coincidence. He glared at his surroundings, momentarily blaming them for his state.

Then, drawing himself together, Krasus pushed aside his frustrations. If there was a reason for his unnatural slumber, he would likely learn it soon enough. What mattered was that he was so very near his destination.

So very near Grim Batol.

Krasus began the transformation to Korialstrasz . . . then hesitated. A dragon was a hard thing to miss, even by the blind. He had a better chance of encroaching on the dread mountain if he remained as he was. Indeed, that had been his likely intention when first he had left his sanctum, but his disturbing sleep had momentarily made him forget. Perhaps he had even transformed into his smaller form for that reason. . . .

"So it shall be, then." Krasus eyed the hillside, seeking a path down. If he hoped to remain hidden from those watching for magical beings such as himself, it behooved him to use only enough of his power to shield his presence. Besides, his current physical form was not adverse to hard effort.

Gloved hands took hold of the rocky hillside as he cautiously lowered himself down into the Wetlands. The difference in the climate became noticeable almost immediately; the land below was far more humid. Fortunately, though he resembled an elf—albeit a very pale one—Krasus had a red dragon's adaptability to heat. The Wetlands bothered him not in the least; the caverns of his flight were far more comfortably hot and, depending on the location, much more moist.

The cries of Wetlands life were oddly muted as Krasus stepped onto the soft, wet soil. In general, a place such as this was teeming with animals and insects eager to vocalize their presence. However, though he heard some of both groups, there should have been much more activity.

It was as if much of the life here was wary of imminent threat . . . something that Krasus also felt.

But nothing reared its ugly head nor attacked him with vile magic. Krasus journeyed deeper into the swampy region, heading on a path directly toward Grim Batol.

The lush growth quickly enveloped him, but as Krasus shoved vines from his face, he noted something about that plant life. It had an ill feeling to it. Outwardly, it appeared normal, but inside, there was a sense that something had become twisted, that the Wetlands were changing for the worst.

The taint from the cursed mount spreads. . . . This cannot go on. He grimly shoved the next several branches and vines, furious with himself most of all for ignoring the benighted land after freeing his beloved queen and ridding the mountains of the orcs and the accursed Demon Soul. It should have been at that time that he personally went into the depths of Grim Batol and eradicated any darkness remaining within. Even while his own flight, which had included some of his offspring, had been guarding the region, Krasus had done nothing. There had always been some other crisis, some other danger, turning him from this task.

But hindsight was ever perfect, whereas Krasus was not. That was no excuse, of course, but it did ease his guilt a little.

Each step of his boots left a squishing sound that echoed much too loudly, but Krasus did nothing to still the sound. That would have required more magic. He still hoped to sneak upon whatever lurked in Grim Batol, though that notion was likely more and more nothing but a dream.

Small insects hovered near him, but then flew off. Most of those who dined on blood could sense that his was not to their taste.

But something else evidently believed that Krasus would make a fine meal. He noted its presence nearby, yet could not sense exactly where without possibly making himself known to anything lurking in the distant mountain. Krasus moved with caution; powerful as he was in this form, he was not invulnerable.

Yet, as he trudged along, nothing attacked. The violet-clad figure moved into the deepest part of the Wetlands and finally decided that it was time to risk sending his mind out toward Grim Batol.

Finding an area relatively far from the shrouded waters of the swamp, Krasus planted himself against a mossy tree and concentrated. Immediately, his view expanded in *all* directions. A human mind could not have coped with such a complete survey, but a dragon's mind was far more complex, far more advanced.

But there was only one direction that concerned him. Drawing his thoughts together, the dragon mage focused on the mountain. Now, he saw all that lay ahead as if he already trod those grounds. He had made better time than he had imagined, but still had far to go.

That, however, did not concern him. Instead, he pushed his mind on to the barren lands immediately surrounding Grim Batol. There, his sense of unease magnified a thousandfold. The wrongness around and within the mountain *screamed* at Krasus to learn its secrets.

Eyes narrowed, he shoved his mind into Grim Batol itself.

Darkness at first filled his gaze, but then fragments of images appeared as Krasus entered the caverns. However, his first full glimpse of Grim Batol's interior was a disappointing one, for all he saw was shadowed stalactites and stalagmites. There were a few bones in the chamber, orc bones, but they were clearly from the battle that had ousted the green warriors from Grim Batol.

Yet, the wrongness was too powerful to ignore. Krasus concentrated. . . .

His brow rose. Something was coming. He quickly withdrew—only to discover that his mind could not retreat from Grim Batol.

Krasus tried, but it was as if he actually stood before the tons of stone and dirt, trying to pound his way through with only his fists. All that he could see was the chamber with the skeletons and the blackness that marked the mountainside through which he wished to pass again.

And worse, because of that, he could not even see what was happening around his own body.

Krasus tried again to retreat, but with no better result. Each moment, he became certain that whoever had set the trap would now strike . . . yet nothing else happened.

But although this snare appeared now to be one set in place and possibly forgotten, Krasus still needed to free himself as quickly as possible. He concentrated on his body as he had last seen it, imagining his mind again within.

Yet, still nothing happened. The dragon mage thought for a moment, then turned his attention to locating the spell matrix that held him. It did not take long to sense, but its complexity dismayed him. It was clearly the work of a skilled practitioner of the arts, possibly, depending on its age . . . possibly even Deathwing himself.

Nevertheless, Krasus knew that he had to find the focus. Only there could he possibly unravel the spell, if there was still hope of that.

His consciousness sank deeper into the binding spell, studying its arrangement. If indeed this was Deathwing's work, that might, ironically enough, be to Krasus's benefit. If there was any being alive who understood the black leviathan's twisted mind, it was Alexstrasza's oldest-lived consort. Krasus had made the former Aspect an extensive part of his long, vigilant watch, Deathwing having played a role in many plots over the millennia.

One by one, the dragon mage followed the threads of the spell. He began to see a pattern, but one more intricate than even he had suspected.

One line showed more promise than the rest. Krasus started to trace it back to its origin. . . .

The thing he had sensed earlier drew closer. It was most definitely coming Krasus's direction. A sudden sense of intense hunger washed over him, a hunger not for flesh, but rather something more significant to him.

What moved toward him hungered for his magic. . . .

Krasus tried to hurry his task. He was a dragon, a creature of magic. To have his magic ripped away would be worse for him than if someone had thrust a sword through his throat. He had seen others of his kind suffer such fates and knew that it was the one death that truly frightened him.

The creature in the caverns closed on his mental location. That Krasus's body was not there did not give the dragon mage any hope. Some devourers of magic needed only the spell link to seize their prey.

The trap continued to evade Krasus's effort. The thread he followed proved a dead end. The second he followed did the same.

The mysterious devourer was almost upon him. Krasus could detect its horrible nearness and knew that when he was finally able to see it through his own spell, it would be too late for him. Yet, nothing he did availed him—

I am a fool! There was one hope, albeit a risky one. It might enable him to avoid the slow, agonizing death dealt by the magic eater . . . but could also end up causing Krasus to slay himself in the process.

In truth, there was no choice. He focused inward. For most magic users, what he intended would not be possible, but Krasus had millennia of training, millennia of practice.

Whether it would still work, though . . .

Krasus felt the beating of his heart. It was a heart that had pulsated through an age when even the dragons as a race were young, through the rise of night elves and that race's dramatic collapse. He had watched the demons of the Burning Legion strike not once but twice and seen entire lands ripped apart.

And now, through his concentration, he tried to slow that heart . . . even stop it.

The beating felt so far away. Still, that he could even sense that much gave him some hope.

Then, the beating eased. Only slightly, but enough for Krasus to hope for success.

A sinister glow entered the cavern of the skeletons.

Krasus concentrated his full efforts on his heart. He hoped that the intense shock would fling his mind from the magical trap. It was something that he had seen done before and had practiced before, but practice was not the same as true emergency.

A vague, hulking form appeared among the stalagmites. Krasus had only seconds—

A shock ran through him . . . but it was not due to his attempt. Nevertheless, it tore the dragon mage's mind from Grim Batol just as the devourer reached out to snare him.

And Krasus discovered that he had only left one hungry creature for another.

The crocolisk had him by his leg and was in the process of dragging the mage back toward the swamp water. The shock that had enabled Krasus to return his mind to his body had been created by the scaly beast's long, toothy maw clamping deep into the flesh. Blood spilled from the ravaged limb, blood that only a creature like a crocolisk, with its stomach protected like a paladin in plate armor, could tolerate.

The irony that he might perish in the maw of so simple a predator as this six-legged reptile after all the powerful struggles he had been through did not escape Krasus. Steeling himself against the agony, the dragon mage smashed his fist on the crocolisk's hard snout.

A blue aura enveloped the swamp creature. It opened its mighty jaws as it roared, enabling Krasus to drag himself free. The crocolisk's body whipped back and forth as the aura intensified.

Panting, the injured spellcaster pulled himself back to the tree and eyed his struggling attacker. This was the beast that had evaded his senses earlier. Even now, Krasus could barely sense its presence. Some force enabled the crocolisk to shield itself from even powerful magi.

But that same force could not now protect it from Krasus's power unleashed. He watched with grim satisfaction as the crocolisk tried to flee the aura by returning to the waters. Yet, with each step, the reptile lost cohesion. Its skin began to slough off, turning to mist before it even hit the ground. The six legs stumbled as they dissolved into ash. The crocolisk let out one more desperate roar . . . and the last of the reptile finally melted away.

Only a few drops of blood—Krasus's blood—remained to mark the predator's passing.

He stared at his twisted leg, an injury that would have meant death by either bleeding or infection had he been a human or any of the mortal races. Even for him, the pain was terrible. Yet, the attack had saved him from a worse and more certain demise, and he was almost grateful to the crocolisk.

Stretching one hand over the ripped flesh, Krasus concentrated. A faint, red glow spread from his palm to the bloody ravine.

The bleeding ceased. Some of the agony faded. The smaller tears made by the crocolisk's teeth shrank. The large one slowly sealed at each end.

Krasus did not simply heal himself outside. There were rumors that *poisonous* crocolisks had been discovered of late. Where they had originated from, he did not know, but Krasus did not want to take a chance. He knew well the dangers of the toxins such a crocolisk's foul teeth might carry. In his current form, he was more sensitive to them. Such poisons could slay a bull in minutes, a man in less. Whether they could do the same to him now, Krasus did not care to discover.

And so as he sealed the wounds from without, he burned away the poisons from within. The strain was more than he expected and for the first time, Krasus sweated. Yet, because of who—or rather *what*— he was, he prevailed.

When it was done, no sign remained. Krasus inspected the leg and found it to be fit. As an afterthought, he waved his hand over his garments, making them whole once more.

He had learned some lessons now. Nothing was to be taken for granted. First he had slipped into unconsciousness and found himself in a place far from his last known location. Then, his mind had been trapped while infiltrating Grim Batol, and now a simple beast had nearly slain him . . . in part because it had gained some ability to shield itself from his like.

A pattern was beginning to emerge that disturbed Krasus immensely, especially as he was not certain of its origins.

But he was almost certain of something else. His arrival appeared to be expected.

So . . . someone awaits me . . . or someone like me. Someone who plays games.

But who?

"We shall just have to see," he murmured to himself. If his unknown adversary wished to play games, Krasus was no novice himself. Let them be aware that he was coming; they would find that knowledge more hindrance than help.

Krasus smiled grimly. "The next move is mine, then, my friend. . . ."
He gestured . . . and vanished.

The dwarves emerged from their new burrow at the exit nearest the
Wetlands. They had no desire to come this way, but necessity had once
more forced their hands. They needed to replenish supplies, especially
water.

"No raptors about," muttered Grenda. "Not much of anything,
actually . . ."

Rom peered into the swampy region. "Let's make this quick." He
pointed at four dwarves carrying small barrels. "You lot go with Bjarl
and his fighters and get to that brook we know is safe to drink from.
Grenda, you and the others come with me. Even if we've got to eat raptor or crocolisk, we're coming back with some fresh meat."

As hardy as dwarves were, none of them were particularly enamored with the notion of chewing on either predator, the meat of both
stringy and tasting as if it were already three days old. However, the
choices were not many, especially of late. It was a wonder that either
of the creatures still haunted the region. Most of the smaller game had
long fled, sensing, like the dwarves, the evil of Grim Batol.

We're getting closer to the truth, though, Rom could not help telling
himself. *There's the blood elf, the drakonid, and the skardyn. And that lady
in black. We know they're there. . . . We just don't know what they're doing
yet. . . .*

He suddenly laughed harshly, startling Grenda. Rom quickly stifled
his outburst. The dwarves just didn't know what the blood elf and the
others were doing. One tiny insignificant point upon which their mission and, likely, their lives depended.

He thought of his missing hand. The wrist, though cauterized,
still throbbed, but being a dwarf he had been able to manage the pain
even after only a short time. Still, it reminded Rom again of how, even
though he had always been the one King Magni could rely on for the

most dangerous of quests, the veteran warrior had initially been reluctant. Naturally, though, Rom had hidden that reluctance from his monarch. Yet . . . *You're a fool, Rom! You should've let someone else command this mission rather than drag yourself back to this dark place . . . back to its hungry, accursed self . . .*

Rom led Grenda and the other hunters out into the Wetlands, his set expression hiding the fact that the deaths of the past ate at him more than ever. Not merely those who had perished since the mission had begun, but all those who had died so many years ago fighting the orcs. He could still see their faces, their bloody corpses.

Could still hear their ghosts calling to him.

Then Rom realized that someone else was calling to him. Grenda, who had sighted something.

"Only saw a movement, but think it might be a crocolisk," she whispered.

"Where?"

"Right there." Grenda pointed at a dead tree far to the right. The branches were long gone and the upper part of the trunk had cracked off. "Just in the deep part there."

"We'll fan out around the area. Watch your footing, everyone." They had lost poor Samm that way. One moment, the young dwarf had been stepping gingerly along the soft soil . . . and the next moment he had been sucked under.

They never *had* recovered his body.

Grenda took half the hunters to the west, while Rom led the other three north. He saw no sign of their prey, yet not only knew how well crocolisks could hide in the water, but also trusted the female dwarf's vision. Grenda had a keen eye for a race that lived much of its life under the surface.

The dwarves moved with a stealth most other races assumed impossible for beings of their stocky build. Grenda's party skirted the water's edge, while Rom had to actually lead his a few steps into it.

The murky water made it impossible to see anything even just below the surface, but Rom knew to watch for the telltale bubbles or the slight odd shift of the current marking a crocolisk's movements. Unfortunately, at the same time, the reptile would likely be watching for signs of them, as well.

He glanced over to Grenda, who gestured with her ax at a spot near one of her party. She had located something. Rom signaled his group to halt.

The next instant, the crocolisk rose up less than a yard from Grenda . . . although not to attack, but rather to flee from her and the others. However, two of her hunters had already maneuvered around, cutting off the reptile's flight immediately. One slashed with his ax. The blade cut deep into the crocolisk's foreleg.

The wounded animal veered around to snap at its assailant, only to have Grenda strike it from behind. Her blow cut through the spine, sending the crocolisk into spasms.

Rom nodded. The beast was as good as dead. The hunt would be a remarkably short one, for which he was grateful. The sooner the band was back underground, the better.

A sloshing sound to his left caught his attention. Two crocolisks, whatever their tastes, would better feed his weary troop. He turned—

But it was not one of the water predators before him . . . it was something ghastly and gelatinous that moved of its own accord toward the dwarves. Within its quivering form floated various objects, but especially *bones*.

"Beware!" Rom shouted. "An ooze!"

One of the younger dwarves with him swung impetuously at the macabre form before their leader could prevent him. The ax head sank in without pause, causing the dwarf to fall face first into the gelatinous shape.

The nightmarish thing sucked the hunter into its midst.

Rom let out a cry of dismay and, hefting his weapon with his one good hand, charged at the creature. He had some horrific memories concerning similar fiends around the Dustwallow Marsh region. If he hoped to save the other dwarf, he had to do something quickly.

With an expert slash, Rom cut at the monster's side . . . but the mark his blade made vanished immediately after. Rom cursed himself for attempting what he should have known would have no effect on the ooze. Inside, the other dwarf twitched but otherwise did not move.

With the crocolisk still struggling against Grenda and her band, it was up to Rom and his two remaining hunters. As the other pair joined him, he circled around, hoping that, if he thrust the hilt of his ax in, the monster's captive could seize it and be pulled free.

"Thorvald's Beard!" Rom gasped. He stepped from the gelatinous fiend, horrified by what he saw.

The front of the captive dwarf's face had already been eaten away.

A skull was all that stared back at Rom from underneath the thick hair. Even as he watched, the hair began to wither and dissolve. It was what he had feared would happen, but from his previous battles against ooze, the dwarven commander had believed that he had more time.

"Get back!" Rom ordered the others, fearful of losing another of his people.

"Look out!" one warrior shouted back.

Rom whirled.

Had he still had his other hand, it would have been lost to him now. The burnt stump sank in to the second fiend's quivering form, and Rom felt his flesh burn.

Crying out, he tried to pull free, but the gelatinous, dripping shape would not release him. He imagined dying as the other dwarf had—

Suddenly, from the tree tops there flew a blazing missile. It struck the creature holding onto Rom dead on. Rom expected the oozing form to douse the flames, but instead the fiend became an inferno.

Rom smelled oil and understood what the archer was doing. He also understood that this was his only chance. He pulled as hard as he could, and part of his maimed limb came free.

Another burning bolt hit the struggling monster. Rom fell back as the thing released its remaining hold on him.

The other fiend started to move into the water, but two more arrows struck it in rapid succession. As with the first, fire engulfed the monster. It shook as if about to explode.

Retrieving his ax, which had fallen from his grip, Rom retreated to his companions.

Grenda rushed up beside him. "Are you all right?"

"As best can be expected," he returned, gladly watching them burn. The second one hit had become little more than a pile of scorched refuse . . . and burning dwarven bones. "Damned ooze! . . ."

She shuddered, a rare display of fear on her part. "I'll be havin' nightmares . . . poor Harak. Is there no way to save him for burial?"

Bronzebeard dwarves preferred to bury their dead, returning them to the ground that so benefited their race. They considered it both an honor and repayment.

But nothing could be done. The fire, fueled also by the ooze itself, would reduce the bones to ash.

"He gets a pyre of sorts, at least," Rom answered, trying to make the best of a grim situation. He glanced around, estimating from exactly where the arrows had come.

Then, something at the edge of his gaze made him whirl about. Grenda tensed, clearly thinking another of the monsters was about to strike.

But whatever it was that Rom had seen was now out of sight. He swore.

"What is it? What did you see?"

"Not nearly enough." A vague shape. That was all. He was not even certain how tall it had been. All Rom did know with any certainty was that it moved much too fast for one of his kind.

But what in this foul realm would lend a hand to the harried dwarves?

And, more of interest to him, what did it mean to his mission?

SIX

"H*e* is near."

Zendarin looked up from the pit into which he had been gazing for the past hour, not for the first time marveling at what he—and the lady in black—had wrought. "Who?"

The veiled lady joined him. She, too, stared down in wonder for a moment, then looked to the blood elf. "The one I have expected. The tests I set before him prove it; any other would have perished or turned back. Only he is determined enough to press on."

"If he's coming here, it's more likely he's a fool."

She tipped her head to the side. "He is that . . . which makes him no less dangerous to us."

Something occurred to Zendarin. "I sensed—"

"Yes, one of your pets almost came across him. That would have proven quite interesting, don't you think?"

As the blood elf was not certain exactly who—or what—sought to encroach on Grim Batol, he merely nodded. Of more concern to him was what this meant. "Do we dare begin again? Is there time?"

She smiled, a reaction that always made him shiver despite himself. "We shall make do with our lone child for now, my dear Zendarin. . . . He shall suffice, if need be."

As if hearing her, from below came a hungry hiss.

The lady in black made a shushing sound toward the pit. Immediately, the thing in the darkness below quieted.

"The poor darling needs to feed. Would you care to do it, Zendarin?"

He shrugged, only one consideration worrying him. "We might kill the nether dragon like this. That creature has an insatiable appetite."

"We shall have another source of sustenance for the dear thing before long . . . if the one so eager to reach us is as clever as he thinks he is. For now, though, we shall just have to risk the nether dragon. It is essential that nothing slows the growth process."

The blood elf bowed. "As you say, my lady."

He strode off to deal with the matter. The veiled female watched him depart, then gazed down into the shadowy pit again.

Below, something flared a deep and unsettling purple before once again becoming part of the darkness.

"Patience, my child," she cooed. "Patience. You shall be fed. You shall be fed . . . and then grow up to be so very big . . ." Her expression turned stony. "Just as your damned father would have wanted."

It was not Krasus who reappeared in the Wetlands, but rather his true self, Korialstrasz. Moreover, the dragon materialized at dusk, the better to make use of the elements of the night for his plan.

The time is nigh, Korialstrasz determined. *Let us see what your next move shall be,* he thought at his unknown and unseen adversary. If it was Deathwing, then what the red dragon planned would outwardly make sense to the black. If someone else, then they would surely follow the same line of thought . . . and that was all that mattered.

He spread his massive wings.

The front part of the great red dragon peeled away. Two Korialstraszes now stood together.

But the spell was not finished. As both exhaled, from each peeled away another copy . . . and then another. Soon, eight Korialstraszes filled the area.

As one, they leapt into the darkening sky, heading in different directions . . . but all with the intention of eventually arriving at Grim Batol.

It was a costly plan Korialstrasz intended. The copies were more than mere illusion; to make all this work, each had been imbued with a tiny bit of himself. Just enough to make those who might be observing him wonder which was the true dragon. They would have to expend precious power determining the truth . . . and by then the real Korialstrasz would be upon them.

Or so they were supposed to believe.

In truth, none of the dragons were real. *All* eight were imbued copies. As the others had been created, the true Korialstrasz had masked his transformation back into the guise of Krasus.

And as Krasus, he once again began moving through the Wetlands. He had learned his lesson from his near-disaster; this time, most of his remaining might was focused on making him invisible both to the eyes and other senses of any watchers. Once more, it was something that few other casters, even dragons, could have accomplished, and Krasus had saved this particular spell for centuries.

Now he hoped the wait was worth it.

The eight Korialstraszes disappeared into the distance. They would fly routes carefully thought out by their creator, who knew the region well enough to make each seem the conscious choice of their particular flyer. Krasus sensed with satisfaction their dwindling presence.

As for him, he pushed on with the knowledge of just how long it would probably take whomever watched to eliminate the choices. By then, the true red dragon would have already infiltrated the dire mountain.

A variety of night creatures crossed his path, but this time none took even the slightest notice of him. Krasus eyed with distaste a second crocolisk swimming through the nearby waters, but otherwise did nothing. He had no bitterness toward the species, however much the one had hurt him. He also found it interesting that, in contrast to the one that had attacked him, this beast had no obvious ability to shield itself from his presence.

Very curious, the dragon mage thought. *Could it be that the first—*

His body suddenly shook. He felt a slight sense of loss and recognized its origins immediately.

One of his duplicates had been just destroyed. Exactly how, he could not say, but in some manner it had involved potent magic. The cowled spellcaster took a moment to recover, then pressed on.

That the first had been struck down so quickly did not surprise Krasus in the least, though he still mourned that tiny piece of him that had been lost. He had expected to be tested quickly. The duplicate had served its purpose and the loss of one among eight was a sacrifice that he could well suffer. Already he had covered a great distance.

However, he had scarcely gone an hour more when again he was hit from within . . . and this time the sense of loss felt tenfold more devastating. Krasus grunted, forced to rest against a tree for more than a minute. He had expected a bit more time to pass before a second was destroyed. Still, there was nothing to do but continue.

And so he did . . . until barely a short walk later a third loss struck him harder than the previous two had. Now the dragon mage staggered. Finding a place to sit, Krasus took several deep breaths. Not only had this one come much too swiftly after the others, but it should *not* have affected him so hard. He had calculated everything to the finest detail. It should not have—

Krasus stiffened. In addition to what was happening well ahead, he abruptly realized that, once again, someone or something was *pursuing* him.

This is not as it was supposed to be! He angrily peered behind him, but saw only the Wetlands. Yet, there *was* something stalking him, and it was no crocolisk. Krasus had raised wards against a reoccurrence of that nature. Indeed, from what little that the dragon mage could sense, what followed wielded a magic different from that to which he was used.

For a region supposedly abandoned by any creature of reason, the Wetlands and Grim Batol were proving quite active. Krasus finally went against his better judgment and sought with his mind to better probe the direction in which he felt the hound on his heels followed.

There was a brief trace . . . and then nothing. The dragon mage frowned. Something was not right—

A cloaked figure suddenly leapt out from among the trees, one obscured foot pounding into Krasus's chest with astounding force. The lanky spellcaster went flying back.

But he was hardly beaten. His body stopped falling just inches from the ground, then immediately righted itself. The cowled mage glared in the direction of his attacker, a spell ready.

The mysterious attacker was nowhere to be seen.

Krasus spun about, arm raised.

He barely blocked the strike coming at his throat from behind, a blow certain to at least incapacitate him, if not shatter his windpipe. Whoever he fought had knowledge of all the most sensitive places to hit. The kick would have left any human, elf, or dwarf unconscious, their breath crushed from their lungs. Only because of what Krasus actually was had he been able to withstand the attack . . . and this one as well.

Yet, even as he deflected that blow, his assailant summoned into being an odd staff . . . the crystal tip of which promptly touched Krasus on the chest.

He let out a roar worthy of any dragon as the pain engulfed him. Wards that should have held against most magical attacks failed utterly . . . because, he sensed belatedly, the forces unleashed by the crystal were unlike the arcane magics of Azeroth.

And only then did Krasus have a suspicion as to just what his attacker was.

Unfortunately, he lacked the strength to stand, much less speak. Legs collapsing under him, the dragon mage tumbled to the ground.

Barely had he done so, when the cloaked form set one foot on his side and the tip of the staff against the very spot that it had just touched.

"Where is he?" a female voice with an accent that verified for Krasus his suspicions demanded. "What have you done with him?"

"I—I have no idea of whom you speak!" he managed. Then, trusting in his judgment, he said in another language, "But a draenei is no enemy to one of my kind, child. . . ."

The cloaked figure hesitated. "No . . . you must be the one. . . . The trail led me here. . . ."

Still speaking the draenei's tongue, Krasus returned, "I have found trails involving Grim Batol may lead anywhere but the truth."

There was another pause, then, "There is much in that. Far too much."

She withdrew the staff, which then vanished.

The dragon mage nodded in interest. "Seldom have I met a priest or priestess of the draenei, and never have I seen one who wielded such a gift from the wondrous naaru. . . ."

Her last bit of uncertainty vanished. Pulling back her hood, she revealed herself to also be one of the youngest draenei Krasus had thus far come across. "I sense in your tone nothing but truth. My name is Iridi. . . ." She extended a hand to help him up. "And when I hear you speak of the naaru, I hear something in your voice that places you closer to them than you are to me. . . ."

"I would claim no such vaunted position. I am a spellcaster of some power, yes." She had clearly not seen him in his true form. For the moment, he preferred to keep that part of his identity even from her. "You may call me Krasus, child."

Her exotic eyes narrowed and a slight smile crossed her face. "Krasus . . . may I put a hand to your chest? I mean no harm by it. It is a sign of trust among those of my particular order."

He nodded. Iridi placed her palm atop his robe, then closed her eyes.

Krasus felt a slight warmth. Startled, he pulled back.

The draenei's eyes shot open. She wore a look of utter astonishment. "You are *not* as you appear, Krasus!"

"No." The dragon mage said nothing more. "And neither are you, it seems." He felt no anger toward her, despite her trick. In truth, Iridi had astounded him in return. He had not experienced such a spell among the draenei, whether spellcaster or priest. Iridi seemed to have abilities rare even among her own kind.

He wondered again about the staff. Krasus knew just enough about the naaru to know that she would not have been given it without a good reason.

The priestess went down on one knee. Her continued reverence made Krasus uncomfortable, for he had no desire for anyone to honor him.

"Rise up," he insisted.

Iridi did, albeit slowly. Her eyes continued to stretch wide, as if she tried to imagine Krasus as he truly was. "Lord of the air, forgive me for attacking you like a fool—"

"There is nothing to forgive, and do not call me by such a title."

She shook her head. "But you are one of the winged ones." Her eyes shut briefly, then the draenei added, "Of those who follow the cause of life . . ."

Krasus was more and more impressed by the priestess. She had learned all that simply by touching him. He made a note to himself to not permit the palm gesture any more should he ever meet another draenei who made such a request.

Although Krasus now at least somewhat understood how anyone could have tracked him despite his wards—and he vowed that from here on that even to a draenei he would be invisible—there was yet the question of what the priestess was doing in this forsaken land in the first place.

However, before he could ask, the dragon mage was suddenly struck as if by an unseen sword through his heart. The sense of loss that he had felt when one of his duplicates had been eradicated overwhelmed him again, but *doubly* so.

"Great one," Iridi gasped, reaching for him. "What ails you?"

Krasus could barely stand. *Two more quickly gone . . . and so close together! What is happening? What is—*

He blacked out.

Iridi grabbed for the cowled figure just before he would have fallen. She was at a loss as to what had just happened. It had been enough of a struggle for her mind when she had discovered that the figure that she had so recklessly attacked was in actuality far more than the priestess had imagined him—and certainly not the slim, elven figure of whom she had only gotten a brief glance from too long of a distance back in Draenor.

One of the lords of the air . . . a red dragon . . . Iridi could scarcely believe that she had taken on such an ancient leviathan. The priestess doubted very much that she had actually bested Krasus—not his dragon name, that much the draenei knew—by herself and now his collapse surely proved her right. He had clearly been weakened from the start, most likely by what had assailed him now.

Gripping the slumped body as best she could, Iridi dragged Krasus to the side of a small, squat hill. The moment that the priestess felt secure with how he lay, she began seeing just what she could do to help.

There were no visual signs as to his ailment. Kneeling, the draenei placed her palms a few inches above Krasus's head. She did not care for what she intended next, but it was her best chance to find out quickly what had happened.

Barely had Iridi begun to concentrate when voices and images flashed through her mind. A red-haired human with the look of a mage on him. An antlered, stalwart figure who appeared to be a night elf—and one of the druids of which she had heard but herself had not yet seen. A female elf of lighter complexion, a fighter whose image seemed bound to the human, oddly enough.

The voices intermingled randomly with the images.

You would sacrifice anything for her, would you not, Korialstrasz?

I had thought you dead. I mourned you for a long time. . . .

They've that much faith left in me? After the others died?

You of all should understand my need to discover the truth.

And more and more faces. A scarred, war-weary orc. Another night elf . . . whose blinded face suddenly reminded her of the horrific tales of the demon Illidan. A noble paladin. An arrogant human noble. A young, blond woman, whose eyes held both innocence and some incredible secret.

And, most of all . . . a face that shifted back and forth between an extraordinarily beautiful woman with crimson tresses streaked with gold and the same sort of pale elven features as Krasus wore . . . and the ageless visage of a gargantuan red dragon. Mingling with the woman's fiery hair were leaves touched by autumn, but what struck Iridi more was that the wild, amber eyes of the former—eyes filled with both a wisdom and humor that the priestess could never attain in her own short lifetime—were somehow the same eyes as those belonging to the crimson leviathan.

They were some of the significant memories of this ancient, this dragon in mortal guise. She knew his true name now and the revered place he held with one that the draenei was aware was a being of great power.

"You are Korialstrasz," Iridi whispered. "First consort to—to the Aspect of *Life*?—and—and protector of the young races . . ." It was impossible to keep the awe from returning to her voice. "You are as much Azeroth's mate as you are hers, for you love them both so much. . . ."

But that was not what she had been seeking. She needed to find the core of what ailed him. Unfortunately, these memories had to be peeled back, first.

Though regretting her intrusion into his past, the priestess had no choice. Not only could Iridi not have abandoned someone in need, but she also felt certain that Krasus—he seemed to prefer that title when in this form—was somehow a part of her search. The elders of her order had taught her that there were reasons for all that occurred, from the slaughter of so many draenei by the orcs during the early days of their encounters to the great calamity—again by the hand of an orc—that had literally ripped apart Draenor. The naaru had emphasized that point as well. No, Iridi needed to help Krasus not only for his sake, but her own.

But other memories kept flowing into her, one in particular disturbing to her. She saw a huge city on the edge of a sinister, dark body of water. A maelstrom formed in the latter and the city was dragged under, countless lives sucked into the water with it before the waters themselves began to follow into the dread gap. Iridi sensed the foulness of the Burning Legion . . . and something older and more terrible than even them lurking in the background.

The priestess fought through the memories and voices, seeking that which was more immediate, more significant to the moment—

She found it. A part of the dragon mage was literally missing. A small part, but the violence of its destruction had been terrible.

And even as the draenei discovered this, that intangible gap within suddenly expanded. Bound to her patient, the priestess was also struck. And while against her the attack was only peripheral, it was enough to throw the draenei back.

Iridi landed hard. Fighting dizziness and pain, she suddenly looked about, certain that whatever was responsible was upon them.

Yet, although she saw nothing, Iridi knew that time was running out. "Great one!" She seized his shoulders in a most unpriestesslike way, shaking them hard. "Great one! Krasus!" Out of desperation, she added last, "Korialstrasz!"

The dragon mage stirred, but did not wake.

The draenei's feeling of impending disaster heightened. With no other recourse left to her, Iridi struggled to raise Krasus up so that she could drag him away from the immediate area to better protection.

A blood-chilling roar filled the darkened sky . . . a blood-chilling roar that was answered a moment later by another, identical one even closer.

SEVEN

In the pit that passed for its nest, that which Zendarin and the veiled sorceress had created digested the energy most recently fed into it by the pair. Despite having been fed well—as the screams of Zzeraku could attest—the thing in the dark still hungered. It hungered for both more of what the nether dragon could give it and also, at last, for solid fare.

But of both, there was none to be had. The small, scaly creatures—the skardyn its "mother" had called them—had learned to stay well away from the nest's vicinity. They had discovered the hard way that, although newly born, that which had hatched from the egg was already a master of its natural magic. With its growing abilities, it had drawn one skardyn to it by causing the ground underneath the vermin's feet to give way. The skardyn had fallen into the pit, where the small morsel was devoured in a single swallow, the food still kicking and screaming as it descended down the gullet.

It was growing fast, faster, in fact, than its "parents" had imagined. They were pleased with that, although not as pleased as it, who yearned to be free, to fly in the sky. . . .

To hunt and devour proper prey . . .

Then, through senses that only it was aware that it possessed, it noted those who had come before it, those who were almost like it . . . but not quite. Now and then, it could feel and even imagine what the other two did, the two who acted as one. They were as close to siblings as it had, and so these glimpses of their freedom were as a feast to a starving man.

They were hunting. They were hunting the proper prey. They not only were hunting it, but, having tasted some little hint of it, now knew where it hid.

The thing in the pit tasted their eagerness. They were not as clever of mind as it, but their instinct was strong.

It waited, eager to savor through them the devouring. Soon, though, soon it would grow large enough to hunt on its own.

And then . . . no force in all the world would be able to stand against its might.

The flapping of wings filled the night sky, but although Iridi had excellent vision, she could not quite make out what it was they presaged. There were *shapes* above, shapes that held a vague likeness to that for which she had searched, but the draenei priestess also felt the wrongness emanating from those shapes. Whatever descended upon Krasus and her should not by rights have existed on either Azeroth or Draenor . . . though, in all contradiction, it also felt as if a part of both worlds.

"Ahh, sssuch lovely-looking morsssels . . ." bellowed a monstrous voice, striking her ears like thunder. "And we are ssso hungry . . ."

"Hungry . . . yesss, we are . . ." echoed a second with equal ferocity. "It hasss been ssso long sssince we feasssted . . ."

"Ssso very long . . ." called the first from what seemed to the draenei directly above her.

The sky there shimmered an unsettling purple. The purple coalesced into the outline of a gargantuan creature.

A dragon. A dragon of such proportion as to leave Iridi gaping at it despite the peril it also presented to her.

"Ssso very long . . ." it repeated. "And we are always hungry . . ."

It descended.

The draenei's hand thrust up, the naaru staff forming in its grip. The crystal flared.

Roaring, the nightmarish dragon suddenly vanished.

Iridi knew that it had not been due to the staff. The crystal had no such ability.

The ground around her erupted, entire trees, huge rocks, and tons of dirt ripped away by what at first the priestess imagined an earthquake but what materialized a moment later as the dragon . . . barely yards from the two small figures.

"We mussst feed!" it declared somewhat more succinctly than previous.

Above, the other voice repeated, "Yesss, we mussst eat!"

It took no stretch of Iridi's imagination to understand that the pair referred to the draenei and Krasus.

She waved the staff at the one on the ground. The shimmering dragon, in the process of tearing up the rest of Iridi's surroundings, drew back in anger . . . and disappeared again.

The draenei immediately seized Krasus and, exerting herself as much as she could, dragged him in the opposite direction.

The Wetlands there suddenly exploded. A second later, the huge form of a dragon appeared. Although Iridi could see no difference between it and the previous visions, she was certain that this was the second of the monsters.

It opened wide its mouth to snap up Krasus . . . and Iridi in the process.

She tried to raise the staff, but it was entangled with the unconscious mage. Iridi concentrated, seeking another course of action.

Krasus's eyes snapped open, the energy of life causing them to glow briefly.

Before she could speak, he shoved her from him. Startled, the priestess tumbled.

A roar split the skies, but it was a different one from those she had heard before. Iridi blinked her gaze clear.

Where Krasus had stood, a huge, crimson form now towered. The red dragon Korialstrasz spread his wings, a wondrous sight of such huge dimensions that his mere presence made the shimmering monster hiss and retreat.

"Yes! You would do best to flee from me!" Korialstrasz proclaimed. "For I show no mercy to those who threaten my friends!"

"Foolisssh morsssel . . ." snarled the cowering monster, but it backed farther yet, clearly intimidated . . . which was as Iridi knew the red dragon desired.

From the previous direction came a roar that marked the second of the two macabre beasts. Korialstrasz immediately turned his huge head, snapping at the air.

He was weaker than either of his foes knew, and the draenei prayed that they would keep their ignorance. If they sensed in the least that his show of might was partially bravado, then they would quickly turn on him.

Korialstrasz roared back at the darkness . . . and the other dragon formed. Like the first, it was cowed. As the red dragon spread his wings wider yet, the shimmering form dropped to the ground, taking up a position like its twin.

Iridi's gigantic companion glanced down at her. "Leave this place," he murmured. "Leave cautiously, without showing any fear, but leave it now. . . ."

"But, what about you?"

He turned his gaze back to the two dread behemoths, his failure to answer the draenei answer enough. Korialstrasz was only concerned with her life, not his.

The priestess could not leave him to face them alone. She had many skills and the staff at her command. There had to be some manner in which she could aid him—

Although his eyes continued to monitor the two nightmarish dragons, Korialstrasz suddenly made a movement with his tail that the draenei realized was directed toward her. The red still desired for her to depart.

One of the shadowy creatures also noticed the movement . . . and proved cunning enough to understand what it meant. Monstrous orbs measured Korialstrasz anew.

A scowl replaced the cowering look.

The amethyst beast let out an ear-jarring cry and launched itself at the red dragon.

The other followed only seconds later, echoing the first's cry.

Letting out a roar of his own, Korialstrasz beat his wings hard. Iridi feared that the two attackers would turn immaterial again, but, so close, they apparently assumed that their prey was doomed. Instead, though, the red dragon not only stood his ground, but struck with all his might.

The heavy wings battered the dark dragons. One spun back, uprooting trees and ripping up more ground. The second dove headfirst into the dirt, its snout drilling deep.

Korialstrasz twisted his head around to the second and bathed his adversary in flames.

The shadow dragon—no, that title did not seem quite right to Iridi, for they did not so much resemble shadow, but rather the day turning to night—shrieked as it pulled its maw free and belatedly returned to a ghostlike state. The amethyst shimmer increased as it shifted.

Twilight! the draenei thought abruptly. *It is as if they are like the twilight of this world's day. . . .*

Then, a savage paw came down where she stood. Only the heightened instincts of one of her order enabled the priestess to leap aside before she would have been crushed into the soil.

Iridi turned the naaru staff against her attacker. This time, the beast reacted too slowly. Blue lightning crackled around the fiendish leviathan. The dragon shrieked.

The draenei's hopes surged. Perhaps she and Korialstrasz would yet defeat this unsettling pair, who felt to her senses so wrong and yet somehow still bound to that which she hunted.

But suddenly the crystal ceased glowing. Stunned, Iridi glanced at the tip.

The dragon against whom she had fought let out a brutal laugh.

"Yessss!" it called. "Feed me mmmmorrre!"

It lunged at her, but Iridi knew that it was the staff that the creature sought. Aware what power still lay in the gift, the draenei feared what would happen if her attacker devoured its full essence.

She would have turned to Korialstrasz for help, but the red dragon was in dire straits of his own. The other monster had not only turned incorporeal, but had vanished beneath the ancient leviathan. Korialstrasz spun about, seeking some trace, however minute.

From behind him rose a purple specter. Iridi tried to warn Korialstrasz, but it was already too late.

The twilight dragon—yes, Iridi found that the name better fit the dread beasts—fell upon Korialstrasz's back. The red fell forward, the sudden weight catching him off guard.

"I will feed!!!" the red's tormentor declared yet again. However, it did not bend down to bite through Korialstrasz's neck, but rather sank its claws into his back and wings.

The ancient flier moaned. A sinister purple aura enveloped Korialstrasz.

The dark dragon gleefully inhaled . . . and a crimson glow arose from the writhing red, a glow that the purple behemoth immediately ingested. The vampiric beast inhaled again, drawing forth more of what could only be Korialstrasz's life energies. Despite clearly trying not to, the red finally unleashed a terrible roar of agony.

Korialstrasz's scaled form began to shrivel, as if he were a fly being sucked dry by a spider. He scraped at the air, trying feebly to escape as his foe ingested his essence.

There was nothing Iridi could do to stop the terrible feasting. Her own pursuer lunged again at her, nearly snapping up both the staff and the draenei together.

The ground shook as the dragon behind her tore at it. Iridi stumbled, then completely lost her footing. She fell forward, the staff flying from her grip.

The twilight dragon let out a cry of triumph that quickly turned into one of childish frustration as it watched the staff vanish. It could not have known that the naaru's gift would soon vanish when not held by her.

"Wheerrre isss ittt?" the beast called. "Wherrrree?"

She felt the monster looming over her. In the background, Korialstrasz continued to moan.

There came from the heavens *another* roar, one whose vibrancy stilled all other sound. The next instant, a powerful force akin to thunder slammed into the monster magically ripping into Korialstrasz. The twilight dragon was bowled over.

The one near Iridi only had time to acknowledge its twin's fate before a new dragon alighted on to it. The twilight dragon immediately transformed, yet although it should have then avoided this startling foe, the new leviathan's claws hung tight. Iridi belatedly noticed that those claws glowed themselves.

"You like to fight those who can't fight you, don't you?" snarled the newcomer. His voice, his tone, were those of a much younger but more hot-headed dragon. From him emanated magical energies such as the draenei had sensed only on one type of dragon.

"You want to feed? Feed on this!"

His unsettling foe shrieked anew as bright, burning energies poured over it. In the light of those energies, the young dragon's flight was identified.

A blue dragon! Iridi had only seen one before, but the memory of that encounter remained burned in her memory. It had not been due to any particular feat by that previous dragon—for, in truth, the priestess had only watched it fly by—but rather the very essence of magic simply radiating from the azure colossus. She felt that now from this one as well, only even more so. Young this blue dragon might have been, but he wielded much power.

And he used that power quite well now. Caught unaware and now knowing that its ability to become incorporeal was of little value to it, the twilight dragon struggled to flee. However, the blue did not give up his prize. He was eager for battle, eager to vent some deep frustration that the priestess sensed on whatever enemy that he could find.

"Not so fast!" the blue bellowed. "I'm not done with you, not at all!"

From seemingly out of nowhere, the other twilight dragon attacked the blue. The younger leviathan was hard-pressed, but still seemed eager for the struggle no matter *what* the outcome.

But he was not alone. Crimson paws seized the second attacker and, making use of the monster's distraction, seared the twilight dragon's wings.

Iridi finally regained enough focus to recall the staff, but was uncertain exactly what she should do. The priestess did not want to feed the two creatures more of the energies for which they hunted. She stood frozen, torn between her choices.

It finally became obvious that this was a battle of dragons, with no place for a puny draenei priestess, however powerful the gift she had gotten from her mentor. Iridi stepped back, only prayer useful to her now.

And it appeared that her prayers were heard. Korialstrasz stood next to the younger blue, the pair aligned as if comrades of old. There was no argument, only action. They struck at the abominations, the blue taking the lead with Korialstrasz feeding his powers to his comrade.

The twin nightmares shrieked, yet they did not flee. With glowing orbs full of madness, they looked upon those who did not feed their hunger, but rather made it grow and grow. . . .

"We must make them use themselves up!" Korialstrasz commanded.

"Is that possible?" asked the blue.

"It must be!"

Under the magical onslaught, the twilight dragons receded. Their forms grew indistinct. Their images wavered and they finally collided.

Iridi cheered silently. The creatures were all but defeated—

The twin horrors *melded* together.

Korialstrasz and the blue fell back in dismay and surprise.

"These are highly unstable creatures!" the red declared. "This is no trick of theirs, but our own power making them even more an abomination!"

"We will feed!" the gargantuan shape clamored. With a terrifying laugh, it enshrouded the defenders in its extraordinarily-wide wings.

"No!" shouted the draenei. She raised the staff, knowing what she must do.

A silver light shot forth from the crystal, a light so pure that it stirred tears from Iridi. She groaned as effort weighed down on her, yet did not surrender. All that she had been taught came to the forefront. She would *not* fail Korialstrasz and the other dragon.

The light touched the humongous creature—which suddenly split back into its two, much smaller parts.

From the folds of the great wings, the red and blue dragons fell free. Neither Korialstrasz nor the younger leviathan appeared able to focus their efforts, but neither did the twilight dragons strike. A momentary lull settled over the Wetlands.

Then, the blue growled. His eyes glowed and the ground around the terrible twins rose up, churning. At the same time, blue bolts of lightning mercilessly beat at the pair.

Again, the twin beasts grew immaterial. The blue started to lunge forward, but the twilight dragons took to the sky.

"We must not let them leave!" Korialstrasz shouted from behind his ally. The ancient red rose up after the pair, lighting the night sky with a vast plume of fire that did not, unfortunately, harm his targets but did at least distract their flight.

The blue was right on his tail. The sky around the younger dragon shimmered much the way their adversaries did when becoming ghosts.

But whatever it was that he hoped to accomplish did not appear to happen. Iridi sensed his frustration. What did and did not affect the abominations remained a question of test and failure.

Gasping, the draenei propped up the staff. She had in her enough for one more effort . . . so she hoped.

The prayer she muttered was the first that she had learned when joining her order. It was designed to draw from within a sense of complete calm. Only in that manner could Iridi hope to survive.

The large crystal flared.

The silver sliver of light stretched out in the blink of an eye, splitting just before reaching the two monsters. As she concentrated, the two new lights touched their targets.

For a single breath, the twilight dragons became silver. They illuminated all and were, in their own way, stunning.

The priestess toppled, barely able to retain consciousness. She could well imagine now how the red dragon had felt, for a part of her had been used up in this attempt.

The shimmering forms swelled. Wise enough to recognize that this was not as it should be, the red and blue hastily dropped toward the Wetlands.

The macabre dragons laughed madly. They continued to swell, now each nearly as massive as the single colossus that they had briefly formed.

They were still laughing as one, then both exploded in a violent release of energies that swept over the area.

As deadly forces rained down, a vast form dropped over Iridi, protecting her from their full fury. She heard Korialstrasz rumble, "Have no fear. . . ."

The Wetlands shook violently . . . and then just as quickly stilled again.

Iridi lay sprawled under the red dragon's wing, barely able to breathe. She both heard and felt Korialstrasz's own labored breathing and knew that he had been through far more than she. It amazed her that he had actually been able to stand for so long against the two abominations.

From somewhere to her side, she heard a voice that was and was not familiar to her. "The danger's passed . . ."

"Yes," replied her protector. "I believe so, too."

As he spoke, the red dragon withdrew from Iridi. She tried to rise, but needed in the end the assistance of a strong pair of hands.

Those hands belonged not to the one she expected, but rather a handsome youth who appeared to be approximately her age. There were elven touches to his looks, but also something akin to the humans whom she had met. He was dressed like a young noble off on a hunt, with high leather boots, *blue* pants and matching shirt and vest.

Indeed, *blue* was clearly not only his favorite color, but a very part of him, for no human or elf of any type had such glittering azure eyes—narrowed in speculation at the moment—or shoulder-length hair of the same brilliant color.

"You're a draenei," he declared finally. "Met a couple of your kind, but no female before."

"You are . . . you are the blue dragon. . . ." Her own statement sounded so obvious that she was ashamed to have even said it, but could think of nothing else. Her mind and body were still battered from her efforts, and if he did not continue to hold her, Iridi suspected that she would have fallen.

"I am the blue dragon," he returned. A smile ever so briefly touched his features, lighting them up, but then he looked to the side and some dark memory clearly reared its head. The smile transformed into a scowl.

A scowl that in part appeared aimed at the cowled figure joining them.

"Miraculous enough to have gained such aid in our hour of need," the dragon mage commented to his younger counterpart. "But more astounding is the familiar shape in which it comes." He bowed his head. "My greetings, Kalecgos."

"Krasus . . ." There was a hint of resentment in the blue-haired fighter's tone. "I thought that it was you, but couldn't believe it at first."

"The fates apparently demanded that our paths cross again."

"The fates? Blame it more on my lord, Malygos. It's he who sent me here . . . and likely sensed that you were also on your way, if I know him." He shrugged. "But it still seems that we were doomed to cross paths, yes."

Krasus took a step closer to his counterpart. "Kalecgos! You know that I wanted only the best for Anveena—"

"You may call me 'Kalec,' " the youth said to Iridi as he purposely turned his attention from the other male. "I prefer it when in this form . . ."

"Kalec . . . I am Iridi."

"Can you now stand on your own, Iridi?" When she nodded, Kalec cautiously released her. "Good."

Krasus sought to interject himself into the conversation again. "Kalecgos—Kalec—it is good to see you—"

"I don't find it so good," the other snapped. "But I couldn't stand by and let even you be preyed upon by—by whatever those were . . ." He looked past them. ". . . and I've no doubt as to where they came from."

"Yes, young one, they had to come from Grim Batol."

"Then, that's where I'm off to." Kalec spread his arms and a look came over his face that Iridi realized presaged a transformation.

But Krasus seized the fighter's arm, a dangerous thing if the depth of Kalec's sudden scowl was anything to judge by.

"It would not be wise to go alone," the dragon mage told him.

"It's not so safe to entrust oneself to you!" He leaned into Krasus's face. "You gave her peace and then you allowed it to be ripped away! You let her live a lie of a life, knowing all too well that it would end in tragedy!"

"But it hasn't, Kalec. You knew what she had to do . . . what she *did*. Anveena's destiny was always written—"

"Don't you speak her name again!" Kalec raised a hand and suddenly a glowing sword appeared in it. The blade looked sharp enough to cut the air itself and the grip had been molded to perfectly match his hold.

Kalec thrust the point toward Krasus, letting it hover just an inch or two from the latter's chest.

Unperturbed, Krasus glanced from the blade to its wielder. "I know how much she meant to you and I mourn that loss . . . but Anveena is still with you always. You should feel that yourself, young one."

Iridi remained perfectly still as the tableau played out. She would have preferred that this argument not take place at all, especially so soon after their battle with the abominations, but clearly this confrontation had been a long time coming and nothing she could say or do could stop it.

Kalec exhaled. Much of the anger dissipated, leaving in its wake resignation. "She said just that right before she sacrificed herself. She was sad and happy at the same time. Sad to leave the grove . . . and us . . . but happy to return that which she was to those who most needed her."

Recalling Iridi's presence, Krasus quietly explained, "Anveena was a young maiden of no guile, only care. She and Kalec met by accident after I worked hard to hide her from the eyes of the Lich King and his agents, especially one Dar'Khan."

The draenei recalled the blond human in the dragon mage's memories. It surely had to be her. "She gave her life so that others might live? A noble fate—"

This for some reason caused Kalec to laugh harshly. "You don't understand, draenei! Anveena never had a true life to give! Her entire existence was a conjurer's trick!" He again pointed the sword at Krasus, but without any intent to use it. "His trick! Anveena wasn't human; she wasn't even mortal! She was the very essence of the high elves' *Sunwell*, their fount of power! She was pure magic manipulated into playing at life so well that she thought she actually breathed, actually had a heart. . . ."

Iridi knew little of the Sunwell, though she had heard it mentioned by others. It was a source of tremendous magic that had been destroyed, that much the priestess understood. There had been a rumor, however, that it had been restored . . . and now it seemed that not only was that rumor true, but there had been far more to it than anyone who had spoken of it could have ever imagined.

"The will of the world shapes us all," Iridi murmured to Kalec in an attempt to soothe him. He had obviously cared much for the human incarnation. "And even through such adversity, we grow stronger."

The azure eyes softened once more. "You would've liked her, draenei . . . and she you."

Iridi bowed.

"I understand why *he's* come here," Kalec went on, referring to Krasus, "but why you?"

The cowled mage also looked at her. "That is a question we were never fully able to discuss, were we? What is it you seek in Grim Batol, Iridi?"

She saw no point in holding back the truth, especially as she was more and more seeing a link with what had happened to them and the object of her quest. They might not believe her, but she would tell them all that she could.

"I am in search . . . I am in search of a nether dragon," the draenei responded.

It was likely rare that Krasus, at the very least, was stunned. Iridi was not surprised that Kalec stood open-mouthed, but even the mage revealed startlement, if only through the raising high of one brow.

"She hunts for a nether dragon . . . in Azeroth!" Kalec blurted. "But there aren't any nether dragons in Azeroth! Those that tried to enter were destroyed by my flight at the portal to Outland! And since then, nothing passes that we do not take note of even from our sanctum . . ."

The priestess shook her head. "One survived the ill-fated crossing. I sensed its presence, but came upon the scene a moment too late. A cloaked figure reminiscent of you, Krasus, found him first, a cloaked figure accompanied by monstrous servants. They carried with them what I have divined is called a chrysalun chamber—"

"A chrysalun chamber!" Krasus looked to Kalec, who nodded. They both clearly understood what the artifact was and, therefore, what it could do.

"The magic they used to shield themselves from the nether dragon they also used to obscure the chamber from those who might notice anything awry in the vicinity of the portal." Iridi saw in her mind the vague vision, the tragic vision.

"No blood elf could wield enough skill to hide from my kind!" Kalec insisted. He opened his hand and, as with Iridi's staff, the blade vanished. Yet, it was clear to the draenei that Kalec's weapon was merely a manifestation of his power, not a true tool, like hers. "None."

"Unless he had some other great source . . ." Krasus suggested, studying Iridi. He had some glimmer of the truth, she sensed, and the fact that he understood that much impressed her.

"There was a source." The draenei held out her hand, summoning the staff. As the large crystal flared to life, Iridi felt a brief pang of grief despite all the training through which she had gone to learn to keep her stronger emotions under check.

Kalec stretched out a hand toward the crystal, the blue dragon trying to understand its workings. "That's not . . . that's not of Azeroth . . . I know . . . I know its origins . . . now . . . from those creatures called the naaru . . ."

"From the naaru it came," she agreed. "I had one. A friend . . . a good friend had the other. They were special gifts that we brought with us to Azeroth, to use for the sake of good. . . ."

"What happened to the other?" Krasus asked in a tone that indicated that he had his suspicions.

"Taken from the corpse of my friend," Iridi replied quietly. "After his slaughter . . ."

"And so that," the dragon mage murmured, "is the source of power that made Malygos's far-reaching senses pay no heed . . . and is also the reason to fear that the worst is yet to come." To Kalec, he asked, "This cloaked figure . . . this blood elf, to be sure, for there are few other than they who would think of this . . . wields the power of the naaru . . ." He frowned. "But it goes far worse than that, if I comprehend you correctly, young Iridi. You hunt a blood elf, wielding the stolen energies of naaru, who has also trapped and kidnapped a nether dragon. . . ."

"Yes." The priestess bowed her head to Krasus's wisdom. He truly did see things as they must be.

"Then, there remains only the question that none of us has yet spoken but that I will to put it to the point." Krasus made sure both of his companions were listening carefully. "A blood elf with naaru energies and a nether dragon as his . . . just what, then, do you think he intends to do with all that at his disposal? I believe that we have just met the answer . . . and it may only be the beginning of something far worse. . . ."

EIGHT

Zzeraku shimmered brightly, but not because of any effort on his part. He was weak, terribly weak, and at times he thought that his tormentors would finally cause what he had been dreaming of doing for the past few days. A creature of energy, the nether dragon was near total dissolution . . . but the spells and magical bonds ever prevented him from being completely destroyed. His captors needed what he was composed of much too much. They needed his essence to work their experiments.

Most of all, they needed him almost constantly to feed the hungry results of that last spell.

Nether dragons knew little about fear, but Zzeraku had learned much since his capture. First, there had been that terrifying sense of claustrophobia when, without warning, he had been sucked into the monstrous box by which they had smuggled him to this faraway place. Then, there had been the shock of discovering that he could not escape the magical bonds.

Now came the greatest of his fears . . . that he would slowly be eaten alive by the thing that their foul magic had created.

Zzeraku had been used to sowing fear, not living it, and so it struck him harder. Yet, at the same time, that fear also fed his rage and his desire for revenge. Given even the slightest hope, he would destroy his captors and devour *their* magical essence.

Unfortunately, thus far there was no chance of that happening. He again tested the strength of his bonds and again found them unbreakable. The agony he suffered in fighting against them was minute compared with the knowledge that he would still be helpless come the next feeding.

Unless . . .

Zzeraku was a creature of energy and the thing hungered for that energy.

An idea formed in the nether dragon's head. The logic of it made him smile as best as his bound jaws could.

Yes, soon they would come to feed their creation . . . and Zzeraku now could hardly wait.

There were dragonspawn about, which pleased Rom to no end. Hefting his ax, he found himself satisfied with how well he was doing with his left hand alone. Let even a drakonid or the foul blood elf come across him now and they would learn what the wrath of a Bronzebeard could be like.

He knew Grenda was watching him close. She was a capable second-in-command, but she was too concerned with his mood of late. Rom was aware that she thought his attitude becoming more and more fatalistic, whereas he only felt it realistic.

Even this foray tonight was not to her taste. Rom had brought them dangerously close to one of the caves leading into Grim Batol, determined to find something that would show that their mission was not a failure. This time, there would be no magical trickery.

The dwarves spread out carefully. Humans and other races thought their kind too hard-headed to learn from their mistakes, yet another myth. Rom had studied the patrol patterns of the dread lady's guards, and this time he believed he knew the variations that they might make. There would be no set-up for a trap, as had happened when he had thought he had captured the skardyn. These sentries would turn out to be exactly what they were, not a blood elf in disguise.

But Rom had another, more pressing reason for such a close approach, one about which even Grenda did not know. With one of the cave mouths so tauntingly nearby, Rom hoped to sneak inside, if only by himself. It was time to discover the full truth about the cries within and only through such daring could he hope to do that.

He also did not feel that he should risk anyone but himself. The obsession was his and his alone.

The soft crunch of feet made the dwarves pause. In one thing they had an easy advantage over the dragonspawn and the drakonid; they were already low to the ground. It made it easy to drop out of sight, especially on such a dark eve. Their foes had good eyesight, but Rom was betting on Bronzebeard eyes seeing better in the darkness.

A bulking figure trundled into sight, a dragonspawn with shield and heavy sword. That it was black was no surprise, for it seemed the blood elf's companion had ties to the remnants of Deathwing's flight. Yet, though the dragonspawn wore also a breastplate, there were no markings signifying its loyalty to one particular dragon or another. The drakonid had been the same. No marking indicating Deathwing himself, nor either of his misbegotten offspring, Onyxia and Nefarian . . . nor any other known black dragon.

But that was a minor point to Rom. What sufficed was that these creatures were willing to serve the two spellcasters. That was enough, along with the terrible cries, to warrant great concern.

"If it can be captured alive," he whispered to Grenda. "So much the better. If it needs to be slain, that's good also. I don't want any disaster like the last time."

The female dwarf grunted her understanding. She signaled another dwarf. The band began to close around the lone dragonspawn.

Then, something caught the scaly fiend's attention. It let out a grunting call, which was immediately answered from just within the cave.

"Down!" Rom ordered under his breath. Grenda managed to alert the others just as another dragonspawn lumbered out.

Rom waited for more guards, but these two appeared to be the only ones. A grim smile played across his lips, one he kept hidden from Grenda. The cave looked more inviting than ever. Two dragonspawn would be tough to take on, but Rom had the utmost confidence in his seasoned fighters.

However, before he could give the signal, whatever had initially caught the first guard's attention now caused that dragonspawn to head away from the dwarves. Rom held his breath in frustration as the four-legged fiend moved from what would have been the perfect ambush spot. He had hoped that the second guard would join the first there.

With the second trotting to catch up, the first dragonspawn readied its weapon as it approached a small cluster of withered oaks. Rom tried to locate all his fighters, wondering which of them might be the reason for the guards' intense interest in that particular location.

An arrow abruptly seemed to sprout from the neck of the foremost dragonspawn. A second, whistling bolt joined the first.

But the dragonspawn only shook a little, then, with a snarl, tore both arrows from its thick hide. The other joined it, the pair eagerly charging the trees.

Another arrow shot at the first abomination, an act that Rom could only see as foolhardy. He changed his opinion a breath later as a tall, slim figure leapt from the trees and, even as the bolt distracted the dragonspawn, cut the massive creature along the chest with a blazing sword that brought to the dwarf bad memories of his hand.

The dragonspawn let out a hiss intermingling pain with surprise. It had an extremely tough hide and that any sword could cut into it so quickly was stunning. Still the guard recovered quickly, attacking its foe with a heavy ax.

The ax, however, was not as sturdy as the dragonspawn's scale and a second strike by the slim fighter cut the weapon in two. Growling, the guard stretched forward heavy, clawed hands as it threw its massive weight up in a clear attempt to crush its tinier foe beneath it.

But it lacked the swiftness of the other, who nimbly leapt aside and then ran the edge of the magical blade across the oncoming behemoth's throat.

The nearly-severed head flung backward, making it appear as if the dragonspawn gaped at the heavens. The huge body was slow in responding to its death, continuing its charge for several paces before collapsing.

The second dragonspawn gaped at the sight of its comrade slain so dramatically, then recovered as the shadowy fighter lunged toward it. Even as the first guard's corpse finally realized that it was dead, the two combatants exchanged several blows. While this dragonspawn's weapon did not glow, it appeared strong enough to withstand whatever magic radiated from the newcomer's sword.

"What do we do?" asked Grenda anxiously.

Rom grunted. "We go and help!"

He was not being altruistic in his decision. Once he was certain that the battle was under control, the dwarven leader intended to slip away to the cave.

The dragonspawn and its foe circled around one another and for the first time, Rom had some inkling of who it was the creature faced. One of the elven races, but it did not look like a blood elf. In fact, what glimpses he saw resembled—

The hood of the figure's cloak fell back, revealing silver-white hair flowing down well past her shoulders. That she was female Rom had figured moments before. She was also very skilled with her weapons . . . as any high elven ranger would have been.

Only . . . there were not supposed to be many high elves left at all.

Even in the dark, he knew the outfit she would be wearing. Knee-high leather boots. Forest-green pants and blouse, with a form-fitting breastplate over the latter. Over her hands and extending to her elbows were thin gloves that still allowed her to perfectly grip the string of a bow, her other favored weapon.

Rom even knew her name, now that he saw her close. It was a name seared into his memory, for she had shared in the struggle to bring down the orcs of Grim Batol.

"Vereesa Windrunner . . ." he rumbled to himself. "Aye . . . Grim Batol is calling in ghosts now, too. . . ."

But she was no ghost, he knew. Rather, she was the mate of the wizard, Rhonin. That much Rom knew. Why she was here, though, he did not understand.

But did that mean that Rhonin, too, was close by?

The other dwarves swarmed the dragonspawn. Between Vereesa and them, Rom saw that the situation was well in hand. It was the moment to make his move.

The dwarven commander slipped away, heading to the cave mouth. Time was limited and it was only luck that the second guard had not had the breath yet to call for help.

Rom scrambled up toward the cave. As a dwarf, he could instinctively ferret out the best places to secrete himself. Then, with caution, he would push deeper, until finally he found the source of—

His plans were cut off by an unnerving glow radiating from within the cave. Rom knew what that glow presaged and now was not the time for a confrontation.

Swearing under his breath, he spun about. They had to retreat, but could not until they had dealt with the second dragonspawn. It was down on its knees but still battling despite several obvious wounds.

Thrusting the ax handle between his teeth, Rom leapt as well as a dwarf could. He landed atop the dragonspawn's back end, then pulled himself up. Legs gripping the monster's sides, Rom took the ax and buried the head in the guard's back.

The blade barely pierced the scaled hide. Flinging another dwarf away, the dragonspawn tried to reach back to Rom. The great claws came within an inch of his face, but could stretch no farther.

The high elf struck again, cutting into the dragonspawn's thick arm. The huge creature turned back to face her.

Gritting his teeth, Rom landed a second blow. With the precision of the veteran he was, he managed to hit the exact same spot.

The ax sank deeper. Thick, dark fluids spurted out.

The guard shook. Grenda and another dwarf managed small but significant wounds to its flank. The high elf severed a finger.

Rom planted a third blow directly where the others had landed.

The dragonspawn gave a shiver, then dropped. Rom all but rolled off, only just managing to cling to his weapon as he landed.

"Let's get you away from here!" he quietly rumbled.

Her long eyes widened. "Rom—"

"The tearful reunions can wait 'til later, milady! There's somethin' coming that you don't want to be around for!"

She had sense enough to nod and follow. Around them, the other dwarves were more perplexed.

"We're bringing her with us?" asked Grenda. "A blood elf?"

"I am no blood elf!" Vereesa snapped with much vehemence for one of her kind. "I am and shall always be a ranger of the high elf people!"

"No time for talk!" Rom growled. "Hurry!"

Even as they started moving, the glow began to radiate from the cave mouth.

"What is that?" Vereesa demanded.

Their leader swore again. "Get a move on it, milady!"

Vereesa hardly had trouble keeping up with Rom. Indeed, he could barely catch his breath, while she seemed not in the least strained.

Daring to glance over his shoulder, Rom saw that the glow had now fully emerged from the cave. The source was a staff with a crystalline head. The wielder was none other than the blood elf. He looked around, but not in the direction in which the dwarves and their new companion had run.

Then, the landscape hid the blood elf and his sinister toy from sight of the dwarf. Rom had an inclination to slow even then, though. The dwarves continued to run at as good a clip as their short, thick legs could stand. Each moment, Rom expected to discover the fiendish blood elf at their heels, but only darkness met his anxious gaze.

At long last, they reached what Rom considered safety. The hidden entrance to the tunnels lay just a few yards ahead. With the ranger beside him, the dwarven commander stepped over to it.

"Rom of the Bronzebeards," Vereesa murmured as the dwarven commander tapped once on a huge rock with the bottom of his ax. The rock slid away, revealing the entrance beneath.

"Milady Vereesa . . . I would say 'tis good to see you, but there's nothing good when it involves Grim Batol. . . ." He gestured for her to slide down. Although she was much taller than them, her slim form easier fit through.

Rom did not enter until the last of his followers had gone down. As he dropped in, he took one last look. Still no glow. Nodding, he slid the stone in place.

Vereesa, almost kneeling, studied the tunnels. "There is much interference in this region against magic."

"Aye, the area for a great distance around is pocketed with these crystal formations."

She touched one of the glittering formations thrusting out of a wall. "Curious. They look perfectly normal . . . but I have never heard of such a thing in such quantity. . . ."

"Be thankful it's here, milady, or that beast of a blood elf would've found us all by now."

She paid the last no mind at all, seizing instead on another part of his dire statement. " 'Blood elf'! You have seen him? He is in Grim Batol?"

"There's a blood elf in Grim Batol, aye! He and the dark lady! They're both—"

The ranger knelt down in front of Rom. Although very much enamored with the looks of his own female kind, Rom could not help admiring her exotic beauty . . . and the terrible concern behind it. "It is the blood elf that I want to hear about!" Anger filled her musical voice. "To think that I was so near! But . . . it has to be the right one! Have you—have you seen him up close?"

Rom let out a harsh laugh and showed her the stump at the end of his arm. "Just before a damned drakonid did this, I was as close to the blood elf as you are to me now. . . ."

"Describe him!"

"He was a blood elf!" That was enough for any dwarf, but Vereesa obviously wanted more. Rom concentrated, trying to recall details. As best he could, he mentioned the shape of the face, the tone of the voice, and even the glowing green orbs. Nothing seemed distinctive to him, but the more he said, the more cold the ranger's expression became.

"That will be enough," she finally said. Her eyes closed briefly in contemplation before she looked again at Rom and muttered, "It can only be him. . . ."

"Him who? You think you know him?" Even as he asked, Rom wanted to bite his tongue. It was very possible that she knew this blood elf, for their foul kind had originated from the high elves. They had taken the ways of demons to fight demons—indeed, actually *draining* the magic from the demons like leeches—and, in the eyes of humans, dwarves, and those few high elves who had held to their old ways, *cursed* themselves for all eternity. This blood elf was very likely an old friend, even a comrade from Vereesa's days as a ranger. Small wonder she would be bitter about him.

"I know this blood elf, yes," she finally answered. "I know him well. I have followed his trail since the night that he tried to steal away my sons, Giramar and Galadin. . . ."

"By the gods!" There were no monsters greater than those that preyed on children, so Rom thought, though he had no offspring himself. "Your sons? But how could any dare take the children of Rhonin Draig'cyfaill—" Rom used the name by which many now called the legendary wizard. Draig'cyfaill—*Dragonheart*. ". . . and you?"

"Rhonin has been busy of late. . . ." She said this without any rancor, only as fact. "There is much to be done to repair things in Dalaran." This she did not explain further, even the dwarves aware of the extensive destruction there. "And as for me . . . this blood elf knew in particular how to disguise himself against me."

"Another ranger . . . or used to be one, eh? Just as I thought."

Vereesa did not listen, her gaze inward. In the light of the torches the dwarves used, her eyes were a bright, bright blue. "Rhonin set in place wards to guard us from those who might want vengeance or merely thought us a danger to their cause. Those wards faced little use for some time, and thus I grew too complacent."

"Complacent?"

"Yes . . . complacent. I, a ranger, had come to enjoy my family and reveled in my children. When the wards shrieked their alarm, I almost acted too slowly. I burst in and sent him fleeing just before he could spirit the children away!"

"What—what would he want with children?" Grenda asked.

"What would *any* seeker of magic want with the children of a powerful wizard and a high elf? Children with so much potential in their bloodlines?" Rom asked her in return, his own questions both rhetorical and filled with dread.

Vereesa nodded. "Yes, that was my thought also . . . and that is why I knew that eventually he would try again . . . and why we had to hunt him down, no matter what the cost." She shook her head. "With all that he has been doing, Rhonin has not slept any more than I. Neither of us will rest until this is over. Our only regret was that we finally had to separate to follow different trails, though we keep in touch through this."

She pulled from beneath her breastplate a triangular talisman with a blue gem at the center. The talisman was attached to a chain that let it hang from her neck.

"That looks familiar . . . somewhat."

"Rhonin took the one you think of and altered it into this design."

Rom grunted. "How long since you last used it to reach the wizard?"

"A day ago."

"Well, it won't work here for the same reason we don't have the blood elf breathin' down our necks."

Vereesa frowned, then replaced the talisman beneath her breastplate. "A small trouble and perhaps the best thing. I now know that he is here. Zendarin *will* pay."

Rom again heard the loathing in her voice. " 'Zendarin'? You know him very well, it sounds."

Her smile was as grim as her tone. "Better than any save my sisters, for his family, too, was named *Windrunner,* as his father and mine were brothers." Her hand caressed the hilt of her sword. "And though we are of the same blood . . . I will put an end to my cousin's abominable thirst for magic, even if it means my own sacrifice."

"Is something amiss, my dear Zendarin?" the dark lady asked with a slight touch of humor.

"You might be interested in these." With the staff, he pointed at a spot near to where she was studying another egg.

The overly-burdened skardyn gratefully dropped the two dragon-spawn carcasses that the blood elf had ordered them to bring all the way from where they had been discovered. As soon as that was done, the scaly creatures quickly retreated from the scene.

"I have seen dead dragonspawn before. You might recall that we have an infestation of dwarves with which you have yet to properly deal."

He ignored her remark. With the glowing end of the staff, he prodded one of the corpses. "This was slain by a dwarf . . . with the help of several other dwarves, judging by the many scars and smaller wounds." Zendarin Windrunner then pointed at the other body. "*That* was done by someone with a weapon of power . . . someone much taller than the Bronzebeard vermin."

She turned her burnt side to him. "And this is of significance to me for what reason?"

"You said that *he* was near, the one you wanted to come! Does this not mean that he's about?"

The ebony-clad woman laughed, a macabre sight. "Is that the best you think he could do? My dear Zendarin, when he comes, it will be in a much more subtle yet still more powerful manner than this. . . ."

"Than what—" He stopped as she strode past him to investigate the one body. One long, graceful hand ran along the area of the body, poising longest by the throat. She smiled as she openly admired the handi-work.

"A skilled warrior did this," the lady in black commented. Her hand suddenly glowed red. It ran once more over the throat. "They located the most sensitive spot with ease."

"What are you doing?"

"Finding a bit of the truth," she replied, standing again. As the glow faded, Zendarin's companion held out her hand to him. "And the truth is closer to home than you might think . . ."

Zendarin did not like riddles save when he was the one telling them. "If you know something, spit it out!"

She gave him a look that immediately cowed the blood elf. "Remember who it is you are speaking to and then consider your tone carefully! There is much insubordination from you that I will tolerate, but there *are* limits to even my fine patience. . . ."

Zendarin wisely kept silent. He bowed his head in respect.

"That is better." She gestured at the cadavers.

A ball of flame erupted from her palm. It split in two as it flew toward the bodies.

The two smaller balls struck. The corpses became tiny infernos, burning to ash in mere seconds.

The lady in black inhaled deeply through her nostrils, her expression filled with dark pleasure. "Ah, what a fine fragrance, don't you agree?"

"You had some answer for me?" the blood elf reminded her.

With her other hand, she dismissed the ashes, which went flying out of the chamber, eventually to descend into the unused lower depths of Grim Batol. In their wake, only one small item remained . . . an arrowhead.

"Pick it up." When he had obeyed, she asked, "Does it look familiar?"

The blood elf sneered. "This is high elven!"

"Yes, but not just. I recognize it. You should, too."

"I do . . ." He turned it over, studying the make. It did not look like any stone, but rather *white pearl*. In truth, it was even much more and would have bore into its target with greater efficiency than any mortal arrow. "This is Thalassian work. These are the mark of a favored of the ranger-general of Silvermoon! No blood elf helped slay the guards, then . . . a surviving ranger was here . . ."

"I find the distinctions between passing phases of elf irrelevant." The disfigured woman eyed him closely. "I do believe that you know exactly who might be responsible. Now *that* is interesting."

"It's nothing. . . ." he grated, tossing aside the arrowhead as if it burned his hand. "And it will remain nothing. . . . I will see to that. . . ."

"You had better. There can be nothing—absolutely nothing—that would interfere." She locked gazes with the blood elf. "You are not worth *that* much to my desires."

With that, she turned from him to study the egg anew. Zendarin was furious at being dismissed like some skardyn, but he held all his anger within a mask of indifference. Besides, there was another upon whom to vent his fury. Typically impetuous—as proven by her tryst with the wizard and the potentially-powerful mongrels they had created—she had come to him rather than wait until he had time to return for her prodigy.

So much the better, my cousin, Zendarin thought as he strode from the lady's lair. *Perhaps you have given me a different path to the magic I crave, one with less danger, more personal potential . . . and no one to bow to . . .*

Then, a roar echoed throughout the caverns. The "child" was hungry again. The lady had—without warning or reasonable discussion—held back with the feedings, suddenly interested in studying other aspects of its growth. However, they had both agreed that it would be fed well come the next evening. Zendarin had even agreed to lend some of the power of the staff to that feeding, to see how it might accelerate certain developments in their creation.

A little longer . . . I can tolerate her a little longer, he decided. *Then . . . then I will be able to deal with her and you, my cousin, and not only reap the benefits of my time and efforts spent in this dismal place, but also finish my plans with your little abominations. . . .*

The blood elf grinned, hungry now himself. Soon, very soon, he would have access to energies in such abundance that he would never feel the withdrawals again.

Soon . . . he, too, would feed to his heart's content.

NINE

As they cautiously approached their destination, Iridi learned more of Kalec and the tale of Anveena. The young blue dragon—like Krasus, remaining in his half-elven form for less visibility—seemed very eager to tell her. Iridi knew that it was in part because of her demeanor and calling, but also perhaps because he wanted to try to hurt the older dragon with his words.

"She was the most innocent soul—yes, *soul*—one could have ever met," Kalec said with a wistful expression. "No guile. No pretense. She was who she was . . . even if she wasn't, in truth." His gaze flickered to Krasus, who walked a few steps ahead of them. The elder male had been silent since they had begun moving again. Whether it was due to concentrating his magic on protecting them or simply because he could say nothing to assuage his companion's bitterness, the draenei did not know.

Kalec spoke of his first encounter with Anveena, who had found him after dragon hunters—led by a vengeful dwarf named Harkyn Grymstone and paid by a disguised Dar'Khan—had almost captured and killed him. Dar'Khan had been part of the reason for the Sunwell's original destruction, although his desire had been simply to wield its power. What he had not known at the time, though, was that the swift defiling and draining of the Sunwell by his master—Arthas—had not caused the total dissipation of its energies. Instead, much had escaped and, after a time, began to gather far, far away.

But there came a point when Dar'Khan had finally sensed its gathering. He had led a band of the Scourge to the location.

Yet, no one had realized at first that Anveena was the key. A tiny creature—a strange combination of dragon and flying serpent—had been found hatching nearby. Anveena and it had instantly befriended one another and she had, in typical fashion, called it "Raac," after the sounds it made.

Although he did not look back or even slow down, Krasus finally interrupted. "Aah, Raac. Does he fly?"

"He vanished right after she did. I assumed that he went to let you know that your worries were over. . . ."

Now Krasus did look, albeit briefly. His expression remained neutral, but Iridi sensed that he felt more than he revealed. "I want nothing but good for all those of Azeroth, Kalec . . . and Raac did not return to me."

"Hmmph! The little one had more sense than I thought."

"Raac was no longer mine. He desired to stay with Anveena."

The younger dragon scowled. "He wasn't the only one."

"What happened after Raac hatched?" the priestess interjected, fearful that a great argument would erupt. This of all places they did not need to have rancor between them.

Kalec told her a tale of adventure, of tragedy, and of hope. With another blue dragon—a female named Tyri—they had gone in search of a wizard called Borel. Their search had brought them to Tarren Mill, where they were met not only by the former paladin, Jorad Mace—another recipient of the mysterious Borel's interference—but by Dar'Khan and the Scourge. After a struggle in which Tyri apparently scorched Dar'Khan to cinders, the three and Jorad had headed toward Aerie Peak to find the cousin of the repentant Harkyn Grymstone, a dwarf with the skills to remove the magical bands Dar'Khan had placed around the throats of Kalec and Anveena. After that, the party had assumed that their troubles would be over.

But the dwarf Loggi was a prisoner of another mad creature, the cunning Baron Valimar Mordis—a Forsaken. He recognized in part what Anveena was and tried to use her to magnify the power of an artifact called the Orb of Ner'zhul, a fiendish sphere that could animate a giant undead. With it, Mordis had already raised a frost wyrm, an undead dragon.

"We barely escaped Mordis and the Scourge," Kalec muttered. "Thanks only to a tauren of all creatures. Trag gave his life to stop his former master. . . ."

"And all was well then?" Iridi asked, sensing that perhaps it had been otherwise.

The blue verified her concerns. "Not in the least. Loggi was killed and Anveena stolen . . . by *Dar'Khan.* . . ."

The supposedly dead high elf then dragged Anveena to where the Sunwell had originally been located. The others had followed, but although they fought hard to save their friend, it proved to be Anveena who saved them. In the process, they also confronted the mysterious Borel, whose machinations Kalec clearly blamed for much of the trouble that had occurred.

The draenei could easily guess the truth about this Borel. "The wizard . . . he was you, wasn't he, Krasus?"

"Of course, he was . . . he has a thousand names, a thousand disguises! He's interfered since at least the fall of the night elves more than ten thousand years ago! He does nothing but interfere—and damn anyone who might be caught up in his intentions!"

Krasus turned. Although his face remained emotionless, his eyes burned. Iridi involuntarily took a step back and even Kalec was stunned into silence.

"I remember the names of *every* brave human, elf, dwarf, tauren, earthen, orc, dragon, and individuals from other races whom I have been forced to need throughout the centuries! I recall all their faces and the manners by which so many of them perished! Each time I sleep, the litany plays in my dreams and I mourn their brave souls!" The air crackled around the dragon mage, an unconscious reflection of millennia of pent-up emotions. "And if my life could bring them all back, I would do it, Kalecgos! Make no mistake about that . . . and remember, among our kind, too many of those lost were my very sons and daughters. . . ."

Krasus's shoulders slumped. The two males faced one another and the priestess felt as if some unheard conversation passed between them. Then, the elder dragon turned forward again and continued the trek. Kalec remained still a moment longer, finally walking with Iridi behind his counterpart.

The draenei made no mention of a concern the confrontation had now created. They were already in great danger of being noticed and the argument between the dragons—especially the potent energies arising from it—had only multiplied that danger. She could not speak up, though, for fear that the pair would only start anew on their differences.

There was so much that Iridi still wanted to know concerning Kalec and his deep devotion to Anveena, especially what had happened with them prior to her "sacrifice." However, not only was it not proper for her to press on the point, but she, too, needed to focus on their journey.

But Kalec apparently could not keep in his memories, even if he no longer punctuated them with rancor toward the red dragon.

"I returned to my kind after . . . after Anveena," he murmured to Iridi. "But I could not stand the caverns. Everything was so cramped together. I—I caused more than one fight, and blue dragons do not just use tooth and claw, we use magic. It finally came to my lord Malygos's attention and he knew that I could not stay among them, any longer. It was almost fate that this mission came up . . . fate or a curse." He stared at Krasus's back. "I know what happened to your people assigned to guard Grim Batol, Korialstrasz. Whatever lies between us, I pray that those you held dearest were not among the ones who suffered most."

"Your concern is appreciated . . . and, yes . . . some were."

Kalec would have said more, but Iridi suddenly tensed. She felt a resonance with which only she would have been truly familiar.

Someone was using the other naaru staff . . . and for a reason the priestess understood all too well.

She tried to dismiss her own, but it was too late. The larger crystal flared bright, but not due to any focus on her part.

"Why are you doing—" Kalec began.

The staff struggled in her grip. She felt its solidity lessen, as if it were dissolving. It was all the priestess could do just to maintain both a physical and mental hold on her gift. Iridi did not even dare direct enough concentration to warn the others.

However, Krasus understood at least part of the trouble. "Kalec! He seeks to bring her staff to him! We cannot permit that!"

The young fighter seized the staff with one hand. Around him there formed a blue aura. Kalec gritted his teeth as he forced that aura to spread to the naaru's gift.

But the crystal's own aura suddenly flared brighter than ever. It engulfed the blue dragon, who let out a scream and fell back.

At the same time, the staff nearly pulled free. Iridi strained, using all her mental and physical training to keep it with her.

Krasus placed a hand on hers. The tall, robed figure closed his eyes. The aura engulfed him as it had Kalec . . . but the dragon mage only grunted. The draenei, who knew the forces in play, marveled at the stamina Krasus yet had considering all that he had been through.

A crimson glow began to overtake the crystal's aura. In seconds, not only did Krasus force the battle back to the staff, but his efforts gained for Iridi the momentum that she needed. Now better able to concentrate her strength, the draenei joined with the dragon mage to cut off the blood elf's insidious attempt to double his ill-gotten gains.

And then . . . the attack ceased. With simultaneous gasps, the priestess and Krasus relaxed.

"Thank—thank you," Iridi managed.

Krasus looked her over. "You are well? You have control of the staff?"

"Yes and yes." For good measure, though, she dismissed the staff, sending it to that place that only the naaru truly understood, that place from which only *she* could summon it.

Or so the priestess hoped. Iridi had not expected the blood elf to be able to attempt what he had nearly succeeded in doing. She knew from others that his kind were not necessarily spellcasters, but he apparently had excellent skills . . . or far too much purloined magic. Whichever the case, the draenei knew that she had been very careless. If alone, Iridi would have now been bereft of the naaru's creation.

And very likely dead.

Her concerns shifted to Kalec, who was just rising. He eyed Krasus and her, then growled to the former, "Nothing is ever simple around you, is it?"

"It would be my fondest wish if for once it would be."

The priestess stepped up to the younger dragon. "Let me see your hand."

"I'm fine," he insisted, showing the palm to her. The last of a tremendous burnt area was just healing itself. "You see? Nothing to fear."

But Iridi was not convinced. She took his hand in hers and touched the palm gently with her finger.

Kalec winced. "What did you just do?"

"I did nothing but locate the point of entry of the staff's energies. I will need a moment to deal with this."

"But I healed it."

"You healed the physical, but in doing so, you let some of the energies be trapped within. You don't want to let it spread."

With a free hand, the priestess again summoned the staff.

Kalec started to pull back. "You are going to use that?"

"Cause may also be cure, so it is written. All will be well." She did not add that such would only be the case assuming that the blood elf did not now try again. "Please. Be patient."

Kalec grimaced but let her touch the head of the staff to his palm. To his further credit, he made no protest when she pricked the area in question with the crystal head.

The crystal briefly flared.

A small tendril of energy akin to the crystal's aura rose from the opening in the palm.

"By the lord of magic!" Kalec breathed. "I never felt that within . . ."

"No . . ." was all the draenei replied. As the tendril disappeared into the crystal, she pulled it back. "You may heal the opening yourself, if you wish."

He did so. At the same time, Iridi once more dismissed the staff. Only when it was gone did she breathe easier.

"What now?" asked Kalec.

As if in response, something howled. Something not all that far from them.

Something that received, from what seemed every other direction to the draenei, an answering howl. . . .

Zzeraku grew impatient. He now had a plan, but not yet an opportunity in which to implement it. The sorceress and the elf thing who pandered to her had foregone the usual feedings for their creation. Zzeraku had all but gone mad waiting.

Then, he suddenly realized that he was not alone. The other was shielded from the sight of the skardyn—as he had finally learned to call the scaly little vermin—but not from his powerful senses. Of course, there was nothing that he could do with that knowledge, bound as he was.

A shadow moved before his eyes, one that flickered in and out of existence. Ever so briefly, it would take a distinct form.

The elf thing. The *blood* elf.

The creature called Zendarin.

You can see me on some level, the shadow marveled. *How unique! The staff is powerful, yet you can see me . . . to a point, that is.*

The nether dragon tried to thrust the voice from his mind, for it aggravated his thoughts as a sharp pin shoved deep would surely aggravate the flesh of the blood elf.

Now, now, my little friend, Zendarin mocked. *This won't take long and it'll be just between the two of us, eh?*

That interested Zzeraku. He had sensed the other's personal ambition, could even appreciate it to an extent.

Let us see what can be siphoned off of you . . .

In the shadow, Zzeraku glimpsed the odd staff that he knew was not of the blood elf's making. Even its glow was invisible to the skardyn. The blood elf was definitely not doing something that the lady would like.

It's close by, his tormentor continued, but more to himself. *I nearly had it, but the others interfered. I need more . . . and I think that you can give me that. . . .*

As the nether dragon had expected, Zendarin wanted to also feed from him. The staff was powerful, but evidently not enough for whatever purpose the blood elf had in mind.

Zzeraku hid his glee. Perhaps he could do with this one as he had planned to do with their creation.

The shadow moved closer. The crystal pointed toward Zzeraku.

Suddenly, Zendarin spun around. With a curse that jolted the nether dragon's mind as if it were thunder, the blood elf slipped away.

A moment later, the only being who truly frightened the nether dragon glided into the cavern. The skardyn quickly dropped to their knees.

"So, my precious child," the dark lady cooed, "and how are you?"

She did not truly expect an answer, as Zzeraku's maw was sealed shut. Unlike the blood elf, she made no attempt to touch his thoughts, although he was not all that certain they were kept from her, regardless.

"Have you regained your strength? I want you nice and strong! You want to be nice and strong, don't you?"

Her tone sent shivers through Zzeraku and much of his earlier confidence slipped away. The nether dragon was almost certain that the female knew his intentions and toyed with him.

"Zendarin!"

The nether dragon did not expect the blood elf to respond—he did not expect the blood elf to even have stayed in the vicinity—but Zendarin surprised him by striding into the chamber. His expression was all innocence . . . or at least as much innocence as one of his kind could possibly display.

"I was just looking for you," the blood elf remarked.

"Looking for me—or looking out for me?"

"I—"

She turned her ravaged side to Zendarin, much to the nether drag-on's relief. Some of the shivering eased. *Some.*

"We are in a very delicate period here, Zendarin. You are aware of that?"

He acted offended. "Of course, I do or—"

The blood elf shrieked as his body suddenly burned as if on fire from within. His blood felt like molten lava and Zendarin expected it at any moment to burst through his flesh.

He dropped to his knees. The staff appeared in one hand, but, if he thought to use it somehow, he never got the chance. It slipped from his grasp and, in doing so, vanished again.

"It makes you want to tear your skin off or bleed yourself dry just to escape the torture, does it not? But you can never escape it. . . . I can never escape it. . . ."

The blood elf rolled on his side, clawing at his chest. She watched him for another minute, then gestured curtly.

The pain abruptly ceased. Zendarin, sweat bathing his body, stopped groaning and, after a time, managed to catch his breath. He peered up at the lady in black, no guile in his face whatsoever.

"A reminder was in order here. The last reminder. You have been offered much by me, but most of all, you have been offered a path to a fount of energy such as your miserable kind can only dream."

The blood elf wisely said nothing.

"I know how much that purloined toy of yours means to you," she added, likely speaking of the staff. "And I sense, as you do, that among those approaching is one who carries its twin. How nice, you no doubt believed, to add it to your collection. . . . Am I correct?"

Zendarin managed a very cautious nod.

"Well, if the other's toy becomes available in the process, it is yours to claim . . . but I will not condone any interference in my desires."

"I—I would never—"

"Think careful of your next words, Zendarin Windrunner. You have already gone far in disappointing me. I hate disappointments. My son and daughter were quite the disappointments. . . ."

"You will not be disappointed. All—all will go as you wish, my lady. . . ."

She smiled, a sight that shook both nether dragon and blood elf. "That is all I ask . . . all . . ."

She whirled on Zzeraku, who wanted to hide from her. However, her words were still directed toward the blood elf, who had wisely not moved.

"Still, your infantile attempt to take that other toy has given me the information I need on *him*. The time has come to move in *that* regard. You may be interested to know that Rask is already out hunting, with a pack of skardyn, of course. I've also made use of your little pet."

This caused Zendarin's gaze to narrow. "Of course . . . I said that it would be available when you needed it for him."

"So glad you approve," she returned with open mockery. "I thought you might be surprised that it obeyed me without your permission . . ."

"Of course not . . ."

The veiled sorceress clapped her hands together in satisfaction. "Shall we go prepare for company?" Her dread smile turned on Zzeraku. "And, after that, a proper feeding. The poor dear *is* growing hungry. *Very* hungry . . ."

She departed with the blood elf in tow. Her parting words left the nether dragon to wonder whether, like Zendarin, the lady in black was just as aware of her captive's intentions and had warned him that, whatever he dreamed he could accomplish, he was sorely mistaken.

And, if that were the case, there was *no* hope for Zzeraku whatsoever. . . .

TEN

The howls were like those of no hound, though there was in them that same sort of bestial determination to hunt down the prey. To those who listened very close, they were more akin to the voices of men . . . or dwarves.

The skardyn raced along the landscape of Grim Batol, more animal than thinking creature. They hopped along the jagged ground, moving with far more swiftness than their stocky shapes would have let on. Others crawled up and over the rocks, even clinging to the underside as they searched for prey.

With eagerness, they sniffed the earth, the air, what life there was around them. They knew, through both their mistress and their hunt master, where exactly the prey had last been located, but there was always the chance that other intruders might be near, such as the Bronzebeards. The skardyn had a special interest in hunting down their distant cousins, if possible.

After all, Bronzebeards made, for them, good eating.

Whether on two legs or all four limbs, whether on the ground or clambering along the rock face, the wild pack quickly covered the distances. Not far behind, a small band of dragonspawn kept pace. They were not the hunt masters, merely the handlers. That position belonged to the foremost of the dark lady's scaly servants, the drakonid, Rask.

Rask was as larger than the others of his monstrous kind as he was more vicious. Yet, he also had a quick mind for a drakonid and, in some ways, a more cunning one than even a blood elf or dwarf. He knew things of his mistress that even Zendarin did not and, because of those, he obeyed her commands with something approaching . . . *worship*.

With as much bloodlust as the skardyn, he led the dragonspawn under his command in search of the prey. His mistress had told him what to expect and, despite the immensity of his mission, Rask was only too eager to confront the intruders.

"Move . . ." he grated at the nearest skardyn, emphasizing his impatience with the crack of a whip. "Find them. . . ."

The skardyn scampered on. They were close now. Very close.

Rask turned to the dragonspawn nearest him. "The signal . . ."

The guard gave him a savage grin, then took the torch he was carrying and waved it three times toward the rear of the hunt.

A shimmering form briefly materialized, then vanished again.

Rask nodded. "Good . . ." He cracked his whip at a nearby skardyn. "We have them. . . ."

"There is no longer any reason for pretense," Krasus declared grimly. "What we seek now actively seeks us. . . ."

"Must you ever state the obvious?" Kalec remarked with some lingering enmity.

Krasus ignored him, instead spreading his arms. The cowled figure began transforming—

But with a sudden groan, he doubled over, still very much looking like some variation of elf and not in the least like his true identity.

As Iridi leapt to his aid, Kalec began his transformation. Unlike Krasus, he suffered no setback as he went from fighter to dragon.

"Keep the old one safe!" the blue dragon ordered. He took to the air.

The draenei knew that there was some mistake in letting Kalec—or Kalecgos now—go, but Krasus again needed her. She leaned over the fallen figure, trying to see what she could do.

"This is . . . all planned," he gasped. "This weakness! This was . . . - begun long before I came here. . . ."

"What do you mean?" the priestess asked as she ran her hands a few inches above his body in hopes of sensing the source of his agony.

To her surprise, he uttered a harsh laugh. "Who—who else would they expect to come in search of the truth? The blues . . . yes . . . - because they are the guardians of magic! But—but more so, they would expect *me!*"

Iridi could make sense of neither his words nor his pain. She thought that she sensed something near his midsection, but it was too vague a sensation, as if either very small or very well masked.

"Never mind me! Do not let—do not let Kalec go to them! I still have the means to turn their plans against them! I need only a moment more!"

She looked up. It was already too late to summon the blue dragon back. Iridi told Krasus that.

"Young fool . . ." The dragon mage let out another gasp, then seemed to recover somewhat. "I was merely caught by surprise. If he only could have waited . . ."

As he spoke, Krasus held up one gloved hand. In it, Iridi beheld a tiny golden shard. It was both beautiful and yet somehow awful to behold.

"Of all places," Krasus continued. "Grim Batol is the only one in which I would dream of using even this, for surely it must still have a tie to the evil within the dread mount." He straightened. "I regret only that Kalec might again suffer when he should not."

His entire frame shook. His eyes rolled up into his lids. Iridi at first thought that he was having some convulsion, but then the draenei realized that he was casting a spell of potent and very dangerous power.

"In addition to the orcs, there were, in the past, other dragons here," intoned the lanky spellcaster. "And among them was the darkest of the dark. I call upon that vile memory to strengthen this spell now—"

But whatever Krasus intended never had the chance to come to fruition. Instead, the golden fragment turned a sudden *black*.

Krasus hissed in pain and, despite his best efforts, finally had to let the shard drop. As it struck the ground, the shard resumed its original coloring and glow.

The priestess immediately reached for it, but her companion shouted, "No!"

Her fingers did not even touch the fragment, but suddenly the draenei experienced a jarring shift in perspective. She saw the shadows of dragons—hundreds of dragons—surrounding her like ghosts. No . . . not ghosts . . . but memories . . .

Then, the image past, and she was again back with Krasus . . . only they were no longer alone.

From all over the landscape, squat, bestial creatures that looked almost like dwarves but were scaled like reptiles and often ran on all fours attacked. As some neared, they straightened and removed from their backs wicked pikes or whips.

Krasus gestured toward the nearest.

On the creature's forehead, a disconcerting rune flashed in and out of existence.

"That symbol should be known by no one here!" the dragon mage blurted. "No one save—"

He got no further, for a lash wrapped around the hand that had gestured. The dwarven nightmare wielding it tugged hard, only to grunt in surprise as Krasus readily kept his ground.

"I am not so easy a target as that even now," he hissed at his attacker. With incredible strength, he used but the one hand to pull his unsuspecting foe forward . . . and into another just lunging.

Iridi, meanwhile, kicked out at another creature seeking to grab her from the side. As that one tumbled back, she struck another at the neck with the base of her hand.

A pike shot past her head, missing by inches. As its wielder pulled back for a second attempt, she followed Krasus's example and grabbed part of the long pole. Utilizing the beast's own mass against it, the priestess threw him up and over her.

However, the winding lash of a whip tugged the pike away before Iridi could make use of it. Undaunted, she summoned her staff, praying only that whoever had the other would not choose now to try again to summon it to them.

To her side, Krasus fought with all the hand skill of one of her calling, but the very fact that he had to do so was of great concern to the priestess. Here was a dragon of clearly tremendous might, yet he could neither become himself nor use his inherent magic.

That made her wonder what she could do. If these creatures were immune to spells due to the rune, then the staff would only be as good as her ability to use it as a physical weapon.

But still Iridi pointed it at the next one to charge her. She concentrated. . . .

The scaly dwarf froze in mid-lunge, his horrific mouth still open in preparation for a bite into her flesh.

Startled by her success, the draenei almost ignored an even more monstrous foe approaching. It resembled in basic shape one of her own kind or even a human or elf, but looked as if one of its parents had been of Krasus's or Kalec's race, although as black as midnight.

"Him!" it hissed. "The mistress wants him! The others are to slay!"

Iridi focused the staff on the drakonid.

A tremendous bellow rocked the sky above.

She looked up to see Kalec, a strange gray aura around him, plummeting.

Krasus pulled her back. "Go, draenei! I will fend them off—"

Then, he stiffened. The blood seemed to drain from his already-pale countenance. He struggled to keep upright.

"No mageslayer has such power!" he snapped. "No—"

The same gray aura overtook him. He let out a groan. Yet, as he teetered, the dragon mage thrust a hand toward the priestess.

"I said *leave!*"

The world around Iridi vanished.

It was difficult to contain the high elf in the tunnels, and not because of any claustrophobia on her account. Rather, Vereesa chafed at not being able to rush out and claim the life of her treacherous cousin.

"He must step out on occasion!" she insisted not for the first time. "I need but one well-placed arrow to finish what must be finished!"

"And 'tis more likely that he'll finish you before you notch that arrow!" Rom argued. "He's like no blood elf I've seen! He's hungerin' for magic, aye, but he's got plenty already to toss at you or anyone else! He's got that staff I told you about, plus a pet mageslayer!"

"I am no wizard like my husband; that would hardly affect me!"

"You've not seen this mageslayer! Somethin's been done to it, and I lay that blame on the dark lady!"

Her eyes narrowed. "You have spoken of this person before! What is she? Another blood elf? A human sorcerer?"

The veteran warrior pulled out his pipe, more to calm his nerves than to smoke any of the foul stuff he had on hand. "Don't know much about her, but I've hazarded a guess or two. She's real pale and what features she has look maybe human, maybe elf, maybe a mix."

"A blending of those races is rare, as I can attest from my sons. What do you mean . . . 'what features she has'?"

Rom recalled the last time that he had seen the lady in black. It had been from a fortunately long distance. "She wears a veil, but it don't hide the fact that one side of her face—by the beard of my grandfather, most of the *whole* damned side of her body—was at some point burnt real bad!"

"She's a Forsaken!" one of the other dwarves interjected.

"She's no Forsaken," countered their leader. "There's life in her, even though it looks to be in the form of madness and evil!"

Rhonin's mate mulled this over. "Does she have a name?"

"None that any of us has heard. They all treat her like she's a queen— and a nasty one, at that. There's fear in the skardyn—"

"Skardyn?"

"Once dwarves of the Dark Iron clan, so it looks to be. More beast than thinking creature. They've become scaled like the dragonspawn and will oft run on all fours."

"Their bite's poisonous," Grenda offered.

"Not poisonous, but it'll make you sick because of the filth they eat. Don't care whether it's rotting or raw, the skardyn."

Vereesa nodded. From her expression, Rom could guess that she was comparing the skardyn to some of the changes in her own race. Finally, she said, "Who do you think this sorceress is? What is she doing in Grim Batol?"

"Me, the best I can guess is that she might be from Dalaran, but that's just 'cause I know she's got magic. As for what she has in mind, if it involves the dread mount, then it's nothin' good, as the roars will attest."

He had already told her about the cries, even the ones that had saved them from the blood elf's trap. Vereesa showed some interest, but only wherever Zendarin was concerned.

"I cannot just leave him be!" she blurted again. "I will not!"

Rom groaned at her obsessiveness, even though he shared that trait far too much.

One of the sentries slipped in among the others.

"Rask's out on the hunt for somethin'!" the excited guard called.

"What'd you hear?" Rom demanded.

"Him shoutin' at a pack of skardyn combin' a trail like a bunch of wolves! There're at least two or three dragonspawn with 'im!"

The dwarven commander rubbed his bearded chin. "Rask don't go out unless that lady's got somethin' special in mind. He's her top lizard, the only one who don't have to listen to your cousin, if he don't feel like it . . ."

"Would he know where Zendarin would be located?"

Rom swore. "My lady! Goin' after Rask right now would be as foolish as goin' after your cousin!"

"Then what is your point in being here, Rom? Those that most might shed light on what you claim your mission seem too much a threat to fight!"

She bit her lip the moment she finished, obviously apologetic for her outburst and the condemnation in it. Silence filled the tunnels.

Tapping his pipe against the nearest wall—and only realizing then that he had never gotten around to filling, much less smoking, it—Rom muttered, "You've not said anything that I've not said to myself. I've been hesitant, yes, because of some of the debacles of earlier, but the time out when we ran across you, I was plannin' to go into Grim Batol myself and there's no lie."

Grenda all but jumped up and down in fury. "I knew it! I knew there was something in your mind—"

"Quiet there! Keep screaming like that and you'll bring the skardyn all the way here!"

"Who would this Rask be hunting?" Vereesa demanded. "Who else is out there?"

"Didn't think there was anyone else but us until you showed up—and that was you who saved me earlier with that blazing bolt, wasn't it?"

The ranger nodded, only half listening. "Rhonin? Could it be Rhonin? He may be danger!"

Rom did not like where this was going. "The wizard? He wouldn't be here and, besides, he's a powerful one that lad is!"

"Perhaps . . . perhaps not." She turned toward the entrance. "He has been straining himself to assist me while still guiding Dalaran's affairs. He never thought to be in command of the latter, but they turned to him in desperation. Weariness is his greatest enemy . . . and you yourself said that this mageslayer is also not like those he has fought in the past."

With some reluctance, the dwarf agreed. "It's a strong one. . . ."

"I must go." She pushed through the other dwarves who, uncertain as to what Rom desired, did nothing.

He let out an epithet. Stuffing away the unused pipe, he checked his ax. "Don't just stand there," Rom growled at the warriors nearest Vereesa. "You think she's going out alone?"

The other dwarves let out a lusty cry and followed Vereesa up. Rom grimaced, feeling too tired to fight, but also too tired not to. He did not quite understand the feeling and gave up trying to think it through.

What mattered was that they were already heading out again, and it was up to him to see that the others did not get killed.

And that now included the ranger.

The guard who had earlier given warning of Rask's hunt was already shoving the stone out of place. He climbed up, Vereesa not far behind.

There came an oath from above. The other fighters hesitated, all eyes on the entrance.

Rom pushed his way to the front. "What is it? Dragonspawn? The blood elf?"

They made way for him. Despite one hand, Rom easily scrambled up.

He gaped. *This is definitely getting too complicated for an old dwarf. . . .*

A body lay sprawled only yards from the tunnels. Yet, it was not any dragonspawn, drakonid, nor even blood elf. In fact, Rom was not quite certain *what* it was, wrapped so well in a wide cloak.

Vereesa knelt beside the prone figure. With much caution—for here of all places a still form could easily be a trap—the ranger turned the body over.

It was female . . . and not in the least what anyone would have expected. Even the high elf, who was surely more familiar with other races than the Bronzebeards, was obviously startled by what they had found.

But at least she could give it the name that, for the moment, escaped Rom's mind.

"A *draenei?*"

Krasus saw no sign of Kalec, the younger dragon's impetuousness very likely doing him in. Still, Krasus could not fault his counterpart, for he was not faring much better.

The mageslayer materialized, utilizing a blink ability of which the dragon mage was very familiar. What he was not in the least familiar with were both its durability—his magic should have overwhelmed the elemental—but also how that magic was also thrown back at him with an intensity no mageslayer had.

He now knew what it was that he had confronted much earlier when sending his mind into Grim Batol. At the time, Krasus had had some suspicions, but he had been unable to completely accept the truth.

Now, the truth was closing in on him.

The mageslayer was a translucent, purple-blue shade with vague hints of spikes or something else sharp jutting from where its shoulders would be and a fearsome, almost avian head. Two blazing white orbs were the only things truly distinct. At times, it seemed to have arms, but other times nothing.

But whatever its true form, it was no mageslayer as Krasus had ever come across in the annals of Azeroth. There was powerful magic in its alteration, very powerful.

As powerful, say, as that of a black dragon?

Could this be . . . could this be Deathwing's doing? Krasus wondered. After all, there were both drakonid and dragonspawn of the black flight involved in this infernal attack.

He stumbled back, seeking some delay while he planned for this unforeseen abomination. A pair of the scaly dwarves immediately attacked, but although he could not fight them directly, at least now the dragon mage knew how to handle the vermin.

He opened his mouth, the lips and jaws stretching farther than mortally possible. From his gullet, a burst of flames struck the ground in front of the dwarves.

The ground exploded, flames, rock, and earth rising up, then showering down on the creatures.

A lash struck him hard on the arm. Krasus winced, but the pain was minor. He turned to confront the drakonid.

"So, your master lives, does he?" Krasus demanded of the fiend.

The drakonid only laughed. He looked not *at* Krasus, but *behind* him.

The dragon mage reacted instinctively, but his reflexes were too slow. He had kept an eye on the mageslayer. . . . Only what he thought was the mageslayer was now only an afterimage, a residue of where it had formerly been.

And now it stood right behind him.

Again, it screamed in his head that this was not the way a mageslayer behaved. Someone had gone to great lengths to make it far more insidious.

He could not transform, but he could still cast. Taking a cue from his success with the dwarven creatures, Krasus focused not on the mageslayer itself, but the elemental's surroundings.

Yet, before his magic could affect the ground and the air, Krasus felt the forces he wielded twist from his control, instead pouring *into* the mageslayer—and right back at their caster.

So close and against such an unexpected extension of the monster's ability to absorb spells, Krasus had no chance to shield himself against his own magic. He was struck so hard he flew into the air and battered against the rocks. As he landed, the ground exploded, another aspect of the attack with which he had intended to at least distract the nearby elemental.

Again, Krasus was tossed about. Under normal circumstances, nothing that he faced would have done him much harm. . . . But there was nothing normal where Grim Batol was ever concerned.

He landed on his back, stunned beyond his belief. He had been careless, very careless. Worse, he had been guided like a bull to the slaughter.

The drakonid looked over him. The black fiend held out a clawed hand to show Krasus something held within.

Though his vision was blurred, the dragon mage recognized it immediately. It was a tiny, golden shard . . . but not the same shard that he himself had earlier wielded.

The drakonid grinned wider. His long red tongue darted in and out as he cheerfully said, "The mistress has been expecting you for a *long, long* time. . . ."

ELEVEN

I ridi opened her eyes wide. She rose to a sitting position, crying, "No! Don't send me away!"

Only after she finished screaming did she notice that she was no longer with Krasus or the young blue. Instead, the priestess lay in a torchlit tunnel surrounded by dwarves.

No . . . dwarves and a more familiar form.

Certain that she was a prisoner, the draenei summoned the staff. Yet, even as she raised it, the elven figure seized her wrist.

Iridi leapt to her feet . . . or tried to. The top of her head struck the low ceiling. Stunned, she fell back.

The silver-haired figure grabbed the staff, only to watch in amazement as it vanished in her grip. "What sort of magic is this?"

"One that you'll not add to your arsenal, blood elf—"

"Use your eyes and call me not by so accursed a name as that, draenei!" the other female snapped. "I am of the high elf people. . . ."

The differences finally registered with Iridi. She had met others of that race and berated herself for not having immediately noticed the difference. The eyes alone should have told her otherwise, for there was no evil green glow here.

"A high elf . . . forgive me for my outburst. My teachers would be dismayed."

"You are a priestess, then."

"I try to pass for one, you mean," the draenei replied with some regret for her deficiencies.

The high elf shrugged off such a remark. "I am Vereesa. The dwarf to your side is Rom, leader of these fighters."

"My lady," the squat, older dwarf grunted.

Iridi eyed him longer than should have been necessary, but only because she began to notice that Rom was *not* as old as he looked. Then, realizing how impolite she was now being to him, the draenei looked away.

"And your name?" Vereesa prompted.

"Iridi."

"Why are you near Grim Batol, Iridi?"

"I came in search of—" The priestess stopped, recalling the last thing that had happened before she blacked out. "Krasus! No! They need my help! Where are—"

The high elf seized her before she could continue. "What did you say? What name did you just call?"

"Krasus! We were attacked by—by scaled, dwarven-looking beasts—"

"The skardyn!" Rom growled. "The ones we heard! They were after you and your friend, eh?"

"Never mind that!" Vereesa interjected. "You said 'Krasus'! Tall, pale, of some unidentifiable elven look and with eyes that speak of an age far greater than his appearance even justifies?"

Iridi nodded. Rom's brow wrinkled deep. "The name. I'd forgotten it. It cannot be . . ."

The ranger leaned close to the draenei. "And from your own eyes, I can tell that you also understand what he truly is. . . ."

"Yes." The priestess said nothing else, her gaze shifting surreptitiously from Vereesa to the dwarves and back again.

The high elf evidently read her thoughts. In a low voice, she said, "Rom, I've already said far too much. Can the three of us speak alone for a moment?"

"Off with the lot of ye," Rom ordered the others. "You, too, Grenda. You've all got duties, haven't ye?"

Vereesa waited until the last of the fighters had gone, then quietly said to Iridi, "It is best that you keep your voice very low even now. Sound travels well in tunnels such as these, and dwarves are very nosy."

The last was said with a ghost of humor. Rom chuckled at her remark, but did not deny it.

"So, is it true, my lady?" he finally asked. "Is this Krasus the one and the same my old memory's stirred up? That would be too fantastic!"

" 'Fantastic' is the appropriate word for him, Rom. I do not recall how much you knew, but you knew quite a lot."

"Krasus of the Kirin Tor," he returned. "And, aye, I know him for what else he is . . . the red dragon."

"The others . . . would any of them know?"

"No and we'll be keepin' it that way. You've my promise on that."

Vereesa frowned. "You sound and look different, Rom. There are changes I do not understand."

"If you mean my speakin', for a time after I was asked to be liaison to your folk and some of the humans. Tried to learn their manner better. Been away from that for awhile, so now my words slip back and forth. Sometimes, I wished I'd stayed with that task, maddening as it was." He gestured at his face. "And if ye—if you mean my appearance, I'll blame Grim Batol on it. I've been poisoned by it from too much time spent furrowing around the damned mount. I've not pointed this out to the others, but a good number of those who fought to free it from the orcs have passed over earlier than they should've. They all aged quicker. Guess I was just a more stubborn cuss, but it's eating at me, the evil."

"You should not have come back."

"I couldn't let anyone else come in my place. . . ." He waved an angry hand. "But that's neither here nor there! If Krasus—Korialstr—*Krasus* is around, then we'll finally be able to put an end to whatever's stirred up Grim Batol again!"

Iridi had stayed silent, but more because her head had begun pounding. Now, though, she used her studies to focus that pain away . . . and finally say what she should have said earlier.

"Krasus and Kalec are in danger! There were the skardyn and dragon men—"

"Aye, Rask the drakonid and some dragonspawn, to be sure . . ."

"But there was also something Krasus called a mageslayer. . . ."

Vereesa did not seem concerned. "A mageslayer should be little trouble for him—"

The priestess recalled Krasus's concern. "There was something different. . . . And Krasus suffered from some other injury or ailment that seemed magical in nature." Now she had their full attention again. "He also seemed to suspect what power was behind it all. He seemed very familiar with it, from the way he acted."

"Gimmel's blood . . ." Rom blurted. His gaze met Vereesa's. "Ye don't suppose . . ." he added, momentarily slipping back to his older ways of speech again.

"It cannot be!" she replied with equal dismay. "Although, perhaps . . . no!"

"What?" the draenei demanded. "Of what or whom do you speak?"

The dwarf used his stump to rub his cheek. "That's right, ye—you aren't from here . . . or anywhere on Azeroth. You might not know the black beast."

"The black beast? The dragon men were black of scale. . . ."

"Aye, for they were created to serve one master and their presence only fuels the possibility that he's alive and behind this."

"A black dragon?" The priestess had never seen or heard of one in the short time that she had been on Azeroth, but it made sense that they would exist. "Is he so deadly?"

"Not just deadly," Vereesa all but hissed. "But death itself."

"Aye," concluded Rom, looking off into his darkest memories. "Aye . . . it may be *Deathwing's* alive and returned to Grim Batol. . . ."

Nightmares assailed Krasus, most of them tied to memories better left lost. He relived again the captivity of his beloved queen and mate, and how the young she bore afterward were forced into servitude by the orcs. Krasus saw red dragons perish in battle, used like hounds by their slavers.

Other images mixed in. There was a darkly handsome noble. Demons of the Burning Legion. A gathering of the great Aspects . . .

Some of the memories had not taken place at Grim Batol, but all were tied to it in one way or another. Krasus tried to awaken, but could not. He felt too weak. The nightmares—the memories—had their way with him without regard to his suffering.

Then, the foul visions faded, only to be replaced by a sense that he was not alone . . . wherever it was his body lay.

"You don't seem like much," remarked a snide voice that finally stirred Krasus toward waking. "And I can't fathom just what branch of our kind you pretend to belong to. . . ."

A jolt ran through the dragon mage. He let out a howl and his eyes snapped open. Unfortunately, through them Krasus at first saw little but his own tears.

He tried to move his arms and legs and found them bound. Mere chains should not have held him, but an incredible weakness also filled the captive.

"Aah, you're awake." The figure looming over him was a blood elf with a sadistic grin. "Much better. I tried to be very gentle. After all, we should be friends. . . ."

Krasus's gaze shifted to the staff the blood elf held. It was virtually identical to Iridi's, and at first he feared that she had also been captured. However, then he recalled what he had done, sending her to the one place in the vicinity of Grim Batol where she might be at least for a moment safe.

But the same could not be said for either him or Kalec.

The young blue, also chained, lay next to him. Kalec was still unconscious. He looked like the warrior, not the dragon, and Krasus had hope that perhaps their captors did not yet recognize what they were.

Unfortunately, the blood elf quickly crushed that slim hope. "So you are a dragon . . . both of you, I mean . . . fascinating. This puts a different slant on things."

Krasus had no time for minions. "Where is he? Where is your infernal master?"

" 'Master'? I, Zendarin, have no master. . . ." The blood elf shifted the staff toward Krasus's chest. ". . . And you'd be wise to speak with more respect to one who offers you hope. . . ."

The dragon mage looked at him with new interest, but then the blood elf glanced behind him.

"That damned timing of hers . . ." he muttered. The blood elf raised the stolen staff . . . and turned to shadow.

Krasus's higher senses still allowed him to see a trace of the blood elf, but he gave no sign as the murky figure disappeared from the chamber. Alone save for Kalec, Krasus surveyed his surroundings in the hope of finding some quick escape.

He found only what he suspected the reason for his weakness. A single golden shard hung high above, well out of physical reach. The spell that kept it there was a clever one, for Krasus knew well what forces were required to maintain the levitation of that particular piece.

Other than the shard, the chamber was unremarkable. It said something for the confidence of his true captor—the blood elf had already verified indirectly that he was not the one in control here—and also of that mysterious figure's identity.

Yet, something he had said also confused Krasus. Just prior to his flight, the blood elf had mentioned "her," not him.

Her . . .

"Onyxia . . ." the dragon mage breathed. Yes, he knew his captor now. Somehow, the prime daughter of Deathwing had survived. Everything made perfect sense now, save how she had managed that last feat.

Of course, she *was* her father's child. Not only had she taken up his cause by raising new eggs in her lair, located in the southern parts of the Dustwallow Marsh, but she resurrected his role as a member of the Prestor line, taking on the guise of Lady Katrana Prestor in Stormwind in order to try to keep the Alliance's leadership fragmented.

However, she had eventually overstepped herself, her plot against King Varian Wrynn turning back on her. In the end, he and a brave band had tracked her back to the marsh and, though it cost many lives, slew her . . . or so everyone had thought.

It was very possible that she had been cunning enough to fool Varian. Onyxia and her brother had been among the most clever of dragons, even if that genius had been misdirected. Nefarian had even managed to take his father's and sister's work to some fruition, creating the chromatic dragons. True, his efforts had ended once he, too, had been supposedly slain by brave fighters, but if Onyxia had learned from him, it would explain much of what was going on in Grim Batol now.

A grunting sound caught his attention. One of the dwarven abominations scurried inside as if to see if the prisoners were still there. Krasus was repulsed by the creature. Seen up close, it was even more a twisted mix of dwarf and dragon, making even the drakonid and dragonspawn handsome by comparison.

The thing rushed up next to Kalec, looking him over in a hungry manner. Krasus had no doubt that it was capable of eating a living being alive and doing so with relish. He summoned what strength he had and stared at it until it looked his way.

The rune burnt into its forehead flared bright. With a chomping of teeth, the creature fled from the chamber.

Krasus had not expected his weak spell to work, but he had wanted to at least frighten away the thing by attempting something. That plan had worked, but it now left him weaker than ever.

And more at the mercy of the damned shard.

Then, he sensed another presence approaching. There was no mistaking what it was, not this close . . .

Into the chamber she strode, a queen before slaves. Through a gauzy veil, she peered down at Krasus with mild amusement in her expression, but great satisfaction in her burning gaze.

"I trust you are well?" she purred. Her attention went to Kalec. "And who is this handsome young blue? Such an added pleasure to receive both of you. . . ."

Krasus frowned. This was not Onyxia. He could sense that well enough. Yet, everything she radiated bespoke the dread black flight and Onyxia had been one of the few known females left.

She turned her face to the side, the better to display the ravaged part of her face. Krasus, aware how the injuries were a reflection of what she would also look like as a dragon, imagined the latter vision.

And only then did he recognize his captor.

"You are dead. . . ." More dead than even Onyxia or her accursed brother Nefarian. More dead, certainly, than he had believed even Deathwing.

The lady in black gave a throaty chuckle. She drew back the veil—which was, in truth, as much illusion as the rest of her current appearance—so that her burnt countenance was utterly visible.

"Have I not changed, then?" she mocked. "A female likes to think she's kept her beauty even after so long. . . ."

"You could never change . . . your evil, that is . . . Sintharia."

"*Sintharia* . . . long has it been since any called me by that name. I've come to prefer the one I've used in this form . . . Sinestra . . . as it has nothing to do with my darling, unlamented mate. . . ." The female dragon leaned over him. "How long has it been, my dear Korialstrasz? Five hundred years? A thousand? How long since we last enjoyed one another's company?"

He did not hide his enmity. "Five hundred or five thousand years would not be enough time to pass before I would willingly look into your face, Sintharia! The marks of your loving Neltharion have never healed, have they? They still burn, do they not, from your last mating?"

Sintharia was more than merely a black dragon; she had been Deathwing's prime consort, the mother of the most foul of his line. Onyxia and Nefarian had not gained all their menace from the mad Earth-Warder alone; Sintharia had been very much her mate's partner in much of his plotting.

But she was also supposed to be dead. Krasus recalled that time as well. It had been closer to a thousand years than five hundred, a time period when the question of Deathwing's demise had also been an important one. Sintharia had been very much alive, though, and she had strived then to spread a contagious spell among the magi of Dalaran that had effectively caused the powers of those infected to cease working. Krasus had been intimately involved in putting an end to that plot and, in the process, it had appeared as if Sintharia had perished when her own magic had been turned on her.

But, as ever, the dragon mage thought bitterly, *the line of Neltharion proves more cunning than death. . . .*

The female dragon's macabre appearance was not due to that incident nor any other plot in which Sintharia had participated. As Krasus had indicated, her horrific burns were the result of nothing less than her mating with the altered Earth-Warder. As the dark magics and darker madness of Neltharion had taken over him, he had physically changed. His body had burned continuously, burned so hot that even his own kind could not bear his nearness, much less his grip.

Sintharia was the only one of his consorts known to have survived those matings, so to speak, though her savage burns clearly still festered after all these centuries. They had perhaps been responsible for giving her a madness equal to her lord's. Certainly, even Krasus could not imagine the tortures through which she had gone.

But whatever sympathy he might have had for her on that one point, it did not in the least enable the dragon mage to condone all else she had done.

"You could not imagine the agony of those times, the burning, the constant burning," she replied to his last comment. A hand Krasus only saw now was as burnt as the face touched the ruined cheek. "It still burns. . . ."

"And despite that, you still work to see his mad dream of a world cleansed of all but dragons loyal to his memory? Or should I say, dragons loyal only to *you*? Are you now to be Azeroth's new god—or goddess, I should say? Sintharia, mistress of a renewed black flight . . ."

Her expression turned to one of disdain, but not for him. "You will refer to me as Sinestra, not Sintharia! I have shaken off that foul past! No new black flight will rule Azeroth! The black flight is dead, and no one shall mourn it less than me, Korialstrasz! There is nothing of it which I cherish, least of all my unlamented lord's memory or our ill-begotten children! They are all anathema to me—Onyxia, Nefarian, or any else who have managed to survive his foolish plans!" Sintharia—or *Sinestra,* Krasus corrected himself, thinking of her current form a separate one, as he did his own guise—laughed at his puzzled look. "Why should I care of the black flight . . . when I can birth into this world a far more *worthy* flight, a new breed of dragons who truly will become *gods*?"

Krasus paused before answering. When he did speak, it was with more than a hint of sarcasm. "Yes—Sinestra—we have seen your results; for gods, they perish quite easily."

"A first test, no more. If there was anything worthwhile in poor Nefarian's pathetic attempts in Blackrock Spire, it was the notion he had at the end—but was unable to follow sufficiently through on—that new *magic,* not merely blood and what he already could wield, was needed for a successor flight. New, unique magic. I have now found that magic. . . ."

"A nether dragon . . ."

"Oh, very good, Korialstrasz . . ." she teased, continuing to use *his* true name despite her distaste for her own. The lady in black bent down so that her face was only inches from his own. "Very good . . . a pity we were never so close that we could have been more. Although you and I both know how strictly dragonflights keep to their own when . . . shall we say 'mingling'? . . . it is due more to tradition and prejudice than because it cannot be done between those of differing flights . . ." When he said nothing, she shrugged, then straightened again. "One way or another, I will have from you what I desire. . . ."

"How long have you been expecting me to come upon your dark deeds?"

"How long? My dear Korialstrasz, I planned on it from the beginning! The red flight is the essence of *life*! What better to stimulate the creation of my perfect children than instill in them some of that?"

Sinestra glanced at Kalec. "Actually, there is an answer to that question and you have kindly brought him to me! The essence of *life* and the essence of *magic*! I *will* be able to create gods now, thanks to the both of you. . . ."

The dragon mage shook his head. "You say you have come to hate Deathwing, but you must truly adore him to embrace his insanity so eagerly. . . ."

She gestured. Krasus groaned as what felt like a part of him seemed momentarily ripped away.

Lady Sinestra lowered her hand. As he sat there, gasping, the female dragon calmly replied, "You have suffered pain for some time now as I worked to soften you for your capture and thus make it easier to draw from you what I need. You will suffer more, my dear Korialstrasz, and there will be nothing you can do about it save beg me to be kind. . . ."

"This is—is not ended, Sinestra! As Nefarian fell victim to his obsession, so, too, shall—shall you!"

"By your hand, perhaps? You know what floats above you, what you yourself have secretly employed despite a declaration by the Aspects that all traces of it be forever buried from the sight of all. You know that there is nothing you can do, for even though the forces it contained when whole have returned to those from which they were taken, the shards all still wield residue of that power."

She turned to leave, dismissing him as if he were nothing—which, Krasus knew—might be the very truth.

"Rest up now, dear Korialstrasz. . . . I shall have need of you and your friend before long. . . ."

And she left him sitting there, staring first at the entrance to his prison in the wake of her departure, then, finally at the tiny shard. It was true that he had played with dark magic in secreting that one other piece in his sanctum, defying even his beloved queen with his interest in it. Now, Krasus knew that, in a sense, he was in this dire strait because he had fallen victim to its seductive evil and had believed that he could control it, use it as a secret weapon against the enemy he had thought he faced.

But not even the slightest fragment of the *Demon Soul* was without danger . . . and because of its vile nature and his own hubris, it was very possible that both he and Kalec would perish for the sake of Sinestra's madness. . . .

TWELVE

The beautiful, sun-blond maiden smiled at Kalec, her arms beckoning to him. He reached for her, but each time he thought that their hands would touch, she seemed just a little more out of reach.

Frustrated, Kalec charged toward her. Yet, although she clearly wanted him to come to her, he never quite made it.

Anveena . . . he called, though his mouth did not open.

Then, other figures materialized around her. A tall, noble-looking human male . . . whose skin was rotting. That ghost faded, becoming the shadow of a huge, skeletal dragon . . . a frost wyrm. Then, even that vanished, to be replaced by a high-elven figure wearing flamboyant albeit dark garments, including a wide-brimmed hat.

Kalec pointed desperately behind her, trying to let her know of any of the fearsome shadows, but, especially this one.

Anveena . . . it's Dar'Khan! It's Dar'Khan—

"It's Dar'Khan!" he roared.

"Kalec!" Krasus's voice cut through the remnants of his nightmare . . . enabling him to see that the waking world was no better.

They were chained tight in an underground chamber that surely had to be part of Grim Batol. He glared at his companion. "So, once again, the great Korialstrasz has saved the world . . . or could I be mistaken?"

The dragon mage showed no offense at his remarks, instead asking, "Do those dreams come often?"

Kalec looked away, not wanting to discuss the matter. However, the other captive would not let it go.

"How often do you dream of her, Kalec?"

He whipped his head back to Krasus. "Every time I sleep or am unconscious for other reasons, such as now! Does that please you?"

Krasus shook his head. "No."

The younger male exhaled. "We're in Grim Batol, aren't we? Is it Deathwing who has us?"

"No . . . it is Sintharia . . . or Sinestra, as she seems to prefer, since she wishes to claim no tie to her dread mate." The dragon mage went into detail on his encounter with Deathwing's consort.

Much of Kalec's anger toward Krasus was pushed back as he listened in disbelief. He looked up at the tiny shard.

"That is what keeps us so weak?"

"That . . . and my little pet," came another voice.

The pair looked at the entrance, where the blood elf who Krasus had said was called Zendarin now stood. Behind him in the corridor beyond was a shining mass of energy, an elemental that could only be a mageslayer. Yet, the blue, attuned to the many aspects of magic, immediately sensed that this was not an ordinary mageslayer, that much about it had been altered dramatically . . . and made the fiend a threat even to dragons.

Kalec could sense that the elemental wanted to draw nearer, but Zendarin waved the creature farther back.

"It's developed some interesting . . . tastes," the blood elf remarked. "There are points to it that now are reminiscent of a mana eater, for instance."

"What do you want?" Krasus asked.

Zendarin grinned. "I want to be your friend. . . ."

Kalec snorted.

"You don't believe me? I've learned several things recently, especially about the dear lady in black. I've a mind that you and I could see eye-to-eye on her in some regards. . . ."

"You play with your doom, Zendarin," the elder dragon returned, "and we will not play with you. Do you not think that she has always awaited your betrayal for your own desires?"

"Of course, she does. That's what makes it more amusing."

The prisoners glanced at one another. Kalec expected his companion to press the blood elf, but Krasus appeared not at all interested in pursuing the only path to escape they had.

"What do you want of us?" Kalec finally asked.

Zendarin waited for Krasus to say something, too, but when the elder dragon remained mute, the blood elf focused on the blue. "There will come a time, when she must be faced. I am mere blood elf. A dragon, though, would be far more able to stave her off for the moment needed. . . ."

"Needed for what?"

"You are interested, then?"

Kalec bared his teeth. "I would not be speaking with one of your kind if I was not, regardless of my current circumstances."

Zendarin's gaze shifted to Krasus. "And what of him?"

Again, the dragon mage remained silent, which infuriated Kalec. Did he think their options so unlimited that he could refuse to even play along with the blood elf?

"He does not speak for me, nor I him," the blue snapped. "I am interested. That is as much as you need from me, yes?"

"Two would be better than one. I give you some time to talk sense into your friend . . . but know that time is very short."

With that, Zendarin slipped out again. The mageslayer did not follow immediately, lingering by the entrance as if still eager to come to them. Only when the blood elf called to it did it finally vanish.

"They have made a minor evil into something far more treacherous," Krasus commented. "Thus is the way of Grim Batol. Evil not only flourishes here, it transforms. . . ."

"What was the matter with you? Why didn't you play along with him?"

"The blood elf is too great a fool to even toy with, young one. His darkness is terrible, but hers dwarfs his a thousandfold. Even to barter with him risks us more than it is worth, trust me."

Kalec glared. "I will never understand you. Do as you wish, then. If Zendarin comes back again, you can rot in your chains alone, staring at that damned shard until she drags you out and sacrifices you or whatever it is she wants."

"She is making an abomination of a dragon, and we are to feed that creation with our lives. . . ."

"All the more reason to take what little possibility of escape we have . . . unless you've come up with some wonderful plan of your own?"

The other's eyes narrowed. " 'Wonderful,' I would not call it . . . nor even truly a 'plan' . . . but . . . but there may just be something I can do after all. . . ."

The younger dragon waited for more explanation, but Krasus merely turned his attention to the entrance . . . and stared.

He is here. . . . Korialstrasz is here. . . .

Sinestra savored the moment again. All her machinations were coming to fruition just as she had dreamed they would. Indeed, she had gained far more than expected, the blue male surely a gift of the fates.

Deathwing's consort strode to the edge of the pit where her favored child rested. It was hungry, very hungry, but had learned finally to trust that it would be fed at the right time in the right manner.

"A pity he could not have come sooner," Sinestra murmured to herself, "or the blue, also. It would have been best if their essences could have been fed into the egg. Now, they will enhance, but not be an integral part of the make-up." She made a tsking sound. "A pity, yes . . ."

But there are other eggs, the voice in her head reminded her. *The next ones will gain the benefit that this one did not! They will be even more mighty, a true legacy to the years of suffering. . . .*

"Yes," she agreed out loud. "The next generation will outshine even Dargonax . . ."

As she said the name, the creature in the pit stirred.

"Hush, hush," the mad dragon murmured to it. "Rest, dear Dargonax, rest. . . . Supper will soon be ready."

Silence settled over the pit again. Satisfied, Sinestra summoned a pair of skardyn.

"Descend below. You know what I need. You will find me in the cavern of the nether dragon."

They grunted understanding, then rushed off to fulfill her command.

Sinestra peered into the black pit one more time, then headed for the cavern. Already, she could imagine what would happen with the next eggs, the magnificent children that would hatch from them.

"At long last!" the black dragon breathed. "At long last . . ."

The thing in the pit stirred again. It—*he*—had discovered long ago that if he pretended to be complacent, he learned much. This time, though, perhaps he had learned more than he desired.

A future batch of eggs . . . new brothers and sisters . . . *better* brothers and sisters . . .

Dargonax hissed.

The dwarves and their two unlikely allies slipped toward Grim Batol. Vereesa it was who had insisted again that they head out, although Rom had convinced her to wait until the next night. In the daytime, the dwarves were too conspicuous a sight; the sentries would easily see them and there were also magical factors with which to deal.

Iridi offered some hope against the latter problem. While it was true that the blood elf might detect her, she suspected that he did not understand the staff's powers to the depths that she did.

"He has not had it long, surely only barely before he also captured the nether dragon," she explained to the others.

The concept of the nether dragon was one that shocked both Vereesa and the dwarves. Even Iridi had no idea of their origins, only that they had suddenly arisen on Outland and, for a time, menaced her kind. Yet, from what she had gleaned, they had not been so much evil as confused. Even they had not understood what they were or how they had come into being.

The nether dragon was still the focus of the priestess's quest. She had even tried to put the other staff out of her thoughts, concerned that some desire to avenge her friend would cause her not to think clearly when the time came. Yet, now Iridi understood that she had made a mistake, that she had only been trying to keep herself from understanding just how great was the peril facing her . . . and how insurmountable her quest might actually be.

But before the band had left on its foray, Vereesa had promised her three things. One was that the nether dragon would be found. Whether to be freed or necessarily destroyed was a question that could only be answered once that happened.

"It cannot be allowed to menace others, if that is its desire, draenei," the ranger had insisted. "Nor, as we all know, can it be used for whatever monstrous purposes they plan. We will free it if that proves a viable option, but we will not let this evil—as those two abominations you described surely must represent somehow—continue."

The second of the three promises concerned the blood elf. In this, Vereesa was adamant. "Zendarin is mine. If you can claim the staff and return it to wherever you need to, so be it, but my cousin is *mine*."

Third—and foremost—they had to *find* Krasus and Kalec. Not only for the sakes of the dragons themselves—assuming they still lived—but for the simple reason that the pair, especially the elder red, gave them their best hope of success . . . much less survival.

The odds were not good, but Rom had made the best of it. "Won't be any worse than tryin' to take Grim Batol during the war! Least there ain't an army of orcs to watch for, either. . . ."

"No, but there are skardyn, dragonspawn, and drakonid," his second, Grenda, had remarked with her usual practicality.

That had deterred them no more than anything else had. All the dwarves serving under Rom had journeyed here expecting to lay down their lives if necessary.

Grim Batol was every bit as dire as Vereesa recalled it. With a shiver, she wished that Rhonin had come with her. However, in addition to his other duties, he was the only one of the two who could be with the children. They were being taken care of by Jalia, a stout midwife with six children of her own who was both like grandmother and second mother to the twins. However, she had no manner by which to protect them.

I pray we will all see one another after this, she thought to her husband and sons. But, if not, she would do all that she could to see that the menace of her cousin never threatened her family again.

Too many of her family had been slain in the previous wars, and of her sister, Sylvanas, Vereesa had learned an even more monstrous fate. Those losses had been terrible enough, but then had come the rise of the blood elves. So many of her kind had turned from their traditions to that dark path, the withdrawals they had suffered after the Sunwell's destruction too much for them to bear. Vereesa recalled her own withdrawals and wondered if she would have joined them had not Rhonin been there to help her recuperate. And much later, when the feeling of loss had occasionally tried to return, the twins had also helped merely by being there for her to love.

She had known Zendarin well when they had both been younger. He had always been ambitious, but in those days that ambition had been an honest one. He had wanted to rise up among his people, no matter how hard it was for any individual to move beyond their caste. As one who had also to a point not fit into the regimented mold of high elven society, Vereesa could appreciate his desire.

But when he had turned to the way of the blood elf, all his ambition had focused on only one thing . . . to gather for himself more and more magic, both to satiate his insatiable appetite and to give him the might to take even more from others. Vereesa heard scattered word of his unseemly deeds, yet had not considered him her problem. As a blood elf, he was part of the Horde and the Alliance was always fighting the Horde. She had expected that sooner or later he would overstep himself and some wizard or paladin would put an end to him.

But then Zendarin had chosen her children as his next prize. Both Rhonin and she knew that there would be something special about them, the rare product of high elf and wizard. One could sense the potential just when standing near them. Even just after their birth, her husband had said something that she now realized was more prophetic than even he had thought.

"I hope they grow up," the red-haired spellcaster had muttered during one of his more sullen moods. "I hope they grow up. . . ."

A simple comment, but complex in its fears.

As she pondered it again, Vereesa readied an arrow. Her sword, a parting gift from her husband, hung sheathed at her side.

"The eyes or just under the base of the jaw . . . at the top of the throat," Rom had told her. "You want to kill a dragonspawn fast or even hope to drop a drakonid, those're your best choices, my lady."

The ranger studied the area carefully. In some ways, her eyes were at least as good in the dark as those of the dwarves. However, the black-scaled hides of the drakonid and dragonspawn made them more murky targets. The skardyn were easier for her, but she considered them a waste of her arrows.

Yet, it was a skardyn she first sighted. The foul creature squatted upon a large rock, sniffing the air like a dog while it chewed on some shadowy piece of meat . . . hopefully nothing more than a hapless lizard.

Vereesa pulled the bowstring tight, then released it.

A shaft blossomed from the skardyn's chest. The scaly dwarf spit out its tidbit and fell face first off the rock. The sound of its body striking below was muted, as the ranger had expected.

In the dark, several dwarven forms shifted position, ever moving closer to the nearest of the cave entrances. Near Vereesa, the draenei waited patiently. The ranger had told Iridi to stay with her at all times, following her lead wherever possible. Iridi had never been to Grim Batol before, whereas the high elf had some recollection . . . and more than a few unmentioned nightmares.

Another skardyn appeared on a ridge higher up. Vereesa swore under her breath. The skardyn were not what she wanted to slay, but, again, she had no choice. Worse, yet, the creature watched from a point that made it very difficult even for the skilled ranger to fire a perfect shot.

The draenei abruptly put a hand on her shoulder, then whispered, "Let me try."

Before Vereesa could stop her, the priestess had slipped ahead. Vereesa watched as Iridi made her way toward where the guard stood. Although the draenei tried to be cautious, the ranger was surprised that the skardyn did not see her and raise the alarm. Indeed, at one point, the creature gazed directly at her, but seemed unconcerned.

Some priesthood trick, the high elf decided. She had heard of priests from other orders who could make themselves either not be noticed or noticed as a threat by those they wished to reach.

Iridi climbed up next to the oddly-oblivious guard. She struck the skardyn a blow on the neck with the edge of her hand.

The sentinel collapsed without a sound.

From the rocks to the ranger's right, Rom gave the short signal to move farther in. The entrance beckoned, yet Vereesa was aware from the dwarf how many times they had gotten this far, only to have some catastrophe strike them.

However, slowly but surely they neared their goal. The dwarves took care of another skardyn and even a dragonspawn without mishap.

We are coming for you, Krasus, Vereesa thought to herself. *We are coming for you.* Then, her mood more grim, she added, *and I am coming for you, Zendarin. . . .*

The ground shook.

A gasp escaped the ranger. She clutched at the nearest rock. The area around her rose up and down as if a massive earthquake were sweeping over the land.

Yet, Grim Batol itself was as still as death.

The dwarves struggled for balance. Although well used to such tremblings, this one was so violent that even they could not in many instances keep on their feet.

She saw no sign of Rom, but did spot Grenda. The female dwarf struggled toward her.

A fissure opened up between them. Fierce gases burst forth, so hot that both fighters had to retreat.

From out of the fissure—from out of other fissures ripping open around them—grotesque figures crawled out.

Figures made of burning rock.

A monstrous gold aura surrounded them. They moved like puppets toward wherever dwarves struggled. Their shapes were crudely humanoid and lacked any features, the latter of which made them more unnerving.

"Undead!" Grenda shouted.

"They are not Scourge," she returned. "They are some animated monstrosity!"

They were a menace such as no one there had expected to confront. Whoever was master or mistress of the mount now had terrible power indeed to raise up such horrific creatures.

One dwarf swung at the nearest of the fiery figures. The head of his ax *melted,* and it was all the fighter could do to keep from burning his hand as he released the weapon.

The rocky creature's molten arm moved with astounding swiftness, enveloping the head of the dwarf. The dwarf's scream and suffering were mercifully short, but the sight of his headless torso dropping sent chills through the defenders.

"We can't fight these! There are too many and our blades are useless!" Grenda looked around. "Where's Rom? He must give the signal to retreat!"

The ranger did not want to retreat. Strapping on her bow, she drew her sword and lunged at the nearest of the animated figures.

The blade easily cut through the soft, molten body. Rhonin had feared that she might encounter some magical threat and had made certain the weapon would be useful against most. The elemental minion collapsed into two separate pieces that still tried to move.

She dispatched a second shambling figure in the next breath. However, Grenda was proving all too correct in her calculation of their chances. The fiery figures were everywhere.

Although she had called for retreat, Grenda had by no means simply turned and fled. A loyal warrior, while she awaited Rom's word the female dwarf did her best with her own weapon. Unfortunately, even the slightest strike meant damage to any dwarven weapon.

And, worse, the fiery fiends kept massing. More important, Vereesa noticed that they were slowly but surely herding the dwarves together. The creatures did not seem inclined to slay the intruders unless the dwarves put up too much resistance.

They want to capture us! the high elf concluded with much dismay. *But why?*

In truth, she had no real desire to find out the answer to that. Aware that her weapon was perhaps the band's best hope, Vereesa leapt over the fissure separating her from Grenda.

"Have as many as possibly can keep with us gather behind me immediately!" she commanded. "I will try to cut our way through!"

"But Rom! I can't find Rom!"

"We cannot wait for him!" It hurt the ranger to speak so about a comrade with whom she shared such a history, but Vereesa believed that his choice would have been the same.

Grenda yelled her orders to the others. Using their axes and swords as best they could to keep their searing foes at bay, the dwarves stayed close behind Vereesa as she swung at one horrific foe after another. Limbs flew and bits of molten earth splashed against her breastplate—and once almost at her face—but she ignored all distractions as, under her effort, the path began to clear.

But then the ground shook anew and yet another fissure opened up before her. A few of the animated attackers fell into the fissure, but their vanishing meant nothing, for the way the ranger had chosen was now no longer open to them.

"We must go to the east!" she cried, but just as she turned that way, skardyn and dragonspawn joined in the attack on the party.

At their head was a particularly grotesque drakonid who could only be the one Rom had called Rask. Vereesa wanted to grab her bow and put an arrow through the creature's throat, but she had no chance.

"Lay down your weapons, you live," the drakonid rumbled. He gestured at the ranks of silent, smoldering rock creatures. "Keep fighting, there be your fate. . . ."

Vereesa could no longer find the space to properly swing her sword. The dwarves, too, had trouble utilizing their weapons properly.

They were doomed, of that the high elf became certain. She looked to Grenda, whose expression matched her own. As Rask had said, there were only two choices. Where there was life, there was hope. . . .

"Lay down your weapons," Grenda ordered the others. She did not get any argument from the other dwarves.

Vereesa tossed down her sword. She prayed that they had not just given themselves up for an easy and awful kill.

The moment the party surrendered, the rocky guardians collapsed. Their bodies liquefied, spilling back into the crevasses as the stunned fighters watched.

In their place moved the skardyn and the dragonspawn. Some of the former quickly snatched up the weapons of their cousins, at the same time making hissing sounds or gnashing their teeth as if in hunger.

One started to reach for Vereesa's sword, but Rask ordered it back.

"Mine," the drakonid declared. He hefted Rhonin's creation. "Good balance . . ." To the other guards, Rask ordered, "To the lower pits. The mistress commands. . . ."

They had wanted to slip into the depths of Grim Batol and their wish would now be granted, albeit not in the least as they had hoped. Vereesa both cursed and marveled at the power of this mysterious mistress of whom the drakonid had spoken. The appearance of the fiery minions certainly gave credence to a black dragon being involved. Was it then Onyxia, the daughter of Deathwing? Surely not, for Rhonin had once mentioned information gathered from other sources that all but verified that the female black was no more. Yet, what other dragon could command this ebony drakonid and his dragonspawn cohorts? Rask had definitely said "mistress," which ruled out either a surviving Deathwing or Nefarian.

Father, son, daughter . . .

Where was the *mother* in all this?

Suddenly the ranger wished that she had not aided in the decision to surrender. In her mind, Vereesa could imagine only that one of Deathwing's consorts lurked in Grim Batol and of his consorts only the name *Sintharia* came to mind.

She had convinced the dwarves to turn themselves over to the mercy of the mate of the mad Earth-Warder.

Vereesa surreptitiously reached for a dagger hidden under her breast-plate. With only living foes with which to deal, she hoped that if she caused a distraction, some of the prisoners stood at least a modicum of a chance of escaping—

The point of her own sword came much too near her throat. The heat from the burning weapon left her sweating.

"The dagger or your head," Rask chuckled, "one or other drops . . ."

The ranger let the dagger fall. A skardyn scooped it up, then wisely handed it to the drakonid.

"Wise," Rask said, sheathing the weapon in a belt around his scaled waist.

The prisoners were ushered into the mouth of the cave.

But above watched one attacker that the drakonid had missed. Iridi could do nothing for Vereesa and the others, although she had nearly climbed down to try. In the end, however, the draenei had determined that she could better help her friends in the long run by not helping them now.

The priestess looked around. Farther up, another opening beckoned. It would require a precarious climb, but it was her best chance of entering the mount.

With the staff dismissed, Iridi crawled like a spider up the rock face. She had no illusions as to her chances; what confronted them was a powerful thing of evil, even more so than the blood elf, whose own dark deeds were even greater in number than she had imagined. Yet, it was now all up to her. That was something that she had sensed from the beginning of her journey, that there would come a point when she would be called upon to make the crucial decision or act, upon which all else would be decided. This had to be that moment.

Krasus, Kalec, Vereesa, and the dwarves were all prisoners. It made perfect sense to her that she should choose one or more to locate and immediately free. As the ranger herself had indicated, Krasus was likely the best choice of all those.

And yet, as Iridi reached the entrance, she knew without doubt that it was the *nether dragon* for whom she was about to begin her search. . . .

THIRTEEN

D o you sense that?" Kalec asked Krasus. "Something is going
on just beyond the mount. . . ."

The dragon mage did not answer, his attention, as earlier,
on the entrance to their prison.

This latest silence only infuriated the young blue more. He had tried
speaking with the other dragon half a dozen times, but Krasus never so
much as nodded. He sat like a statue, and while Kalec understood that
his companion had something in mind, he had given indication more
than once that it would have been good if the other had included him
in the details.

Krasus knew that Kalec still leaned toward the blood elf's offer, although only long enough to regain the upper hand. There was merit in
that, but not enough considering that it was Sinestra who was the true
darkness of Grim Batol.

And so, Krasus did not argue with Kalec, but chose to work on what
was possibly an even more remote hope.

"We're no better. . . ." the blue remarked bitterly.

Despite his current task, Krasus could not help but be curious. "What
do you mean by that?"

"My lord Malygos, now that he's whole again, has had nothing good
to say of the mortal races and their abuses of magic. He proclaims
that only dragons are worthy and capable of wielding magic *properly*."
Kalec shook his head. "Right now, to me it seems like dragons wield it
worse than anyone else. . . ."

Krasus was about to reply, when he sensed a presence moving down the corridor in their direction. It did not radiate the magic that permeated Zendarin, the mageslayer, or, most important of all, *her*. Perhaps it was finally what he hoped it would be.

A skardyn strode into sight.

Rather than be disappointed, Krasus's hopes rose. He made a grunting sound identical to some of the speech that he had heard them use earlier.

The scaly dwarf looked his direction.

Krasus caught the creature's gaze . . . and held it. He did not do it by any true magical means, but by sheer will.

From Kalec there came a brief, muted sound. The blue now had some inkling of what he planned.

The skardyn stood motionless for a few seconds, simply staring back. Then, slowly, it entered.

Yet, it was not toward Krasus it went, but rather the nearest wall. Eyes ever tied to the dragon mage's own, the skardyn began climbing.

Krasus guided it with his gaze. Over the space of several millennia, he had become very adept at mesmerism. It was very rare for him to use this skill, for he despised any who willingly enslaved another even for a short time, but there were times of necessity, such as now.

Despite its squat form, the skardyn was an agile climber, not at all surprising considering it lived in the caverns within and below Grim Batol. Krasus had it continue its ascent until it was now near the ceiling.

At that point, he turned his gaze to the shard floating in the air.

The skardyn leapt.

The heavy dwarven body enveloped the shard. As it touched the magical fragment, the skardyn's form flared golden. Despite clearly being in immense pain, the creature did not release its hold.

Skardyn and shard finally dropped to the floor.

"Is it still alive?" Kalec asked.

"Its death was unavoidable," the dragon mage replied somewhat sadly. As one who served and defended life, he regretted when circumstance demanded such cold manipulation of another creature on his part, even a creature such as this. Shaking off his regret, he asked in turn, "Can you feel the difference around us now?"

At first, Kalec did not look as if he understood. Then, the blue suddenly frowned.

"The shard . . . its influence is lessened . . . just a little, but it is less."

"It was a hunch I played. The very rune that makes it immune to much magic is also what enables it to act as a buffer, so to speak, of the shard's powers."

Kalec struggled with his bonds. Krasus could detect the blue using his magic, but to no avail.

"You will not be able to do anything," the red explained.

Kalec frowned. "Then what is the point, old one? Why did you go through so much trouble if we still can't escape this chamber?"

"But we can . . . if only we work together."

The other dragon did not look confident. "There is still some other force besides that shard keeping us so weak . . . and something else keeping you even more so, Korialstrasz."

"Do not concern yourself with that last. Sinestra planned long for my particular coming, knowing—as you might put it—that I *must* interfere. I was assailed by storm and sea monster and magic from various dark elements, including naga whom I suspect had the choice of serving her will or suffering terribly. All of it, including a wound that does not completely heal, were to make me weak enough to overcome once I came here . . . and I willingly let that happen." Krasus straightened. "But I am not so weak as any of you think . . . and that is why, with both of us together, we should at least be able to free ourselves of these bonds."

"But what else wearies us?" Kalec persisted as he readied himself.

"I have my suspicions, but to speak them would be to only add more uncertainty to our situation. Should we escape this chamber, we can deal with that and all else as needs be."

"Murky as ever. Your queen must love mystery. . . ."

Krasus did not show how the last comment sent pangs of remorse through the older dragon. The red was not all that certain that he would survive this to see his beloved mate again. True, he had often been in dangerous situations, but evidently age was catching up even with him.

That did not mean, however, that he had any intention of abandoning his self-chosen role as Azeroth's protector until death truly did claim him.

"Let us concentrate our wills together," he said to Kalec.

It was not something the blue obviously desired, but he nodded, then closed his eyes. Krasus did the same.

The magic of a blue dragon was different than that of a red, but even Krasus was surprised by the particular traits of his companion's. There was a touch to that magic that did not feel at all akin to any other blue's with whom Krasus had been in contact throughout his existence. That even included Malygos himself.

And then Krasus knew what it was that made Kalec unique not just among the blue flight, but *all* dragons.

He was touched by the power of the Sunwell.

Kalec did not know this himself; that was obvious to Krasus immediately. The influence was subtle and deep. Indeed, it blended so much into the blue's very essence that Krasus could think of it only as done on purpose.

Before she had resumed her true destiny, Anveena had left with her champion a token of her love. Unbeknownst to Kalec, she would always be with him, even in his darkest time.

In some ways, the two were even closer than he and Alexstrasza.

He felt Kalec's sudden impatience, the other dragon not aware what Krasus had discovered. Anveena had had a reason for him not knowing and the red respected that.

Concentrating, he bound what power he could summon with that of the other prisoner. Together, they focused on one of the bonds holding Kalec. The choice of that was Krasus's; if something happened, he at least wanted the blue free to hopefully warn the dragonflights.

At first, nothing happened. There was magic involved in this part of their captivity, too. Fortunately, though, it had evidently been assumed that the shard would be sufficient. Krasus and Kalec found the weak link in the spell and eradicated it.

The blue's wrist was freed.

The other bonds were simple to remove after that. Within a minute, the pair was standing, albeit with some aching.

"What now, Korialstrasz?" Kalec asked, insisting on calling his companion by his full dragon name rather than by the identity the other currently preferred. Krasus always favored the name that matched that shape, something the younger dragon evidently did not appreciate. "Should we take the shard?"

"It took me months to gather that one shard and learn the spells enabling me to wield it. Sinestra's made that foul piece hers." He kicked over the body of the skardyn. The shard had left the front badly burnt. "There is only one thing to do with it and that is to leave it here."

"Not what I'd prefer."

"Nor I . . ." But despite saying that, Krasus headed to the entrance as if the shard no longer existed. After a moment, Kalec hurried after him.

"Which way is out, do you suppose?" the blue asked in the corridor.

"That does not matter as much as the way deeper."

Kalec considered this, then nodded. "Of course."

"It is the captive that we must reach, the nether dragon, as Iridi called it. We must decide whether it can be safely freed or, if not that, how to quickest destroy it."

"Not a simple choice, considering our odd weakness."

"And that is the other thing that we must locate, which I believe must be not that far from the nether dragon. That shard of the Demon Soul was strong enough to deal with us, but this very mount radiates a foulness that sickened and slew my kind. One little shard, even of the Soul, cannot do that. Sinestra has something more vile."

The younger dragon agreed. "We will probably have to separate at some point."

"My company is surely something you do not desire much, so when the time comes, that should be no trouble."

Kalec chuckled, but the chuckle died as he realized that Krasus was making no joke.

Meanwhile, the dragon mage had finally determined which direction might best lead them where they desired. He had been in portions of Grim Batol in the past, but his current condition had had some effect on his memory.

"This way," he said, pointing where they had last seen Zendarin go.

Kalec steeled himself. "As you say."

"Can you create any sort of shield to block us from Sinestra's senses?"

"It would be a weak one, Korialstrasz."

The dragon mage considered as he walked. "She is distracted by her work. Even a weak shield may be enough to preserve us."

The younger dragon drew a circle in front of him. Krasus could have perhaps done as well himself, but he was already using what power he had to divine what lay ahead.

The circle that Kalec drew grew to fill the rocky corridor. It then swelled, becoming a sphere that engulfed both males. At the same time, it gradually faded from visibility.

"It should at least help us with the drakonid and dragonspawn," the blue remarked. "And maybe the blood elf and that altered mage-slayer."

"If it helps with any, it helps. . . ."

The passages were not lit for the most part, but neither dragon was bothered much. What illumination there was came from crystals intermittently set in the walls.

"How far down do these caverns and tunnels go?" Kalec quietly asked.

"I know of no creature living or dead who could answer that question save perhaps Deathwing himself. Even the orcs did not descend into the caverns' true depths."

"Nor dragons, either?"

"Nor dragons, either . . . save again, perhaps, Deathwing, for the mad can survive what sanity says is suicide." Krasus did not add that, depending on how matters turned, he, at the very least, might have to brave the lowest depths.

They journeyed for some time along the same passage, but then it broke off into three directions. Krasus paused at the juncture, smelling the air.

"The smell of skardyn is everywhere, which negates seeking the currents. However, we can at least make some judgments on what is visible each way. The path to the right will most certainly climb again. The one ahead seems to go down another level at least and may eventually lead us to our goal, but I cannot say whether we should follow it or take the one on the left—"

A thundering roar filled with pain shook the entire mount. Krasus and the blue pressed themselves against the walls as rock fell here and there.

The roar ceased. The tremor passed a moment after.

"That came from the left, Korialstrasz."

"Yes, our choice has been made."

The two crept slowly in that direction. Krasus would have liked to have moved faster, but with both of them not at all in any condition for a prolonged battle with Sinestra, they had to be very, very cautious.

There came another roar suddenly, one that sent shivers even through Krasus. He had never heard its like before, even among all dragonkind.

Even including the two unstable abominations they had fought.

"What—what is that?"

"Sinestra has a new child, it seems. . . ."

Kalec looked at him in shock. "You mean like those things we ran into earlier?"

"I would think that they perhaps pale in comparison. She would not wish to repeat mistakes." He considered. "That roar came from the same general direction as the pained one."

"It sounded closer, too."

"Indeed . . ." They waited a moment longer, but the roars did not resume. However, voices began to arise.

Without a word to one another, the two dragons slipped back down the passage. Krasus pointed down an unlit side tunnel. What he could sense of it gave indication that it had not seen recent use.

Kalec continued maintaining the shield. The pair finally paused at another juncture, then stilled.

The black dragon was near. Very near. Krasus prepared himself to fight her with what might was left in him. The tunnels prevented all of them from resuming their true forms, but that would not keep Sinestra from unleashing power such as neither of the escapees had, even combined.

Then, both the voice and the presence of Deathwing's consort faded again. Krasus waited longer than necessary before finally heading back.

With Kalec close behind, he headed to where the roars had originated. They entered another chamber that immediately made Krasus wary. To one side of the chamber, a great pit descended into utter darkness. The dragon mage cautiously peered into it, but, despite his best attempts, could sense nothing beyond the inherent evil permeating all of Grim Batol.

"Very odd," Krasus murmured to his companion. "I would have thought that—"

Kalec suddenly gripped his arm and pointed farther on.

Two dragonspawn entered from the other side of the chamber.

The dragonspawn were more startled than the prisoners. Kalec leapt forward, a magical blade already summoned. It was fainter in its glow than Krasus knew that it should have been, but it still cut through thick scale well enough to badly wound the first guard. As the massive creature tried to rally, Kalec cut through both its arm and its chest.

As the one collapsed, the second started to call the alarm. Krasus gestured, hoping that at least he could spare enough magic to prevent that.

The dragonspawn's long mouth opened . . . but no sound escaped. The guard clattered his ax against the rocky wall nearby, with the same lack of results.

Expression almost murderous, Kalec battled the survivor. The ax came near his skull, but his weapon severed the head of the ax from the shaft.

As the guard registered the loss, Kalec slashed again.

The dragonspawn's muzzle dropped to the floor.

The monstrous guard stumbled back. Even for a four-legged giant, the loss was a terrible one regardless of the fact that the sword had also immediately cauterized the wound. The dragonspawn clutched at his ruined face.

The blue dragon drove his blade through the guard's chest.

Krasus joined Kalec, who was panting, but not from effort. The elder dragon saw that the younger had relived some past, critical moment.

"We need to dispose of them quickly," Krasus whispered to him, more to shake Kalec from his reverie than because he really had to tell him what was obvious.

"This pit seems very handy." Kalec created a blue-tinted glow sphere. He sent the sphere down into the pit for some distance, but when the bottom remained invisible, finally summoned it back to him. "It's huge . . . and there's a tremendous drop on the right side, Krasus. This would be as good a place as any for these two."

Krasus had no argument. The farther into the depths of Grim Batol, the less likely that anyone would find the bodies. The disappearances would still be noted, but there would be some question of what had happened, buying the escapees precious seconds.

Gritting his teeth from effort, Kalec used his magic to tip the first dragonspawn into the pit, then joined Krasus in disposing of the second in the same manner. It was not until the second slipped over the edge that they heard the first strike bottom.

Kalec smiled grimly. "That definitely should be deep enough."

Krasus nodded, but felt even more unsettled somehow. Suddenly he wanted to be very far from this chamber.

The other dragon noticed. "What is it?"

"This is no unused chamber . . ." the red pulled his younger counterpart from the edge of the pit. "That second cry . . . it had to be from somewhere near to here, Kalec."

"And so?"

The unsettled feeling magnified. Krasus felt as if something lurked all around them, watching, judging.

His eyes narrowed as he studied the darkness of the pit again.

"Come! Hurry!"

There came a low, ominous sound that shook both to their core. It was a laugh filled with the promise of terrible things, terrible things that even dragons could not face.

From out of the pit arose tendrils of energy a dark and foreboding amethyst in hue. The monstrous waves of purple illumination were not an attack in itself, but presaged something terrible to come.

Kalec suddenly slipped. His body slid back, heading toward the pit as if pulled by an invisible hand. Krasus seized him, then pulled. At the same time, he felt something trying to drag him over as well.

"Leave me!" the blue shouted. "Leave me!"

"Never!"

Kalec's feet tipped over the edge. Despite his best efforts, Krasus doubted that he would be able to save either of them.

Something tugged hard on the blue dragon.

Krasus could not maintain his grip.

With a shout, Kalec vanished into the sinister light below.

Krasus felt himself also dragged closer to oblivion. The edge of his feet crossed. He knew that in another breath, he would join the unfortunate blue.

And then . . . just as suddenly as it started, the threat vanished. The sense that something huge was about to rise up over the edge of the pit ceased. The dark amethyst glow winked out.

Gasping, Krasus dragged himself away from the pit. He did not go far, though, still hopeful that Kalec might have somehow survived. The red crouched, then concentrated his will on the pit—

A powerful burst from the other end of the chamber sent him flying through the air. He collided with the far wall. Half-dazed, Krasus slid to the floor.

Sinestra loomed above him. She was terrible to behold, all pretense of propriety gone.

"You are troublesome," Deathwing's consort quietly declared.

She held up a small container, a dread thing with four sloping sides that appeared to have been made from black and fire-red crystals that pulsated in what seemed a perfect imitation of breathing. The front side was the narrowest, the two flanking it longest. The lid bore a pattern of alternating crystals shaped to form a symbol that matched the shape of the box and, to Krasus's horror, identified its origins and use. The symbol represented a volcano, the ancient mark of the power of the earth . . . and the black flight, whose master had created it.

It was a chrysalun chamber. . . .

Sinestra slid back the lid halfway—as far as it could actually move— revealing a v-shaped gap barely large enough to allow for a nut or some other tiny tidbit.

Krasus raised a hand before him in what he knew was a feeble attempt to stave off the inevitable.

The chrysalun chamber swallowed the dragon mage whole. The lid then slid shut of its own accord and the crystals began their slow, steady breathing again.

Tucking the artifact under her arm, Sinestra turned to the pit. She peered over the edge.

Dargonax stirred.

"You have been naughty," she murmured to her creation, her ultimate child. "Such a waste! I will have to find a proper punishment for you . . ."

"Forgivvveee . . ." a ghostly voice—like that of the wind on a chill day—replied from below.

"Your first word!" Her anger dissipated. "Your first word . . . how delightful . . . you are almost all grown up now . . ."

Sinestra glanced at the chrysalun chamber, then into the pit again.

After another moment of thought, she laughed and carried the magical prison off.

Her child was almost ready to leave the crèche. There was much to prepare.

The landscape where Vereesa and the dwarves had been captured lay deathly quiet. The fissures remained open and from them sulfuric gases continued to rise.

A pair of strong, leather boots made only slight sounds as another newcomer to Grim Batol looked over the ravaged scene. He shook his head, then went in search for something in particular that lay among the ruined earth.

It was here, somewhere. He sensed it, sensed it as well as if it were a part of him . . . or *her*.

The evil that was the dread mount did not go unfelt by him. There were things even now that should be watching his every move, but they could not because they had been told by him to look other ways, at other things.

He had come prepared for the worst, and the worst he had found. Still, with him were not only his own tricks, but some added strength passed on to him by others. It was ironic that he, once reviled, now could ask for them what he needed and they would give it to him.

But then, so much had changed. It was for him interesting to think that one of the most consistent factors in Azeroth was that Grim Batol would be filled with menace. There was almost a twisted comfort in that knowledge.

Suddenly, he detected the nearby presence of that which he sought. A shiver ran through him as he pondered the impending discovery. There was a limp shape right near where the object should be. Could that shape belong to—

Never one to care for proprieties, he ran for all he was worth to the body.

"Praise be!" he hissed. It was not her, merely an oddly-shaped mound of upturned rock and dirt.

But underneath it was that which sent his heart pounding. He lifted up the talisman. The broken chain dangled limply. After all the care that he had put into remaking it so that it would keep them tied together no matter what the distance, it had now proved as useful as any one of the rocks that made up the landscape here.

He looked around again, but there was no sign of her. No sign of his Vereesa.

The wizard Rhonin swore.

FOURTEEN

The nether dragon was near. Iridi could sense him better than almost any other creature around her. After all, were they not both strangers to this world? Had they both not come to here from Outland?

Now that she was so close, the draenei asked herself what she expected of the nether dragon. Did she think it would be grateful to see her? Draenei had never been friends to the nether dragons any more than other races. For all Iridi knew, it was just as likely to eat her.

But something within insisted that the priestess try to reach the creature.

Pressed against a wall, her training making her seem almost invisible to the skardyn, Iridi peered around the next corner. A vast cavern opened up before her and in it crawled the savage dwarves in large numbers. They scrambled up the walls, clung from the ceiling, or scampered over the floor, all to keep, in her estimation, their sole prisoner from moving so much as an inch.

So astounding was the nether dragon's prison that the draenei almost walked out and stared. She had wondered how they could keep the great beast secure once it was freed from the terrible box and now she knew. The strands of energy choked the nether dragon as if the leviathan were corporeal like her or the skardyn. They looked almost flimsy, yet it was clear that their power was incredible.

Finally looking beyond the shackles to the prisoner himself, Iridi could scarcely believe that he still survived. The nether dragon was more ghost than ever, so much so that there were areas where it was more difficult to see him than whatever lay behind his hulking form.

She almost went to him then, but a familiar evil approached. The blood elf strode into the chamber. With him floated an insidious-looking creature that was the mageslayer Krasus had confronted.

Zendarin approached the nether dragon. He appeared as if he did nothing but observe the prisoner, but the priestess sensed that more was at play.

A skardyn came up to Zendarin, growling and hissing something that apparently he could understand.

"Then next time see to it that it doesn't happen!" Zendarin snapped peevishly. "Would not want to get another of your stinking little ilk swallowed up, would you?"

Only then did she notice that four of the creatures were adjusting crystals near the nether dragon's great maw. That now explained one of the tremendous roars that she had heard. Something had clearly happened that undid those particular strands. She eyed the skardyn's work close, trying to discern just what. Perhaps there would lie the key to freeing the leviathan.

But would she actually free it? That was a question for debate, debate Iridi had been having since the beginning.

There is only one way. I must try to judge this nether dragon. . . .

Even Krasus would have looked at her in disbelief had he known of her decision. The draenei knew well that there was not one of her recent companions—and few of her own following—who would have chosen such a course. What there was known of nether dragons did not urge trust in them.

But still Iridi felt she had no right to do otherwise.

The blood elf departed, his mageslayer behind him. The priestess glanced around, but saw only more skardyn. Those, she believed she could handle. The runes that protected them did not appear to work against the staff, although she would use that as a last resort. For now, the draenei trusted in the teachings of her order.

Think their gaze away. Let them look around you, not at you. A seemingly impossible thing, on the surface, but with those words her teachers had also taught her techniques to better blend with her surroundings. She had used them to her advantage outside and even in the corridors, but here there were more skardyn than ever.

Nevertheless, the draenei stepped out. She kept herself close to the nearest wall, letting her cloak help mask her.

The skardyn continued with their tasks. They were eager to keep the crystals in place. Iridi could sense their anxiousness whenever they got very near the nether dragon.

One of them happened to glance her way. The priestess froze.

The skardyn gnashed its teeth, then resumed its task. Iridi waited a moment more, then started to descend.

Then, a dragonspawn entered.

It pointed at the nearest several skardyn. "Come. Mistress commands. . . ."

Half a dozen of the creatures followed the dragonspawn out. Iridi gave thanks; their departure left the area near the head virtually devoid of skardyn. The rest were farther away now. This was her chance.

With great nimbleness, the draenei descended to the level where the nether dragon lay bound. She waited there for a moment as two skardyn climbing along the wall passed into a side tunnel, then slipped toward the massive prisoner.

Even the nether dragon did not appear to notice her, although his condition likely had much to do with that, too. Iridi frowned. She knew that the staff might help her, but feared to summon it.

In the end, there was again no choice. Looking to see where the nearest skardyn currently were, the priestess called it forth and focused it on the captive leviathan.

The eyes of the nether dragon opened wide.

In that instant, a flood of memories and emotions flowed from the behemoth's mind into hers. She saw him in Outland and saw the evil that he had done. Yet, that evil came in part from misunderstanding and as the emotions and memories continued to pour into the priestess, she sensed his regret over his betrayals and the hope to make up for them.

Iridi also sensed that there was something redeemable in this dark giant . . . and, knowing that, determined that it was *freedom,* not death, she sought for the nether dragon.

The priestess glanced around at the skardyn. Thanks to her efforts, they still paid her no mind. She kept the staff low, hoping to be swift.

Can you understand me? the draenei anxiously thought.

Zzeraku . . . hears . . . you. . . .

Iridi breathed just a little easier. The naaru had given some indication that the staff would help her communicate with some creatures, but she had doubted that it would be of use with a nether dragon.

But the link was faint, the reason for that either her wielding of the staff or the nether dragon's obvious weakness or both. Iridi concentrated harder.

Do you know how these bonds can be removed?

The nether dragon visibly stirred at this question. The draenei realized that he had expected her to be yet another of his captors. His hope and gratitude radiated bright in her thoughts, solidifying the priestess's beliefs that she was doing the right thing. This was not an evil creature, only a creature who had mistakenly done evil. He had the potential to be so much more.

The crystals . . . he finally answered. *The frequency . . . Zzeraku is not . . . not strong enough to change them. . . .*

But he had tried, she sensed, and in his most agonizing moments had been nearest to success. Yet, even then all his might had not been enough.

Not being restrained herself, the priestess had hope that she would be more successful. Iridi looked around, debating what she should first attempt to free. A paw would have made much sense, but the maw was closest and possibly the simplest to do without being seen.

Yes . . . Zzeraku said.

The nether dragon had chosen for her. The draenei went to the nearest crystal.

A skardyn dropped down from the wall to the side. It stared at her in surprise.

Iridi released the staff, which vanished. She seized the monstrous dwarf by the arm and pulled the creature forward. As he flew into her, the priestess struck the skardyn at a predetermined point on the side of the neck.

The skardyn collapsed. Iridi hurriedly shoved the body behind part of the wall's natural formation. The skardyn would be found, but she hoped to be finished before then.

Recalling the staff, the priestess focused the point on the first of the crystals keeping Zzeraku's jaws sealed. She felt the crystal's vibrations and understood what the nether dragon had meant. Concentrating, Iridi tried to do as he had suggested.

The crystal resisted. Sweating, the draenei pushed herself to her limits. If she could not do even this one, then there was no hope whatsoever of freeing the immense captive.

The crystal's frequency altered. It was very slight and not enough as far as Iridi was concerned, but it was a start. Just a little more effort, she believed, and this one would be finished—

A howl of alarm echoed through the chamber.

Iridi had been discovered.

The priestess made one last concentrated attack on the crystal, then stepped back. Skardyn came at her from all sides.

She used the staff to fling the nearest pair away, then dismissed it and fought the ones that followed with her hands and feet. While the skardyn outside had used whips and pikes, those here for the most part wielded no weapons. Why should they have? They had obviously never expected a foe to appear in this particular chamber.

But that one advantage was short-lived. Iridi caught sight of more skardyn emerging from holes above. Some of them had whips bound around their waists; others carried a large piece of mesh . . . a net for her, no doubt.

One of the dwarves leapt onto her back, its sharp claws ripping at the cloak. The draenei slipped free of the travel cloak, at the same time using it to entangle both that foe and another just reaching for her.

But they were continuing to swarm from everywhere around her.

Iridi struck another in the chest with the hard part of her palm. The skardyn had hard, muscular torsos like their cousins, and the draenei's own bones shook.

She quickly looked up. The skardyn with the net were nearly in position to toss it on her and the ones surrounding the priestess kept her from moving out of the way.

Then, the skardyn suddenly hesitated. Several glanced past Iridi.

She felt a wave of energy fill the chamber and feared that, in addition to the skardyn, the blood elf was now upon her.

But the skardyn scattered, forgetting her as if she were nothing. Even those above quickly crawled like spiders back into their holes, dragging the net with them.

She turned . . . and faced not Zendarin . . . but the monstrous mage-slayer.

Vereesa and Grenda hunched together as the skardyn watched over their captive cousins. They had no idea why they had been taken alive, only that it behooved them to find some manner by which to quickly escape. Clearly, whatever fate the creatures' mistress had in mind would not be a pleasant one.

"No one's seen Rom anywhere," Grenda murmured. "He and five others are missing. One of those, I know for sure is dead and there's those that can claim seein' two more slaughtered out there."

The ranger nodded. They both assumed the worst. Now what mattered was what to do next and, with Rom no more, Grenda was in charge of the dwarves.

"We are inside," the high elf said.

"I'd be happy with that if we weren't locked up in here like pigs waitin' to be slaughtered."

Indeed, the band was sealed in a set of cramped holes dug into the side of the dimly-lit cavern. Old but still reliable iron bars hammered into the rock kept the prisoners secure. More than half a dozen skardyn acted as guards, with one bored dragonspawn overseeing them.

Rask had been thorough in having the captives searched. None of the Bronzebeards could volunteer anything useful to deal with the locks, much less the guard beyond.

But Vereesa was still not sad to be inside. She was close now to her quarry and, she hoped, also close to wherever Krasus was being held.

"Keep watch for me," she whispered to Grenda.

As the dwarf obeyed, Vereesa reached to her right boot. She slowly and casually felt for a small depression near the calf area. . . .

"The guards are straightening!" Grenda hissed. "Someone approaches!"

Vereesa moved her hand away just as a shadow passed across the bars. Her eyes widened as she saw who it was.

"Hello, my dear cousin. . . ."

"Zendarin." The ranger did not rush to the bars, which she hoped at the very least would disappoint the blood elf, who no doubt desired such a reaction.

"Ever the calm, calculating ranger," he mocked. "Are you still that much one of us, anymore? With so much human taint in you, it would be a surprise. . . ."

"One should not speak of taint who has taken to draining the foul magic of demons."

"You find that distasteful? We are doing more for Azeroth than all the Alliance combined! We are the most feared of foes the Legion has!"

Still seated, Vereesa shook her head. "You are *becoming* the Legion, Zendarin . . . and the only reason any of you do this is because you hunger for that magic. You need it. Without it, you would wither. . . ."

He sneered. "Not all of us have such a ready source with which to indulge ourselves daily . . . and nightly, cousin. . . ."

"I have been free of the hunger for quite some time, Zendarin . . . thanks especially to my husband, the *human*. He did more for me than any of my own kind could have. My children are a sign of my freedom, for I would never have dared bring them into this world if I had remained *sickened* like you. . . ."

Zendarin scowled, then snapped his fingers. A skardyn stepped up to the cell door.

The blood elf opened his hand. A staff akin to Iridi's materialized in his grip.

"Step out, cousin," he ordered as the skardyn unlocked the door. "Unless you'd like to watch one of these others skinned alive."

Vereesa had no choice but to obey. Waving off a silent protest from Grenda, the ranger left the cell.

Her cousin looked her up and down. "Still fit. You must revel in your human pet. Good! The stronger you are, the better you'll serve her."

"What do you mean?"

"She's in constant need of laborers, the death rate running very high. . . ." Before Vereesa could retort, Zendarin suddenly ordered, "Still your tongue and put your hands behind you." He emphasized the order with a thrust of the point of the staff at her throat.

The ranger did as she was told. Zendarin pulled the staff back, then brought the crystalline point up to the top of her head. Slowly, he lowered the point until it finally aimed at the floor beneath her feet.

"Ah." He raised the staff a little higher, the point now leveled with her calf.

Vereesa gasped. Her calf felt as if on fire.

"Surely you are stronger than that," her cousin remarked coldly. "You don't know what it is like to truly burn. . . ."

There followed a tearing sound—and the slim, metal blade that the ranger had kept secreted in her boot flew out. It landed next to Zendarin, the metal still orange-hot.

Favoring her other leg, Vereesa simply stared at the blood elf.

"I knew that there would be something. Not only is a ranger versatile, but so is the line of Windrunner. . . ."

"You are a stain on the line, Zendarin."

He scoffed. "Any more than one who sleeps with a human, even breeds with them? Any more than a banshee, perhaps? I am far from the darkest stain on our family; in fact, I am its future!"

She said nothing, still bitter about his comments. The ones concerning her were not so terrible; she had faced the prejudices of both her kind and Rhonin's and, for the most part turned those with the prejudices into believers. No, it was more his comment about something so accursed as a banshee.

A banshee, like her sister, Sylvanas.

But Sylvanas was a situation for another time, perhaps another life.

"Silence becomes you." Zendarin gestured for her to return to the cell. He briefly pointed the staff at the dwarves while Vereesa rejoined Grenda. "Ah. Everyone else is being good, I see. No other hidden blades . . ."

The skardyn had been good about searching their cousins, but not with Vereesa. Now, Zendarin had dealt with that situation.

"Your poor, poor children," he added, staring at her through the iron bars. "How will they feel when they discover that their mother has abandoned them? Well, soon they will have their uncle to console them . . . and raise them after their father, too, fails to return."

This time, Vereesa let out a cry of rage. She leapt back to the bars, her hands seeking Zendarin, who had already stepped back. He laughed, the skardyn and the dragonspawn joining in.

"I have enjoyed this family reunion," he finished. "It makes me more eager than ever to renew my acquaintance with my nephews. . . ."

Dismissing the staff, he left the prisoners. The dragonspawn moved to the cell, whipping Vereesa back.

"Sit!" the behemoth roared. Then, satisfied that they were under control, the dragonspawn returned to its post.

The ranger scowled at her captors, then grudgingly returned to Grenda.

"I'm sorry about all that," the dwarf whispered. "Maybe your male will be able to stop him, being a wizard and all. . . ."

"Rhonin's skills aside, I have no intention of placing all my hopes on that," Vereesa answered, her expression far more calm than moments before. "We will be escaping and I will face Zendarin again . . . of that I will at least swear."

Her hand slipped to her other boot. There, she carefully slid out of another slot another small blade. However, where the other had been crafted of metal, this one appeared to be of iridescent pearl.

"Gimmel's blood!" Grenda murmured. "But how did you hide that from your cousin?"

"He searched for weapons, seeking those made as one might expect. Rhonin crafted this for me, a simple but strong blade made from the bounty of the sea. There is no magic in it. Unless he knew to look for the blade in particular, the chances were small that he would find it, for his spell would simply think it part of the boot's crafting."

The Bronzebeard shook her head. "What wizards'll conjure up!"

"The suggestion was mine. The crafting his." A moistness escaped one eye. "Together we are stronger than each is separately." Steeling herself, she continued, "We must escape at the first opportunity—"

They were interrupted by another arrival . . . this time a drakonid. Vereesa studied the creature, but it was not Rask.

"Take one!" the drakonid ordered.

The skardyn unlocked the door. With whips they drove their cousins back, then cut off a lone warrior from the rest. Two skardyn dragged him out.

The moment the rest of the guards had retreated, the dwarves charged forward. Unfortunately, they were not able to keep the cell from being locked again, nor could they do anything for their comrade except shout angrily as he was taken away.

Skardyn began whipping at the bars. The dwarves finally fell back.

The drakonid laughed. "Your turns. They will come. All serve the mistress."

With that, the black beast followed after the others.

"What'll they do with Udin?" asked a younger dwarf.

"Torture 'im to see if there's any of us still out there, most likely!" answered another fighter.

Grenda turned on the second dwarf. "Are you daft, Falwulf? Didn't you hear what that blood elf said before? They're not interested if one or two of us are still out there; they want to make us into slaves. . . ."

An uneasy rumbling spread through the prisoners. Dwarves were fighters; give them an enemy with a weapon, and they would do battle even to their deaths. There was no honor in slavery.

Grenda looked to Vereesa. "If you've got an idea of how we can escape and escape fast, now would be a good time to start on it. . . ."

The ranger's gaze went from her companion to the skardyn keeping watch. "It may cost some lives. . . ."

"Better that than what we're lookin' forward to."

"As you wish, then." Vereesa hid the blade in her palm. She leaned back so as to not stir the guard's interest. "Get everyone prepared to act on my signal. We must all move together . . . even if only in the end we buy ourselves a quick death."

"Aye." Grenda casually turned to a comrade. As the high elf watched, the dwarf began to pass on word. There would be no hesitation from any of the Bronzebeards. As Grenda had indicated, what other choice did they have?

From beyond the chamber where their cells lay, there came a hideous cry. It was mercifully short, but the sound remained burned in all their minds.

"That was *Udin,*" uttered the younger warrior who had asked about the other prisoner earlier.

Among the skardyn, there was rough, mocking laughter. One of them leaned close to the bars and, for the first time, spoke something intelligible.

"All fight gone from him. He good slave now . . ." The feral eyes surveyed the captives. "Who want to be next?"

The other skardyn laughed again.

FIFTEEN

The mageslayer towered over her. Iridi knew nothing of its kind save what she had gleaned from Krasus. By rights, she should have been fairly safe from its abilities, but this creature had been transformed into something more menacing.

She seized a rock and threw it. As the priestess expected, the missile flew through without pause.

The draenei had no choice. She summoned the staff even knowing that its power might be used against her.

The mageslayer moved in silence. That made it all the more unnerving. Iridi pointed the staff and focused.

A blue light erupted from the staff, striking the mageslayer—

And immediately after, flying back at the startled draenei.

Iridi was sent hurtling away. She released her grip on the staff, and quickly twisted in the air. A moment later, the priestess crashed into the ground.

Most would have been left unconscious or even dead, but the priestess's training enabled her to land rolling, then end up in a crouched position. Even then, though, Iridi was left disoriented. It took her a moment to locate the mageslayer, a moment she did not have.

A second burst of blue light almost crushed her into the floor. The draenei barely dodged out of the path. It did not seem right to her that the monster could send the staff's power back *twice*; that should have been an impossibility. She could only assume that this was another benefit of the transformation.

Skardyn in her vicinity ran off as if on fire. That none of these foul creatures—supposedly serving the same entity—desired to be any-where near the mageslayer did not bode well.

Iridi suddenly noticed that the nether dragon sought her attention. The draenei summoned the staff back.

There . . . there . . . Zzeraku managed. *That . . .*

"That" was an altar whose base included what appeared to be carv-ings shaped like dragons. Resting on it was a cube of some bluish tint. There was something about the cube that made the draenei hesitant to draw near it.

The staff . . . the nether dragon struggled to continue. *It might stir the cube . . . might begin the feeding . . .*

Iridi had no idea what he meant by the last, only that the cube was possibly her only hope. She dismissed the staff again, then, as the mage-slayer neared, performed an athletic leap *over* its very head.

What vaguely resembled a clawed appendage grabbed for her, barely missing. The mageslayer turned as the draenei landed. Its midsection had turned darker.

A black light shot out at her.

The priestess avoided being struck, but a skardyn seeking to flee from behind her moved too slow. The light enveloped it—and with a squeal, the skardyn went spinning into the nearest wall, striking so hard that Iridi could hear its bones crack. The dead skardyn slid in an ungainly lump to the floor.

Before the mageslayer could strike again, the draenei reached the altar. Praying that Zzeraku had not steered her terribly wrong, Iridi summoned the naaru staff.

The center of the mageslayer darkened again.

Iridi pointed the crystal at the cube.

Think . . . think of the creature . . . Zzeraku suddenly warned. *Then use . . . the staff . . .*

She did as told, imagining the abomination in her mind.

The staff fed power into the cube. The cube flared bright—

An eerie, whistling sound filled the chamber. Iridi belatedly realized that it came from the mageslayer.

The monster lost all cohesion. As a swirling mass of energy, the mageslayer flew toward the draenei . . . then suddenly sank into the cube without a trace.

The priestess stood there disbelieving.

Beware! Zzeraku warned.

Some of the skardyn began recovering from their own surprise and fear enough to recall that there was still an intruder. They started for her.

She spun around. They were coming from all sides again. She raised the staff—

And suddenly there was a robed figure with red hair standing next to her. He wrapped his arms around the draenei before she could react.

"Damn it! You're not her!"

Before she could respond, the cavern chamber disappeared. Iridi cried out in frustration. "No!"

She was outside again. Outside the mount that she had so desperately tried to enter.

"No!" the priestess repeated. "No!"

"Be quiet!" The robed figure spun her around. For the first time, she saw that he was human. Under the thick, fiery hair, eyes of bright emerald green stared back at her. He was not unhandsome for one of his kind, although his nose had clearly been broken sometime far in the past. He had a strong jaw and angular features and a stubborn expression that well matched his red hair.

On the breast of his robe had been sewn an eye of gold on a field of violet. Below the eye were three daggers, also gold, that pointed downward.

Iridi recognized the symbol of Dalaran.

"You are the wizard Rhonin, mate of the high elf, Vereesa," she quietly declared.

"You know her? You know where she is? I tried to locate her and sensed some magical forces in play. Vereesa's always in the middle of such things. . . ." He cursed at himself. "I tried something and it failed. But at least you're safe."

"But I need to get back inside! I was trying to free the nether dragon—"

The spellcaster looked as if she were mad. "Why in the world would you do something that mad? I've heard from those who've seen what they can do! Destroy the creature, maybe, but *free* it?"

"I've seen into his mind. Zzeraku means no ill. He's done terrible things in the past, but he's changed now. . . ."

"As simple as that, is it? And you're absolutely certain you read him true?"

"I am . . . and I will not back down on this. He must be freed and for many reasons. . . ." The draenei dismissed her staff. "He is the key to whatever is going on. They're using Zzeraku to create some terrible creature. . . ."

Rhonin grimaced. "It never ends, does it? Never any true peace for Azeroth . . . gods, I wish Krasus were here at least!"

It did not surprise the priestess to learn that the wizard knew the red dragon. With some trepidation, she said, "Krasus is also in Grim Batol . . . as a prisoner."

"That's not possible. Not him . . ."

"He sent me to safety just before he and a younger blue dragon— Kalec—were captured. There was a mageslayer—"

"That wouldn't stop him," Rhonin scoffed.

"There was something different about it, he indicated. It had been enhanced by those in Grim Batol."

A sound from the direction of the mountain made them both still. Rhonin took hold of her arm. "I should be able to do this one more time. Jumping into Grim Batol took more than even I thought."

"We're going back inside?"

He gave her a harsh laugh. "Not at the moment, not if you don't want to end up a part of the mount itself for the rest of eternity. No, I'm sending us somewhere safer . . . relatively speaking."

Rhonin's brow furrowed in concentration. Iridi started to protest again. Surely, he, of all people, understood the need to return to Grim Batol.

But it was too late. The air around the pair crackled . . . and both vanished once more.

Krasus floated in an oppressive darkness, the sense that it was seeking to crush him ever prevalent. He had heard stories of confinement in chrysalun chambers, horrible tales of dragons and other magical beings driven mad by years, decades, even centuries of entrapment. Time, after all, did not flow inside as it did in the true world. For all he knew, his friends and comrades were all long dead and whatever evil Sinestra had birthed in the pits of Grim Batol had wreaked havoc all over Azeroth.

No! That has not happened! Not yet! The dragon mage berated himself for such dire assumptions. Deathwing's consort intended to use his magical essence to feed her abominations; therefore, there was still hope . . . at least for all save Kalec.

He mourned the blue's violent passing. The thing in the pit, the thing already so well-adapted at shielding itself from powerful dragons, had surely made a grisly meal out of Kalec. It infuriated Krasus that he had been unable to do anything to save his companion, infuriated him more that no one had been able to depend upon him. He had no idea what had happened to Iridi. In desperation, he had transported her to the one area that he knew of around Grim Batol—knowledge gleaned from those of his kind who had stood guard over the evil mount—where magic was difficult to use. There, she would have at least had a chance to recover and, if wise, abandon the area as soon as possible.

Krasus doubted that she had done so.

Not for the first time, the dragon mage tested the limits of his prison. It was ironic that, in here of all places, he was more at his full strength than anywhere else in and around Grim Batol. The chamber was a pocket universe in itself, one that drew upon the victim's own magic to keep the latter imprisoned. Yet, it also cut him off from Sinestra's spellwork and whatever truly kept him so weak in the mount.

But he could not just wait here until the black dragon freed him for her diabolical spells. Krasus was no ordinary prisoner; he was well aware of the history of chrysalun chambers, for were they not the work of dragons, after all?

Initially, the chambers had been designed for varied purposes depending on which dragonflight had created them, but first and foremost they had all been intended to trap creatures and beings of magical threat . . . demons, mad spellcasters, elementals, and the like. Those specifically created by the black flight had been intended for use against wild energies and the like that threatened the very earth itself.

Yet, that had changed forever after a newly-insane Neltharion, furious at his loss of the Demon Soul over the Well of Eternity, had sometime afterward altered those created by his flight for the foul purpose of trapping his imagined enemies. The other flights had quickly moved to locate the chambers and, in addition to those of the Earth-Warder, had supposedly forever sealed them away where they could not be found.

But over the centuries, a few had made their way back into the world . . . and perhaps this one had never even been uncovered before.

Krasus grew frustrated. Perhaps he had been wrong. Perhaps his knowledge of the history of the foul boxes was *not* something that would serve him after all—

The dragon mage hesitated. Or *would* it? One particular point suddenly struck him. Chrysalun chambers required much effort, which was why there were thankfully so few. Even some of those had not been entirely stable. They had had *faults* . . .

It was a desperate hope, but the only hope he currently had. Krasus focused his mind and reached out.

But at first, all he sensed was his oppressive imprisonment. Krasus shuddered and briefly the hope that Sinestra would need him quickly for her experiment flashed through his mind. He immediately rejected the notion, but wondered, if he failed to escape, how long it would be before he prayed for it again.

Once more, Krasus concentrated. For the most part, it was his own magical essence he sensed, but gradually, he noticed another.

It was not of Azeroth in origin.

Hopes raised, Krasus fixed on it. There was something familiar about it, something that reminded him of—

Yes, that was it. This was, of course, the *very* chamber in which the nether dragon had surely been contained.

Whether or not that bettered his chances, the dragon mage could not say. The nether dragon's energies were like nothing that the creator of this hellish prison could have imagined.

Krasus probed deeper into the design. There were odd variations that could only be the work of the original caster, perhaps Neltharion or even his consort. Krasus grew less confident that there would be any advantage after all. Whoever had created this particular artifact had been eager to experiment.

But still Krasus had to try. He inspected the magic foundation of the box, seeking some disruption from the nether dragon's incarceration that might have created a flaw. That flaw would be his best chance of escape. He needed to—

The dragon mage frowned suddenly. There was another variation in the spell matrix of the chrysalun chamber. It had not been forged by the same hand that had created all else. However, it made no sense . . . - unless it had been caused by the nether dragon.

Krasus inspected it further.

His prison suddenly shifted, throwing him about. The darkness turned to gray, then black again. Krasus was sent spinning—

He reacted instinctively, his body contorting and his arms and legs stretching and bending at angles not conforming to his elven shape. Claws burst from his fingers. Scales covered his skin as his nose and mouth stretched forward into a long, sharp muzzle. Wings sprouted from his back as his robes faded to nothing.

Beating his massive wings, Korialstrasz slowed, then *halted* his flight. The red leviathan roared from the painful effort.

As he regained his equilibrium, Korialstrasz tried to make sense of what had happened. His simple probing of the area in question had turned his entire prison on its head.

Clearly, the nether dragon had come much closer to freedom than he had imagined. Unfortunately for the creature, he had not had the cunning or knowledge to benefit from his very uniqueness.

But now Korialstrasz's hopes heightened. There was great risk, but risk was better than either eternity or awaiting his captor's summons. Sinestra would surely be well prepared for him when she opened the chamber again. It behooved the red to make his escape, if he could.

With much more delicacy, Korialstrasz surveyed the weakened area again, observing carefully how it weakened the overall matrix. It did not surprise him to quickly discover that the odd energies of a nether dragon could affect the matrix almost like a virus in a mortal body. The two forces were enough alike that now the essence of the former captive had restructured the original spellwork into a pattern never conceived by the chrysalun chamber's creator.

And where the spell matrix had been most affected, there the red dragon found what he felt was the weak link, the point where he needed to concentrate his efforts.

With the eye of one who had studied the workings of magic perhaps second only to the greatest of the blue dragons, Korialstrasz slowly picked his way through the aberration. He finally found the thread that he felt would, if removed carefully, cause the rest to become undone and, theoretically, open the way for him.

Already feeling claustrophobic, Korialstrasz began gingerly severing the link. Immediately he felt the entire chamber quiver. The darkness became slightly grayer again. The red dragon grew more bold in his work. Freedom was close—

The aberration completely disintegrated, not at all what he had wanted. The matrix became frayed, with the frayed area spreading. Korialstrasz quickly sought to rebind it, but the damage was already more than he could overcome. The strain on the rest of the spellwork keeping the chamber intact increased a thousandfold.

The chamber collapsed, the grayness pressing in on the red dragon from all sides. Korialstrasz screamed, his prison's abrupt destruction unleashing new and terrible forces that threatened to rip him apart. Korialstrasz was caught in a maelstrom that grew to horrendous proportions. Try as he might, the dragon could do nothing to keep from spinning toward it.

That this was all taking place in a container not even large enough on the outside to seemingly hold much more than an apple did in no manner assuage Korialstrasz. For him, it was as if Azeroth had been destroyed and the universe were about to join it. He had wanted to be free of the chrysalun chamber and he had gotten his wish . . . perhaps much to his eternal regret.

The great wings beat again and again, the strain of fighting against such powerful primal forces quickly bringing Korialstrasz to the point of exhausted panting. The eye of the maelstrom loomed before him, a swirling mass of gray, black, and crimson.

As he neared the eye, invisible forces pressed down ever harder on the dragon. His bones felt as if ready to crush to powder, his flesh as if about to be squeezed to pulp. In all his long existence, he had never known such unendurable agony.

At that point, the dragon decided that there was but one thing he could do. It offered the potential for even greater suffering and a much worse death, but also the slightest of hopes.

Concentrating as best he could, Korialstrasz focused all his magic on protecting himself. The effort strained him more, and he nearly blacked out. Yet, in the end his spells held.

The red leviathan studied the maelstrom, seeking the *exact* center. It had to be exact. Anything else was certain suicide.

Beating his wings as hard as he could, Korialstrasz no longer fought against the maelstrom's pull, but rather *embraced* it. He soared forth, speeding into its maw and praying that whatever happened, it would happen swiftly.

And as he entered it, Korialstrasz screamed again . . . and again . . . and again—

SIXTEEN

Sinestra slept.

That she might do so even when her senses warned her that there were other intruders about spoke not of her exhaustion, but of her confidence. She was certain of her impending triumph, certain that any of the vermin seeking to prevent it would soon be either eradicated or serve her in some manner or another.

She slept, as she always did, for but only a few minutes at a time. There had been periods when she had gone more than a century without slumber. This was not normal for most of her kind, but Sinestra had only contempt for the others, even those of the black flight. In her mind, the only dragons worth existing in her imagined world were herself and her new children.

Still in her mortal form and lying atop a bed of stone, she slept alone in a vast chamber deeper than any other she currently used for her experiments. Down here, there was nothing to disturb her.

Down here, she could listen to the voice in her head far more clearly.

All goes as planned, it said over and over. *All goes as planned and Dargonax grows larger. . . . The next generation will dwarf even him . . . and be a thousand times more powerful . . .*

"A thousand more times . . ." Sinestra murmured in her sleep. "A thousand more times . . ."

A thousand more times powerful . . . and they will crush the other dragons . . . crush them all . . . the day of the dragon is at an end . . . now comes the twilight . . . the night . . .

"The night . . ."

But the night shall be followed by a new day . . . the first day of the children's rule . . . the first day of a new golden age of dragons . . .

"A new . . . golden age—"

Sinestra started. Her eyes flashed open and a look of intense anger spread over her face.

"Korialstrasz!" the black dragon roared. She leapt to her feet. "But how could he—how could he—?"

And then, oddly, Lady Sinestra's expression transformed. Instead of shock, anger, and outrage . . . *satisfaction* spread across her maimed features.

"Yes . . . of course . . . how delicious . . . how perfectly timed! Thank you, Korialstrasz . . . thank you . . ."

With a smile, she hurried out to find Zendarin. . . .

Another dragon stirred at that same moment, a dragon who was certain that he was dead. It was not Korialstrasz, though, but rather the blue, Kalec.

His first discovery was that he was not, after all, dead. That, though, did not explain the darkness that surrounded him, a darkness that felt . . . in some obscene way . . . almost alive.

And then Kalec recalled what had happened to him before he had blacked out. He remembered the pit where they had dumped the huge corpses and the discovery that the pit was not empty.

Not empty . . .

Kalec summoned his blade. The blue-tinted weapon materialized, but only as a dull shadow of what it should have been. The next moment, it simply faded away.

"Must not . . . must not do that . . ."

Each syllable literally struck a chord of fear in Kalec, even though he was not one given to that emotion. The blue dragon tried again to call for the blade, but this time there was not even a hint of its existence.

"Must not do that . . ." the voice repeated. ". . . or she will know . . ."

She. There was no question as to whom the voice referred. It could only mean Sinestra.

"Who—who are you?" Kalec finally asked.

"I am her child. . . ."

"Where are you? Let me see you!"

"I am here before you. . . ." There was a deep amethyst glow and in it Kalec beheld an immense shape. It was dragon in form, yet seemed to flow as if not entirely solid. It resembled somewhat what he knew a nether dragon was supposed to look like, but was also more.

Shimmering orbs observed the blue dragon in turn. Kalec suddenly felt as if those eyes had been staring at him all the time that he had been unconscious and that notion sent new chills through him.

"What are you?" he asked.

"Her child . . ."

Kalec grimaced. He was not certain whether the vaguely-seen creature was as naive as he sounded or simply toying with the blue dragon.

He decided to try a new tack. "Do you have a name?"

There was a pause, then, "I have a name. . . . She calls me *Dargonax.* . . ."

" 'Dargonax?' " Kalec's wariness magnified a thousandfold. He knew the meaning of that name from the tongue of his kind.

Dargonax . . . *Devourer* . . .

"Do you like it?" the murky form asked. "I like it."

"It is a . . . strong name."

"It means 'Devourer' . . . in the dragon tongue, she says," Dargonax added, quickly destroying any hope the blue had that the creature was ignorant of the foul meaning. "You are a dragon. . . ."

Kalec surreptitiously tried to summon a magic blade, *anything* that he could use against the creature. Now the blue knew that he was being toyed with.

"I am a dragon, too. . . ." Dargonax moved forward, the murkiness peeling back as just enough to allow Kalec to see that the shape was definitely that of a dragon, but not one of the nether ones. Dargonax was much, much more.

But the mysterious dragon did not fully reveal himself. Indeed, he pulled back, growing once more akin to a shadow. Kalec had no idea whether it was some ability of his, some spell, or some trick of the pit, for there were unsettling energies in play around them and not all were directly associated with Dargonax . . . although surely he was affected by their presence.

Kalec wondered if even Sinestra understood what she was growing in this pit.

He steeled himself for what would surely be his imminent end. "We are both dragons, yes."

"Then we should be friends. . . ."

The statement took the blue dragon aback. He could fathom no reason why Dargonax would need his assistance. Surely it would do him more use to swallow Kalec whole, an easy task considering that, in addition to being unable to use his inherent powers, the blue could not even shapeshift. He had already secretly attempted to do so more than once and the only explanation for his failure had to be something that his surreal companion was doing.

It occurred to Kalec then that Dargonax was surely only days— perhaps a few weeks at best—old.

How terrible would he be as he further matured? And did he even need to mature? The beast seemed already huge.

Krasus had warned Kalec against even pretending to deal with the blood elf and surely would have counseled against doing the same here, but the blue doubted that he had any real choice. Dargonax had dragged him down here in the first place, and the only reason that he had not devoured Kalec as he had the dragonspawn—for there were no signs of the corpses anywhere—was that the behemoth did truly need him.

But exactly for what was the question.

"Yes," the blue finally responded. "We should be friends."

"Good . . . good . . . and friends, they help friends, yes? Is that right?"

For a being who had likely never been out of the pit, Dargonax was already well-versed in many of the nuances of life. Sinestra had wrought something terrible.

"Friends help friends," he agreed. "Both help each other."

"So they do—" Dargonax broke off. Then, much to Kalec's shock, the other's voice resonated in the blue's head. *She comes! Be silent and still!*

Although still recovering from his surprise at Dargonax's ability to speak to him through his mind, Kalec nevertheless managed to obey. There was no need to ask just who the creature meant. Since Anveena's sacrifice, Kalec had become very reckless where his life was concerned, but he also still held tight to his sense of duty. He would not serve Malygos well by letting Sinestra know that he had survived. The blue planted himself tight against the wall and tried to summon the shield that he had earlier created.

But still nothing happened.

Then, he felt what almost seemed a wing cover over him. Kalec was immersed in shadow . . . shadow with hints of amethyst in it.

Barely a breath later, he heard Sinestra . . . and another.

"*He* is missing," she hissed at her companion.

"Your old 'friend'?" The other voice was that of the blood elf. "From the chrysalun chamber? How is that even possible—unless—perhaps his companion survived. Maybe he let the other out."

Kalec grimaced, caught between hope and concern. He suspected that they spoke of Krasus, which meant that the red had somehow escaped a *chrysalun chamber* of all things. That was all for the good, but now Zendarin had, by his mistaken notion, put into Sinestra's mind the thought that the blue lived.

"Dargonax has feasted on that one," Sinestra replied. Yet, there was a hint of question in her tone. Then . . . "Besides, the chamber was destroyed from the *inside*."

"I've never heard of such a feat! How could he manage that?"

"He is who he is; that is how he could manage the impossible! Make no mistake of it, my dear Zendarin; he is the one fact that I consider a concern."

"And yet you brought him here."

"He would have come," she retorted. "He *always* comes. He *always* interferes. That is his nature. The best way to deal with that was to make him come on my terms, at my urging." There was another pause, then, "He must be even weaker now and if I know him, he will have fled below. He knows that must be where to go. I want you to send your pet after him—"

"I'd do that, my lady, except that the damned beast hasn't responded to an earlier summons! The last I traced it, the thing was in the vicinity of the nether dragon and since then . . . *nothing.*"

Sinestra let out a long, angry hiss. "How cunning! Korialstrasz must have slipped around and sought to free the nether dragon! Go! Seek your mageslayer—"

Kalec did not hear the blood elf depart, but assumed that he would be wise enough to obey her. The blue started to speak, but then sensed that his unsettling companion did not wish him to do so.

"My sweet child . . ." she cooed in a manner that turned the blue dragon's blood cold. Her fury had now been replaced by a malevolent confidence. It was as if she had become an utterly different being from the one the moment before. "Come to me, my sweet child. . . ."

Dargonax moved upward, ever keeping his indistinct form between Kalec and the dark lady. "Missstresssss . . ."

The shift in Dargonax's speech startled Kalec nearly as much as Sinestra's odd, abrupt change in attitude. The creature sounded much younger, much less developed.

Much less of a threat?

"My Dargonax . . . my firstborn of a new world . . . is there anything you would tell your *mother*?"

"Hungrrrrry . . ."

Sinestra chuckled. "Of course, you are. Fear not, my darling. Soon you shall be fed, fed as you never have been before, oh yes . . . but from thereafter, you must learn to stave off your hunger. There will soon be others to feed, brothers and sisters in multitudes. . . ."

Brothers and sisters in multitudes. Kalec imagined a dozen, a *hun-*

dred more like Dargonax. What would become of Azeroth, then? He doubted that these newer ones would be as unstable as the pair that he and the others had fought. And even if they could eventually be stopped, how much bloodshed and destruction would they have committed by then?

Kalec thought of the sacrifice that Anveena had made to help her world begin the road to recovery. All that might be for naught if more of these dragons hatched.

He recalled a brief conversation that he, Krasus, and Iridi had had shortly after the struggle. While eating, Iridi had mentioned her impressions of the dragons, who were not black, blue, or nether. The word *twilight* had come to her, a word very apt in so many ways to these monstrous beings, if Dargonax and the pair were even the least of their example. The draenei had called them twilight dragons.

And they might just be the vessels by which Azeroth's own twilight would happen.

Caught in such thoughts, he missed what Sinestra said next. Only Dargonax's reply enabled him to figure out what it was.

"Yes . . . mother . . ." the creature answered in his false child-talk. "Want to share . . . want them strong . . ."

Sinestra had obviously been emphasizing the fact that Dargonax could no longer expect to be the focus of all her efforts, that he would have no choice when she began feeding him less magical energy so that she could use it on the next generation. But even if Dargonax's creator did not notice the tiny hint of ire in the twilight dragon's voice, Kalec certainly did . . . and now he knew why his shadowy companion left hidden to Sinestra his rapid maturing.

Dargonax was jealous of the siblings to come.

Suddenly, although he had made no sound, no movement, the blue dragon sensed a change in Sinestra. That was verified all too well a moment later, when she snapped, "What is that in there with you?"

"Nnnothing . . ."

"Nothing?"

Dargonax screamed and only because his roar was so loud did Kalec's own cry go unheard. The blue dragon suddenly felt as if molten earth rather than blood now flowed through his veins. It was all that he could do to avoid adding to the other scream. Dargonax roared again, his cry ending in a whimper.

"Do not lie to your *mother*. It hurts me more than you when I must punish you. Show me what you have there, my child. . . ."

"Yesss . . ."

Kalec prepared himself to be tossed up to the lady in black, there to be subject to a fate that would make his recent pain a blessing. Yet, it was not he who flew upward—perhaps raised by Dargonax's paw; he could not tell—but a heavy lump that he had not noticed previous in the dark.

"So . . ." Sinestra said in an almost disappointed tone. "Is that all, then? One of the missing guards. They left them to you."

"Yesss . . ."

"Consider him an appetizer for what is to come. You will be obedient from here on, will you not, my darling son?"

"Yesss . . ."

"Yes *what*?"

Dargonax did not hesitate. "Yes . . . mother . . ."

"Very good, Nefarian. Finally learning . . ."

There was the brief sound of movement away from the pit's edge and then silence. In that silence, Kalec pondered the interesting fact that Sinestra had called Dargonax by her prime son's name. Whether it had been accidental or not, he could not say, but it made him think of something.

It was another minute at least before Dargonax quietly rumbled, "She has left."

"I must get out of here," Kalec immediately responded. "Korialstrasz needs me. . . ."

"He's the other? He is a . . . friend?"

"Yes," the blue replied quickly. "And he could be of great help to you. You want to escape her, don't you? You want to be free of her. It would be best if Korialstrasz is also able to help you."

Dargonax considered this, then replied, "Yes . . . that makes sense . . . it does . . . who is *Nefarian*? You know. I sense that you know. . . ."

So, the twilight dragon had been as quick as Kalec at noting Sinestra's use of the name. "He was also her son, the son of she and her mate, Deathwing. Nefarian was the eldest and most powerful of her children. . . ."

"I would meet Nefarian," the creature murmured. "I would meet my brother. . . ."

"Nefarian is dead." At least, that was as far as Kalec knew. Taking advantage of the mention of Sinestra's murderous offspring, the blue dared add, "He failed her and she abandoned him to his enemies. . . ."

There was silence. Dargonax either did not understand or was digesting the information. The twilight dragon was very, very clever, but perhaps it did not understand all things, being secluded here.

"My brother is dead. All my brothers are dead."

The finality in Dargonax's statement shook Kalec as much as the last part itself did. *Brothers* . . .

"They escaped her. They escaped her just before I was born. We were far, far apart, but we could feel one another, yes, we could feel one another inside."

He was speaking of the two other creatures Deathwing's consort had created, the two whom Kalec shared some responsibility in destroying.

"But they were not like me," Dargonax continued, a slight hint of contempt arising. "They did not think well. They only hungered. They let the hunger think for them. They were foolish and they died foolishly. . . ." The shadowy head leaned a little closer, but still not enough to be distinct. "I will not die foolishly. . . . I will not die . . . and you will help me . . . friend . . ."

"Yes . . . of course, I will—"

Without warning, Dargonax once more spoke in Kalec's head. *I will send you to find our friend. You and he will free me of her. I will not be cast aside. . . .*

Kalec was thrust up into the air much the way the dragonspawn corpse had been tossed. He shot out of the pit and landed on his feet next to the fetid body. No sooner had he landed than he saw the corpse—carried by Dargonax's magic—float back into the pit.

Kalec turned toward the pit—and an invisible force arising from within shoved him toward one of the passages leading away from the chamber. Dargonax's will was incredible and, at the moment, something against which the weary blue could not fight.

She is the other way. You go this one.

With no choice, Kalec obeyed. He wanted to find Korialstrasz, although he feared thinking too much concerning the reasons exactly why. Kalec was not certain how much of his thoughts Dargonax could read or sense. Indeed, he might have already given all his secrets away.

The blue dragon felt a surge of magic rush through him again, his own magic once more there for his use. However, it was not his will that next raised his hand and created his sword.

Go . . .

Gripping the weapon tight, Kalec exited.

SEVENTEEN

Vereesa and the dwarves remained prisoners. They had not given up on their plan of escape; they had simply not been allowed to implement it as the ranger had intended. Even now, even after hours had passed, they all sat ready to move on her signal.

But there was one very large reason why the high elf could not yet move. Now standing guard with the skardyn and the dragonspawn was another drakonid. He was neither Rask nor the one who had taken Udin, but had a similar sharpness of eye that warned Vereesa that he would be more difficult to fool than the dragonspawn. Indeed, he watched the ranger most of all, and the one time that she had started to rise, he had immediately reached for his weapon.

Vereesa had not given up, but she had to wait. With the drakonid as wary as he was, the high elf would not even get to the door, much less open it.

She and Grenda had communicated by glance, the dwarf acknowledging her understanding that everything had to wait, no matter how long. Fortunately, dwarves and high elves could be far more patient than humans.

Then . . . Rask stuck his scaly snout into the chamber. He located the second drakonid and growled, "Come!"

The two vanished a moment later, leaving the anxious dragonspawn back in command. The bulky creature obviously wanted to follow Rask, but had been given no order. It clearly chafed at being kept from something that had to be more exciting than guarding a bunch of prisoners safely secured.

That worked to Vereesa's advantage. She slipped toward Grenda—

Another drakonid entered. The same drakonid responsible for Udin's fate.

"You," he rasped, pointing at the ranger.

Doing her best to keep the tiny blade secreted, she faced the creature.

"The door," the drakonid commanded of the skardyn. Several of the squat fiends rushed up to fend away any heroic dwarves while another unlocked the cell. As the skardyn swung the door open, the drakonid approached. In his other hand, he held a long rope, which he began unwinding.

"Come—"

The tiny blade buried itself in his eye.

The ranger charged into the skardyn before her, bowling them over by sheer surprise more than anything else. Striking their bodies was like striking rock, but she used leverage in her favor.

And behind her poured out the other prisoners.

The first two dwarves perished quickly, pikes in their guts. Their sacrifice helped those behind them, for Grenda and others seized on the pikes and tore them from the grips of their foes. That created a further opening that allowed the rest of the prisoners to flee the cell.

Vereesa paid no mind to the skardyn, the drakonid still her greatest concern. Even as he pulled the blade free of the ruined eye, the ranger fell upon him. With no weapon of her own, she grabbed for the rope.

Still dealing with his awful wound, the drakonid let his grip on the rope slacken. He belatedly tried to grab the high elf by the throat, but Vereesa had already darted to his side.

The dragonspawn came lumbering at the pair. Vereesa looped the rope and before the drakonid could turn to face her, tossed the loop around his throat. She pulled tight.

With a savage croak, the drakonid tried to free himself from the makeshift noose. The ranger tightened her grip on it as she turned to face the dragonspawn.

The four-legged behemoth swung hard at her, its ax chipping away at the ground as it just missed. The ranger used her weight to kick at the guard while at the same time also adding it to the force she was expending on the rope.

There was a terrible cracking sound. Vereesa felt the drakonid grow limp, its neck broken.

But being caught between the two foes now left her at the mercy of the dragonspawn. The bestial warrior snagged her leg and dragged her in closer for the kill.

Still clutching the rope, the high elf tried to use the dead drakonid's weight to keep her from the dragonspawn. Unfortunately, the strength of the latter was so great that both she and the corpse easily slid toward her eager adversary.

Vereesa released her hold. The sudden change in resistance caused the dragonspawn to go stumbling back. The ranger went sliding under the heavy feet as the dragonspawn collided with one of the walls.

She twisted out of what remained of the creature's hold, then rolled under and to the side. The ax came down, but the dragonspawn, still off-balance, missed by a wide margin.

Scrambling away from the behemoth, Vereesa came up behind a skardyn with a pike. Moving with the swiftness of which her race was famed, the ranger ripped the pike from the creature's claws before it knew what was happening, then kicked it into the waiting hands of a pair of dwarves. She spun around just as the dragonspawn closed on her.

The pike thrust into his shoulder, but, thanks to the scale hide, did nothing more than leave a small scar. The dragonspawn tried to chop her weapon into pieces and only by rapid maneuvering did Vereesa keep that from happening. She wished for her bow, certain that she could have planted arrows in both eyes and the throat if given only a few seconds. As it was, the pike was an unfamiliar weapon, one at the moment more suited for humans or sturdy fighters like the dwarves or skardyn.

Around her, the dwarves were pressing their savage cousins. The skardyn had more of the weapons, but they did not have the numbers.

Grenda had seized a whip from one fallen foe and used it now to good effect on those wielding pikes. She would let the whip lash around the weapon's long pole, then use a skilled flick of the wrist to wrench the pikes forward.

However, one skardyn managed to slip behind Grenda. The scaly dwarf raised an ax at her back. . . .

Another figure shoved his way between them.

"Grenda! Beware!" shouted Gragdin. Grenda's brother had no weapon, only his own body. "Bewar—!"

The skardyn eagerly chopped into Gragdin's chest.

Grenda let out a howl of pain that matched her brother's brief one. The female dwarf dropped the whip. She did not grab for Gragdin's blood-soaked body, but rather at the weapon that had done him in. Dwarven rage gave her the strength to tear it from the skardyn's hand, then immediately use it across his throat.

The skardyn's head went rolling away. His body collapsed atop Gragdin's.

With a berserker fury, Grenda cut down two more skardyn nearby. The other dwarves followed her lead, decimating what was left of the guards.

Vereesa, meanwhile, continued her combat against the dragonspawn. The giant swung high, nearly clipping her head. In the process, his weapon finally chopped the pike in two.

But Vereesa immediately leapt for an ax lost by a fallen enemy. Seizing it, the ranger ducked under the drakonid's guard and attacked not the torso, but one foot.

The ax bit through the scaled flesh, severing the toes and part of the front. Blood poured from the wound.

The dragonspawn hissed. It reached down to press the ranger into the rock floor, but again Vereesa wriggled free. She slipped past the guard, ending up near the entrance.

At that moment, a pair of skardyn came rushing into the chamber. They spotted Vereesa, let out hisses, and charged her.

The dragonspawn began to turn. In close quarters, the massive body was more ungainly, especially with the long, thick tail to consider.

Vereesa slapped the tail with the side of the ax.

Her adversary reacted instinctively. The tail swept back and forth, a deadly club to whatever was in its range.

But the high elf had already made certain to avoid being near. The tail instead swatted both approaching skardyn, sending them flying in opposite directions. The savage dwarves crashed against the walls and lay still.

And as the dragonspawn continued to turn, Vereesa leapt onto the back just as Rom had done with an earlier one. The dragonspawn tried to twist its upper torso around enough to reach her, but she moved with it, keeping directly behind.

Jumping up, the ranger planted both arms over the dragonspawn's shoulders. She brought the ax around with one hand and, as best she could, gripped the top with the other.

Summoning as much strength as she could muster, Vereesa jammed the ax blade into the softer tissue of the throat.

The dragonspawn grabbed at her arms, pulling at them with such force that she thought that they would be torn free. The ranger struggled to press the ax deeper. She felt a moisture on the hand holding the top.

Then, the guard managed to tear her free. It threw the high elf over its head. Vereesa tried to guide herself as best she could, relying on her natural nimbleness and ranger training to keep her from breaking her neck or skull.

As she struck, she went into a roll. The roll ended abruptly as she collided with one of the dwarves.

Vereesa dared not take the time to check on the other prisoner, certain as she was that the dragonspawn was coming for her. She located the ax and turned to face her adversary.

Indeed, the guard was lumbering forward, but in a haphazard, almost random manner. Not only was the wound to the one foot causing it to sway, but the entire upper torso was bathed in blood from the wound the ax had made.

Dwarves with pikes suddenly surrounded the dragonspawn. Grenda thrust first, her pike reentering the wounded throat. The dragonspawn slapped the weapon away, only making the rip bigger.

The guard teetered, crashing to one side. A dwarf ran in for the kill.

With a titanic effort, the dragonspawn seized him. Before anyone could do anything, the guard used one thick fist to crush in the dwarf's chest.

Grenda screamed and thrust with the pike again. Her momentum was such that she buried the point deep enough that the tip thrust out of the scaled hide behind.

The dragonspawn waved one bloody hand . . . then died.

Of the guards, only a pair of beaten and bruised skardyn remained. Grenda had them bound and tossed into the cell. That she let them live was no act of charity, to hear her explain it.

"When they're found like that with all the others slain, you can be sure they'll pay for their failure," she said grimly.

The female dwarf went back to the body of her brother. Her other brother, Griggarth, stood at her side, staring at his dead sibling as if not certain that he himself lay there instead.

Grenda touched the forehead and chest once, then her demeanor shifted. "Let's move before more guards arrive. . . ."

There remained one problem with that. Even Vereesa's trained senses could not identify which direction they should head. Grenda thought she knew—dwarves well versed with reading tunnels and judging their ultimate rise or fall—but could not swear in the case of Grim Batol.

"Rom told me that the tunnels here have no rhyme or reason that he could recall. Those that would've made sense one way often suddenly banked, then went the opposite. 'Tis as if a bunch of mad diggers randomly carved it out."

"Probably a bunch o' Dark Irons," snorted Griggarth.

"These tunnels are older than even those bastards," his sister replied.

She touched the corridor floor, studying it. "If these traces read right, I'd say we go left."

"What are you looking at?" the ranger asked, fascinated despite their situation by the dwarf's own tracking abilities.

"The striations, the patterns of the rock and stone, for one. They can sometimes tell you the right direction. There's also tiny bits of dirt and scrapings that these fiends've brought from outside." She grunted. "If there's anythin' we dwarves know, it's rock and dirt."

"Then, we go as you say. Lead on."

Nodding, Grenda guided the weary band. They were armed with everything that they had been able to take from the dead. Vereesa had not accepted any ax or other weapon, preferring those to go into the hands of the ones who best knew how to use them. The only defense she took was the small blade that Rhonin had forged for her.

As Grenda led her people on, Vereesa fell toward the back. She followed on, growing more confident in the female dwarf's sense of direction. Surely, with her at the forefront, the band would reach the outside safely.

And, with that thought in mind, the ranger slowed more. When it was clear that the dwarves were completely focused on the passage ahead, Vereesa suddenly turned. As silent as the night, the high elf vanished down the deeper end of the tunnel.

Somewhere down there, Vereesa was certain, she would find Zendarin. . . .

"Surely, we must reenter Grim Batol this very moment!" Iridi urged the wizard. "Each breath we delay, the others may suffer!"

"You think I don't know that?" Rhonin snapped. He sat with the draenei on an old log, his hands before him. A faintly lit blue glow arose from the ground before both, the wizard's version of a campfire that would not be seen from far away. "My wife's in there, priestess. There are no more important people to me in the entire world than she and my sons. None."

"Then, why do we not just materialize there as you did previous?"

He spat. "I don't know how magic works with draenei in general or you in particular, but that sort of thing takes a lot out of a person, especially as it wasn't my first or even second attempt! I'd been in two other locations there, using this to hunt for her!"

Rhonin held up the talisman that Vereesa had been wearing. Iridi could not sense anything from it, but then, she was not its creator.

He was growing more upset. The priestess berated herself for adding to the pressures on the human. She was showing many failings as a priestess these past few days. The draenei wondered how she could have ever considered herself the one who needed to find the captured nether dragon. Such hubris in the face of her results was laughable.

The pair sat in the wilds of Grim Batol, near an area Rhonin had called Raptor Ridge. The name had shaken a weary Iridi, for she recalled the battle at Menethil Harbor. However, the wizard had assured her that most of the raptors had moved toward the direction of the dwarven settlement.

"They sense what's going on in Grim Batol," he had told her. "That's why they're giving the dwarves so much trouble right now."

He had provided her with simple fare from a pouch on his person, a pouch with incredible depth, it appeared. The red-haired wizard pulled out much more food than should have been able to fit inside, and even after that the pouch had not looked flattened.

"There're some benefits to my calling," Rhonin explained as he and she devoured some unleavened bread and cheese that was actually cool and creamy. "But a lot more burden."

"You have great responsibilities among your kind."

"You mean wizards, the Alliance, or humans? Take your choice; I seem to be bound to all in more ways than I like. The Alliance is still looking to Dalaran for a lot and the wizards are looking for me to think different than they've been doing for the past several hundred years. As for the humans in general . . . I've seen too many die and I want it to end . . . I just want to be with my family. . . ."

But Rhonin would never willingly abandon any of the groups that he had just mentioned. Iridi could sense that. The wizard was much like Krasus, striving to make Azeroth better for all, even though it cost him so much.

Even though, at present, his beloved mate might already be dead.

"You are a being of destiny," the priestess quietly declared. "You will do great things, I know that."

"I haven't even been able to keep my wife and sons safe." He shook his head. "I've fought demons, dragons, orcs, and more, but the scariest part of my life has been trying to be there for those I care about most."

She put a comforting hand on his shoulder. Although Iridi had no close family with which to compare her situation to his, she was empathic enough to understand his trials. "It's often the most frightened of folk who do the greatest deeds."

"You sound like a demigod I once met called Cenarius—" He cut off, suddenly tense.

"What—?"

Rhonin hushed her. His left hand tightened into a fist as he whispered, "I think this should do the trick. It's more startling than it is anything else, but . . ."

The dim blue glow suddenly flashed a thousand times brighter, yet its intense illumination was limited to an area just a dozen or so yards in diameter, with Rhonin and Iridi at the center of that lighted circle.

But in that bright glow, the pair were revealed not to be alone.

More than a dozen tall, reptilian creatures surrounded the vicinity. They were not drakonid, although, like them, they walked on two legs. These were more primitive and more bestial and, to Iridi, the return of a nightmare.

"Raptors . . ." Rhonin breathed.

The brilliant light had stunned the beasts. Several still had their heavy muzzles turned away. More than one hissed. Tails swung back and forth in what was clearly anxiety.

"Stand next to me," the wizard ordered.

Iridi trusted his judgment, although she also prepared to summon the naaru staff. The raptors paced back and forth, slowly adjusting to the glow, which the draenei noticed Rhonin had decreased in intensity.

As she studied them more, Iridi noticed that most of them were scarred and, in some cases, freshly injured. Iridi recalled again the battle at Menethil Harbor.

The raptors continued to pace back and forth. Occasionally, one would call out. The throaty growls had different nuances, depending on the raptor who spoke. Iridi held out her hand to summon the staff, wondering if it would help her understand them.

"There're more out there," Rhonin told her, interrupting the thought.

"More? How many?"

"Difficult to say. Enough, would be my personal taste." He peered around. "They've had a tough time of it with Menethil Harbor, from the looks of it. Dwarves are short, but they pack a lot of muscle and fight in their compact bodies. Even speed and good claws and teeth aren't a match." Rhonin straightened. "Hmm. Looks like the 'chief' is approaching."

From the edge of the light emerged a larger, sleeker raptor with more feathers than the rest. Its body was a bright red with golden and blue stripes running across. It walked with all the confidence of a king . . . or a queen. Iridi could not mark which sex it might be.

The other raptors bent their heads low as they watched their leader progress toward the duo. Several of the reptiles twisted their necks so as to display the more soft, easily torn areas.

"They're marking its dominance over them," the wizard explained.

"Is it male or female?"

"A damned good question."

Iridi waited, but he said nothing more on that subject. What mattered most to both of them was what the lead raptor wanted . . . and whether the two could escape if the entire pack attacked.

"I have some tricks, so don't worry yourself," Rhonin muttered, as if reading her thoughts. "I'm just curious why a bunch of meat-eating lizards would treat us as if we were something bigger and nastier than they are."

The lead raptor paused at just the other side of the glow's source. It peered first at Iridi, then at the wizard.

At last, it growled at Rhonin.

The priestess would have acted, but Rhonin gently tapped her arm with his fingers.

"Our friend here wants to talk. Let's see if we can figure out what it's saying."

The raptor growled again, this time the tones changing. Iridi listened closely and thought she detected no aggression in the sounds.

"I think it seeks peace with you," she suggested to the wizard.

"I had the same notion. Curious concept, speaking peace with a carnivorous monster. Of course, I've experienced odder things."

To her surprise, he took a step toward the raptor. Rhonin kept his gaze directly on the creature's own. As he adjusted his position, he called back to her. "Always look them straight in the eye. There's always a battle for dominance and if you slip, you lessen yourself in their opinion. That's hard to reverse." He chuckled. "Something I learned during a few years as a diplomat . . ."

The human and the raptor continued their staring contest for more than a minute . . . and then the reptile ever so slightly glanced to the side. Rhonin nodded once.

This momentary movement on his part seemed to signal a new point in the confrontation. The raptor dipped its head low, then glanced in a different direction.

Despite the risk of doing so, Rhonin casually glanced the same way.

"It's looking at Grim Batol," he said. "What a surprise."

"Do they want us to go back? Are we supposed to be prisoners to turn over to the blood elf and her?"

"I doubt that." The wizard studied the lead raptor again. "It would be nice if we spoke whatever it was they speak."

Iridi again thought of the staff. "There may be something I can do."

She summoned the naaru's gift. The raptors hissed, but did not otherwise react. Rhonin said nothing as the draenei cautiously pointed the large crystal in the direction of the leader.

"Do you understand what I'm saying?" she asked of the creature.

The raptor growled.

In the priestess's head, a series of images suddenly formed. The raptors on a hunt for food. A sudden uneasiness. Grim Batol's dark outline.

Two fearsome, batlike raptors diving from the sky, clutching the hapless ground folk and taking them up to devour in the air.

Iridi recognized the monsters even despite the different perceptions. She was seeing the twin twilight dragons that she and Krasus had fought, but as the raptors identified them. These images were the best that the staff could translate the reptiles' method of speaking.

"Fascinating!" Rhonin breathed, at the moment sounding much like the dragon mage. It surprised her that he also apparently saw the images, but then the staff continued to reveal new elements to its abilities.

More images. The ground folk—as best a term as the priestess could come up with from the way the raptors described themselves—fled toward the west. The vision of Grim Batol kept returning between the various scenes and the draenei could only assume that the reason had to be the raptors' constant sensing of the evil arising from it, an evil that even they were too afraid to ignore.

There came next the battle at Menethil Harbor. *Battles,* in truth. The raptors had attacked the dwarves in the past, but never in such numbers as they had now. Many packs had joined together . . . the reason for that again an image of a dark Grim Batol.

But the battle to take new and safer lands had not gone well. The dwarves were seen well defending their territory, although at first Iridi was hard-pressed to identify them for what they were. The raptors' vision of the dwarves made them resemble the skardyn, which they knew of also.

There were images of the raptors moving back and forth between the mount and the harbor. The creatures did not stop. First they went one direction, then the other, then back again.

And then *Rhonin's* face appeared among the scenes, but not quite the same Rhonin. He looked slightly fresher, younger—and he was shown facing a green-skinned giant.

"I'll be damned!" the wizard blurted. "That's me around the time the orcs were kicked out. . . ." He pondered that, finally saying, "Some of the raptors must've been near, possibly this very one since it's older—" He cut off as a new and puzzling image played out.

It was still Rhonin and the orc, but now there was also a raptor—and one that indeed did remind the draenei of the leader—involved in the battle. Yet, it was not seeking the wizard's blood, as one might have expected, but rather the orc's.

And then the orc transformed into a skardyn, which, in turn transformed into one of the bat-winged raptors that were the twilight dragons. No matter which foe faced them, the wizard and the raptor fought it side-by-side.

The lead reptile pulled back slightly. The visions ceased.

"What did that all mean?" the draenei quietly asked, watching as the raptors patiently eyed the wizard.

Rhonin took a long time to answer and when he did, it was to verify the priestess's suspicions. "To be honest, I think . . . I think that they want our help. I think they want some sort of alliance, if you can believe that. . . ."

Iridi nodded. If the raptors were as intelligent as they seemed, perhaps the idea was not far from the truth. After all, their lands were very near Grim Batol and she already knew that they had become so desperate that they had launched the attacks on Menethil Harbor. Perhaps they somehow sensed Rhonin's power—even seen him materialize with her—and instinctively looked to him as a possible savior.

Whatever the truth, Rhonin looked willing to believe in his version so much that he stepped toward the lead raptor. The huge creature lowered its head again, as if not wanting to do anything that would offend the human.

The wizard stepped within biting range. With continued calm, he stretched out his hand. "Come on, my friend," Rhonin murmured, "Come on. . . ."

The reptile sniffed it, the jaws large enough to snap off Rhonin's entire arm keeping respectfully shut. The great nostrils ran along the length of the hand and even the arm, in some cases leaving traces of mucus that the human patently ignored.

Then, the lead raptor stepped back and let out an odd, barking sound to the other assembled creatures.

As one, the assembled creatures lowered their heads nearly to the ground . . . and then turned their baleful gazes to Grim Batol.

Rhonin chuckled darkly. He looked back at Iridi. "It appears we have a ready-made army," the wizard commented with a twinkle in his eye. "I wonder how best we can use it."

EIGHTEEN

Vereesa wound her way from one passage to the next, aware that she descended deeper and deeper into the mount without yet any sign to show that her quarry was near. She had thought that she would find some trace leading to Zendarin, but instead the passages through which she journeyed seemed more and more unused, and when the ranger attempted to navigate back from one, she only ended up in yet another unfamiliar tunnel.

Sometimes it is as if Grim Batol itself is alive and toying with all of us, good and evil, Vereesa thought. She knew of legends of such places, areas said to have intelligences of their own, often because they had been repositories for great magic. Certainly, that qualified Grim Batol. There were few places in Azeroth so drenched in such energies for so long.

Determined to find her way, the high elf began using the tiny blade to leave small marks in the walls that she would recognize. Each time she turned a corner, Vereesa also made certain to mark which side was on her right. In this way, the ranger was certain that she would not remain lost.

But when one passage abruptly ended—forcing her to turn back— Vereesa was unable to locate her marks. She stepped back, reaffirmed what direction she should head, and stubbornly pushed on.

However, Vereesa soon saw nothing she recognized and, worse, an attempt to return proved just as vexing as before.

Then, somewhere in the distance, the ranger heard what sounded like skardyn. While at one point she would have kept from their presence, now the high elf saw them as her best hope of not only locating her cousin, but finding out just where she was in general.

The hissing, growling voices seemed to move away from her. Even when she picked up her pace, Vereesa could not get any closer. More worrisome, her path continued to descend far more than she had originally desired. She had no notion as to what lurked in the lowest depths of Grim Batol and, at the moment, had no interest in finding out unless Zendarin proved to be there, also . . . which she doubted.

For the most part, Vereesa had been relying on both her eyesight and the small gems that lined the walls every now and then to guide her way. That they had been set by some hand was obvious and that had kept her concern from growing too great, for clearly she was still in passages used by the current or former inhabitants.

Indeed, in one small chamber, she had even found the remains of a troll, likely one who had served here at the time of the orcs' occupation. The cool underground had kept the body fairly intact, so much so that she could still see some of the tattoos on his long, lanky body. The pointed face was stretched into a death's-head grin. There were even a small ax and a dagger, both of which were in a usable state and thus claimed quickly by the high elf.

Yet, as she abandoned the corpse to its endless sleep, it bothered Vereesa that she had found no mark that explained why the troll had perished. Other than being amazingly thin, he had looked almost alive.

Had the troll lost his way here and starved to death so near and yet so far from his comrades? That hardly boded well for the ranger.

Still, with the hand ax and the dagger, Vereesa at least felt better prepared for any foe that she did come up against. She also continued trying to mark her way.

Then, the path she was on grew less and less illuminated until she finally turned into a passage utterly devoid of any of the glowing crystals. Frustration growing, Vereesa retreated to the previous tunnel and went on until she found another.

That, too, was unlit.

Twice more, she paced down some length of the lit passage, only to find side tunnels filled with darkness. Now she was certain that either some entity—Zendarin, perhaps—or even the mount itself was toying with her.

She paused before another black tunnel, debating her choices. Seemingly trapped into entering one or another, the ranger simply stepped into the one she faced—

From within its depths, the ranger heard a faint voice.

What it had said, Vereesa could not tell. It had sounded pained and weary.

Despite the likelihood that it was a trap, the high elf picked up her pace. She listened carefully as she moved, but did not hear the voice repeat. That it might have been a figment of her own tired mind, Vereesa could not deny. However, now that she was committed, she had no intention of turning back. Wielding the ax in one hand and the dagger in the other, the ranger pushed through the darkness.

With each step, she felt herself descend deeper and deeper. Her grip on the weapons tightened. Ahead, she thought she detected a slight illumination. . . .

Sure enough, what started as just a faint haze began to fill the passage the more she headed toward it. Vereesa was finally able to make out details in the walls, details that indicated that this passage had been far more crudely carved out than those above. That in itself bespoke of its ancient construction and the likelihood that most of those above did not know of its existence.

But then . . . to whom did the voice she believed that she had heard belong?

The high elf slowed. Ahead radiated a low, red glow . . . as if a chamber lay just a bit further beyond. Her jaw tightening, the ranger very cautiously approached.

She suddenly noticed that the closer she got, the cooler it became. Much cooler than it should have warranted. In fact, in Grim Batol, she would have expected such a chamber to emanate *heat*, not cold.

Despite how far she had come, Vereesa debated turning around. Yet, something would not let her.

Crouching, the high elf peered inside.

Her eyes widened.

She stared into a huge chamber that was both fire and ice. The former was from where the crimson glow originated, vast pools of molten lava constantly bubbling. The smell of sulfur suddenly filled her nostrils. There were more than a dozen such pools that the ranger could see, from those as tiny as her hand to others wide enough to have engulfed her and the dwarves without the surface hardly shifting.

The chamber should have been so boiling hot that sweat should have already covered Vereesa. Yet, it was actually so cool that she could just see her breath.

The explanation for that came from above. There, massive daggers of ice thrust down from the ceiling. Yet, they were not by any stretch of the imagination of natural origin. As Vereesa moved farther into the chamber, she saw how absolutely white they were inside and even felt the coolness pulsating against her skin.

And then the "why" for this magical arrangement became obvious. The high elf spotted one, then another, then another . . . and realized that every rounded mound she saw was the exact same thing.

There were eggs everywhere. Eggs so large that they had to come from only one creature.

A dragon.

Vereesa approached the nearest. At first she thought that the egg was cracked, for what she could see of it was covered in some sticky coating that reminded her of part of a yolk. However, as she studied it closer, she saw that the egg was not broken. The odd resin simply covered it completely.

Probing the substance with the dagger, the high elf had her answer. *Myatis.* Her people had used the magical coating to preserve sacred relics and rare living things like seeds. Someone had decided to use it for a more ingenious purpose; keeping these eggs from rotting.

But while the myatis coating was excellent for preservation, Vereesa understood now the constant battle between heat and cold in the chamber. It was not enough to preserve the eggs; sticking her finger into the coating, she determined that they were just the perfect temperature to guarantee the life within stayed absolutely viable.

And then Vereesa noticed just how many eggs had been arranged in such a perfect balance. Not a handful. Not dozens.

Hundreds. So many hundreds that she could only imagine that they had been gathered over centuries . . .

The high elf spun around. It had gone unnoticed by her at first because the myatis coating tended to make everything look gray, but not all the eggs were of the same type. It was not simply a matter of some difference in shape or even size, but also color and patterning.

By the Sunwell! These are not just the eggs of a black dragon. . . . They are surely those of reds and others, too. . . .

Vereesa could not believe what she beheld. When she and Rhonin had helped aid the queen of the red flight to escape from the Horde, there had been ample opportunity to see pieces of that flight's broken egg shells. Afterward, her husband, constantly seeking to keep himself educated in all magical matters, had shown her egg fragments from other flights, including those of the black. Certainly, eggs of Deathwing's kind dominated the chamber, but there were many akin to the red and those that looked like neither had to have been stolen from the blue flight and others.

"Centuries . . ." she whispered to herself. "Yes, it must have taken centuries. . . ."

Then, something odd about the eggs made the ranger peer closer at a couple. They looked strangely swollen and there were tiny pustules all over the shells.

Whatever these eggs had once held, they no longer held the innocent young of dragons.

A shiver suddenly overtook her, a shiver that had nothing to do with the fierce, magical stalactites. She knew well Deathwing's desire for a new, more terrible dragonflight and how his children had carried that foul legacy on. But all the while Nefarian and Onyxia had been delving into their own plots concerning that flight's creation, someone else had been patiently and methodically collecting all these different eggs—no doubt often by deceit—for the time when it would be absolutely certain that the chances of successfully creating the monstrous dragons desired were almost perfect.

And with so many eggs, there would be more than enough of the abominations to sweep over every last bit of defiance Azeroth's natural creatures might muster.

The horrific images filling her head were suddenly swept away by the sound of movement from farther in the great chamber. Ax held ready, the ranger moved toward the direction from which she thought the brief sound originated.

But as she neared, all Vereesa saw was yet another of the bubbling pools. This one was so vast that a sailing ship could have been set down in the middle of it, although from there it could not have gone very far. The high elf studied the edges of the pools, searching for anyone who might be near. Despite the constant bubbling, she was certain that it had not been that noise that she had mistaken for much more.

From the center of the pool burst forth a huge, monstrous head. The heat of the molten lava colored it a bright, burning orange. It opened its reptilian maw—

"Ve-Vereesa?" it rasped.

With a groan, the giant rolled toward her end of the pool. The ranger stumbled back as several tons of steaming dragon fell free of the lava and onto the ground before her. She continued to retreat, stunned by the massive girth of the beast. Rarely had she seen a dragon so huge save the queen of the red flight or Krasus in his true form of Korialstrasz—

Korialstrasz?

The steaming leviathan continued to collapse in her direction. The ranger turned and ran, realizing that the dragon was even larger than she had first calculated.

His shadow loomed over her. Vereesa knew that she was not running fast enough. She braced herself for the inevitable—

But Korialstrasz did not fall upon her. Indeed, the massive crash she expected did not happen, instead only a slight thud behind her marking the end to the dragon's fall.

The high elf dared look back.

Steam still rising, Krasus the mage lay sprawled at the edge of the pool. His generally-pale complexion was, for a moment, bright red and his body was clearly burning an imprint into the stone floor. Curiously, his cowled robes were untouched . . . but then, they were a false image, the results of the dragon's conjurations and thus far more durable than any true garment.

Getting over her shock, she ran to his side. Fortunately, despite his still appearance, Krasus breathed.

However, she could not wake him. Not certain what else to do, Vereesa tested to see how warm his body was. While still far more than was normal, she could at least touch him without fear of burning.

Lifting the slumped figure as carefully as she could, the ranger pulled him over to one side, where the floor of the cavern rose up. There she set him in a sitting position and pondered what to do next.

Krasus saved her that trouble by at last opening his eyes.

"V-Vereesa of the high elves," he managed. "You were not one of those I expected—" The dragon mage went into a coughing fit. He looked older, more emaciated. "—but it is good to see you, albeit not so good to see you here."

"I should have expected to find you, though," the ranger returned. "With so much evil at hand, who would come to see to its end but you?"

"You—you and Rhonin—have done more than your sh-share, young one." He waved off her protest. "Be-besides, that is neither here . . . - neither here nor there." His eyes narrowed. "Do you know what is going on in Grim Batol?"

"Just enough to be confused, great one." As he winced from pain again, she eyed him in renewed concern. "Krasus . . . what ails you?"

"I have been to a place of a hellish kind I hope never to suffer again. I barely managed to escape, but in doing so nearly tore myself apart.

I was cast back from limbo into the very mountain itself . . . the very *rock* of the mountain . . ."

He quickly described for her as best he could the awful moment when, escaping a magical trap, he was randomly thrust by its unleashed forces into a part of Grim Batol. His body and the foundation of the mount became part of the same. Only the dragon's incredible magic and powerful will kept him from becoming forever entombed.

"It was all that I could do to thrust myself into the nearest chamber. I burst through, still in my true form, and crawled without care from one cavern to the next. I needed heat to revive my body, incredible heat. Yet, the only source that I could sense close enough to reach felt like so little. However, I had no choice. I went there, forcing the change to this body when the tunnels proved too narrow. . . ."

He had not even paid any attention to what lay all around him, his suffering mind only knowing that, despite the heat seeming so little, there were pools of molten lava within sight. Dragons were not, by nature, generally found diving into lava and, had he stayed in much longer, he would have eventually burned to death. However, it said something for the critical state of his life that this was the only way that he could quickly recuperate. Aided by what magic he could muster, the incredible heat revived him far swifter than normal means could have.

"But the trick is to know when to escape the pool. I was originally so undone that I nearly overstayed. I had thrust up twice to call as secretly as I could to any who knew me as friend, for I knew that I would unfortunately need help yet. I expected another, either one of the dwarves or a draenei—"

"Iridi?"

His brow arched. "Ah? You have met. Yes. She seeks not one impossible quest, but two. She hopes to either free or destroy a nether dragon—"

"Yes . . . and also take from a blood elf a staff that he stole from a friend's murdered corpse." Vereesa's expression turned cold despite the nearby pool. "But Zendarin is mine and no one else's. . . ."

He studied her face in concern. "A personal quest, a personal feud. I will not ask you why, but remind you of the folly of such."

"You are hardly one to judge that," the ranger curtly replied, standing. She glanced around at the monstrous display. "And what do you make of this? Is this left over from Deathwing or his children?"

"No . . . this is the obsession of the mother of Nefarian and Onyxia, an obsession whose depth I have only just begun to appreciate . . . and fear. How long she must have collected these eggs, collected them and then corrupted each—no doubt with the aid of the accursed, still malevolent Demon Soul—for her own foul desires! And how—and how much effort she must have gone through—to move them here to Grim Batol after my own kind had abandoned their guarding of it."

"You think she and this were not here already?"

"She—she could not have been here, done all this evil, and not be noticed by those keeping sentinel. No, Sinestra has only recently come to this forlorn place, but she has—has settled in very, very, well!"

He did his best to push himself up. Vereesa quickly aided him when it became clear that he was about to drop again. "Thank—thank you. I am growing stronger by the moment, though I hope never to go through that again. That is more the way of the Earth-Warder, Deathwing's lot. But fire in any form is a valued part of life and that enabled me to do what I did." The dragon mage scowled at the many eggs. "And, as a servant of life, this hideous mockery of it—" Krasus gestured at one of the swollen eggs. "—fills me with such rage that I could destroy this chamber and all in it with little regard for my own destruction!"

Vereesa looked aghast, fearing that he would follow through on his dire notion. She saw herself perishing with him, leaving her children and Rhonin without her and Zendarin able to go hunting the twins at his leisure. Much as she, too, thought that this cavern deserved razing, she was selfish enough to want to at least protect her family first.

But Krasus shook his head. "No, that I cannot do just yet. That would leave Sinestra to still plot. She has the nether dragon at her mercy and one abomination already born. She may find another blue or red dragon—magic and life—to further her creation's horrific powers—"

"Why would she even need to do that? She has eggs from your flight and likely ones stolen over the generations from even the blues, rare as they are. She could raise her own."

"The raising would require more trouble, and she would need a mature adult, well into their power for years, to even hope to achieve what she desires. Sinestra has patience, but not in all things. Besides, there have been many generations in which she herself has had to hide as much as plot." He smiled slightly as something else became apparent. "And there are few enough eggs of the other flights. They would be more valuable to her than her own . . . which is surely what all these black flight eggs are."

"All from one dragon alone?"

"It looks like so many, but these have been salvaged over many centuries. . . ." He shook his head. "The tremendous range of years Deathwing and his blood use for some of their plots ever amazes me. . . ."

Vereesa shivered. "Do we destroy them one by one, then? The two of us together—"

"Would take far too long. I am still weak, young one, and I think I know why. . . ." Krasus gestured further into the bizarre cavern. "And if I am correct, we need to go that way *now*."

Wondering what could be of such greater importance to the dragon mage, Vereesa aided him in heading in the direction indicated. As they left the vicinity of the eggs, the heat from the pools began to take over, so much so that it grew harder for the high elf to breathe.

The area also took on a more crimson cast, the pools now the only source of light. While she had usually trusted Krasus in the past, the ranger began to wonder if he actually knew where he was going.

The cowled figure suddenly groaned. "Yes . . ." he gasped. "We are very close."

"Close to what?"

But Krasus did not clarify, instead peering at something ahead. Even with the eyes of a high elf, Vereesa could not see what it was until several more unsteady steps.

The glow was barely perceptible at first, only a slight, golden glimmer. It emanated from a chamber whose entrance was a crack that, when finally reached by the pair, had to be entered one at a time and sideways.

Krasus hesitated. "I will go first . . . but I need you to follow quickly after. I do not know how well I will be able to withstand what is in there."

"What is it?"

He looked back at her as he began to slip through. "One of my nightmares . . ."

And with that, the dragon mage vanished into the chamber. Aware that Krasus was not one to overstate a situation, the ranger immediately followed after. She pressed her back against the rock and slid from the previous cavern, wondering what she would find.

"It is as I suspected and feared," Krasus whispered, staring at what lay ahead. "And it made only too much sense, especially with *her.*"

Even as he spoke, Krasus started to lose his legs. Vereesa quickly leapt to his side and helped him right himself.

The dragon mage swore with a vehemence the ranger had never before heard from him. She could see the bitterness in his face, a bitterness focused in great part, Vereesa knew, at himself.

Her gaze turned to a small platform carved from the very stone of which the mount was composed. Set atop it was the source of the glow . . . a horrific artifact that she recognized despite its odd state.

"One shard I had," Krasus rasped. "Another tiny one I found. Of the rest, I saw nothing and feared nothing of . . . but only she could resurrect even this much of that abomination . . . only Deathwing's consort could even dream of trying to recreate any aspect of the *Demon Soul.* . . ."

NINETEEN

Grenda did not notice Vereesa's disappearance until well into the trek to freedom. When she did, the dwarf debated calling for a halt, then decided against it. The ranger had made her own choice; Grenda had to concern herself with her own people's well-being.

This did not mean that she only intended to lead them out of Grim Batol. After all, the Bronzebeards had come to the mount on a mission. Grenda sought an exit, yes, but she was also on a lookout for anything relating to the goings on in the dire place.

And, at last she found just that. The chamber was huge and in it was a sight both fearsome and striking.

The great beast bound by magical strands could only be the cause of the great roars of anguish that the Bronzebeards had heard on and off over the recent days. It was like no dragon that she had seen and appeared more apparition than substance.

"What're they doin' with that thing?" muttered one dwarf near her.

"Something foul," remarked another.

Grenda shushed them both. As concerned as she was about the imprisoned beast and the purpose for that situation, the female dwarf also needed to study the chamber's layout.

The first things she noticed were the five skardyn taking care of various tasks in the vicinity of the dragon. They seemed greatly engrossed in their efforts, almost as if their lives depended upon it. After the dragon and them, the next point of interest to her was a long ridge running along the side of the cavern, one that she saw led to another passage that, to her best estimation, had to lead to some exit.

Grenda came to a decision. First and foremost, she needed to get the band outside. They had some weapons, true, but mostly pikes and whips, not their favored axes or short swords. They were also worn and beaten. Better to escape, then send word to the king of what they had discovered. They had gathered enough information that those with sharper minds would likely be able to put two and two together and come up with the complete picture.

"We go for that passage," she ordered the others. There was no disagreement; Grenda was their leader now and her commands would be followed as if she were Rom.

Rom. She wondered what had happened to him, where his body lay. They would probably have to pass near where the others had perished; perhaps among them she might discover his corpse.

If there's any way to bring you back for burial, I'll do it, she swore to his shade. Although Grenda could not even admit it to herself, she had fallen in love with the veteran fighter. It had started as admiration for his deeds and reputation, turned to respect as she had followed him on this mission, and became much more the longer she had been around him and learned of the dwarf behind the legend.

Grenda gritted her teeth. With only five skardyn about and none of them near the ridge, it was time for action, not regrets. She waved two of the others up to her.

"On my mark, you move as quickly as you can to the other side. Keep low, keep running."

They nodded, then braced themselves for her signal. Grenda glanced from one skardyn to another, watching where their attention lay.

"Go now!"

The two warriors scurried forth. Grenda watched with anxiousness as the pair wended their way along the ridge. The two made it a quarter of the way, then half, then two-thirds . . . and, at last, to the other side.

By that time, she already had two more ready. As soon as the first two were nearly across, the dwarven commander sent them.

In sets of two, her band crossed, but much too slowly for Grenda. Each second, she waited for one of the skardyn to look up, but they never did. Where all the others were, Grenda did not know. She wondered whether they were hunting the high elf or the draenei, who no one had seen in almost as long a time as they had Rom.

As she thought of the others, Grenda sent two more of her people on. However, they had barely gotten a third of the way when the escapees were finally noticed . . . but not by those below.

The skardyn who sounded the alarm had crawled out of one of the openings well above, one which no Bronzebeard would have been able to use. The scaly creature climbed along the high cavern wall like a spider. It had quickly seen the two fighters racing along and had opened its mouth to let out a guttural shriek that sounded as if from the grave.

The other skardyn immediately turned to stop the escapees. Worse, others began pouring out of holes everywhere, no longer reminding Grenda of spiders but a legion of poisonous ants.

"Everyone across! Now!"

The rest raced forward, Grenda taking rear guard. She wielded one of the pikes, which now felt highly ungainly as she sought to reach the other passage. The dwarf took some solace in the fact that most of the skardyn would not be able to reach the ridge before the party left the cavern. There was also the benefit that neither the whips nor the pikes would be of any use until that moment—

A small object whistled past her head. At the same time, one of those just before Grenda let out a cry and toppled off the ridge to the floor far below. Grenda could see that he was already dead long before his body hit.

She glanced at the wall next to her, where the object had struck and stuck. It was a tiny stone ball with spikes at least two inches in length. Grenda knew the material from which it had been carved and understood immediately how deadly it was even for a dwarven skull.

Another of her people let out a howl and fell. This time, though, the body lay sprawled on the ridge, blocking the path.

There was no time for niceties. "Shove her off!" Grenda shouted. "Do it!"

The dwarf next to the body knelt to do just that—and another spiked ball caught him in the throat. He fell into the corpse and both slipped from the ridge.

The skardyn were using a device that looked almost like a tiny crossbow. Grenda recognized the weapon from historical records. The *dwyar'hun*—the name literally meant "star bow" in the older dialect, the spiked ball being the "star"—had been used by Bronzebeards long ago, too, but had eventually been discarded. The skardyn still apparently favored this weapon, though.

The one disadvantage to the dwyar'hun was that, while the skardyn could apparently cock it using one hand and their teeth—a necessity when one was clinging to a cavern wall—only one ball could be loaded at a time and that slowly, as it required manipulation by the same hand. Indeed, the salvo that had slain three of her number was all but over and the dwarves now had at least some breathing space before the next possible shot.

But that momentary respite was quickly shattered as those at the other passage began piling together instead of moving on. The reason for that was soon evident; another group of skardyn had come from elsewhere to block the path. More adept with their particular weapons, they were forcing the escaped prisoners back to the cavern . . . and certain doom.

However, the Bronzebeards would not go down easily. They used the pikes and whips as best they could and managed some well-struck blows themselves. Grenda's remaining brother used his pike to shove one climbing skardyn down atop another, sending both to the rock floor far below. Another dwarf, this one armed with a whip, caught a skardyn above as it crawled from a nearby hole. The lash circled one arm enough so that when the dwarf pulled, his target lost hold.

Unfortunately, the Bronzebeards still could not break through. Grenda looked back, wondering if the rest should retreat.

Skardyn burst out of the other passage. The dwarves were trapped between them on a narrow ridge where, one way or another, they would be picked off until they either surrendered or perished.

And then, to the utter surprise of everyone—but especially the skardyn—a new menace materialized near the captured dragon, a menace of the likes Grenda could only imagine out of her nightmares.

A raptor . . . *raptors* . . .

Grenda counted two, then three, then four or more. She could swear that they literally popped into existence, for what else would explain their sudden, impossible presence in here of all places.

The raptors faced away from the dragon, striking at the nearest skardyn with wild abandon. Caught off-guard, the nearest skardyn perished in a quick ripping of flesh.

And as the reptiles turned the battle to utter chaos, a more familiar figure appeared near the bound leviathan: Iridi, the draenei, but not alone. With her was a human who bore the look of a wizard, a human with thick, red hair.

Grenda knew of only one wizard with red hair and although there might be more, she had to assume that there was only one daring— perhaps foolhardy—enough to leap into Grim Batol. Rom had told her the stories of the human, and the ranger had mentioned him, too, albeit in a much more intimate manner.

Rhonin Dragonheart had come to their rescue.

But that was not quite the case, Grenda thought the next second. First, he could not have known that they would be here at this moment. In Grim Batol, yes, but not here. Indeed, both he and the priestess looked far more concerned with the unsettling dragon than anyone else. Iridi was working feverishly at one of the crystals that marked each end of the strands holding the massive prisoner in place. The female dwarf understood that they were trying to *release* the behemoth.

She thought them both insane, but had to assume that they knew something that she did not. What mattered more to her, though, was the sudden turn of events. With the skardyn now forced to take on not one but two zealous foes—and a wizard besides—she had hopes for her people's survival.

Then, from one of the lower passages, half a dozen dragonspawn led by a drakonid charged toward Iridi and Rhonin. A raptor materialized next to one of the dragonspawn and immediately attacked. Grenda noticed that Rhonin had gestured at the same time. He looked determined, but weary, and she knew that he had already spent himself much to create this fantastic scenario.

Two more of the raptors turned to attack the newcomers. A dragonspawn with an ax cut down the first, but then the second closed with the four-legged giant.

A heavy figure suddenly dropped down on the female dwarf. Captivated by the events below, Grenda had forgotten to watch her own back. The skardyn pressed down on her, trying to push the dwarven commander off the ledge.

Grenda twisted, managing to turn on her back. The monstrous countenance of the degenerated Dark Iron loomed inches from her own face. The sharp teeth tried to snap at her nose.

"You—are—one filthy—beast!" she snapped. Her left arm collapsed, as if weak. The skardyn—it was impossible to tell whether the scaly thing was male or female—hissed in anticipation, a hiss that ended in a choking sound as the skilled Bronzebeard warrior slipped her left hand under its guard, formed a strong edge with the fingers, and jammed them into his squat, short throat.

The skardyn pulled back as it tried to breathe. Grenda used her body to shove the gasping fiend off both her and the ridge.

She rose to find her comrades holding their own. Below, the raptors and Rhonin kept the other guards at bay, but Iridi appeared to be having difficulty with what she was attempting. At the very least, it seemed to Grenda that the draenei was no further along than she had been moments before.

Suddenly, thunder shook the cavern, thunder so powerful that it sent skardyn plummeting from the walls and dwarves from the ledge. Grenda had never heard such thunder and was amazed that it could be felt so deep within Grim Batol.

But then the dwarf realized why she had never heard such thunder . . . because it was *not* thunder at all.

It was a roar.

The time has come, Zendarin Windrunner had decided but minutes before. *This is no longer worth my efforts. . . .*

He had always known his partner in this affair was mad, but apparently madness was commonplace when it came to anything revolving around this accursed lump of dirt called Grim Batol. He himself must have been mad to have ever accepted her offer to reveal to him new sources of magical energy in exchange for his assistance with her spells. Their creation would have given him access to more magic than a thousand blood elves could gather in their not inconsiderable lifetimes . . . magic and dominance.

But now was the moment to begin what he had intended all along. The thing in the pit had grown rapidly; it was surely near its full potential.

All Zendarin had to do was give it that final push . . . and at the same time seal his *own* mastery over it.

He stepped to the pit. Although he gazed hard, their creation was still difficult to make out. The creature radiated a unique, fascinating energy that the blood elf hungered badly for, but that was a feast for a better time. Now . . . now he had to be the one to do the giving.

Through the cerulean cube in the other chamber, the nether dragon was ever bound to the thing here. However, the link had to be purposely opened, generally by Zendarin and the dark lady together. Zendarin had always indicated that the staff he had stolen could do no more than it had in that regard.

Naturally, he had lied.

The staff was fascinating. He had tricked the draenei into revealing the secrets of its use while in another guise. He had discovered how to make the staff work for him and him alone so that no one could think to take it from him in turn. If *she* had tried, the staff would have returned to its creators, the beings called the naaru. That was what should have happened when he had slain the draenei, if not for the fact that he had learned the secret of transfer, a secret even she could not peel from his mind.

That was perhaps the greatest reason why she had never actually followed through with her threats against him. Despite all her hubris, Zendarin knew that he had still been an essential element of the spell-work.

But where she desired domination over all, he would be satisfied with domination over some and the satiation of his eternal hunger. Zendarin leaned over the edge more and pointed the crystal at where he best estimated the bulk of the creature—Dargonax, she had so grandiosely called it—and concentrated.

The staff's astounding energy flowed into the pit. As it struck, it outlined for the first time Dargonax's full glory.

Zendarin gasped and almost lost his focus. It was far more huge and powerful than he had thought! Surely even she did not comprehend the full scope of what they had wrought.

And that only made the blood elf grin more eagerly. As he fed the staff's power into the beast, he also used it to awaken the cube, awaken it and demand that it take from the imprisoned dragon all that it could and feed that also into Dargonax.

As both magical streams poured into the essence of the creature, it suddenly let loose with a tremendous roar that shook Grim Batol. However, caught up in his lust for the greater magic with which he believed his betrayal would reward him, the blood elf only laughed. He was master of the situation now.

He was master of *everything*. . . .

But as Zendarin continued with his traitorous act, he did not notice a shadow that separated from others in the chamber.

Sinestra watched the blood elf commit to his betrayal. She smiled in satisfaction as he worked to take all that she had set into place as his own. When Sinestra was certain that there would be no going back for Zendarin, she sank into the shadows again and vanished.

All was going just as Deathwing's consort had planned, all save for the question of Korialstrasz.

But that was a problem easily remedied. . . .

There was another who heard the roar and feared what it meant, especially as the voice in his head was no longer there. Kalec sought hard for Dargonax's presence, but not because he desired the creature to stay with him. Rather, now that it appeared that he was free, the blue had his own interests with which to deal. They did not directly deal with the missing Korialstrasz, but if Kalec ran across the red, he would by no means avoid him.

Kalec still had reservations concerning the other dragon. He did not trust many of Korialstrasz's choices, although he did have to admit that the red was more than willing to put his own life on the line for those choices. That was something that he had not so much believed until this point. Kalec had always thought Korialstrasz more of a manipulator, in some ways as callous as even Deathwing.

No . . . he's no Deathwing, the blue thought with some shame. *But neither is he me. . . .* Kalec would have never risked his friends or loved ones. Never.

He followed a trail that he did not understand. It was not the one he had begun under Dargonax's guidance. Rather, the blue felt as if someone had called to him, someone who suddenly had ceased doing so. Yet, Kalec did not feel that he could ignore it.

Lower and lower he descended. He was near, very near, to *something.*

What he thought a movement in the shadowed recesses of the passage caught his gaze. The blue cautiously turned toward it.

A blue glow sphere burst from his empty hand. In its light, the younger dragon saw nothing but rock wall.

Cursing his own anxiety, Kalec continued on. He hoped that soon he would find whatever it was he was meant to find.

Then, a golden glow radiated from some point far ahead. Kalec gripped the magic blade tight. As he moved closer, he saw that there was some chamber there.

The golden glow brought back memories he had tried to keep down. Anveena's face appeared before him, both beautiful and innocent. She had touched him as no other had or ever could . . . and now she was gone.

His earlier ire at the red dragon burned anew. It was Korialstrasz—in the guise of the wizard Borel—who had caused Anveena such grief. It was the red's fault that Kalec had lost her forever. It was—

He stepped into the chamber . . . and saw Korialstrasz as the mage Krasus being guided by a high elf toward a strange broken crystal.

Rage overwhelming him, Kalec let out a roar and charged the red.

Both Korialstrasz and the high elf looked his way. The high elf— a ranger—released the dragon mage and moved to block Kalec from him.

The blue had no quarrel with her. She was clearly another of Korialstrasz's dupes, likely thinking his guise as Krasus made him a trusted friend, not an insidious, uncaring plotter. Kalec gestured and, despite some sudden, unsettling weakness that he blamed on his counterpart, his spell sent the high elf flying to one of the walls, where the rock sealed around her wrists and ankles. There she would keep until he had dealt with his foe.

"Kalec!" Korialstrasz started. "You live! I thought—" The blue's rage suddenly registered with him. "Kalec, listen to me! There is something wrong with you—"

But Kalec was aware of the danger of letting the cunning red's words infiltrate his mind. Gritting his teeth, he swung at the cowled figure.

However, his blade was met by a fiery orange-red sword that sprouted from his foe's hand just as Kalec's had. Kalec had taught Krasus the spell during a quiet moment on the journey and the irony of that was not now lost on the red. The two shared one stinging blow after another, most of the offensive ones on the blue's side. Yet, not for a minute did Kalec think Korialstrasz's hesitation against attacking in turn anything more than a ploy. He had to strike down the older red before the latter could put whatever trick he had into motion.

"Kalec! You are not thinking for yourself! Another is doing that for you! Gaze upon the foul artifact near us and understand the reason!"

Despite himself, the blue dragon did glance for just a single breath at that which Korialstrasz had mentioned. For the first time, he saw the oddly-cracked, glowing sphere. Shards of it were missing here and there, yet, some force held it together.

Moreover, that same force seemed to also be the source of a strange pulsation. As Kalec's and Korialstrasz's magic-wrought swords clashed again—sending off showers of energy—the pulsations magnified.

But although he saw that there was likely a link between the actions, Kalec assumed that they could only be from one source . . . the cowled figure before him.

"A master of trickery as usual!" he growled. "But not a master of magic . . ."

Kalec's blade, about to meet the other yet again, suddenly curled around as if a tentacle. It wrapped around Korialstrasz's arm and burned bright.

With a cry, the red dragon released his own weapon, which faded to nothing.

The younger dragon tugged hard, pulling Korialstrasz toward him. In his other hand, a second weapon formed.

But the rock beneath Kalec's feet chose that moment to sprout life in the form of great vines that burst through cracks to tangle his feet. He managed to slice some, but in the end lost his balance.

Both opponents tumbled to the floor. Korialstrasz grabbed the younger dragon's arm. "Hear me! We are being manipulated! Sinestra has drawn us together into the very place she intended we end up! Do you not feel yourself getting weaker yet? Do you not recall the tales of my people's sufferings when they chose to stand guard over Grim

Batol? The very reason for that hovers near us, a reborn and redesigned monstrosity that surely still earns the title *Demon Soul*!"

A part of Kalec registered what the other dragon said, but it was not a great enough part to overcome the intense fury and mistrust he felt for Korialstrasz. "Spare me your lies! This is just as likely your devious trap as it is that witch's!"

With each passing moment, Kalec's strength waned more, but his unchecked anger kept him fighting. He would not give in to Korialstrasz! He would not!

The blue dragon focused all his magic on one spell. He did not seek to conjure any intricate attack, but merely wanted to make certain that when it hit Korialstrasz, there would be no doubt as to the outcome.

The cowled figure's pale visage distorted in clear recognition of what his younger foe intended. Korialstrasz's dismay further fueled Kalec's pleasure. In the blue's mind, Anveena's face smiled at his impending triumph.

Kalec smiled back at her, all the while ignoring Korialstrasz's entreaties.

"For you, Anveena . . ." he whispered.

The blue dragon unleashed *everything*.

Grim Batol shook again. Dwarves, skardyn, drakonid . . . *all* were tossed about as if tiny toys.

The pain! Zzeraku suddenly roared in the draenei's head. *The pain! It tears me apart!*

"What happens?" Iridi shouted out loud to the dragon.

"Keep at it!" called Rhonin, thinking she was speaking with him. "Keep at it—"

His voice failed him as the bound nether dragon suddenly shimmered. Zzeraku's body all but faded away for a moment. A terrible moan escaped the suffering leviathan.

The pain! I am being eaten!

Have courage! the priestess told Zzeraku. *Have courage!*

Her words, her strength, cut through his suffering. Zzeraku stared at her. *Why do you do this for me? The draenei have love for my kind, after all that has happened!*

Iridi was steadfast. *I do it because you don't deserve this. . . .*

I—do not?

Then, elsewhere, yet another horrific roar sent further chills down the spines of all. Even the raptors cowered at its force.

"I have this terrible feeling that we're too late," Rhonin said.

TWENTY

He was alive. Krasus was not surprised by that miracle, but neither was he entirely pleased. Kalec's attack had failed, but failed for a darker reason.

"Ah, the great Korialstrasz . . . defender of the lesser races, savior of Azeroth . . . the grandest fool ever born . . ." declared the voice of Deathwing's consort.

Krasus could barely move. It was painful just to lift his head enough to see her stride toward the re-crafted Demon Soul and touch it as a loving mother would a cherished offspring. The dragon mage doubted that Sinestra had ever treated Nefarian or Onyxia so, but then they had not existed solely for her ambition and madness. The Demon Soul had no mind of its own, no potential dream of independence. . . .

"It shall—it shall never w-work!" he managed to croak. "In the end— you shall only have—have disappointment—and death . . ."

"Preach not to me, Korialstrasz," the black dragon mocked, now peering up in amusement at a stunned Vereesa. "Yes, my darling, you are also alive, albeit temporarily. You should thank me for that miracle. All the force this impetuous young fool sought to unleash was steered elsewhere through my good efforts. . . ."

Krasus snorted. "It was—it was your vile whispering in—in the blue's mind in the first—first place that made him cast such a force of violence."

"Of course! He made such a wonderfully delectable choice! You can imagine how enjoyable it was to find out not only that he was alive, but that his thoughts were in such distress that I could easily manipulate them against you! Your continual interference in the affairs of the world has left you with many like him, Korialstrasz. . . ."

"And you are—are breeding your own destruction, S-Sinestra! You cannot—cannot control what you have wrought! Think upon that before it is too late—"

She gave a curt wave with her hand, and he went flying up against the ceiling. Krasus screamed as he hit, but not only because of the force.

The point of a long, wicked stalactite—a stalactite reinforced by the black dragon's power—thrust through his chest.

A stream of the red's life fluids drizzled onto the chamber floor. Krasus gasped, yet, despite what seemed a mortal wound, he remained conscious.

"All goes as I desire, my darling Korialstrasz, and always has! I have adjusted for every eventuality and although I will grant you some surprise on my part at your ability to escape the chrysalun chamber, your act only served to enable me to bring matters to a swifter and more satisfying conclusion!"

"You will—you will only bring yourself to—to a swifter doom, I tell you! Even now—"

"Even now, your other companions are trying in vain to either escape or, in the case of two, actually dare to free the nether dragon. . . ." She smiled at the expressions of both the dragon mage and the ranger. "Ah! Some of this is not known to you? You, my dear high elf, should be especially interested, as I do believe that with the draenei who is known to both of you, there is a human wizard . . . a human with the red hair marking him as Korialstrasz's favored lackey!"

"Rhonin?" Vereesa gasped.

"Such a loving mate . . ." The veiled figure's expression momentarily hardened. "Such a *loving* mate . . ." The sense of triumph returned. "But they are both merely readying themselves to add to the reservoir of magical energies I have been collecting for my new children. . . ."

A savage roar shook the chamber, almost sending Krasus falling to the floor. At the last moment, Sinestra reinforced his agonizing captivity.

"Listen—listen to that—Sinestra! Each time he cries out, your creation sounds larger, stronger. . . ."

"But, of course! That is the point! Really, Korialstrasz, I think your mind is finally going."

The cowled figure managed to shake his head. "You will never understand until it is—" He groaned. "—is far too late . . ."

She laughed. "Do you feel the weakness spreading? Do you feel the numbness embracing you? When I gathered up what fragments there were of the Demon Soul, I found within it a residual energy like none I had ever seen. More interesting, the pieces appeared to be trying to draw in more energy, as if seeking to rejuvenate my dear, unlamented mate's creation." Sinestra caressed the gleaming construct. "It was as if fate had granted me its favor. I already had Balacgos's Bane, which would work so hand-in-hand with what was left of the Soul that it was almost as if I had planned it myself!"

Krasus knew of Balacgos's Bane, a cube of cerulean created by one of Malygos's elder offspring. All blues were caretakers of magic, but Balacgos had gone one step further; he had designed the cube to deal with a situation that he thought endangered Azeroth . . . the unharnessed latent magical energy that was spread throughout the world, magical energy that no one controlled, but that could be used by any unscrupulous practitioner of the arts who came upon them.

The cube had been designed to seek and take into itself any such energies that it sensed. One only had to activate it with their own power. The cube was intended to be a reservoir, keeping that magic available for when the blue flight might need it.

But upon first using his grand creation, Balacgos had discovered a small error in his calculations. The cube had sensed nearby magic and absorbed it . . . but that magic had been the dragon's.

The other dragons had found him a dried husk, blues being so much a part of magic itself that it was as much their life as their blood or other life fluids.

This had been in the ancient times when Malygos had still been truly sane and Deathwing had yet been the trusted Earth-Warder,

Neltharion. Krasus recalled with some irony that, in order to keep the cube from doing harm to his people, Malygos had, on Neltharion's suggestion, passed it on to his trusted friend to bury deep within Azeroth.

It had been like giving an assassin a dagger and telling him not to use it.

Still, like what remained of the Demon Soul, Balacgos's Bane had obviously had its purpose altered. Now, the two artifacts gave Sinestra the ultimate matrix for absorbing the energies she needed to create a dragon such as had never flown *any* world's sky.

"It will not take much longer for both of you to be drained of what I need," Sinestra explained. "In the meantime, I shall see to the draenei and the human. Their powers with yours will make a delightful mix! A shame you will not be alive to see what I create with it, Korialstrasz! I think that even you would find it most interesting. . . ."

Krasus tried to retort, but the combination of his wound and the weakness from the draining were too much. He could only stare at the black dragon . . . and the infernal artifact.

"Oh, yes," cooed Sinestra. "One other thing you should know. You would have never managed to destroy it, anyway. I have worked hard to make certain that no power born of Azeroth can shatter the Soul this time, including *any* black dragon's scale, much less my late lord's. . . ."

"You have—only made matters more terrible—then."

"You are persistent, are you not, Korialstrasz? I shall miss your blind determination, I shall. . . ."

The dark lady laughed once more . . . and vanished.

"Krasus!" Vereesa called. "Is there nothing that you can do?"

He shook his head. It was all that he could do to keep conscious and soon that would even be beyond his ability. The dragon mage eyed Kalec. The blue's face was very pale and even the red's sharp eyes could barely detect movement of the chest.

"Then . . . I must hope that—that this will work!"

Krasus heard a scraping sound from the ranger's direction, but could not see what might be the cause. Then, there came a sharp crack—

"Unnh!" The clatter of rock filled his ears. A moment later, the dragon mage heard footsteps.

A figure moved below him. Krasus managed to focus enough to see *Vereesa* standing there.

She held up a small, odd blade. "I was holding this when the blue cast the spell sealing me to the wall. I was fortunate; he seemed only to want to keep me away, not harm me."

"Kalec—Kalec is no evil force."

The ranger studied his situation as she continued, "I managed to move the dagger about enough to cause a weakness in the rock he created, but it was only a moment ago that I sensed my struggling was finally too much for that weakness."

"Rhonin . . . Rhonin made that for you."

"Of course." Vereesa frowned. "I do not know how to free you, great one."

"My life . . . my life does not matter . . . drag . . . drag Kalec from this chamber. It is—is my hope that in the chamber of the eggs, he might recover. The eggs must be—must be protected from the draining or they would all be useless to h-her."

Rhonin's mate nodded. "Being dragon eggs, they have magic in them, too. You must be right. Then, when he recovers, Kalec can help you."

Krasus did not argue with her, although he knew very well that his wound was beyond Kalec's ability. Alexstrasza might have had the power to heal her consort, but she was far, far away and even should they have somehow carried the wounded red out of Grim Batol, he would have been long dead before they could get him to her.

But if I can save these two and they can warn others, then my death will have been worth it. . . .

He watched as Vereesa took hold of Kalec and started tugging him in the direction of the other chamber. There was a good chance that, if Sinestra did not come to investigate, what he had said concerning the blue dragon would prove true.

They were soon out of his sight. Krasus continued to force himself to stay conscious. If not for the fact that he was of the red flight, the guardians of life, he might have already welcomed the relief of death. As it was, despite the inevitable, Krasus sought some miracle. Not for himself, but for all the others.

And, most of all, for Rhonin and Iridi, whom surely Deathwing's consort intended to capture next.

Barely had the roar faded away when another chilling sound filled the cavern.

This time, it was laughter.

Rhonin and Iridi turned in the direction from which it had come to see the tall, slim lady in black. The scars on the one side of her face were evident to them even through the veil.

"You're a dragon," Rhonin commented.

Iridi showed no surprise at this; after what had happened to Krasus and Kalec, that this female was more than she appeared made perfect sense.

"Very good, Rhonin Redhair," the dragon in mortal guise purred. "And do you know *what* dragon?"

The wizard shrugged, his demeanor quite calm considering that he stood amidst a chaotic battle of dwarves, skardyn, dragonspawn, drakonid, and raptors. "You have that admirable disposition and manner of dark dress that means you must belong to Deathwing's flight." He pursed his lips in thought, then nodded. "And since you're not the rabid dog or his two worst pups, I'd hazard by your grand posturing that you must be one of his prime bitches. . . ."

The lady in black scowled, taken aback by the human's daring affront. Iridi gripped the naaru staff tight, awaiting any signal from Rhonin. The draenei instinctively kept herself between Zzeraku and the malevolent figure.

Flee! Zzeraku warned the priestess. *Flee! She is monstrous! Forget me!*

I won't! Iridi found Zzeraku's concern for her heartening, even under the circumstances.

The disfigured dragon recalled herself. Once more acting as if empress of all she surveyed, she replied, "I am Sinestra, first and greatest of the Earth-Warder's consorts. . . ."

"That would explain your lovely complexion. Mating with Deathwing must have literally set your heart on fire."

"Is it wise to speak to her so?" the draenei whispered.

"He speaks so because he is a fool confident in his master, are you not, Rhonin? You think Korialstrasz—pardon me—*Krasus*—will save you. But your master is *dead,* human, his life essence a contribution to the birthing of a new era!"

The priestess caught just a hint of anger at the corner of the wizard's mouth, but Rhonin quickly smothered it. "Oh, yes! The great family plot! Let's rebuild or recreate or create anew a wondrous flight in our image—or something close enough to it—that will—dare I *say* it?—*take over the world!*"

"You remind me of my Nefarian . . . arrogant, blind, and doomed."

Sinestra gestured.

A shockwave rushed over all there, including the black dragon's own minions. Not one creature was left standing, so powerful was the invisible wave.

Not one creature . . . save Rhonin. His face was pale, yes, and his legs wobbled, but he still stood.

"If you think . . . me the same impetuous upstart . . . who came here to deal with your mate," he rasped. "You're . . . you're only half-right."

His gaze shifted to the cerulean cube. It suddenly glowed.

But Sinestra only chuckled. "Very good! You know Balacgos's Bane . . . your master taught you well!"

Sweat dripped down Rhonin's forehead. Through gritted teeth, he answered, "He's not . . . my master . . . he's my . . . *friend.*"

The cube flared bright . . . and then melted in on itself, leaving a blue puddle from which sinister vapors of a like color arose.

Sinestra's eyes narrowed to slits. This time, Rhonin could not keep from being thrown to the ground.

"A powerful, valiant attempt . . . but only an attempt." She pointed at the melted Bane . . . and it formed again. "The secret of it is mine, as are so many other secrets."

The raptor leader had by this time managed to reach its feet. With a hiss, it leapt with claws bared and maw wide open at Sinestra.

With a contemptuous glance, the black lady pointed at the raptor.

The ground rose up beneath the leaping reptile, catching it. Molten earth engulfed the raptor leader. The reptile's scaled hide blistered horribly, then burned away, quickly followed by the muscles and sinew beneath. The raptor had no time to shriek. By the time the creature collapsed on the chamber floor, it did so as a loose pile of still-smoldering, scorched bones.

"The right temperament," Sinestra clinically commented. "But lacking in so much else." She returned her attention to Rhonin and Iridi.

But the priestess was no longer there.

For the first time, Sinestra showed some puzzlement. Her ire immediately focused on Rhonin, who was struggling to rise.

"Where is the draenei? Where is she?"

The wizard managed a grin. "I don't know. . . ."

Zendarin fell back, gasping. He was finished at last, finished with the final step toward his never having to hunger again. It had cost him much of the staff's power, but for that he would have that which would gain him more than he could desire in a hundred lifetimes.

He leaned over the pit. "You understand me, don't you?"

"Yes . . ." came the rumbling voice.

The blood elf smiled. "It is time."

"Yes . . ." A dark form began to rise toward Zendarin. "It is time . . ."

"You will obey my will in all things," the blood elf went on. "You will—"

A monstrous sound arose from the pit. It was not a simple roar, as had erupted more than once during Zendarin's efforts, but rather *laughter* . . . laughter that reminded him too much of the dark lady's.

"I do not obey you. . . ." Dargonax replied with mockery also akin to hers. "You are little more than the dirt beneath my feet. . . ."

The blood elf could not believe his ears. Enraged, he shouted, "You've no choice but to obey me! I have made absolute certainty of that—"

The murky shape stretched above the pit, expanding, growing, until it filled all of Zendarin's view. The head of a huge, amethyst dragon coalesced.

"You have made certain of nothing, but that you are a fool. . . ." Dargonax declared.

Zendarin threw his will into the stolen staff, hoping it had enough power left.

Jaws open, Dargonax lunged.

The blood elf vanished.

The gargantuan dragon immediately halted his lunge. He did not look angered or disappointed, but instead, amused.

Dargonax suddenly looked up at the ceiling. His long, pointed ears twitched as if he listened.

"Yes . . . I come, my mother . . . I come . . ."

And once more, the behemoth laughed.

His arm was broken—he thanked the small favor that it was the one minus a hand—and he had somehow gotten far more lost than any dwarf ever should have underground in any cavern. Rom could swear that the tunnels shifted of their own whim and always to keep him from the ones leading back up. He wanted to go back up because, in one passage, he had heard the cries of some of his people. They were dying, Rom believed, and all he could do was keep walking in circles.

But he had to keep trying.

He stumbled into another passage that looked exactly like the passage before and the one before that and so on and so on. The veteran fighter swore under his breath, even his mounting frustration not enough to make him alert any possible foes to his nearby presence.

Was that a mistake, though? Perhaps if he shouted his head off, he would finally get some action.

Rom snorted. He would also end up perishing without doing his comrades any bit of good.

When the other dwarves had been attacked, Rom had not abandoned them, as they likely thought. Rather, he had been twice struck hard, the first enough to shatter the bone in his arm and the second knocking off his helmet and battering his head. He had then stumbled, dazed, into one of the crevices that had opened up. There, Rom had lain as one of the dead for hours.

By sheer luck, the other end of that crevice had proven to have an opening into the mount. Upon awakening, he had taken no joy in discovering that his long-desired dream to infiltrate Grim Batol had come to pass. In his eyes, he had failed the others. Rom could only pray that Grenda—capable and probably more level-headed than he—would keep the rest alive, with or without him. As for Rom, he had retrieved his helmet—which had fallen in with him—and simply marched off to see where fate would lead him.

But now he cursed fate for keeping him from his comrades.

A grunting sound made him still. Rom prayed that the echoes of the tunnels were not turning him around again. If they were not, then the source of that grunt was only a few short yards away.

He picked up his pace . . . and immediately back-pedaled as the voices of several skardyn heading his way warned him that he was about to run into far more than that for which he had bargained. Rom rushed back to the nearest side passage and threw himself in just as he heard the foul creatures enter the one he had abandoned.

The skardyn came rushing past, the scaly fiends crawling along the floor, the walls, the ceiling. Rom pressed himself against the rock, certain that he should have headed deeper into his own tunnel but aware that any movement now would only attract their attention.

A skardyn paused near the opening, smelling the air. It leaned in, seeking anything in the darkness—

A black fist seized the suddenly-squealing skardyn and threw it in the direction the rest were heading. The drakonid cracked his whip as he drove the rest on.

The dwarf recognized Rask.

"Move . . ." the black beast hissed. "The lady commands. . . ."

Rask and the skardyn moved on. Rom hesitated just long enough to ensure that they would not be able to see him, then followed after.

At last, he thought, he was getting somewhere. But *exactly* where, he would have to wait to find out.

And, by then, Rom suspected it would be too late to turn back.

TWENTY-ONE

Iridi had not abandoned her companions, at least, not according to Rhonin's back-up plan. The draenei felt otherwise, though, and prayed that she would soon be able to return to help the wizard and the others.

And, by helping them, she had to either finish freeing Zzeraku—whom she especially felt ashamed of leaving behind—or, miracle of miracles, find Krasus and Kalec.

If they still lived.

The trouble was, the priestess had no time to do any of what she desired. She could sense Sinestra's monstrous creation converging even now on the cavern and, through the staff, that it was more powerful than ever. Indeed, some of that power came from a most disturbing force . . . the energies of the other staff. Iridi wondered if the murderous thief realized just what he had done.

As for the draenei, it had not been by her own staff's power that she had vanished, but rather a one-time spell that Rhonin had given to her just for this emergency. All she had had to do was think of the need to escape and then stare in the direction she wanted. Rhonin had purposely created the spell so that she and only she would know her destination.

However, she had not gone where she had expected. While the wizard himself could take her from one point to another, the spell he had given her had for some reason not been as efficient. Now Iridi stood in the midst of some tunnel somewhere within Grim Batol with no notion as to her location or how she might manage to help *anyone*.

Then, a noise that she by no stretch of the imagination would have desired to hear filled the tunnel. By now, she recognized the savage growls and hisses of the skardyn and, if she estimated correctly, there were more than a score heading her way.

And barely had the priestess thought that than the skardyn poured toward her from a side passage. They clearly had not been hunting for her, but, the moment that her presence became clear, the monstrous dwarves let out hisses and howls of anticipation. They raced toward her, teeth bared.

Iridi turned the staff, using the lower end to catch the first skardyn in the throat. As that one fell, a second seized the staff by the long handle and clung to it. The weight forced the draenei's arm down.

Another skardyn leaped at her as she was pulled down. The priestess stretched out her foot, letting the creature's own momentum be the force that knocked it out when its head struck. Iridi then swung the staff around, using the skardyn clinging to it as a weight against its comrades. She bowled over three, then let go of the naaru gift.

It vanished, sending the skardyn who had held onto it rolling down the corridor. However, the scaly dwarf did not go far, for almost immediately it collided with an immense, black form.

"Draenei . . ." he rasped. "Keep her alive . . . barely . . ."

The remaining skardyn closed on her. Iridi raised her hand to summon the staff—

With startling reflexes, the drakonid lashed her wrist. Iridi's hand jerked and the staff, just materializing, faded to so much mist.

Rask pulled and the draenei fell forward. As she did, she managed to summon again the staff, but by then the skardyn were almost upon her.

Then, a battle cry filled the passage. From behind the drakonid lunged a single dwarven warrior who appeared to have only one good arm . . . and one hand at that.

Iridi could not believe her eyes. "Rom?"

The dwarven commander swung hard at the drakonid, who ducked at the last moment. The flat of the ax head caught Rask on the side of the skull and while from most warriors that blow would not have been enough to even bother the drakonid, from the powerful dwarf it managed to stun his much larger foe.

But Rom did not follow up, instead, racing toward the draenei. Iridi, meanwhile, had taken advantage of the dwarf's appearance to regain her footing. She kicked at one startled skardyn, then tripped another with the staff.

However, in the low, narrow tunnel, the naaru gift proved as much impediment as help. It was too long to properly maneuver with so many skardyn around. Iridi finally dismissed it, instead relying on the battle arts taught by her order to all its members.

The momentum of a skardyn enabled her to send the creature into one of its comrades. The priestess leaped over another foe, then kicked back with one leg as she landed, sending the skardyn into a wall.

Rom, meanwhile, simply cut his way through the bestial figures like a farmer scything grain. Three skardyn fell before he reached Iridi, with two more propped against the walls, clutching their wounds.

"That way!" he growled, indicating the opposite direction from which he had materialized.

"Where does it go?"

"Somewhere! 'Tis all I know or care! Going back's not an option, my lady!"

He spoke truly. Rask had recovered and the black drakonid even now shoved his way past skardyn, the whip once more ready. For the first time, Iridi also paid attention to the heavy ax the senior guard had strapped to his back. Rask could not use it well enough in this tunnel, which was why he needed the whip. However, she did not think it wise for her or Rom to be near when the ax would prove more an option. The drakonid looked capable of chopping either adversary in half with but a single swing.

Rom pushed her ahead of him, although whether that was a safer position was debatable. Iridi said nothing, more than willing to defend them from any who attacked from the front.

"Gods!" the dwarf burst out. "Wish I had my hand back! I'm itchin' all over! Figures those damned things would have fleas!"

But fleas were the least of their concerns, for although they had left many skardyn behind, more than enough pursued, Rask either urging them on or, if they were too slow, tossing them out of his path.

A spherical missile shot passed her head. Glancing back, Iridi saw that some of the skardyn were armed with the sinister crossbow devices she had seen in the great cavern. Now and then they would pause to fire, then continue their chase.

The two still had no idea where they headed, but they ran there as fast as they could. However, the way was not entirely clear, as skardyn dropped out of holes in the ceiling or popped out of those in the ground. Word had evidently been passed on ahead, although Iridi could make no sense of the snapping and growling the creatures made.

Behind her, Rom let out a grunt as a skardyn leaping out of a side passage snagged his leg. A second joined it, the two quickly dragging the dwarf back.

The draenei summoned the staff, thrusting the crystal into the feral faces. So near to Rom, she dared not use the staff's power to its fullest, but a sudden blaze of light called up by her was enough to make both skardyn squeal, then release their holds and slip back into the comforting dark. Even more so than dwarves, the mutated creatures were sensitive to brightness.

As she helped Rom to his feet, a hulking form loomed over both.

Grinning, Rask pulled back the whip.

Iridi thrust the staff up. Rask easily avoided it by leaning back.

But the drakonid was not her target. Rather, it was the ceiling above him. The staff broke loose some of the rock . . . causing more to collapse.

Releasing the staff, Iridi grabbed Rom and pulled him forward. Rask made a belated snatch at the dwarf's boots, but missed.

The draenei and the dwarf ran as the passage caved in where Iridi had struck.

"You know, ye could've brought the whole damned thing down on us!" Rom commented, his manner of speech slipping to older habits under pressure.

"I perceived a fault that I thought would work for us just as it did," the priestess explained. "I followed the same principles my teacher used when showing novices like myself how to defend against physical attack."

"Well, any dwarf who's lived in tunnels most o' his life will tell ye that fault you hit could've just as easily buried us rather than block the drakonid's way."

She did not respond, suspecting that he did indeed know better than she. Still, the fates had been kind to her, at least for that moment. How long that might remain the case, though, Iridi could not say.

They came to an intersection, where they paused to choose a path. Neither she nor Rom could here tell which might be the better choice.

The dwarf glanced behind them. "The skardyn'll still be digging their way through . . . unless they know a better way to reach us." He eyed the draenei. "I know I was lost, but what were you doin' here, my lady?"

Iridi quickly told him her tale, finishing with Rhonin's spell that had enabled her to vanish in the face of Sinestra's wrath.

"So, the wizard's here, eh? I'd say good, but what you've told me makes me wonder if anythin' has a chance against that bitch and her damned creation!"

"I believe Zzeraku can help us . . . and will be willing to."

"Zzeraku—that what you call that thing they got tied up?" He gave her a wide-eyed stare. "You really think freein' that thing's a good idea?"

"Yes. Rhonin also believes that we need to free him. That was why he wanted me to be able to flee even without him. Zzeraku is key. . . ."

The dwarven commander rubbed his bearded chin. "Lettin' loose another terror in hopes it'll stop the other! I must be mad to believe you know what you're doin'. . . ." He considered the two tunnels. "Pick one."

Frowning, the draenei hesitated, then indicated the one to their right.

"My luck's been bad for the past hours and since I'd have chosen the left, I think we go your way."

"As simple as that? We take a guess?"

Rom snorted. "You're a priestess of some order. I bet your teachings have something to say about luck or guesses. . . ."

She nodded. "One makes their own luck, good or ill . . . and there are no guesses, merely faulty concentration."

"Yeah, that sounds like something a priest would say." And, with that, Rom started down her choice.

With one quick look over her shoulder, the draenei followed.

His roar again shook Grim Batol. Heedless of the presence of their mistress's enemies, the skardyn in the great chamber scattered for the nearest holes. The dragonspawn and the one drakonid remained, but even the black behemoths looked as if they wished they were elsewhere.

The reptiles his "mother" had called raptors cowered, fear so unknown to them that they suffered the greater for it now. Even the skardyn's cousins, the dwarves, pressed themselves against the walls as if hoping not to be seen.

Dargonax laughed. Creating fear in others was a sensation he found he enjoyed.

There were only three who did not cower. Dargonax had never seen the nether dragon before, although he had tasted much of the captive's essence. The nether dragon could not move, but rage clearly ruled him. Dargonax admired that aspect of the other dragon, if nothing else. He was far, far more than this pitiful prisoner, far, far more than anything . . . except those that his "mother" had promised would come next.

She, of course, was the second of the three. Still in her mortal guise, she smiled with pride at what she had wrought. Dargonax spread his vast, leathery wings as best as the chamber allowed, the needle-sharp points at each end *scraping* the very rock. His amethyst form could have filled it completely had he stretched himself to his fullest. He was two, perhaps three times the size of the nether dragon. The edges of his body had a misty glow to them, as if they were not of substance, but shadow.

"This is my child," Sinestra informed those who could still listen, but one in particular. "Is he not magnificent?"

But the third of those who dared be without fear curtly replied, "He's a damned obscenity. . . ."

Dargonax thrust his massive head at the insulter. A hundred teeth each the length of a sword filled a mouth capable of swallowing a dozen raptors in a single gulp. At the front of the mouth, monstrous fangs twice as long as the other teeth gave the twilight dragon an even more nightmarish "smile." Atop his head, curled horns that thrust back, vied with wicked barbs and spikes that descended down the skull and neck and then seemed to explode in incredible number all over the rest of Dargonax's humongous form. Each time the twilight dragon breathed, he also seemed to swell a little more. His pupilless orbs, larger than a giant's shield, reflected the puny robed figure about to die.

"No, my Dargonax!" commanded Sinestra, her tone showing no concern for the behemoth's victim. "Not . . . yet . . ."

He drew back. His body pulsated, shimmered. He looked at the black dragon. "But, Mother . . . you do not command me, anymore. . . ."

The gargantuan beast started to lunge again—and suddenly pain wracked his body. He twisted and turned, but could not escape it. It felt as if his body were about to rip into a million tiny pieces. . . .

"Now did I not warn you about behaving?" Deathwing's consort purred. "Did you think that you had outgrown my control? You know that you can never escape what is within you. . . ."

He could not answer, the agony too much for him to do anything but scream. He, the most monstrous of beasts, fell upon the chamber floor, writhing.

★　★　★

And a watching Rhonin, who knew the powers wielded by one of the Earth-Warder's flight, wondered just what spell she had cast, for it was not normal. Indeed, knowing there had been a familiar foulness about it, one that he had not felt since . . . since he had destroyed the Demon Soul during the fall of the orcs here.

The wizard's eyes widened. *Since the Demon Soul . . .*

As for the behemoth, he finally recovered enough to gaze at his creator and tormentor. "You tricked me! You tricked me!" he managed. "But I am stronger! Stronger! I am Dargonax! I am—"

He screamed once more, then stilled. His body continued to shimmer . . . its glow at one point almost perfectly matching that of the insidious creation of Deathwing.

"You are what I say you are. . . ." Sinestra said with a mad smile. "My loving child . . ."

Vereesa ran back into the chamber where Krasus hung. "Did you hear that?"

"Yes, it has begun. She has unleashed doom upon all of us."

"Great one—Krasus—is there anything I can do for you?"

The dragon mage managed to focus on her. She knew the truth, that he could see. There was no sense telling her otherwise. "No . . . it is up to you and Kalec. . . ."

At that moment, they both heard a groan from the other chamber. The high elf looked from Krasus to the sound and then back again. She appeared caught between conflicting desires.

"Go to—go to him—" The effort was too much. The red's world swam. Vereesa became a blur.

"I will return shortly!" she called to him. "I swear!"

But as she departed, Krasus began an accounting of his own life. He did not have long and he wanted to know if he had actually done much of worth to Azeroth or if he had merely been pursuing a vanity of his own. Would those who recalled him after he was gone think of him with good thoughts . . . or curse his memory?

Yet, barely had he started when a light filled his eyes. A brilliant, soothing light that took away all of his agony.

So . . . there is no more time . . . I am already dying.

A voice called to him, then. There was a distinct familiarity to it and, since it was female, he chose it to be the one that meant the most to him.

"Alex-Alexstrasza?"

A figure formed in the light.

Vereesa rushed in among the eggs and molten pits, fearful that the blue's weakness had turned his condition for the worse. However, upon seeing Kalec, the ranger stopped short.

A bright illumination surrounded the younger dragon, but it differed from that of the chamber or of the Demon Soul near Krasus. It had a pleasant warmth that even Vereesa could feel, a warmth that reminded her of the rising sun.

Kalec murmured something. One hand reached up as if to caress an invisible figure leaning over him.

At the same time, the ranger heard a voice from where Krasus hung . . . a feminine voice.

Thinking that Sinestra had returned, Vereesa did not hesitate to rush back to the red dragon's aid. She knew very well the odds were against her, but did not care.

But when she entered, there was no sign of Deathwing's insidious consort. Indeed, there was at first no sign of the dragon mage, either. The stalactite hung perfectly clean, not even a trace of Krasus's life fluids clinging to it or pooling on the floor.

Confused, she turned around in search of him—

A powerful fist caught her in the chin. Vereesa spun about, then fell.

"Well, what a delight to see you, my dear cousin," Zendarin

growled. "That makes *two* objectives still dealt with before I depart this
madhouse. . . ."

Stunned, Vereesa rolled onto her back. "Where—what have you
done with him?"

The blood elf glanced contemptuously at her. "If you're referring
to that mongrel creature you call a mate, I've done nothing with him,
although since he's come to your 'rescue,' I imagine he'll soon end up
in the gullet of *her* beast!" He swung the staff at her, the crystal point
just barely grazing the ranger's thigh. Vereesa let out a howl and rolled
farther away as if blown there by a fierce wind. "I'll deal with you in a
moment, cousin. I've something far more important than you awaiting
me right here."

Zendarin turned on the reconstituted Demon Soul. With the staff,
he began drawing a circle of light around the dread artifact.

He meant to steal it, Vereesa saw. Steal it from his own ally. The
ranger was tempted to let him do it without any trouble, for surely
it would weaken Sinestra's efforts, but she had no idea what had happened to Krasus or whether she might, in the end, need the Soul to find
or cure him . . . assuming that he was even alive. More to the point,
surely nothing good could come of her cousin wielding the artifact.

If only there was some way to destroy it! But Vereesa believed Deathwing's
consort when she said that nothing born of Azeroth could now affect
the evil object.

Her gaze narrowed. But the same could not be said for Zendarin
himself . . .

She gripped the tiny blade, waiting for the moment. As Zendarin
finished his circle—and the glow of the Demon Soul grew muted—the
high elf threw.

But something made her cousin turn at the last moment. He brought
the staff between him and the soaring blade. Vereesa's missile deflected
off the staff.

Zendarin hissed as the blade left a dripping crease along his left
cheek. He aimed the staff at his cousin—

The ranger was already on the move. The blood elf's strike only decimated rock and dirt. He spun around to face her just as Vereesa leapt at him.

Zendarin had all the lithe grace of any of their kind, but he was no practiced ranger and, despite her recent shift to motherhood, Vereesa was still more than fit enough to be one of the best of her calling. She fell upon her cousin and the two struggled, the staff the only thing between them.

They crashed against the base of the Demon Soul's resting place. One side caved in, showering them a moment later with limestone and more. However, the artifact itself—still surrounded by the energy of the staff—remained exactly where it was even though it no longer rested on anything.

With a glare, Zendarin tried to send her hurtling away. However, Vereesa gripped the staff tight, the results being that both were spun around and around and around.

Again, they fell into each other, this time with the blood elf atop.

"You're weak!" he growled in her ear. "A fading memory of a fading people! The high elves are gone. . . . The blood elves are ascendant!"

"Do not dignify yourself by thinking that you are even worthy of being called a blood elf, much less the race you forsake for that foul role!" Vereesa retorted. "I have faced others before you and they had more worth, more honor, than you! You are a thief, a murderer, and a parasite! Nothing more! All elven lines would reject you, just as I reject any blood tie between us!"

"How terrible for me! Spurned by my dear cousin who sleeps with animals . . ."

She shoved them both to their feet. "You are not fit to walk in Rhonin's footsteps. . . ." The ranger spit in his face. At that moment, a desperate notion came to her, one so wildly improbable and yet the only hope that Vereesa had. "And without that stolen staff, you are nothing to *anyone*!"

He grinned. "Aah, but I *do* have the staff . . . and it can do many things for me, even while you cling to it . . ."

The large crystal turned as bright as the sun.

Vereesa threw her weight into thrusting the staff to her right. At the same time, she said a silent farewell to Rhonin and her sons.

The crystal struck the Demon Soul just as Zendarin unleashed the former's energies.

Someone grabbed the ranger from behind, tearing her from her cousin.

Zendarin Windrunner shrieked as both the head of the staff and the Demon Soul *shattered*. He was enveloped by energies from both, energies that tore him in opposite directions even as shards from the Demon Soul went flying throughout the chamber and the ruined staff burnt to ash. Zendarin, his face spreading wider and wider, reached for his cousin as if seeking her help.

The staff and its power were of Outland, not Azeroth. The ranger had prayed that its unusual energies would do what Sinestra had prevented her own world's magic from accomplishing—destroy the Demon Soul once and forever, even if it cost the high elf her life.

"You have all the magic you could ever hunger for," Vereesa murmured unsympathetically. Her own life meant nothing now that she had made certain of her cousin's demise. The children, at least, would be safe. "Why do you not savor it, Zendarin?"

The blood elf ceased shrieking as his body tore in two, the halves quickly dissipating in the spiraling energies. As the unleashed magic more and more filled the chamber, the ranger suddenly recalled her mysterious rescuer.

"We must keep moving!" Kalec shouted in her ear. "Hurry! There's not much time!"

He looked and sounded far healthier than when Vereesa had seen him last, but she knew that could not be due to the Demon Soul being reshattered. Not even the blue dragon could have recovered in the space of a single second, much less have also seized her before the energies could do with her as they had her cousin. Still, Vereesa was glad to see Kalec and grateful for his quick action.

He dragged her toward the other chamber, but the intense energies began to pull them back. Kalec cast a shield around them, yet that barely slowed their backward movement.

"It's too much for me!" the blue shouted.

"What can we do?"

"You do *nothing*!" shouted another voice.

Krasus's voice.

And in the next breath, the unleashed magic suddenly condensed, then rose up through the very rock, vanishing. As it did, both the high elf and Kalec fell forward.

A stillness settled over the chamber, a stillness broken by gloved hands raising up both of them by the arm.

The dragon mage smiled grimly at the pair . . . and the miracle of Kalec's recovery was minute compared to that of the red dragon. Krasus was whole, utterly whole, although he did not seem so pleased by that.

"Praise be!" Vereesa hugged him. "But how? Where did you get the power to do all this, especially bind such a wound—"

"I am not responsible."

"Then, it was Kalec, after all!"

"I've done nothing for him," the blue piped up. "I don't even remember him having any wound. It was a bad one, I take it?"

"Sinestra drove a stalactite through his chest and left him dying upon the ceiling!"

Krasus grimaced at this recollection. "It was very nearly my time."

Kalec shook his head in wonder. "I'd think that I'd recall doing anything like that, if I even could *do* it. It was no miracle on my account that he's alive—"

"Ah, but there you are wrong, young one." As both looked at Krasus in puzzlement, the dragon mage solemnly explained, "Even though you have felt the loss of Anveena, you have also always felt that she was in your heart, your soul, have you not?"

"I have. What of it?"

"I shall tell you as we move! There is much at stake!" As he led them toward another passage, Krasus said, "She left you a small token of her own love, Kalec. A tiny part of her that did not return to being the Sunwell. It was what kept you alive when, under Sinestra's influence, you sought to slay me."

"Great Korialstrasz . . . I never truly meant—"

"There is justification to your anger, but your violence was not by your choice. I know that. Sinestra was all at fault. The incident is forgotten. As I was saying, what Anveena left in you helped preserve, then save you. That says much."

"Anveena . . ." Despite their situation, the blue smiled. His gaze looked to the unseen heavens.

"And, because I was near . . . and because she sought me to help protect you afterward . . . that same essence also *healed* me. It took all of its power to save us both and it shall never be able to do more now than remind you of her love. I sensed it earlier on, but never knew it—she— was capable of this much."

Kalec grabbed his wrist. "You talked with her—"

"She *spoke* to me. I have told you all she said during her brief materialization . . . and when I say her, I mean that which she left to protect you."

"Anveena . . . I'm glad she was able to bring you back from so near the brink. If I'd had a choice, I'd have had her take care of you before me."

The dragon mage guided them into a darkened corridor. "And that is why she had the power to do that much, I believe." He grunted. "But as ungrateful as it sounds, I would wish that she had more to give us yet, for we will sorely need it."

"But why?" asked Vereesa. "With both my unlamented cousin's stolen staff and the Demon Soul no more, this surely puts to an end Sinestra's mad dreams!"

"There are variations upon variations to that mad dream as Deathwing's foul family has shown time and again . . . and one of those is the reason we must hurry! Have you not thought of what happened to all that was released by the destruction of both creations? Kalec, have you?"

The blue hesitated in mid-step. "Do you mean—"

"Yes—" At that moment, there was a rumble from above. It shook the passage so much that Kalec had to quickly shield them before they would be buried under a small collapse. Krasus wasted no time on gratitude, instead remarking, "It has reached what has been waiting for it. We are too late again."

"But where did it go?" Vereesa demanded. "Where did it go?"

Yet, it was not the dragon mage who answered that, but rather, Kalec.

"It's gone to Dargonax . . ." he said. "It *has* to have gone to him. . . ."

TWENTY-TWO

Rhonin could not believe the size of the behemoth. Other than Korialstrasz and the great Aspects, this Dargonax was the hugest dragon that he had ever seen. It had, in truth, been all he could do to stand before it with his expression unfazed. Indeed, only his experiences fighting Deathwing had made him able to face such a monster.

Krasus, I could surely use you now, the wizard thought. However, there was no telling where the dragon mage was and Rhonin could not stand there hoping that his mentor would suddenly materialize to save the day. It appeared the fate of everything was in his hands.

So be it, then. The crimson-haired spellcaster did not wait. He struck, but not at Dargonax.

It was perhaps audacity that enabled his spell to have some effect. After all, Sinestra no doubt expected him to attack her creation, not her. Thus it was that she was suddenly encircled by green bands of energy that pinned her arms to her sides and her legs together.

But Rhonin's relief was short-lived, for, with a look of anger, the black dismissed the rings.

"You are cunning and powerful . . . for a human," she declared. "And if I thought you intelligent enough to see matters as they will be, I would let you live to serve and worship me."

"How generous of you."

"Your impertinence is no longer amusing. Dargonax, you may feast upon him."

The gargantuan fiend roared. The huge head lunged at Rhonin, who cast a powerful force spell. Much to his dismay, though, the magic seemed instead to *feed* the foul creature.

The cube, damn it! he thought as the horrific maw filled his view. *The blasted cube must be doing this!*

He was going to die . . . and without knowing if Vereesa was at least safe. Someone had to be there for the children—

And then a terrible blast of energy struck Dargonax full in the face. The leviathan roared, but more from frustration than pain. He glared in the direction of the attack's source.

Zzeraku was free.

No, not free, not entirely, but enough that he could attack utilizing some of his magic . . . and the reason for him being able to do anything at all took the form of the draenei and, wonder of wonders, Rhonin's old comrade, the dwarf Rom. The pair stood near the rear of the imprisoned dragon, where Iridi even now sought to destroy one of the remaining crystals. Rom kept guard behind her, beating off a pair of skardyn whose fear of Sinestra's wrath had apparently been greater than their fear of either behemoth.

The priestess looked exhausted . . . and no wonder. She could not have been standing there for more than a handful of seconds, yet, in that time, she had managed to do far more than before.

Dargonax shook off the effects of the spell. The Devourer leered not at Zzeraku, but rather Iridi. "What have we here? Another morsel of power?"

The draenei could have fled during Zzeraku's attack, but had remained behind to finish her task. She turned at Dargonax's voice and prepared to make a stand against him, which made the behemoth laugh. As she raised the staff, he exhaled at her.

A ring of foul red energy struck her, sending the draenei hurtling back. She crashed against the rocks near the last of the bonds and lay still.

And from Zzeraku there came an angry roar that caused even Dargonax to pause.

*   *   *

His savior had been attacked. The one creature who had believed him to be something worth saving lay as if dead.

Zzeraku shrieked his fury. This tiny, insignificant creature had shown more value than he ever had. She had stood where he likely would have fled. Shame filled the nether dragon.

He strained to be free, to be able to throw his full might at Dargonax . . . and this time the remaining strands could not deny him.

With great glee he felt them shatter. Freedom was his at last, but Zzeraku did not waver in his choice. He was not afraid of the larger dragon, whose size and relative solidity in the nether's mind only made him that much more easy a target. Indeed, he flew with eagerness to confront his foe.

"Foul vermin!" he roared at Dargonax. "You are good at harming the little ones, as I once blindly did, but Zzeraku is not little! Zzeraku will teach you that they are worth far more than you or I! Far more!"

However weak he had looked previous, Zzeraku was now a mighty fury. Lightning crackled all around Dargonax, sending the twilight dragon into a startled retreat. The walls shook as, in his surprise, Sinestra's massive creation collided with them . . . and a nether dragon learned what it meant to fight for others, not himself.

But if Dargonax was occupied, that still left Sinestra. Furious at what she beheld, she roared. Her mouth distorted, becoming more reptilian. One clawed hand thrust out at the draenei—

Rhonin put all his will into a shield between Iridi and the oncoming spell. When the black dragon's power struck, it jolted the wizard as if he were the target. Rhonin cried out, but held his ground even as Sinestra fed more and more into her assault.

At that moment, the priestess stirred. She managed to push herself up. . . .

But as Iridi rose, Rhonin noticed a new danger to her. A drakonid had slipped out of one of the tunnels and in one hand he held a small weapon like a crossbow.

A weapon aimed at the priestess's back.

Rhonin would have warned her, but then a monstrous black paw came out of nowhere to smash the distracted wizard against a wall. A raptor leapt to his defense, only to be crushed in the jaws of a great, ebony dragon . . . an ebony dragon with one side of its face covered in grotesque burn scars.

The true Sinestra spat out the reptile's remains, then leered at Rhonin. "Much too sinewy . . . I prefer a tidbit a little more soft . . . like you . . ."

She bent to swallow Rhonin—then suddenly looked away. The black dragon let out a mad snarl . . . and disappeared.

Krasus paused.

"What is it?" Vereesa asked.

"Kalec, you and she go on ahead!"

The younger dragon frowned. "If you—"

"Do as I say!"

Kalec shut his mouth. After a moment, he nodded. To Vereesa, the blue said, "We'd better listen."

The ranger looked to Krasus. "You're heading back the way we came . . . why?"

In reply, the dragon mage gritted his teeth . . . and vanished.

The high elf spun around to face Kalec. "I know how much that cost him to do! Neither of you are strong enough to really transport your-selves yet! Not in Grim Batol! Why is he heading back—"

"Because he must . . . just as we must hurry on!" Kalec eyed her close. "All the evil of Grim Batol has come to a boil. . . ."

Because she could do nothing else—and because she feared some-how that Rhonin was here and in the midst of it all—the ranger reluc-tantly nodded.

But as she and Kalec picked up their pace, Vereesa could not help but imagine why Krasus now risked so much . . . imagine it, and shudder.

A gasping Krasus materialized in the chamber of the eggs. The hundreds of misshapen eggs immediately sent a new wave of revulsion through him as he once again thought of the lives within that would never become what they should have. He cursed Sinestra for what she had wrought here.

This horrific chamber was his chosen destination, but not his final one. That, of course, had to do with the next cavern, the one that had housed the reconstructed Demon Soul.

And, as the faint golden glow emanating from it indicated, a foul artifact yet again seeking resurrection.

"More than enough pieces, more than enough, I promise," he heard Sinestra muttering. "You'll be better and better than ever, you'll see. . . ."

He stepped into the chamber to find the immense black dragon ever so gently plucking up the shards of the Demon Soul one by one with the great claws of her right paw. Each time Sinestra did this, she then set it floating before her. On the ground, the shards were still, lifeless, but once they floated, a hint of their vileness returned.

The secret for her ability to recreate it had to do with the cube she wielded in her left paw. It took Krasus a moment to recognize Balacgos's Bane, and he marveled that this other artifact, as dangerous as it was, could enable Sinestra to rebuild the second and far worse one, even if the Soul would still be a shadow of its former infamy.

What mattered was that it would exist *at all* and that Sinestra could continue her experiments.

"Soon, very soon," she murmured to the floating shards. "Almost enough! Almost—"

With a roar, she turned her head toward Krasus and unleashed a torrent of molten lava from her gullet.

But Krasus had been expecting such an assault from one of the black flight, the followers of the Earth-Warder. He swept his arm before him and cool light wrapped over the monstrous outpour.

The lava cooled, creating a gray-black wall between Sinestra and him.

"I will remake it again and again and again!" Deathwing's consort shrieked. "And each time it will be more terrible! I will do it! I will!"

Krasus had known her to be mad, but now the veneer of imperious calm threatened to forever be banished. The destruction of the Demon Soul had done far more to her mind than the dragon mage could have ever imagined.

And then he thought he knew why.

"This did not begin as your plot, did it, Sinestra?" the cowled figure asked as he slowly wended his way around the cooled lava. "Long ago, Deathwing compelled this desire on you, did he not? Should he perish, you would always seek to recreate his dreams, no matter what?"

The black dragon's breathing quickened. "No! This is my dream! My grand vision! Yes, I will make over Azeroth into a realm ruled by the ultimate dragonflight, but it will be *my* creation, nothing of his! Mine!"

He readied himself for her next attack. What was most important was to get a little nearer to both the shards and the cube. Too many times, the Demon Soul had lived again, and that had to end.

Even if it ended with all within Grim Batol slain in the process.

"But the legacy of Deathwing will forever be found in the blood and magic of those dragons, Sinestra! After all, it is the Demon Soul that acts as part of their creation! What more speaks of your Neltharion than that?"

She opened her mouth—and hesitated. Krasus wondered if perhaps she actually believed him. He had, after all, truly spoken as he believed.

"Azeroth will be mine. . . ."

The ground rose around him, swallowing Krasus in a single second. Darkness surrounded him and he felt his prison sink below. He knew that Sinestra intended he be sealed forever in the heart of the world.

But the dragon mage had also expected that. Pushing his will to its limit . . . he transformed.

His expanding body pressed against the interior of his prison. Sinestra had expected him to attempt this. If he continued, he threatened to crush himself to death. With most dragons, this would have certainly been the case.

But Krasus refused to yield. His body strained. His bones felt as if about to crack in a hundred places. His skull threatened to flatten—

The earthen shell cracked. Like a newborn, Korialstrasz the dragon thrust his head out and roared his defiance to the black dragon.

Sinestra was in the act of using the cube. The cerulean artifact pulsated and, in reverse of its normal function, now fed forth the power it had accumulated.

Korialstrasz rose up, at the same time sending the pieces of the hardened shell at the black dragon. As they bombarded her, he whipped with his tail from below her blocked view.

The tail sent the cube flying toward him. Korialstrasz expertly caught it in one paw. Following the example related to him by Vereesa, Korialstrasz threw the cube into the other artifact.

"No!" the black roared. Sinestra grabbed for the cube.

The cube and the Demon Soul utterly annihilated one another. Both had been too unstable for such close proximity; their doom had been certain the moment that the cube had touched, for now Balacgos's creation tried to both feed and feed upon what would not surrender what it was absorbing.

The final, absolute end to Deathwing's creation was a burst of magical forces that, while not as horrific as when Vereesa had shattered it with the naaru staff, were fearsome enough to any in the near vicinity.

Sinestra turned away, but too late. Even her scales were not sufficient to keep her from being scorched. The stench of burning flesh filled the cavern.

And as the black roared her pain, she did so with a face perfectly matched in horror on each side.

Despite her agony—or perhaps because of it—Sinestra flew at her rival. Korialstrasz met her head on. In truth, he was still weaker than she because of all through which he had been, but not once did he concern himself with that.

Sinestra sought to clamp her teeth upon his neck. Korialstrasz twisted his head back and forth, trying to avoid that while at the same time steering her toward the chamber of the eggs. The two crashed against the wall next to the entrance, sending down a rain of stalactites on both.

But just as Korialstrasz was about to succeed in getting her in among the eggs—and hopefully turn their battle, whatever its outcome, into the destruction of her most prized resources—Sinestra pulled back from him.

"Clever, clever, my dear Korialstrasz! I do applaud you! Would that you had been Earth-Warder rather than Neltharion! Such more valued offspring we would have produced!"

"Rather would I have spawned with a kraken!"

Despite the open and very definitely painful sores on her face, the black dragon laughed.

Behind Korialstrasz, the way to the eggs sealed tight. When he struck the former opening with his tail, it was like hitting diamond.

"I would not want my new children getting singed," she mocked.

The ground beneath them rumbled.

Korialstrasz recalled the lava pools in the next chamber and knew that they had to have a source below.

A source that no doubt stretched under the entire expanse of Grim Batol.

The floor of the cavern erupted. A flood of molten lava rushed up—

The dread mount shook anew, but the two other leviathans locked in conflict paid no mind to it. Dargonax and Zzeraku fought with abandon, the former occasionally crashing into walls when struck by the latter's magic . . . and then both sinking into them as the Devourer, too, turned incorporeal and better learned to strike back with his own fearsome energies. The cavern filled with bright and deadly light as tendrils sought to strangle, starbursts tried to rip through ghostly torsos, and phantom jaws attempted to bite through equally ethereal throats.

But all this meant little to Rom, who had stood with Iridi while she had attempted to finish freeing the nether dragon and now sought to reach her after Zzeraku's horrific foe had sent her flying. At this point, the dwarf wanted only to get the draenei and his people out. As the priestess leaned against her staff, he spotted Grenda in the distance.

She also saw him and the pleasure in her eyes was enough to make the veteran warrior blush under his beard. He waved for her to lead the others to the nearest passage, then saw that she was pointing past *him*.

Spinning about, Rom saw Rask aiming a dwyar'hun. The drakonid had likely seized it off one of his minions, for he had not been carrying it earlier. Rask had no doubt calculated that he might not come out near enough to those he pursued to use any other weapon.

The drakonid fired even as the dwarf registered him. However, the target was not Rom, but the draenei. Yet, not at all caring what risk he took, Rom threw himself between the drakonid and the priestess, at the same time raising up his ax.

The spiked missile deflected off the flat of the ax head, but instead of flying off in a harmless direction, it hit Rom in the shoulder right between two segments of padding. He grunted as some of the spikes went in at least half an inch.

Hiding his injury from the draenei, he roared to her, "Run for Rhonin! He's our best bet of makin' it out of here alive! Hurry! Go!"

He started after her for a few steps, then, when he was certain that she was committed to reaching the wizard—and thinking that he was the same—Rom turned.

But he did not turn soon enough. The head of a heavy ax sank into his side. The dwarf fell, his one hand trapped under his body. He felt his blood simultaneously spilling over his torso and growing cold as it sluggishly attempted to keep flowing.

A heavy clawed foot stepped on his maimed arm and although it was broken, it still very much felt the new pain as Rask purposely pressed enough to make a new, sharp break.

"Dwarf filth . . ." The drakonid stepped past Rom, the ax now gripped for tossing. Only a creature as powerful as Rask could throw such a large ax with accuracy.

It was time to die, Rom knew. The ghosts of Gimmel and the others who had perished in and around Grim Batol gathered in preparation of his joining their ranks.

But Rom struggled to his knees, keeping as silent as he could. Wavering, he moved behind Rask, who was aiming not at Iridi, but an unsuspecting Rhonin. There was no doubt in the dwarf's mind that the drakonid would deliver unto the unsuspecting wizard a fatal blow despite the distance.

Rom sought for the dwyar'hun, but Rask had apparently discarded the weapon right after firing the one shot. He left the wounded warrior with only one chance.

Rom threw himself under the much taller drakonid's arm, shoving Rask's arm upward. At the same time, he twisted the creature's wrist, trying to drive the sharp blade into Rask's head.

But although still strong by human standards, Rom was too weak to achieve his desperate goal. The ax head instead turned toward Rask's jaw, slicing it open.

With a hiss of rage and pain, the scaly guard shoved him away. Blood dripping from his mouth, the drakonid swung the ax at Rom. However, the swing was an awkward one, the flat instead striking against the dwarf's helmet.

Rolling away, Rom located his own ax just as Rask staggered over him. The drakonid's breathing was ragged, but he was far from slowed. He adjusted his grip on his weapon and came at the dwarf.

With a mighty roar, Rom raised his ax.

The drakonid's reach was greater than his. With a grunt, Rask chopped at the fallen warrior, the blade cutting deep into the dwarf's chest.

The dwarf cried out, aware the blow was a fatal one. Yet, instead of giving in to his death, Rom used the incredible pain to add to the force of his own swing. With the skills of one who stood among the elite of Bronzebeard's warriors, he guided the ax expertly past Rask's guard. And with his remaining strength, *severed* the drakonid's head from his body.

As Rask's body tumbled to the side, Rom collapsed near the head, which even in death still wore a snarl. The roars of the fighting dragons nearly shattered the dying dwarf's ear drums. He heard a crack from above and knew that a section of the ceiling had broken loose, but was not concerned. By the time the collapse would reach him, Rom would be beyond any pain.

He suddenly noticed figures standing around him. Gimmel, his comrade from the war, stood among them, offering Rom a pipe.

The ghosts of those other dwarves whom Grim Batol had claimed welcomed into their ranks their old comrade and vanished to the great halls of the afterlife . . .

The two titans clashed again and again, using their spells to toss one another about the cavern. Dargonax paid no mind to the tiny creatures around them, but Zzeraku did. He saw the dwarves and the wizard and, most of all, the draenei—Iridi, he knew through their contact—struggling not only to survive, but to defeat the evil in this place, an evil akin in many ways to what he had once embraced but was now utterly revolted by.

Whereas Zzeraku had been brought here by force, they had come *willingly* to this place, come willing to sacrifice themselves. Zzeraku struggled to understand that willingness even as he battled Dargonax. They fought for something that meant more than their lives, something that would help *others* more than themselves. . . .

That knowledge made him all the more ashamed at what he had been in the past . . . a twin in spirit of the grotesquerie against which he now struggled.

No! I will not be like him! She found me of worth! I will not be as this one . . . I will not be!

And although he sensed just how powerful Dargonax truly was and just how much chance he *really* had against him, Zzeraku knew that, if only for Iridi, he would fight to the end . . . *whichever* end fate decreed.

For her . . .

Most of the dwarves had fled and Rhonin had managed to indicate to the raptors that they should follow. Only a few skardyn remained, but they were a threat easily contained by the wizard, who gathered them up with a single spell, then threw the lot into one of the farthest crevices. Whether they survived or not was of no interest to the wizard, only finding Vereesa and, assuming that he was alive, Krasus.

Iridi ran toward him, the draenei constantly looking over her shoulder as if expecting someone to be right behind her. Rhonin looked past the priestess and saw only the rubble of the collapsed ceiling.

"*Rom* . . ." he murmured, starting forward. The last he had seen of the dwarf had been when a drakonid had also appeared.

"He was supposed to be with me!" the draenei uttered the moment they reached one another. "He was—"

"Acting like a true dwarven warrior," Rhonin returned. "He did what he had to. There's nothing we can do. . . ."

Iridi's expression changed abruptly, becoming very solemn. "I knew him only a short time, but I'll do my best to honor his sacrifice and follow his example. . . ."

The wizard started to reply, only to suddenly need to grab her before another section of the chamber could fall upon *them*.

But although he managed to keep them from avoiding that threat, the ground now shook with absolute abandon. The tremors that Rhonin had felt a few moments before magnified a thousand times over.

Cracks spread throughout the cavern floor, hot gasses hissing out of them. The cavern became stiflingly hot.

Rhonin looked to the nearest passage, which was still too far away. A part of him thought of Vereesa, but he knew what he had to do.

He seized the draenei in his arms. "Hold tight and pray I've got the will and strength to do this one more time!"

"But Zzeraku needs me! He knows that he can't fight Dargonax alone! He is sacrificing himself for us! For me! I feel it! I must help him! I will not let his sacrifice be in vain—"

"No time for arguments! Hold tight!"

The last of the dwarves and raptors were out, not that Rhonin could have done anything for any still lingering. He shut his eyes and concentrated—

An explosion filled his ears . . . then almost immediately dulled.

It was dark around him, but he did not need to see well to know that the two of them were outside. In addition, the wizard could hear the dwarves as they abandoned Grim Batol without reservation. Hisses mixed among their calls gave hint of several raptors also escaping the carnage.

But even outside, the ground shook. Rhonin was too weak to risk another leap after so much spellcasting over the past hours, but he prepared himself nonetheless.

However, it was not the ground that finally erupted, but a side of Grim Batol.

And with it came Dargonax and Zzeraku.

A plume of lava shot into the pair—and through them. The immense burst of molten earth meant nothing to them. Yet, all was not clearly well with Zzeraku for some other reason. In the fiery light of the eruption, the nether dragon looked more translucent than Rhonin thought healthy, and he seemed always on the underside of the struggle.

"Zzeraku is losing," Iridi suddenly said, verifying the wizard's fears. "He has been too long a prisoner, too long drained of his essence . . . and I think Dargonax yet still somehow feeds . . ."

"That doesn't surprise me a bit!" But other matters were already on Rhonin's mind, matters that had him staring at the ravaged mount. To the draenei, he said, "Iridi, you'll be safe here with the dwarves. Stay with them, all right?"

"You're going after Vereesa, aren't you?"

"And after Krasus, if he still lives, but, yes, Vereesa most of all . . ."

The priestess nodded. "Go. I know what must be done."

He nodded his appreciation, although he also felt some guilt at focusing only on the personal in the midst of what might prove calamity for all Azeroth. Dargonax needed to be stopped, if that was at all possible.

But he *had* to find his wife first . . .

Rhonin gritted his teeth and tried to focus entirely on her. He prayed that he was close enough to be able to transport himself to the one whom he knew best of all and who knew him just as deeply. If she was alive, Rhonin would find her.

And if Vereesa was not, even Sinestra and her abomination would learn how great could be one wizard's fury . . . whether or not in the end all Rhonin accomplished was to get himself killed.

TWENTY-THREE

There was lava everywhere and although Korialstrasz had earlier used it to heal himself, as he had explained to Vereesa, there were limits to how long he could survive in it in general.

He had just about reached those limits.

Where Sinestra was, the red dragon could not say. There were too many primal forces and energies around him. Grim Batol was so saturated with magic that it was impossible to ever fully comprehend the magnitude of those energies. Each time Korialstrasz had thought he knew all, the mount proved him wrong.

The heat began to take its toll on his body as he fought ever upward. More than one patch of scales was already burnt. Korialstrasz began to doubt his chances of escaping this particular menace—

But then his head burst through cooler rock and dirt, followed almost immediately thereafter by precious air. Korialstrasz let out a roar that was more a gasp for that air plus a pleading to escape the burning. The red dragon tumbled haphazardly over the top of the ruined mount, then, unable to keep his momentum, he crashed into the far side of it . . . and rolled down to the base.

There were two others desperately seeking their freedom from the catastrophe wrought by the black dragon. Kalec shielded both he and Vereesa as best he could, although after all his trials, the young blue was more than willing to admit he was near to being finished. Yet, visions of Anveena in his head combined with his concern for the ranger to keep him pushing on.

And then, with lava seeping around them and no good place for the weakened blue to transform, a startling figure materialized. A human wizard with red hair. Kalec knew enough from both Vereesa and his own flight's information on mortal spellcasters that this had to be Rhonin Draig'cyfaill . . . although in the eyes of the great Malygos, calling him "Dragonheart" was a rather sweeping statement since, rightly or wrongly, the Aspect of Magic saw him as the most tolerable of an intolerable order.

In this and other things, Kalec had found himself much in disagreement with his lord, but at the moment he only cared that this human was the mate of this high elf and might be able to get her out.

"Vereesa!" Rhonin shouted the moment he saw her. Like Kalec and the ranger, he was, for the moment, shielded. However, his shield was even closer to collapse than the blue's. Kalec had to act fast.

"Take her with you!" he ordered, thrusting her into his arms. "Get her out of here! This passage is about to join those below in being deluged!"

"What about you?" demanded Vereesa. "What about you?"

Seeing the pair together, the young blue wondered what might have been, if the destinies of he and Anveena had been meant to be the same. That decided matters for him. He did not wait for the obviously weary human to attempt to take the high elf to safety. Kalec did it for them.

The transparent, blue orb encircled both. It was a visible variation of the shield already around him. Rhonin and Vereesa looked ready to protest, but Kalec gave them no chance.

"With your magic, you can guide this out! Go!" As an impetus, he sent the sphere on its way, assuming that the wizard was smart enough to keep it moving afterward. The orb and its occupants burrowed up through the crumbling walls.

Now at last Kalec could try what he had dared not to for fear of endangering his companion. It would require all his focus, all his remaining might . . . and all the faith Anveena had ever had in him.

He transformed, at the same time molding a greater shield around his expanding form. As this all happened, the blue also sought to rise up.

Kalec tore through ton after ton of hard rock and earth. He did not go directly up, but on more of a slant, for it was his desire to reach one of the vast caverns he knew pocketed that side. That was where the nether dragon had been secured and it was the blue's intention to see if the other leviathan was still imprisoned there. Kalec knew that he alone could not take on Dargonax, but with the nether dragon's aid—assuming that was possible to gain—there might be hope.

The lava continued to explode through Grim Batol. This was no natural eruption, that he knew. The mount should have been far more stable. He could only think it the work of Deathwing's consort, likely as a strike against the red dragon. Kalec wished that he could go and help—assuming that Korialstrasz still lived—but he felt Dargonax the greater threat. Sinestra did not know what she had created. Somewhere, somehow, the abomination would turn from servant to master.

The rock before him suddenly crumbled away. His snout entered a shattered cavern, but one that also was not yet flooded by lava. Grateful for that, the blue dragon burst through.

A powerful black radiance washed over him. Kalec roared, then crashed against one side of the cavern. His limbs froze. He could not move at all.

"Well, not the fool I was expecting!" Sinestra crowed from somewhere in the darkness. "But you will do . . ."

Her claws wrapped around his legs and she carried him away with her.

Zzeraku was dying. Iridi could both see and sense that. She knew that a nether dragon's essence was finite and, after so much torture, there was not much left. He surely recognized his imminent doom, but not in the least did Zzeraku appear eager to escape it.

And it was not because of pride or simply that Dargonax had to be stopped. No, as Iridi had discerned earlier, it had to be because the nether dragon hoped to somehow save the others—save *her*—from death.

But I can't let that happen! I won't let him sacrifice himself for me or anyone! the draenei desperately thought. Thus it was that she slipped around the dwarves and even the raptors—who were clearly headed back to the ridge that took its name from them—and wended her way to a spot where she could observe the two giant combatants as closely as possible. Iridi had no idea whether or not her plan would work, only that surely if Dargonax could feed on the staff's power, then so could Zzeraku.

Summoning the staff, she pointed the larger crystal at the nether dragon. The priestess recalled all her training in the area of inward focus; she could have no distraction. All her concentration had to be on this moment.

And on preventing Zzeraku from giving his life for her.

Eyes fixed on the crystal, she channeled the power of the naaru's gift into the great beast . . . and prayed.

A great rush of energy filled Zzeraku. With it came wonder at this miracle, wonder and then understanding. He knew the source and knew exactly what it was costing the draenei.

And the fact that she was willing to give of herself again to save him filled Zzeraku with something else he had never truly experienced . . . pride in not only what he was, but what he had become. Nether dragons had no true past, no true legacy upon which to draw; they were, he had discovered from another, the product of the warped eggs of the very same black dragonflight from which Dargonax had also been created.

The only difference was that, unlike Dargonax, Zzeraku now rejected any such tie. He was not destined to be evil; his fate was his choice, whether it be life or death.

Glowing bright, the nether dragon summoned his magic again. A new and more turbulent storm of lightning bolts assailed the Devourer, who withdrew in surprise.

Zzeraku laughed . . . and dove forward in pursuit.

The two titans swooped over the burning mount like a pair of huge carrion crows fighting over the dead of a battlefield. Dargonax dropped down upon the nether dragon, but the two once again passed through one another.

Iridi felt that Zzeraku was still not strong enough to defeat Sinestra's creation. The draenei dropped down on one knee in order to preserve her strength as she forced the staff to give of itself—and her—even more.

As the new burst of energy filled him, Zzeraku roared to the draenei, "You must not do more! Go! This one is mine now to fight!"

But Dargonax, peering down at the priestess, roared back to the nether dragon, "Fear not for your little pet! She and the power she wields will make me a fine meal soon enough. . . ."

Iridi knew that most dragons were highly intelligent, but Dargonax had a cunning far in advance of his meager life. All about the twilight dragon was more than should have been possible. Sinestra had accelerated both his physical and mental growth beyond any measure. How deadly would Dargonax be if allowed to live even a year?

That fear made her all the more determined. The priestess looked into herself for that tiny part that in almost any mortal creature always held back. Yet, for the sake of Zzeraku, Iridi could no longer permit that.

And so she gave that part of her, too. Through the staff, all that she was helped feed the nether dragon yet more.

Zzeraku swelled again. More fearsome than ever, the nether dragon beat his wings, creating with both them and his magic a gale force wind that buffeted Dargonax. The twilight dragon reverted to ethereal and yet still Zzeraku's wings battered at him, for in that wind was also the powerful energies that the staff—and Iridi—provided.

On one of Dargonax's wings, a spark of light burst into being. A second materialized on his lower right leg and a third on his torso. Each time, the twilight dragon groaned.

It's working! Although Iridi felt as weak as death, her heart leapt. Zzeraku was moments from destroying Dargonax.

But then, from the fiery mount shot forth a black radiance. The draenei expected it to strike the nether dragon, but instead it hit Dargonax from behind.

Yet, the twilight dragon did not roar in pain, but rather *bellowed* in pleasure.

"Yesss!" He called to all that could hear. "More! I would have more . . ."

And before a startled Zzeraku could move, Dargonax flew forward, grasping the nether dragon by the wings with claws that glowed onyx. Despite the fact that Zzeraku was incorporeal, the twilight dragon suddenly had no trouble keeping a savage grip on him. The nether dragon tried to twist free, but his monstrous foe held fast.

"You've fed me many times," Dargonax mocked. "Now you feed me one last feast!"

The twilight dragon drew back his head. Zzeraku shrieked and his body rippled as if not real. His shape then twisted, as if beginning to melt to mist.

"No!" screamed Iridi. She had been so close to saving Zzeraku. "No! Please!"

Zzeraku felt himself slipping away. He was doomed. His only desire now was to keep the brave little draenei from perishing with him. How grand she was! How brave and loyal! He cursed himself for having thought so disdainfully of not only her but all the tinier creatures! Despite their size, despite their soft, easily-crushed bodies, they were far more admirable than he.

But although he tried to break the link, Iridi refused. She was still as determined to help him as he was her.

He had only one other chance. With a last defiant roar, the nether dragon tried to disrupt the spell that enabled the Devourer's claws to hold his incorporeal form.

As Zzeraku attacked, he felt something within Dargonax react to his power. The Devourer shrieked in turn, then, almost immediately pulled himself together.

"No . . ." sneered the dark beast. "No, you will not . . ."

Zzeraku felt tendrils of power tear at his very being. He was literally being torn to pieces and there was nothing more he could do to stop it . . . or help the draenei. The nether dragon tried to maintain his cohesion, but felt himself slipping away. As the twilight dragon took in more and more of what was his foe, he now swelled to horrific proportions. Zzeraku's mind splintered. He no longer even looked like a nether dragon, but rather some grotesque, monstrous blob. He managed one last coherent thought focused at the draenei.

I am sorry! I am sorry . . . friend—

And as Dargonax absorbed Zzeraku's full essence, he also took into him from the staff . . . and Iridi.

The draenei shook. She tried to keep to a kneeling position, but even that was not possible, anymore. With a groan, Iridi fell forward. The staff dropped from her grip . . . but this time did not vanish. Instead, it clattered on the rocky ground several times, then came to rest near her feet.

The light of the great crystal faded, leaving only a dull stone.

I've failed . . . the priestess knew. *All that, and I've failed you . . . brave Zzeraku . . . friend . . .*

She forced her head up, hoping against hope that Zzeraku could still prevail—

But with a wail, the nether dragon dissipated into a swirling cloud of energy, which Dargonax took in with a single inhalation. As the twilight dragon roared his pleasure, he seemed to swell even more.

More than her own suffering, this last terrible vision was too much for Iridi. Her body wracked with pain, she laid her head down . . . and lost consciousness.

The sphere carrying Rhonin and Vereesa alighted on the ground near the dwarves, then opened. As the two stepped through the gap, the huge orb vanished.

Grenda rushed up to the pair. "Vereesa! Wizard! Praise be! And the others?"

Rhonin shook his head. "I can't say with any certainty about anyone . . . except Iridi and Rom."

"Rom?" The female dwarf looked fearful. "Do you say—?"

"He perished in battle, bringing some drakonid with him."

"Rask, most likely," Vereesa added.

"He—he shall be honored," Grenda replied, her face flushed as she fought to contain her burning emotions. Clearly trying to set her mind on other things, she asked, "What about the draenei?"

"She should be out here somewhere. . . ." The fiery illumination sprouting out of Grim Batol made it possible to see quite far, if in odd intervals at times.

At that moment, a roar made all peer up. Dargonax fluttered above the landscape like some infernal god. In the eruption's glow, he was frightening to behold.

"What happened to the nether dragon?" the wizard asked.

"A terrible black force shot forth from Grim Batol and it strengthened the beast. There was a pale blue light that touched Zzeraku and made him stronger for a time, but it wasn't enough—"

"A pale—Iridi! She must've been trying something! I hope she wasn't hurt by—"

But before Rhonin could say more, Dargonax looked down at the tiny figures and laughed. "Gaze well upon this wretched place surrounding you and savor that view, little morsels . . . for it is the last sight you will live to see . . ."

The wizard grunted. "Why do they always say something like

that?" He stepped in front of Vereesa and Grenda. "All of you scatter! There may be a chance I can hold him off long enough for the rest of you—"

"I will not go without you!" the high elf declared.

"And no dwarf runs anymore from an oversized lizard!" Grenda cried, her remark sparking shouts of agreement from those warriors nearby.

Rhonin had no time to argue. Dargonax was already descending. The wizard thought of everything that he had learned about dragons and hoped that something would give him a notion of what to do. He was already exhausted and even at his best, he doubted that he was good enough to beat back a behemoth such as this.

But still he cast.

White tendrils materialized around Dargonax. They were akin in look to what had held Zzeraku at bay, but with a more intricate matrix to their design.

They enveloped the twilight dragon, binding the wings that had stretched out for as far as the eye could see. Dargonax roared his fury as he fell toward the ground.

But suddenly he grew translucent. Rhonin's magical bonds continued their descent without their prisoner.

Dargonax shimmered momentarily, then solidified once more. Shaking his head, he continued his dive toward the tiny figures below.

We're doomed, Rhonin realized. *We are about to die and I don't even have the strength to cast Vereesa to safety. . . .*

Dargonax opened his huge maw.

A sharp pain was what finally caused Korialstrasz to stir, a sharp pain in a familiar place.

The red dragon raised his head and stared at the area where he had been wounded by the black crystal. Yet, it did not strike him that the crystal was to blame . . . but rather something that had been hidden by the crystal's more obvious presence.

And now, here in Grim Batol, away from all else, he could finally sense it. Korialstrasz could finally tell what it was.

Ever you haunt me, child of Neltharion! The crimson behemoth concentrated his sudden fury on the spot. He twitched as renewed pain coursed through him, but did not give in to it. This time, Korialstrasz would cleanse himself.

From his scaled hide there suddenly shot out a small group of tiny shards. Most were of the black crystal and, thanks to his earlier efforts, absolutely harmless.

But with them was one golden piece no larger than a tiny pea.

"Curse of my life!" Korialstrasz growled. "Damnable Demon Soul!"

Dismissing the other shards, he summoned the lone piece of the Demon Soul to him. It landed in his paw, so tiny and yet so insidious. With it now discovered, the red dragon could sense the secretive spell cast around it.

Already he felt stronger. Korialstrasz prepared to destroy the lone shard—then shut his palm around it. He looked to the chaotic fury going on atop Grim Batol, then stretching his wings full, rose into the air.

Sinestra watched with glee as events unfolded. In her mind, all went exactly as she desired. That Grim Batol itself was in dire turmoil did not matter. What did was that her creation had proven to be all she had hoped for and more . . . and would be outshone by the next generation she created once all those who sought to interfere were eradicated.

The black dragon leaned over the blue, who lay frozen at her feet. In her hand, she held one shard of the Demon Soul. It was all Sinestra needed to achieve her glorious future. Let a hundred dragons come; so long as Dargonax obeyed her, they would perish as Korialstrasz had . . . and the blue eventually would.

A steady golden glow surrounded Kalec. He was not unconscious, merely unable to move. Worse, once again his very essence was being drained, albeit in a more indiscriminate manner than previous.

But with her other devices and spells unavailable to her, Sinestra now used herself to help focus the energies to their final destination. Through the shard and herself, the mad dragon sent them forth in the form of the black radiance to Dargonax.

The nether dragon was no more, but his essence had not gone to waste. Again, thanks to her efforts, Dargonax had been able to ingest that essence and make himself even more powerful.

"Perfect . . ." she murmured. "It has all come to pass. . . ."

Then, the one thing that could shatter her insane confidence suddenly flew up from seemingly the dead to approach Dargonax. Sinestra roared her fury at the sight of Korialstrasz. The red was moments from reaching the monstrous figure.

And even from where she stood, Deathwing's consort could sense through the shard she held what Korialstrasz carried with him. It was no longer where her long-ago plotting had dictated. Secreted by the sorcerer under her control, under the guise of another magical attack. Now, her cunning trick to see to it that Alexstrasza's meddling consort would never face her with his full strength or faculties was coming back to haunt her.

If Korialstrasz willingly carried with him the piece of the Demon Soul once infecting him, there could be only one reason. It was a mad plan and surely could not work.

It surely could not . . .

Sinestra leaned forward. Korialstrasz was no match for Dargonax, no match for what she had wrought. There was no need to do anything but continue draining the blue and using it to feed her child. Dargonax would devour the red much as he had the nether dragon. There was no doubt of that.

And yet . . . it *was* Korialstrasz . . .

Sinestra glared at her creation, seeking any hint of trouble . . . and found something. Something that had been altered in Dargonax and gave Korialstrasz a chance after all . . .

Something that only the unique energies of a nether dragon might have caused . . .

With an outraged shriek, the black dragon held her own shard close to her as she soared after the hated red.

Sinestra's foul get was gargantuan. He was not quite as huge as an Aspect, but he certainly was as massive as Korialstrasz and certainly much more refreshed at the moment.

Nevertheless, the red leviathan did not hesitate. Indeed, it was vital that he close with Sinestra's abomination. Only then could he use the shard and hope that he had guessed right. At this point, there could only be one manner by which Deathwing's consort could control such a monster, the same manner by which Korialstrasz hoped now to destroy the fiend.

The hope was a desperate one and not likely to work, but it was all Korialstrasz had. He doubted Sinestra would leave such a weakness in Dargonax and yet . . .

The other dragon did not see him, the creature in the midst of diving down to terrorize and destroy the dwarves—and Rhonin and Vereesa, Korialstrasz sensed. That further spurred on the red dragon; he was already certain that Kalec was dead, Kalec who had rightly claimed that too many of those who had become involved with Korialstrasz over the centuries had paid the price for that association. The red dragon could not let that happen to the wizard and the high elf, *especially* not them.

He bellowed as loud as he could, demanding his foe pay mind to him, nothing else.

The amethyst leviathan obliged him.

"The red one . . ." Dargonax hissed slyly. "Krasus or Korialstrasz, yes? I sense your great power . . . your *energy* . . ."

Korialstrasz said nothing, soaring toward Dargonax. The fiend sounded as mad as his creator.

The twilight dragon's eyes became slits. "The blue told me you were cunning, but I see only a fool! I will enjoy devouring your essence as I did the nether's—"

"Would you rather not be free?"

Dargonax came up short. Hovering before the oncoming red, he growled, "What do you mean? What trickery is this?"

"She will always command you, always keep your head bowed to her! Would you rather not be free of her mastery, you who are clearly more than any dragon ever born?"

"Oh, yes, I would be free . . ." Dargonax shimmered. ". . . but not as you'd like!"

He turned ethereal just before Korialstrasz, with a last, sudden burst of speed, tried to thrust the shard into him. The red dragon flew through his foe.

But even in failure, Korialstrasz learned much. First was that there was *no* shard inherent in Dargonax's physical form. The second was that the shimmering was *not* a part of his transformation to the ghostly form. Indeed, when it had happened, the red had sensed something altered at Dargonax's core, something that hinted of another force . . . one akin to the energies of the dead nether dragon.

The red dragon's hopes renewed. Banking, Korialstrasz turned for a second attempt.

A plume of lava struck him full in the chest. Stunned and out of control, he spun around and around. Only barely did he continue to hold onto the shard, although a part of him wondered if it was worth it.

As his head cleared, he saw Sinestra above Dargonax. The twilight dragon looked from one to the other and the loathing he had for the black was clear to Korialstrasz, although Dargonax was careful to hide it from her.

"For shame, Korialstrasz!" she mocked. "You'll not take my Dargonax away from me!" The black dragon held her paw forward. "He will always be mine . . . as Azeroth shall be . . ."

"Your insane dream stops here, Sinestra! *Deathwing's* insane dream stops here!"

As he had expected, mention of Neltharion threw her into a rage. Wings outstretched, she looked to Dargonax. "He is—" Sinestra unexpectedly paused. "Ah, well done, Korialstrasz! You did want me to send him at you, did you not?" She cocked her head. "No answer from you? Perhaps *this* will open your mouth!"

The red dragon roared as his paw suddenly thrashed uncontrollably. He opened his paw—

The shard that he had hoped to use on Dargonax was now no more than a puddle that dripped through the air . . . and with it went Korialstrasz's last hope.

TWENTY-FOUR

The moment that the red dragon appeared, Rhonin tried to get the others to flee. Vereesa, however, had another concern. "We must find Iridi. . . ."

With a nod to his wife's sense, the wizard and she rushed off to where he had last seen the draenei, while Grenda reorganized her people in preparation for any attack, even by Dargonax or his creator.

"She should've been near here," the wizard muttered, eyeing the area in exasperation. "She was supposed to stay out of danger. . . ."

The sharp-eyed ranger studied the ground. "Iridi went this direction."

"That leads her back toward Grim Batol. Of course."

With Vereesa in the lead, they raced to where the trail led. Above, the dragons roared, but Rhonin kept his focus on finding the priestess. At this point, the outcome above was in the hands—paws—of Korialstrasz.

But while Rhonin had often had confidence in his mentor, he wondered exactly what the red could possibly do under these extreme circumstances.

"Rhonin!"

Vereesa pointed at a rocky formation just ahead . . . a rocky formation that was in actuality a body. The two ran to Iridi, certain that she was dead.

But as Vereesa gently turned her over, the draenei let out a low moan. Her eyes fluttered open.

"Does it . . . still . . . fly?"

They knew what she meant. Vereesa answered, "The monster still flies, yes."

"Twilight . . . dragon . . . that's what I called it . . ." She coughed. "Twilight of the . . . dragons . . . of all Azeroth . . ." Iridi coughed again. "Perhaps . . ."

Rhonin noticed her hesitation on the last. "What do you mean?"

"The staff . . . it still lies near me? I can't feel it, anymore." The draenei grimaced. "I miss that. I miss the closeness."

Vereesa located the naaru creation. "Here it is."

Iridi managed to grasp it with one hand. She looked at the crystal. The draenei grimaced. Rhonin started to speak to her, but suddenly the crystal glimmered.

The priestess stared at him. "There's something . . . left in it, but it reacts . . . reacts to you, wizard . . . the naaru . . . have you . . . have you communed with them before this?"

Rhonin gave both her and his wife a puzzled look. "I've never spoken with one of them, if that's what you mean . . ."

"Yet . . . something deep in the staff . . . woke . . . something I can't sense . . . you are touched by someone, if not the naaru . . . I . . . - wonder . . . perhaps there is something . . . please, can you . . . can you help me up?"

Rhonin was reluctant, but Vereesa urged him to help. With the pair's aid, Iridi managed to stand.

The draenei pointed at Dargonax, who at the moment hovered near Sinestra, a new arrival to the trio.

"This just gets better," grumbled Rhonin. "Vereesa, you stay with her! I've got to go and do what I can for him—"

But Iridi managed to take hold of his arm. "Wait! You can't go! There's something . . . you need to see it . . ."

"See what?"

"Look there!" the priestess suddenly called.

However, the wizard saw nothing save impending doom for Korialstrasz. He looked to the high elf.

With a frown, Vereesa said, "I thought—I thought that for a moment—the twilight dragon shimmered—"

" 'Shimmered'?" Rhonin gazed at Dargonax. To Iridi, he asked, "Is that significant?"

"P-praise Zzeraku . . . he did more than . . . than he imagined . . ." The draenei looked grim. She was clearly dangerously near her end. "It may mean our salvation . . . or it may not . . ."

"For the final time, Sintharia," Korialstrasz began, purposely using the name that the black dragon no longer desired. "I warn you to reconsider—"

"You are simply laughable, Korialstrasz! Indeed, there is no more need to tolerate your existence! Dargonax. . . ."

The twilight dragon looked as if he would have preferred to devour his creator, but he certainly had no qualms anymore doing the same to the red. After all, with his mistress guiding the matter, Dargonax stood to gain all that was Korialstrasz . . . and thus become an even greater terror to Azeroth.

That left only a lone option for Korialstrasz . . . to take Dargonax with him.

If that was at all possible.

The amethyst leviathan fell upon the red—only to be unexpectedly struck in the side by a sleek, blue-tinted form.

Kalec and Dargonax exchanged furious roars. The pair slashed and snapped at one another. The blue glowed, possibly seeking to further protect himself from the twilight dragon with a magical shield.

But although the younger dragon fought zealously, Korialstrasz could see how weak he truly was. That Kalec had also come from the same direction as Deathwing's consort explained to the red how she had been able to feed Dargonax so much more power when he had been fighting against Zzeraku.

Korialstrasz knew that he should try for Sintharia, but he could not let Kalec fight Dargonax alone. Torn between the two choices, he finally threw himself into the struggle alongside the blue.

His intervention only made the twilight dragon laugh. "Come then both of you to me . . . I will merely feast greater . . ."

He seized Kalec and threw the blue into Korialstrasz. The red could not veer out of the way in time. The pair collided with a sound like a thunderclap.

Wasting no time, Dargonax battered the tangled pair with his long tail. The amethyst beast then brought his tail to Korialstrasz. As he did, the twilight dragon turned ethereal. Dargonax thrust his tail through the red—

And turned solid again.

Korialstrasz barely realized in time what his foe intended. He twisted in mid-air, seeking to escape the tail.

He was only partially successful.

The red dragon cried out in pain. Already twisting, he ripped open a gap in his side where the tail had stuck in.

As terrible as the agony was, it surely would have been worse if not for Dargonax quickly reverting to an incorporeal form. The twilight dragon had wanted to slay his adversary, but not at the cost of being dragged down with him.

From his maw, Kalec unleashed a blue cloud. It enveloped the ghostly giant, then crystallized around him.

Dargonax briefly writhed, as if freezing solid. Then, the Devourer opened his mouth—and immediately sucked in the magic that Kalec had unleashed. The cloud vanished.

As he finished swallowing, the twilight dragon momentarily shimmered, then solidified again. At the same time, he caught a stunned Kalec hard in the side with one vast wing.

The blue went hurtling down toward the lava. Korialstrasz dove after him, only to be snagged from behind by Dargonax's claws.

"You first I'll feed upon!" the gargantuan beast declared. "Then his essence will I take! Then . . . then nothing will there be as powerful!"

"There—there will always be *her!*" Korialstrasz reminded him.

He sensed Dargonax's ire rise at mention of his creator. "There will come a day . . ." the twilight dragon murmured between them. "There will come a day . . . she made me too great to be her slave . . . I am destined to rule all. . . ."

"Until she creates more . . ."

"She no longer can! The eggs are destroyed!"

"She protected them! You know she would!"

Dargonax shook. He threw Korialstrasz from him, shouting out, "I save you for last! The blue's magic I'll taste first!"

As the red dragon sought to recover, Dargonax dove down in the direction of Kalec . . . but Korialstrasz knew that the monster was not actually pursuing the blue, who hovered weakly over the burning mount.

And to verify that belief, Dargonax became incorporeal again.

But just as he was about to reach Kalec—and continue on through him, Korialstrasz was certain—a golden glow surrounded the twilight dragon.

Dargonax struggled, but could go no farther. He twisted around to face his creator.

"Do not be a bad child," Sintharia intoned, holding high the shard of the Demon Soul. "I have had enough bad children. . . ." The black dragon thrust a clawed digit at Korialstrasz. "This one first! As for the other . . ." She glanced at Kalec, who had crash-landed near the base of Grim Batol. "There may be some pickings left on his corpse by the time you are through with the red. . . ."

"Yesss, Mother . . ." And with the golden glow still surrounding him—no doubt, Korialstrasz believed, to discourage any further rebellion—Dargonax charged the red.

"There will . . . be . . . be . . . only one chance," Iridi managed. She looked to the high elf. "You're certain of what happened?"

The ranger nodded. "I saw it happen."

"Then, we must try now." The draenei sought to stand on her own, a questionable proposition at first.

Rhonin and Vereesa exchanged glances behind the priestess. "Iridi, what do you intend?"

"I know how to . . . how to guide the staff . . . but . . . but I've nothing left . . . to give . . ." The draenei peered at the faint glow from the crystal. "But you . . . you might be able to provide the power. . . ."

"If it can stop that thing, you'll have everything I can give—"

"Beware!" Vereesa interrupted. "She sends the beast at him again!"

Iridi immediately stepped forward and thrust the staff in the direction of the battling dragons. She wobbled for a moment, then murmured to herself, "I made a vow." To the wizard, she gasped, "I need you . . . now . . ."

Rhonin stepped up beside her and placed a hand on the staff. The crystal flared as bright as it ever had.

The draenei focused . . . and prayed.

Dargonax again tore into Korialstrasz. The red tried to fend him off, but so many events had worked to weaken him, and the twilight dragon was at his peak.

Then, there came from Sintharia a maddened shriek. A great burst of light enveloped Korialstrasz and Dargonax.

And the twilight dragon swelled to even more grotesque proportions.

"Yesss!" Dargonax cried. The twilight dragon let out a roar of pleasure.

He threw a startled Korialstrasz back . . . and turned upon his maker. Even as he did, he continued to swell.

Korialstrasz fought to stay aloft. He glanced at Sintharia.

Her hand was burnt badly, another addition to her macabre beauty. Yet, the black dragon clutched tight what so burned her . . . the shard. It was also what fed Dargonax more and more power. . . .

No! Korialstrasz thought. *Do they not know what they are doing?* He looked down at the source of the energies flowing through the shard into the twilight dragon.

Iridi . . . with Rhonin beside her. He was the source of the energy now powering the staff. Rhonin should have at least known better what would happen. Why would they—

"No!" Sintharia shouted to the sky. "I will not give it up!"

He looked back at the black dragon and saw that her clenched paw was straining toward Dargonax, as if she—or rather *it*—sought desperately to join the amethyst juggernaut.

And suddenly Korialstrasz understood what the others hoped to do. They were making use of the same aberration he had sensed in the other dragon.

Dargonax converged on his creator . . . but seemed to be caught at the end of an invisible leash only a few scant yards. The behemoth strained, but could not go any farther.

It is because she still wields the shard . . . always because she wields the shard . . .

Disregarding the consequences to himself, the red dragon pushed with all his might to do what Dargonax could not . . . reach Sintharia.

His plan would have been certain to fail if not for Dargonax so near and the shard continuing to scorch the black dragon's paw. Deathwing's consort had eyes only for those two situations, nothing else. So long as she had mastery over the twilight dragon, the fate of all else was literally in her hand.

Korialstrasz came up from under her, his snout aiming for her paw. Sintharia noticed him at the last moment, but her reaction was too slow.

With all the force he could muster, the red dragon barreled into her, taking special aim for the paw. His snout slammed into the underside.

Already straining, Sintharia could not maintain her grip. The lone shard from the Demon Soul flew out of her hand . . . and with astounding speed and accuracy, drove straight into the maw of Dargonax.

"You fool!" she growled at Korialstrasz. Her tail wrapped around the base of his throat. The sharp scales dug in deep as the muscular tail—fueled also by her insane fury—threatened to crush in his neck. "I will tear your head off!"

"No . . . I will tear *yours* . . ." said the twilight dragon's voice.

No longer restrained, the monstrous dragon attacked her. Sintharia's eyes widened in disbelief and even as Dargonax seized her, she roared back, "You are mine! I birthed you! You will obey!"

The amethyst beast's eyes narrowed dangerously. "I obey no one but myself . . . I am Dargonax, the Devourer of all, including *you*. . . ."

He tore at her mid-section with his fearsome claws, now twice as great as hers. Sintharia shrieked anew as scale and flesh went flying. Yet, she showed no fear, only fury, and spewed forth from her gullet a torrent of molten lava that matched in intensity that still bursting below.

Dargonax turned ethereal, but not before being slightly burned. Still, he ignored his wounds, so eager was he to claim the life of his hated creator.

Korialstrasz, meanwhile, wondered why the others did not finish what they surely knew was not complete. Glancing down, he saw in the eruption's light that the draenei, clearly the guide, was on her knees. Rhonin, too, looked weak.

Crawling toward them was another figure, the blue dragon. Kalec clearly understood what Korialstrasz did, but weak as he was, it was possible that he would not have the will to successfully help the others.

The red dove as swiftly as he could. Just before he would have crashed, Korialstrasz pulled up. As he landed, he transformed into a more practical form, that of Krasus.

And as Krasus, he helped a changing Kalec to Rhonin and Iridi. Vereesa stood with both her husband and the draenei, keeping them from losing their grips.

"It—it must be destroyed—" the priestess declared to Krasus and Kalec, not needing to explain just what "it" was. "We must . . . we must focus on the weakness . . . Zzeraku created! I will guide . . . guide all the power! But you must give me whatever you can!"

Krasus understood what the flow of their combined energies was doing to her, as did Kalec. The blue hesitated. "No! I won't—"

Iridi stared at him. "You must!"

The dragon mage took the blue's hand and guided it to the staff. The four gripped the naaru gift tight, with Vereesa now helping Iridi to keep the staff pointed where it must.

"Let this . . . be done," the draenei commanded.

The staff's glow surrounded all of them. Krasus, Rhonin, and Kalec grunted. Iridi made no sound.

A great stream of energy shot up into the air . . . but this time it struck Dargonax.

As Krasus strained, he knew that the knowledge on which this desperate plan was based was due in part to Vereesa. She had seen the power of Zendarin's staff destroy the indestructible. Why would the same principle not hold true now, even with the shard safely—so the twilight dragon believed—in his gullet?

But it *had* to be inside Dargonax for what they wanted, nowhere else.

"He shimmered again!" Vereesa called. "Does that mean—?"

"It means nothing for us unless the shard is also destroyed!" Rhonin responded.

Dargonax suddenly twisted. His body shook and briefly lost cohesion. He was apparently trying to divest himself of what pained him.

And then . . . a brief golden explosion burst through Dargonax's body. The twilight dragon bellowed. He forgot Sintharia and looked to the ground.

Without a word, Krasus leapt from the group, changing as soon as he was far enough away from the others. As Korialstrasz, he raced into the sky. Now, more than ever, he dared not let the monster reach the others.

Dargonax shimmered. He visibly concentrated, pulling himself together. The twilight dragon eyed Korialstrasz with venom.

"You . . . I will feed on you slowly, enjoying your torment—"

Korialstrasz cut him off. "She is escaping you!"

Dargonax's reaction was immediate. He turned back to the departing Sintharia—and shimmered again.

"What is—" The gargantuan fiend glanced back at Korialstrasz, who stared determinedly back.

With a mad roar, Dargonax glared at the red dragon . . . then swooped after Sintharia.

Her wound slowed her too much. Deathwing's consort managed to fly above Grim Batol, but got no farther before Dargonax caught her again.

"Release me!" the black dragon demanded. "Release—"

Dargonax clamped his claws onto her torso and wings. The twilight dragon shimmered again and as he did, Sintharia's expression became one of dread.

"Release me! I—"

But the Devourer only laughed darkly. "At last!" he shouted. "At last I am free of you—"

Dargonax shimmered once more. He grew as bright as the sun.

The power that he contained burned both him and Sintharia away.

The last shard of the Demon Soul had fed him, but, once destroyed within, it had set loose a chain reaction that fed the slight instability that Dargonax had shared with his twin predecessors but that would not have otherwise proven as fatal as with the pair.

Sintharia managed a muted roar, one that did not hint of fear, but anger. Korialstrasz could almost swear that her last glance was at *him*, but it might have only been a trick of the flickering light from the eruption below.

And as he thought of that eruption, the red dragon saw with disbelief the flow recede as if some great force sucked it back into the depths of the mount. Wherever there was a crevasse or some other opening through which it had originally flowed, the molten rivers returned.

The eruption was stirred by her power. . . . Without her, it is receding, for it should have never been in the first place. The magic of the black dragonflight amazed the red dragon and he yearned for the era when once that flight had been friends and allies, not a threat.

But that day has long past. Indeed, we are in some ways very much into the night for our kind. . . .

Shaking off such thoughts, Korialstrasz banked. He descended to the others . . . and as he neared, the red dragon saw what he had feared might happen.

The others surrounded the draenei, who lay on her back. The priestess still clutched the staff, which glowed ever so faintly, though from what source now, the descending Korialstrasz could not say.

Kalec leaned over her, the blue running his hands above her face and heart. He looked upset and as Korialstrasz transformed into Krasus, the blue muttered a name. *Anveena.*

The dragon mage immediately touched Kalec's shoulder, whispering, "I am sorry. What she did once, she can do no more. Now, Anveena is with you alone."

"I'd rather that she could save Iridi—"

"Fate apparently says otherwise. . . ."

The draenei must have heard Krasus's voice even though he tried to be quiet. Her eyes opened and turned to him.

"It—it's over?"

"Yes, Iridi," Krasus responded, kneeling by her side. "Hush. There is a chance that if I take you with me now, my queen can save you—"

She coughed. "No . . . my . . . my quest . . . it ends here . . ." The priestess smiled. "With Zzeraku . . . praise be to his part in ending this. . . ." Another cough followed, this one harsher. "Azeroth . . . Azeroth is a world of . . . of marvels . . . but I miss . . . I find I miss *Outland* . . . even with . . . even with so much struggle . . . there . . . I wish . . . I wish I could . . ."

She trailed off. Her head fell to the side, the eyes still open. Her grip on the staff failed.

The naaru's gift rolled away with a clatter, the last of its light gone forever. Vereesa started for it, only to have the staff shrivel as if a living thing suddenly desiccated. In mere moments, there was nothing left but a gray, powdery pile vaguely shaped like the original staff.

The four stood quiet for a moment, honoring the draenei for her sacrifice.

"Shall we bury her here?" asked Rhonin, finally breaking the silence.

Kalec reached for the body. His voice shaking, he said, "No. I'll take her there. She deserves that."

Krasus knew exactly where he intended to go. "Is that wise? Will you be permitted by Malygos?"

"Permitted or not by my lord, I'll take her to Outland. That's what she wanted." Carrying Iridi in his arms, the blue transformed. As he stretched his wings, he bowed his head to Rhonin and Vereesa. "I'm honored to have met you both . . . and am more than a little envious." To Krasus, the blue added, "I understand you better now. I don't agree with all you do, but I understand why you do it. . . ."

Krasus bowed back to the blue dragon. "She will always be proud of you, Kalecgos."

"I still prefer Kalec. She preferred Kalec."

"Then, fare you well, Kalec . . . and thank you for what you have done. . . ."

The blue dragon rose into the dark sky. Kalec circled over the other three for a moment, then headed in the direction that Krasus knew would eventually lead him to the portal to Outland.

At that moment, they were approached by Grenda and some of her warriors. She saluted the trio with her ax. "I've accounted for everyone." To Rhonin, the female dwarf hesitantly added, "As for the raptors . . . I don't know about 'em."

Rhonin chuckled. "I'll deal with that situation. With things calming down around Grim Batol, they should be happy to remain around Raptor Ridge and not encroach on Menethil Harbor. Keep apart and things should be calmer."

Grenda snorted. "Don't know how well that'll actually work . . . and is that damned mount really calm finally? Have we seen the last of its evil?"

"That shall remain to be seen," Krasus interjected. "But for the moment, at least the dreams of Deathwing are at an end. When Sintharia perished, the spells protecting the chamber of the eggs would have failed. The receding flow will have destroyed them."

"Then our mission's done," Grenda decided. With a slight hesitation, she added, "We head back to our people come morning, there to report to the king and to honor our dead . . . especially Rom."

Krasus frowned. "Tell your king that the red flight will also honor your fallen warriors, including my comrade of old."

She brightened. "That will mean much for his memory. . . ."

The dragon mage turned to Rhonin and Vereesa. "You would be with your children as soon as possible, would you not?"

The wizard and high elf nodded. "We'll rest until morning," Rhonin replied, "then I should be able to bring us back there . . . and spend a little time before I need to return to Dalaran."

The red-haired spellcaster said nothing more and his expression indicated that Krasus would hear nothing from him as to what was being planned in the shielded city.

"Your lives and your choices are yours," he told the couple, but especially Rhonin. "I am only grateful for your aid here and . . . and for your continued friendship."

"You will always have that," Vereesa said.

Krasus pulled himself together for one more spell. "And as a friend, allow me this . . ."

The wizard and the high elf vanished.

"They are home with their children," the dragon mage responded to Grenda's dumbfounded expression. "I may be able to send some of your people in such a manner if given time to recuperate—"

But the dwarves all shook their heads. With an anxious grin, their leader answered, "If it's all the same to you, great one, we of the earth folk prefer solid footin' under us!"

That made him smile. "Of course. The ground is to you as the sky is to me. I understand very much." He stepped back from Grenda. "I leave you, then. May your axes be sharp and your tunnels strong. . . ."

The Bronzebeards went down on one knee as Krasus again changed into his true form. As Korialstrasz, he dipped his head in homage to the dwarves' own deeds, then leapt into the sky.

Once there, Korialstrasz arced not away from Grim Batol, but *toward* it. He passed over the damaged mount, marveling that, despite Sintharia's eruption, from beyond its walls Grim Batol looked more or less as it always had.

It perseveres, this place. It always perseveres.

He concentrated as best he could, seeking to assure himself that what he had told the others was true. Korialstrasz surveyed as much of Grim Batol's interior as possible, sensing only emptiness and that same residual evil that had permeated it for centuries.

And of the area where the chamber of the eggs would have been located, the red dragon sensed utter ruination. As he had said, without Sintharia, it had no longer been protected. Perhaps an egg or two had survived the destruction, but even the myatis coating he had seen on them would not be enough. Dargonax was the last of the twilight dragons.

Korialstrasz turned in the direction of home. He, too, missed his family. It was time to return there for awhile before again renewing his eternal vigil over Azeroth. . . .

And behind him, Grim Batol sat as silent and as still . . . as death.

Yet far, far below the dread mount—deeper than even Sintharia had ever gone—it was not completely still. In the sunless cavern, a huge form finally moved about. The intruders were all gone. It was safe to begin.

Around him were gathered the eggs that Sintharia had thought sealed in her special cavern and that the accursed red dragon believed were now destroyed. There were many places to store them down here, many places to keep them viable until things were ready.

You were a useful puppet for a time, he thought of Sintharia. *You were so easily drawn here, to this of all places, and made eager to fulfill a dream you thought your own! Envy and hatred made you my greatest tool, yes . . . and from your mistakes, I now know better what to do. . . .*

Deathwing laughed, the only mourning he would do for his former mate. She had been manipulated well, even in dealing with the damnable Korialstrasz, with whom there would yet be a reckoning.

Dismissing his ancient adversary, the mad Earth-Warder eagerly toyed with one of the eggs. Dargonax had been a flawed but quite interesting creation. Deathwing's consort had chosen an interesting path with her experiments. However, he understood where Sintharia had gone wrong. *His* twilight dragons—so appropriate a name, he thought and thanked the voices he had heard echo it to him—would be perfect. They would be *him.*

And since everyone assumed the Earth-Warder dead, Deathwing had all the time in the world in which to "hatch" his grand design . . . all the time he would need to erase the blunders of his children and his mate and ensure that *no one,* not even—not even *Korialstrasz*—would understand what was happening until it was far, far too late.

The day of the dragon is over, Deathwing thought to himself with anticipation for the imminent future. *Its night is almost upon Azeroth . . . and after that night has swept away the old flights . . . there shall come a new dawn . . .*

The dawn of my new world . . .

ABOUT THE AUTHOR

Richard A. Knaak is the *New York Times* bestselling author of some forty novels and numerous short stories, including such series as *Warcraft, Diablo, Dragonlance, Age of Conan,* and his own *Dragonrealm*. He has also scripted a number of mangas for *Warcraft,* including the top-selling *Sunwell* trilogy for Tokyopop, and has also written background material for games. His works have been published worldwide.

Currently, he is at work on his next *Warcraft* novel, finishing up *The Gargoyle King*—the third in his *Ogre Titans* trilogy for *Dragonlance*—and writing the first volume of the *Dragons of Outland* saga for Blizzard and Tokyopop. Some other projects include adapting some of his *Dragonlance* short fiction for the new *D&D* comic, more background work, returning to *Diablo,* and penning several shorter pieces for other *Warcraft* manga. He is also at work on projects to be named later.

Currently splitting his time between Chicago and Arkansas, he can be reached through his website at www.richardaknaak.com. While he is unable to respond to all his e-mail, he tries to read it all. You can join his mailing list on his website for e-announcements of upcoming releases and appearances.

WORLD OF WARCRAFT®

Arthas

The new novel from
CHRISTIE GOLDEN

Available April 2009

Turn the page for a preview.

The wind shrieked like a child in pain.

The herd of shovel tusks huddled together for warmth—their thick, shaggy coats protecting them from the worst of the storm. They formed a circle with the calves, shivering and bleating, in the center. Their heads, crowned with massive antlers, drooped toward the snow-covered earth, eyes shut against the whirling snow. Their own breath frosted their muzzles as they planted themselves and endured.

In their various dens, the wolves and bears waited out the storm, one with the comfort of their pack, the other solitary and resigned. Whatever their hunger, nothing would drive them forth until after the keening wind had ceased its weeping and the blinding snow had worn itself out.

The wind, roaring in from the ocean to beat at the village of Kamagua, tore at the hides that stretched over frames made of the bones of great sea creatures. When the storm passed, the tuskarr whose home this had been for years uncounted knew they would need to repair or replace nets and traps. Their dwellings, sturdy though they were, were always harmed when *this* storm descended. They had all gathered inside the large group dwelling that had been dug deep into the earth, lacing the flaps tight against the storm and lighting smoky oil lamps.

Elder Atuik waited in stoic silence. He had seen many of these storms over the last seven years. Long had he lived, the length and yellowness of his tusks and the wrinkles on his brown skin testament to the fact. But these storms were more than storms, were more than natural. He glanced at the young ones, shivering not with cold, not the tuskarr, but with fear.

"He dreams," one of them murmured, eyes bright, whiskers bristling.

"Silence," snapped Atuik, more gruffly than he had intended. The child, startled, fell silent, and once again, the only sound was the aching sob of the snow and wind.

It rose like the smoke, the deep bellowing noise, wordless but full of meaning. A chant, carried by a dozen voices; sounds of drums and rattles and bone striking bone formed a fierce undercurrent to the wordless call. The worst of the wind's anger was deflected from the taunka village by the circle of posts and hides, and the lodges, their curving roofs arching over a large interior space in defiance of the hardships of this land, were strong.

Over the sound of deep and ancient ritual, the wind's cry could still be heard. The dancer, a shaman by the name of Kamiku, missed a step and his hoof struck awkwardly. He recovered and continued. Focus. It was all about focus. It was how one harnessed the elements and wrung from them obedience; it was how his people survived in a land that was harsh and unforgiving.

Sweat dampened and darkened his fur as he danced. His large brown eyes were closed in concentration, his hooves again finding their powerful rhythm. He tossed his head, short horns stabbing the air, tail twitching. Others danced beside him, their body heat and that of the fire that burned despite the flakes and wind that drifted down from the smoke hole in the roof keeping the lodge warm and comfortable.

They all knew what was transpiring outside. They could not control these winds and snow, as they could ordinary such things. No, this was *his* doing. But they could dance and feast and laugh in defiance of the onslaught. They were taunka; they would endure.

The world was blue and white and raging outside, but inside the Great Hall the air was warm and still. A fireplace tall enough for a man to stand in was filled with thick logs, the crackling of their burning the only noise. Over the ornately decorated mantle, carved with images of fantastical creatures, the giant antlers of a shovel tusk were mounted. Heavy beams supported the feast hall that could have housed dozens, the warm orange hue of the fires chasing away the shadows to hide on the corners. Carved dragon heads served as sconces, holding torches whose flames burned brightly. The cold stone of the floor was softened and warmed by thick pelts of polar bears, shovel tusks, and other creatures.

A table, long and heavy and carved, occupied most of the space in the room. It could have hosted three dozen easily. Only three figures sat at the table now: a man, an orc, and a boy.

None of it was real, of course. The man who sat at the place of honor at the table, slightly elevated before the other two in a mammoth carved chair that was not quite a throne, understood this. He was dreaming; he had been dreaming for a long, long time. The hall, the shovel tusk trophies, the fire, the table—the orc and the boy—all were simply a part of his dreaming.

The orc, on his left, was elderly, but still powerful. The orange fire- and torchlight flickered off the ghastly image he bore on his heavy-jawed face— that of a skull, painted on. He had been a shaman, able to direct and wield vast powers, and even now, even just as a figment of the man's imagination, he was intimidating.

The boy was not. Once, he might have been a handsome child, with wide, sea-green eyes, fair features, and golden hair. But once was not now.

The boy was sick.

He was thin, so emaciated that his bones seemed to threaten to slice through the skin. The once-bright eyes were dimmed and sunken, a thin film covering them. Pustules marked his skin, bursting and oozing forth a green fluid. Breathing seemed difficult and the child's chest hitched in little panting gasps. The man thought he could almost see the labored thumping of a heart that should have faltered long ago, but persisted in continuing to beat.

"He is still here," the orc said, stabbing a finger in the boy's direction.

"He will not last," the man said.

As if to confirm the words, the boy began to cough. Blood and mucus spattered the table in front of him and he wiped a thin arm clad in rotting finery across his pale mouth. He drew breath to speak in a halting voice, the effort obviously taxing him.

"You have not—yet won him. And I will—prove it to you."

"You as foolish as you are stubborn," the orc growled. "That battle was won long ago."

The man's hands tightened on the arms of his chair as he listened to both of them. This had been a recurring dream, over the last few years; he found it now more tiresome than entertaining. "I grow weary of the struggle. Let us end this once and for all."

The orc leered at the boy, his skull-face grinning hideously. The boy coughed again, but did not quail from the orc's regard. Slowly, with dignity, he straightened, his milky eyes darting from the orc to the man.

"Yes," the orc said, "this serves nothing. Soon it will be time to awaken. Awaken, and move forward into this world once more." He turned to the man, his eyes gleaming. "Walk again the path you have taken."

The skull seemed to detach itself from his face, hovering above it like another entity, and the room changed with its movement. The carved sconces that a moment before were simple wood undulated and rippled, coming to life, the torches in their mouths flaring and casting grotesque dancing shadows as they shook their heads. The wind screamed outside and the door to the hall slammed open. Snow whirled about the three figures. The man spread his arms and let the freezing wind wrap about him like a cloak. The orc laughed, the skull floating over his face issuing its own manic peals of mirth.

"Let me show you that your destiny lies with me, and you can only know true power through eliminating *him*."

The boy, fragile and slight, had been knocked out of his chair by the violent gusts of frigid air. Now he propped himself up with an effort, shaking, his breaths coming in small puffs as he struggled to climb back into his chair. He threw the man a look—of hope, fear, and odd determination.

"All is not lost," he whispered, and somehow, despite the orc and the skull's laughter, despite the shrieking of the wind, the man heard him.